THAT LAST
Secret

JENN MCMAHON

BOOK FOUR OF THE

Firsts in the City

SERIES

Cover Design: Emily Wittig

Copy Editing: Caroline Palmier

Developmental Editing: Salma R, Amy Pritt

Proofreading, Formatting: Cathryn Carter

———

For anyone who's ever felt like they needed to go through things alone out of fear of what people might think of you. You're not alone. You're never alone.

You are stronger than anything you're fighting inside of you.

Also for Lauren Brooke. I'm sorry for edging you to death for three whole books. Logan Bennett will always be yours.

A NOTE FROM THE AUTHOR

This book was probably the hardest book I've written to date for so many reasons. Their story did not come easily to me. And if you pair that with the life challenges I went through along the way, it only built up all the reasons this book was almost never done. Through my health issues that happened, to losing a baby with a miscarriage, and just overall life happenings—it all contributed to the reason I almost didn't finish writing this book.

But we did it. Logan and Emiline are in your hands now.

It's been my goal through this series to write you a story that leaves you laughing, blushing and maybe with a little tear along the way. However, I always want my readers to be comfortable picking up one of my books. With that being said, if you want to be aware of any possible content warnings, please see the link below. Please know, these content warnings do contain spoilers for the book as well. But your mental health is more important to me. If you don't need this, you can move forward.

Either way, I hope you enjoy this book. I'm sorry in advance for the tears if you shed them. If it makes you feel better, I've shed just as many writing this story.

Content warnings can be found here:

http://jennmcmahon.com/pages/trigger-warnings

PROLOGUE

Emiline

I HAVE a love-hate relationship with my job.

I enjoy helping people and using my placement as a foot in the door for future opportunities in nursing.

But I *hate working* in the Emergency Room.

Every night is unpredictable. You never know what will come through those doors.

Stroke alert.

Code STEMI for a heart attack.

Code blue.

Will we be prepared for whatever comes in?

Will we be able to *save* them?

The unknown always causes my stomach to churn with anxiety each passing hour.

Yet, despite all that, I love my job.

"It's only one hour into our shift, and I'm already over it," Brooke groans to my left as she sits at the open computer next to me. She throws her head back and swivels back and forth next to me. "Hear me out, okay? What if you take the empty bed from room three and accidentally run me over so I can go home?"

I choke out a laugh. "It's a little early in the shift to be this dramatic."

Brooke has become one of my best friends since we started nursing school. We met on the first day of classes after we sat beside each other. When we had time to chat that day, we discovered we lived only a block from each other and were both obsessed with iced coffee. We also have similar study habits, and if there's an area where one of us struggles, the other understands.

After our first study session, we felt utterly lost. We agreed we needed more hands-on experience than school offered us. So we both got a job working in the Emergency Room at City General.

A few months into this job, we can confidently say it was the best and worst decision ever. It's the worst because working nights while in school is not fun. But despite that, the nurses we work with are some of the most supportive people we've ever met.

When a patient would come in, they'd explain to us what they had, what to look for, and which treatments are commonly used. It was a perfect way to experience what we learned in school firsthand.

Brooke isn't just a coworker or a nursing school buddy anymore, I'm lucky to call her my best friend.

"I was considering asking you to run me over five minutes before the shift started," she scoffs, sitting upright in the chair. "And then I got stuck on the B side. You know, the opposite side of the ER from you. Which is so rude, by the way." She dramatically rolls her eyes. "Tonight seems to be filled with people who have no respect for common coughing etiquette. I'm taking a blood pressure test on the patient in room eighteen, and instead of turning his head away from me to cough, he turns and directs his face toward me and lets it out. I felt the germs spray my face."

"Say it, don't spray it." I chuckle.

"Tell him that, *please*," she begs, with her hands joined in prayer.

"There's not much happening here on the A side. But it's still early." I lift a shoulder.

Brooke's eyes widen in my direction as she smacks her hands on the table in front of her. "You just jinxed yourself. You never talk about the *Q word* or so much as insinuate it. It's Nursing 101. You've worked here long enough to know that."

She's right.

It's one of those, *if you know, you know* things. You never say the word 'quiet' and talk about how it's not busy. When you do, the universe sends the bat signal out, and we're flooded with patients.

"At least if we're busy, tonight will go by fast. It's my last shift this week. I have to study for my board exam. It's two days away, and I'm already freaking out about it."

"Please." Brooke leans her forearms on the counter to level with me. "You've been at the top of the class since day one of the nursing program. You could take that test with your eyes closed and get the highest score in the state. You'll go from maroon to blue scrubs with an RN beside to your name by next week."

I open my mouth to respond, but our nursing team leader comes rushing behind the desk. "Listen up," Kim announces, her tone laced with concern. "We have two serious motor vehicle victims five minutes out. Brooke, I know you're on B side tonight, but I need you in room one with Lisa. Joyce and Emiline, I need you both in room six for extra hands. You all know what to do. Be ready when they get here."

"I hate this," Brooke mutters as she retreats to room one.

Me too.

Because this is one of those unknowns that we both worry about.

I run to grab supplies we might need before wheeling the wound cart to my designated room. Next thing I know, two ambulance stretchers are being rushed in.

The first one through the doors heads in my direction. One

paramedic has two hands over another man's head to keep pressure on the wound and prevent it from bleeding profusely.

I assess how much blood is in the field and run as fast as possible to grab the extra gauze dressings from the supply room. When I return, I take over with fresh gauze and apply pressure to the man's head, where it looks like shattered glass left a gaping wound.

The smell of alcohol engulfs my senses, telling me this had to be a drunk driving incident. I don't like making assumptions, but the scent is so strong.

I have to fight back the bile rising in my throat with each second I hold pressure.

Another nurse starts an IV in his arm while the doctor assesses him from head to toe. He's unconscious, and there's barely a pulse.

In the quickest ten minutes of my life, we successfully stabilize him. The doctor irrigated the wound on his head before applying a dressing, while the other nurse administered a cocktail of medications to help get his heart rate up and control his pain.

I exhale a sigh of relief as I remove my gloves while exiting the room. Only to hear the steady ring of a flatline coming from room one, where they took the second victim of the accident.

The sound is jarring and heartbreaking.

I rush to the room to see if there's anything I can do to help, or if they need an extra set of hands.

But the minute my eyes land on the patient, I realize there's nothing I can do.

I can't breathe or even see straight.

My senses are so dulled I don't even hear Brooke calling my name or any noises filling the room. I faintly hear her say, *"Get her the hell out of here,"* before I'm pulled out of the room.

My stomach curls, and I think I might vomit right here on the floor.

Because I can't fucking breathe.

The person lying in that bed without a pulse is the man I'm deeply and madly in love with.

He's the man who knows me better than anyone else.

He's the man who holds all of my secrets.

Part One

THEN

CHAPTER ONE
Logan

The Beach House - November

"OKAY, do we all know how to play?" Peyton's grandmother, Gigi, announces as she shuffles the cards for the game *Cards Against Humanity* before passing everyone their starting hand.

"Yes, Ma'am," I answer, rubbing my hands together. I'm ready to dominate this game because if there's one thing I'm good at, it's card games.

Work has been exceptionally hectic for everybody, probably because we're heading into the holiday season soon. My best friend, Thomas, had the idea of taking a trip to the house he owns on the Jersey shore. He invited everyone to tag along since it's also his birthday weekend. I didn't think his nanny and her friends would join us, but they've proven to be fun as shit.

This trip with these people was exactly what we all needed.

"Relax, Logy," Emiline says with an exaggerated eye roll. "It's not that serious, and you're going to lose anyway."

I give my best friend's baby sister a wink before I say, "I never lose, Emmy."

That earns me another eye roll.

"Peyton," Gigi says. "You're up first to pick from the deck.

Read it out loud, and then we'll all look at our cards and put them in the center. Then you can pick your favorite and whoever played that card is the winner of that round."

Peyton does as instructed. "A successful job interview begins with a firm handshake and ends with *blank*."

"Oh, fuck." Peyton's friend Avery laughs as she picks through her hand of cards. "I have a good one."

"You can't beat mine, Princess." Marc chuckles from his seat.

I want to smack him in the back of the head at how he calls her *Princess*. It's fucking weird.

"I'm blowing all you bitches away." Gigi laughs.

My eyes dart to where she sits along with everyone else sitting around the table. For an older woman, Gigi's got a mouth on her. My favorite type of person.

"What?" Gigi chuckles. "I'm a pro at this game. You're all going down."

With that, we all break out into a fit of laughter.

This is my first time meeting her, but I love her already.

"Well, Gigi," I say, but quickly stop myself, narrowing my eyes as I point in her direction. "I can call you that, right?"

"Of course, sweetheart." She winks at me. "A fine young man like yourself can call me whatever you want. Just don't call me late for dinner."

"Well, well." I sit up straighter in my seat with a smirk plastered on my face. "I'll have you know that my card will be a favorite of yours."

"I bet it will, *Logy*," Gigi mocks the way Emiline said my name just moments ago.

Peyton clears her throat, directing the attention back to the game. "I'll read the first card and then the answers. 'A successful job interview begins with a firm handshake and ends with'"— she picks up the first card—"*a plunger to the face*."

We all laugh, and Emiline almost spits out her drink next to me. "That was even funnier when you read it all together." Emiline chokes, grabbing a napkin to wipe her mouth. "I gave myself away, but that one is mine. It's what I would like to do to Logan."

"First of all," I say with a pointer finger in the air. "You're not supposed to tell her it's your card. Second of all"—I lift a second finger—"you fucking love me."

"Never in this lifetime, Logan," Emiline scoffs.

"Shush, you two," Peyton says, grabbing the next card. "A successful job interview begins with a firm handshake and ends with *Fuck Mountain*," she says. "That's a good one, guys." Peyton puts the card down and pulls up the next one. She rereads the leading prompt before finishing the sentence with the card she's holding. *"Blowing some dudes in an alley."*

"Oh, fuck yeah!" I clap my hands together. "But that wasn't mine. It was a good one, though." I turn to see Gigi with her hand over her mouth, laughing in her seat. It was definitely hers.

Peyton rereads the prompt, and I take another sip of my whiskey, and she reveals the following answer. *"Just the tip."*

"That's all you need." I laugh out loud, nearly choking on my drink.

"I beg to differ," Avery adds in a serious tone. "Just the tip is a tease. You want to get a girl off, give her all the meat, Logy."

Out of all of Peyton's friends, Avery is most definitely the wildest of them. She has no filter and always says whatever is on her mind.

I scowl at her because this new nickname is annoying as hell.

"I second that," Peyton's other friend, Kali, chimes in.

"I know how to get a girl off," I defend myself, placing a hand over my chest, even though I know I don't need to. "And multiple times. Thank you very much."

Marc says something, but all I hear is Emiline's following words.

"I have to agree with them," she says. "Just the tip does nothing."

"My ears are bleeding, Em," Thomas adds. "Please don't talk about your sex life, I'm begging you."

"She doesn't have a sex life," I scoff. "She's just a baby."

"I'm fucking twenty-one, you Lincoln Log," Emiline says defensively.

My eyes widen. "Since when?" I groan, rubbing a hand down my face. "Good gracious. How have you two not tied her up and locked her in the basement to protect her?" I gesture to Thomas and Marc.

"Because the last two people I want to be tied up by are my brothers," Emiline answers.

My brain is reeling, and I suddenly feel light-headed.

I stare down at my cards, thinking about what Emiline just said. I'm not entirely naive. She's obviously not a child anymore. But twenty-one? When did that happen? I mean, I hang out with Thomas, Marc, and Oliver often. She has always had her own life with her own friends. It's not like I would have known this because she doesn't hang out with us.

Peyton is still reading cards, but it's drowned out as I look from my cards to Emiline and back. Thankfully, no one at the table catches on, but now that I see her, I can't stop staring. I'm captivated by her radiant smile and how her eyes light up as she laughs with her friends.

What the hell is wrong with me?

How have I never noticed any of this before tonight?

I drown the rest of my whiskey and look back at her again. She's still laughing with everyone and most definitely doesn't notice that my eyes are on her.

She's... beautiful.

I already knew that, but now, it feels different.

Way different.

That short back and forth with Emiline just flipped a switch in my brain. I'm seeing her in a new light, and I don't particularly care for the consequences that might come with it if I'm honest.

I'm now noticing how her light blue eyes sparkle when she laughs, causing a small crinkle around them. And the way her wavy, blonde hair cascades down her back, and when the breeze blows in through the windows, it flows effortlessly.

And how her plush, pink lips move with every word out of her mouth. If she was anyone else, I'd want to see them wrapped around my—

"I'm not picking anyone," Peyton says, interrupting my thoughts. *Thank God.* "You all told me who laid down what cards. It's not fair for me to choose now."

"Come on." I stand, throwing my hands in the air. My reaction is over the top, but I'm aggravated by how my brain works through this revelation from just moments ago and because I hate losing games. "I totally won that shit. *Just the tip* is the perfect fill in the blank."

"Would you give it up already?" Emiline huffs, her voice grating my ears. It's annoying the shit out of me that I'm even *hearing* her differently. "Just the tip is never perfect. In any aspect of life."

I grind my molars together and look toward Thomas and Marc. "I swear to God, please stop. How the fuck did you allow her to grow up?"

My reaction is insanely irrational.

I have no reason to feel this way about this newfound perception.

It's fine, right?

After this trip, I'll go back to looking at her the way I did before.

"I'm allowed to do whatever I want." Emiline stands, snapping at me. "I'm a grown adult, whether you like it or not."

"I don't like it," I sneer at her, moving to close the gap between the two of us and bringing my face to hers. The scent of honey and vanilla engulfs my senses, only making the turmoil inside build more. "I really don't fucking like it," I whisper, only for her to hear.

"We've accepted it." I hear Thomas say. "You can too."

Avery and Gigi both say something, but it goes in one ear

and out the other because I can only focus on Emiline. The way she stares at me with such intensity. The way she refuses to pull away or back down from this fight.

Until she does.

She pulls away, and I release a breath I didn't realize I was holding.

I think I'm as torn as I am because I don't want her to be another temptation added to my list.

She's off limits.

Her brothers have told me that from the day we met, and I assured them they had nothing to worry about. Especially because I never really saw her around much. It was always in passing or when she was watching Thomas' son for a quick interaction. Nothing more. I promised myself that I would honor their wishes, and there hasn't been a single time when I thought about wanting her or saw her in a different light.

Until tonight.

"I'm getting a headache," I say, closing my eyes and rubbing my temples with my fingers.

I retreat away to the kitchen to pour myself another glass of whiskey. Marc joins me in the kitchen but says nothing as he pours himself one too. I definitely can't tell him or show him I'm feeling any sort of way for his sister.

Is that what this is, though?

No. I can't go from seeing Emiline as my friend's younger sister to feeling anything for her.

That's just downright crazy.

Marc talks to me about work while we engage in mundane conversation at the kitchen counter. An hour later, "Breakfast at Tiffany's" blasts over the kitchen speakers. Avery, Kali, and Emiline are in a tequila-induced haze and jump on the counter, belting every word of the song.

My eyes never leave Emiline.

The way her body moves.

The way I *notice* how her body moves.

She might as well be the only one standing on the counter.

I take a long pull from my whiskey and wonder if my drinking tonight has caused these thoughts.

I shake myself out of it and glance over at Marc, who has his eyes fixed on Avery. I let out a relieved sigh, thanking the heavens above he doesn't notice how I just tracked every curve on his sister's body as she danced in her short jean shorts on the kitchen counter.

At that moment, I make a pact to myself that I will never think about whatever short-circuit my brain went through after tonight.

Emiline is off limits, and I need to keep my distance.

CHAPTER TWO
Emiline

March

"HOW IS it almost halfway into this semester, and it's kicking our ass more than our first semester?" I groan as we walk to class.

Starting nursing school was the hardest thing I've ever done. People always tell you how hard it is, yet it's something you can only understand once you're in it yourself.

I'm constantly reminding myself that this is all temporary, that classes will only take over my social life until I get this degree.

I *know* I can do this.

"At least you're passing," Brooke scoffs to my side. "I'm barely making it."

"Girl, you have a B+."

"Again, barely making it." She laughs.

"I'm glad we have a good professor this semester," I tell her. "I think we lucked out because the one teaching the other cohort scares me a little."

"Girl, they *all* scare me." Brooke shivers before tightening the hold on her jacket and adjusting her hat while she looks at me.

"Aren't you freezing? We are walking five blocks, which isn't short enough to be in a sweatshirt. This weather is much colder than usual for March."

"I forgot to grab a jacket before I left."

The cold doesn't bother me the way it bothers some people. Growing up in the city, I learned to adapt to this weather. Brooke had only been here for a few years when she moved in with her now ex-boyfriend. The unsupportive guy couldn't handle the busy schedule of our classes.

But she stayed because she discovered the allure of the fast pace of living here and the convenience of not needing a car to travel everywhere.

"I worked last night and rolled out of bed after two hours of sleep with enough time to shower, throw my hair in this top knot bun, and I still remembered my jacket," she says.

"Shit. That's right. I saw the work group chat going crazy. It sounded like it was a busy night for you guys."

"That's an understatement. I could have stayed in bed for three days after that shift, but it still wouldn't be enough," Brooke emphasizes.

"Oof, it was really that bad?"

She shoots me a pointed glare out of the corner of her eye. "We had patients in the waiting room for almost four hours. Maybe more. I don't even know. When one person left, another came in. To top it off, they brought in some bar fight last night around midnight. Six grown men. I swear I thought they'd continue the brawl in front of the nurse's desk. And one was so messed up that his eye was so swollen shut that we couldn't even see if there was actual damage to his eyeball."

"Jeez," I sigh.

"Yeah, you're lucky you weren't there. I wish I was sleeping soundly like you were last night," she jokes, bumping my shoulder as we walk.

I force a smile because I don't want to tell her what I was really doing.

I was having a panic attack over the content we haven't even touched in class today.

No one knows the struggles I deal with and I'd like to keep it that way.

I've always been afraid of someone looking at me like I'm weak because I freak out before a class or a significant test or if I'm overwhelmed. Being the only daughter in the family, not to mention the youngest sibling, there's a lot of pressure on me to live up to the standards my older brothers have set.

All three of them are insanely successful and wealthy. Granted, we all have a decent amount of money from the inheritance my father left us when he passed. I didn't get mine until I was eighteen. After discussing what to do with the money with my older brother Thomas, we invested it for a few years until I was ready.

This worked out well because once I turned twenty-one, I moved out of my apartment and into a new one. The money was enough to cover two years of rent and furnish this place I call home. It's nothing crazy, but it works for me.

I love it because it's quiet and all mine.

After that, I applied for the accelerated nursing program and got in almost instantly. I was set on making something happen for myself, even if it wouldn't make me a billionaire like my brothers.

"Oh, I forgot to tell you, I saw your hottie officer." Brooke wiggles her eyebrows.

The thought of *that* particular person sends chills through my body.

Logan Bennett.

My brothers' best friend.

A man older than me by a few years and insanely hot.

"Please stop calling him that."

"What?" a smirk plays on her lips. "I just call it like it is."

I roll my eyes.

I hate that she's not wrong.

Prior to getting my job at the hospital, I only ever saw him in passing with my brothers. Now I get the pleasure of seeing him more and more because he's one of the many officers that brings people into our emergency room here and there. I say pleasure with as much sarcasm as possible because ever since that one weekend we took a trip to Thomas' beach house for his birthday, Logan's been so different. He went from looking at me like his best friend's younger sister to looking at me like he hates my guts.

Brooke picked up on the way he was looking at me one night. All I saw was a scowl, but she was so delusional that she saw something more. Hence her calling him 'my hottie officer.' This is precisely the reason why I dread when he has to bring someone in.

I've been thankful that our paths haven't crossed again since he brought in our regular, Jerry, last month. But that's not surprising since I only work a part-time schedule while in school —two twelve-hour shifts a week—and it's really hit or miss when they show up with someone.

In January, when my brothers, Peyton, and Kali took me out to dinner for my birthday, I half expected him to be there because we always do everything as a group. Marc said he invited him to join us but that he picked up a shift.

I was relieved but also partially irritated.

Not that I had any right to be. However, it *was* my birthday, and Logan suddenly hated me so much that he had to 'pick up an extra shift' just to stay away from me?

I might be completely wrong and assuming the worst, but he didn't even text me to wish me a happy birthday. And I know he has my number because we're in a group chat with everyone, and because he's always wished me a happy birthday in all the years he's been friends with Thomas.

At first, I thought I was overreacting to the entire thing, as I do in many situations. Admittedly, I'm constantly worrying if someone is mad at me. It's one thing I hate about myself because nine times out of ten, it's just me reading a situation all wrong.

That changed when he brought in Jerry. It was awkward, and Logan couldn't leave the room fast enough. That's how I knew fully that I was not reading our situation wrong. It was a moment of painful clarity.

I wanted to be mad at him, ignore him, and maybe even confront him.

As I navigated the patients room that night, I could feel his gaze on me, a silent force I struggled to resist because I've always had a crush on Logan. From the moment he first started hanging out with Thomas, I thought he was the hottest man to ever cross my path.

That crush has been long gone. It's as if it had never existed.

I had a good look when he walked in and fought to smile when I saw his dark brown hair brushed to the side like he'd been running his hands through it for hours.

When I saw those chocolate brown eyes, they burned me to my core, and any feelings of wanting to smile disappeared. I watched Logan's jaw tick like seeing me was the worst part of his night, forcing him to avert his gaze as fast as possible.

At that moment, I truly grasped his disdain for me, and any concern I had for his feelings vanished.

"You really need to stop calling him that and thinking something's there when it's not. Even if you were right, I cannot date him. Nursing school is my only focus."

"I said nothing about dating the guy," Brooke chokes out. "Besides, you know the unspoken rules at work. No dating any of the four P's... paramedics, physicians, firefighters, and police officers."

I narrow my eyes as I glare at her from the corner of my eye. "Firefighter does not start with a P."

"Pff," she says, making a noise with her mouth to emphasize that when you sound it out, it could very well start with a P.

This time, I bark out a laugh.

Even the thought of dating makes me ready to break out in hives. I've only been in one serious relationship, which was enough for me.

We started dating in high school and ended things the summer before I started this program. Well… *we* didn't end things.

He did.

Apparently, summer isn't the time to be locked down in a relationship, and he wasn't ready to settle down.

To be honest, he was just an uptight, rich kid. He wasn't my type, but he was the kind of person I felt like I was supposed to end up with because of the wealthy lifestyle I grew up in.

After that ended, I realized that morning tea with men wearing sweater vests and golfing on their days off was *not* my thing.

Unfortunately, he was also the first and last guy I slept with. What's even sadder is that I rarely had my needs met in that relationship.

Did I get off during sex? Well, sometimes.

The first red flag I should have noticed in that relationship was that he never once went down on me despite all the times I'd gone down on him. But we got into a routine, and I thought that it wasn't as common for guys to do so.

I shake myself from my thoughts and try to change the subject before she keeps bringing up Logan. "Want to stop for coffee?" I ask.

"That's the dumbest question you've ever asked me."

"You should know that no question is stupid."

Brooke barks out a laugh. "That one is. The answer will always be yes when coffee is involved."

I shake my head, and we stop at the small coffee shop on our way to campus.

"I'm getting the largest cup of iced peppermint mocha they have," I announce proudly.

"Like that's nothing new for you, you caffeine addict. You'd drink peppermint mocha in the heat of the summer."

We both burst into hysterics as Brooke graciously holds the coffee shop door open for me. However, my laughter is abruptly cut short as I collide with something… someone. I feel a searing pain in my chest and struggle to draw in a breath.

"What the hell," the voice yells.

Burning hot coffee is poured down the entire front of my sweatshirt.

"Shit, shit, shit." My voice trails off while I pull the fabric off my chest to avoid first-degree burns. "Ahhh."

"Are you okay?" the now familiar voice asks.

When I look up at the set of eyes staring back at me, alarm bells ring in my head, and suddenly, it's like I've stepped into the inferno. His mouth morphs into annoyance as the realization hits him as well.

"Don't you watch where you're going, Lincoln Log?" I snap.

He has no right to be annoyed right now. I'm the one with coffee down the front of my shirt.

"Me? That's rich, considering you're the one who wasn't paying attention to where they were going. You barged in here like you own the place." When I don't answer immediately, he continues. "But none of that matters right now. Are you okay?"

I groan loudly in frustration. I'm not okay, but Logan doesn't need to know that. I turn to Brooke, and her eyes are wide in shock at my exchange with Logan.

Good, maybe she can drop the hottie cop comments and see it for what it truly is.

"I can't go to class like this." I gesture to the enormous stain down the front of me.

"If you had an actual jacket on, you could've avoided your sweatshirt getting soaked," Logan cuts into the conversation. When I turn to face him, his shoulders lift in a shrug. "You realize it's like thirty degrees out, right?"

"What are you, my dad?" I fire back before giving him a

sarcastic puppy eye. "I'm so sorry, Daddy. I left the house without a jacket again." I school my features before I continue. "Unlike your ice-cold soul, I'm warm-blooded."

His eyes narrow, but something else flashes through them. I can't tell if it's because I mockingly called him daddy or because I told him he had an ice-cold soul. Either way, I feel heat skate across every part of my skin with how he looks at me.

And it's definitely not because of coffee this time.

I break his stare before sidestepping him to follow Brooke into the line so we can order. She already has napkins in hand, helping to dry me off. A few little napkins would not help this mess right now.

"Well, that was some run-in," she deadpans. "No pun intended, of course."

"You could say that again."

"Well, that was some—"

I throw up my hand to stop her. "Don't start," I say as I attempt to pat some coffee off my chest. "Do you think I have time to run back to my apartment to change my shirt? I can't walk into class late with Professor Mathis smelling like I bathed in coffee grounds."

Brooke looks down at her phone to check the time. "I think we can make it. You having this insane need to be in class twenty minutes earlier than we really need to be is a plus right now. We just have to book it."

A throat clears behind me, and I see Logan still standing there.

"What?" I practically growl.

"Still trying to make sure you're okay. Judging by the growl in your voice, you're fine. I'm also here because I need a fresh cup since mine was spilled." He grins mockingly. "So relax, Emmy."

"Don't call me that," I grit out through clenched teeth. He rolls his eyes in annoyance before I turn to face forward.

Brooke and I each order a coffee. No sooner do we finish

telling the barista our order, when Logan jumps in and reorders as if he's part of our tab.

"Excuse me," I say as I spin around quickly. "I'm not paying for the coffee you negligently spilled all over me."

"You're not," he says flatly.

The barista hands over his coffee first because, of course, he got a straight black coffee. Seconds later, the second barista comes to the counter to hand me the two iced coffees we ordered. Once she does, Logan hands her a twenty-dollar bill.

"This should cover the order," he tells her.

"Oh," Brooke coos. "Thank you. I'm Brooke, by the way." She extends a hand out to greet him, a smile covering her face. "We've probably met briefly in passing at the hospital, but I figured I would introduce myself anyway."

He raises a brow at her, and I can't help but roll my eyes. Logan doesn't say a single word back but shakes her hand. Leave it to my best friend to make things extra uncomfortable when I'm supposed to hate him as much as he hates me right now.

"Thank you," I say, conceding to how nice he is right now despite my entirely rational frustration. "To answer your question, I'm okay. But now, I'm extra late for class. I can't make Brooke late too. So, if you'll excuse me." I move to sidestep Logan, but he doesn't move an inch, forcing our bodies to collide. The coffee down my shirt has already run cold, but my body is instantly hot all over again. "Move. I have to rush home, get changed, and literally run to class."

Instead of moving out of the way, he says, "I'd offer you a ride, but sounds like you have everything under control here."

"Would you have flashed the lights and everything for us?" Brooke laughs.

"No lights," he answers her before turning to look at me. "I have my motorcycle today—"

"And here you are lecturing me about how it's thirty degrees out," I scoff, cutting him off. "Don't you think it's a little too cold to be riding your motorcycle in this weather?"

Logan's jaw ticks before he scoffs. "I'd ride it in the snow if I could."

"Great. Good for you," I say.

"*Great* for me," he says sarcastically without aggravation laced in his words.

"We have to go now so I can get changed before class. This is wasting my time."

I turn toward the door, and Brooke pushes it open before me so we can get out of here.

I don't even give Logan another glance to see his reaction before turning around and walking towards the door, and he doesn't stop us either.

As we hustle back to my apartment, my brain buzzes, replaying our entire interaction. He used to be so nice to me in all the years I've known him.

This is not the Logan Bennett I used to know.

Something has definitely changed.

And none of it is sitting right with me.

CHAPTER THREE
Logan

I DOWN THE rest of my coffee before getting on my motorcycle. The engine roars to life under me as I watch Emiline and her friend, who I recognized from the ER, hustle down the street. This morning was anything but what I expected. I just wanted to get my coffee and meet my partner, Silas, at the gym. Instead, I had a *literal* run-in with the girl I've been trying to avoid at all costs.

Shaking off the intrusive thoughts, I pull down the visor on my helmet and steer my motorcycle in the opposite direction.

Once I arrive, I park my bike, quickly unclasp my bag from the back, and hustle inside. Silas is waiting for me, tapping his fingers on the receptionist counter as if he's been waiting for hours.

"Bout' time, Bennett."

"Relax," I reply casually, with a grin. "I just had my four-dollar cup of black coffee spill all over the place as I left the coffee shop and then got into a fight with the recipient of said spilled coffee."

His eyes widen. "Well, okay."

I love that he never asks more questions or pushes for information.

"I'll go get changed," I say as I walk toward the locker room.

After I change into a pair of gym shorts and an old T-shirt, I find Silas already in the ring and ready to go. I'm determined to make the most of this session, to push myself further than before, both physically and mentally.

"Let's do this." I nod, taking my place in the ring with him. I don my gloves, and Silas holds up punching mitts as I throw light jabs and hooks to warm up.

Some people run or take up a hobby to escape whatever demons they fight. But not me. I'm not the type of guy who likes to talk about emotions. I've never talked about my dad with any of the Ford siblings. They know he died when I was young but never asked for more details. We've always had a silent understanding, a bond that doesn't require words.

Boxing is my escape. It's become an outlet for me after tough shifts at work or when I need to release pent-up emotions. It's a testament to my resilience, showing that I can face my demons head-on and come out stronger.

In my line of work, I've seen some shit I never want to see again. Some things are so jarring and heavy on the mind that their images are forever embedded in my brain, no matter how hard I try to eliminate them.

But that's what I signed up for when I became a police officer.

I've wanted to be a police officer since I could walk. It feels like it's always been in my blood to follow in my dad's footsteps. He was the former police chief, and I've looked up to him my entire life. Hell, I still do, even years after his passing.

The current chief, Bob, is actually his old partner, and he's finally talking about retirement. The thought of taking over his position fills me with excitement and nervousness. I want the job more than my next breath.

It's partially because I would love to no longer be on the streets as much as I am, but I also want to make my father proud. His dedication to his work and family has always inspired me, and I feel that by following in his footsteps, I can honor his memory.

Silas introduced me to this gym about six months ago. He's been coming here for years and finally talked me into joining.

He might be older than me, but he started on the force long after me. Like many people, he didn't know what he wanted to do with his life after high school. During our first shift together, I learned that after graduation, he was a single guy torn between becoming a police officer or going into accounting.

He initially chose accounting, and after a few years of hating absolutely every minute, he realized the desk job life wasn't for him and went back to school to study criminal justice.

He's genuinely one of my best partners since I've been here. And I've gone through my fair share of them. I'm not sure if it's because I'm an asshole or because I drive them away with my intense work ethic. Either way, Silas puts up with my moods, never asks questions, and *wants* to work.

My mind is a whirlwind of thoughts as my punches grow stronger and stronger.

Work, my dad, and a specific blonde-haired, blue-eyed woman.

It still feels weird to think of her like that because she's always been my best friend's little sister. Emiline Ford was always Thomas, Marc, and Oliver's kid sister. Three best friends who have become more like brothers to me.

I wasn't dumb about the fact that she's older now, but something shifted during our weekend trip to the beach house for Tommy's birthday.

After our little argument over the card game, my brain rewired itself.

Now, my mind is constantly invaded by thoughts of an undeniably off-limits woman.

Thoughts I don't fucking *want* to have.

Months later, I still cannot rid my mind of them.

Which is why Emiline infuriates me now.

It doesn't help that prior to that trip, I only saw here in passing. Now she's unavoidable in my line of work since she works at this hospital. It's not like she works in another part of the building, and I don't have to see her. She works at the front line of the ER, and she's one of the first faces we see when we bring someone in.

The last time I brought someone in and saw her, my steps faltered and I fought a silent battle inside of me to maintain my composure around her.

The minute my eyes landed on her, I couldn't look away. Her long blonde hair was pulled back in a ponytail, and she was wearing a pair of deep maroon scrubs. The color complemented her ivory skin and made her eyes shine brighter, if possible. An image burned in my brain for no reason. It made her look almost angelic as she sat behind the desk, sipping her iced coffee.

Emiline has this pureness and innocence to her that a part of me craves to corrupt, a desire that burns within me like a forbidden flame, but I can't allow it.

I ended up trying to get out of there as fast as I could.

Now, I'm constantly wondering what it is about her and why she's always on my mind.

I'm mostly curious about her.

She's sassy and strong-willed.

But is that a way for her to hide some form of trauma from the world the same way I do by being the funny guy around friends?

I could be overthinking it.

I could be wrong.

I can't help but wonder.

I release everything I feel, punch by punch, until I have nothing left.

"Jesus, Bennett." Silas stops me, stepping back. "You're wound up worse than usual today. And to think that was just the warmup."

My hands fall to the side and I release a sigh, working to

control my ragged breaths. "I don't know, just a lot in my head," I admit.

When I don't hear him immediately respond, I glance in his direction, and the look on his face is passive and unreadable.

"Has nothing to do with blondie in the emergency room, does it?"

"I don't know who you're talking about," I say with a dismissive tone.

Silas holds up his hands in defense. "I won't make you talk about it, but if you want to, you can."

How do I explain my thoughts to someone when I can't wrap my head around them myself?

I can't put words together to explain that I can't eat pizza anymore without thinking of my dad never coming home. Or how my best friend's little sister is so deeply buried under my skin that I can't stand the way I see her now.

I can't say any of that.

Not to him. Not to anyone.

"I'm good. Let's go one more round," I say, swiftly changing the subject before Silas can probe further. "Then we can hit up the East Side dive bar for some burgers."

Silas smiles and raises his mitts to his face. "Give me all you got, Bennett."

And I do just that.

CHAPTER FOUR
Emiline

"WELL, THIS WAS LONG OVERDUE," Peyton says, placing her napkin on the table after finishing her meal. "I feel like it's been forever since we got together for our Tuesday night dinners."

"It really was what we needed," Kali agrees.

When Peyton moved to the city last fall, she, Kali, and Avery started a weekly tradition of going to Old Jose. It's this little hole-in-the-wall Mexican restaurant with the best atmosphere and food where we meet for tacos and tequila.

Avery claims that combining the two solves all of life's problems. Since Peyton started inviting me to their weekly nights, I can confirm it does. Having a group of girlfriends to talk or vent to about whatever is going on in your life is like a breath of fresh air.

I had a handful of friends before these girls, but they all moved away for college, which turned into one of those things where we just never kept in touch.

At first, it was disappointing because we had gone through so much together during high school. But I quickly learned that maybe those people weren't meant to be in my life long term. I've seen what real friendship is like with these girls.

It's carefree.

It's filled with laughter and a great time.

These girls have become everything to me, and I'm so grateful for their presence in my life. They've shown me the true meaning of friendship and I couldn't be more thankful.

"How's school going, Em?" Kali asks. "You're almost halfway done with your second semester, right?"

"Yeah, I am. It's a lot tougher than I thought it would be." I laugh lightly.

It's challenging to explain nursing school to someone who hasn't experienced it. It involves constant studying, feeling overwhelmed by clinical work, and moving from one topic to the next without fully grasping the previous one.

It's only intensified my panic attacks.

Not a soul knows I deal with them in the first place.

Not my brothers. Not Peyton, Avery, or Kali.

Not even Brooke.

I'd like to keep it that way too.

It's such a pathetic thing to keep a secret, but I don't want anyone to worry about me more than they already do. My brothers and friends already worry so much about me. I want to be able to stand on my own. Anyone knowing I have them would make things so much worse for me.

I put a lot of pressure on myself and worry about things out of my control.

Working in the emergency room doesn't help. The unknown causes me considerable anxiety before every shift. Even when I try to nap before work, my brain runs a mile a minute thinking about what we might see on shift.

Then, when I have to sleep after work, my brain runs through feelings of guilt for sleeping instead of studying.

I'm at the top of my class, but it hasn't come without hard work. I put sleep, my friends, and my family all on the back burner.

I'm also the type of learner who has to study extra hours, read more material, and write things down. Then, to grasp the material, I have to find supplemental videos supporting what I just read.

Yet, all of that preparation still doesn't ease my nerves.

Once a test is approaching or we're about to dive into new content, fear crushes me like an elephant sitting on my chest, and I fall into a total panic.

It's easier to deal with alone than have people asking questions.

Or worse, people treating me like a porcelain doll.

"But I'm managing," I add before they can question me. "I can't wait for spring break in a few weeks to get myself a little ahead so I don't constantly feel behind."

"You're doing amazing." Peyton beams with a smile. "I'm really proud of you, and I know Thomas is too."

Just hearing her say that fills me with an overwhelming sense of pride.

She may not be my sister, but she's the closest thing I have to one, being she's engaged to my oldest brother. Knowing that she's proud of me means everything.

"That means a lot." I sigh, and change the subject before I get emotional. "Has anyone heard from Avery? How's her mom doing?"

"She's doing good," Peyton answers first. "Her mom's recovery is going well, and she says she should be back in the city by June. That's her goal."

"I miss that ball of energy," Kali adds.

I laugh. "Speaking of balls of energy, I need to make it over to your place to see James soon."

"You know you're welcome anytime." Peyton's smile radiates warmth, making me feel instantly at home.

I will always be thankful for stumbling upon a 'nanny for hire' ad that Peyton placed when she moved here, even though Thomas definitely didn't want to hire someone. He didn't understand that school would take over my life for a while and I wouldn't be able to watch my nephew anymore, so I took it upon myself to find someone.

Peyton agreed to meet me one morning. When Thomas showed up to meet the possible nanny, it turned out that she and my brother already knew each other, which was wild to me.

Her getting hired led to the greatest thing that happened for both of them.

They are now engaged and will get married this fall. They even bought a house in New Jersey, right outside the city.

Every time I think about James or hang out with Peyton like this, I feel guilty for how I haven't made an effort to get out there and see them as much as I'd like.

It's mostly because I'm terrified of stepping away from the books.

I hate that I've let myself get like this.

"Once I get myself caught up with school, I am so making the trip to see you," I tell her.

"Have you been seeing anyone?" Kali asks randomly. She holds up her hands in defense. "I know you're busy with school, but we weren't sure if there was… someone *else* keeping you busy."

I toss my head from side to side. "Absolutely not. I don't have time for a relationship or seeing someone casually. Not to mention, the moment they find out what I deal with, they would run for the hills."

"What do you mean?" Peyton cocks her head in confusion.
Shit.

"You know." I wiggle my hands in the air and laugh nervously. "Studying for hours on end and night shifts in between. It's a lot for someone to handle. It's a lot of late nights and many sleepless days."

Now I'm rambling nervously.

"Yeah, I guess." Peyton shrugs before she picks up her phone, buzzing on the table, to read her text. "Oh, Thomas is almost here." She reaches for the check the server placed on our table moments ago. "This one's on me tonight, girls."

"I'll leave the tip today," I say, reaching for my bag.

By the time I finish shuffling through my purse and wallet to place some cash on the table, my brother walks in to pick up Peyton.

I can't help but watch how Thomas' eyes light up when he sees her in a room. It's almost as if everything around them fades, and all he sees is her. Peyton moves from the table and leaps into his arms as if they haven't seen each other in days.

One day, I want that kind of love.

Someone who looks at me like I'm the best thing that's ever happened to them.

My lips curve into a smile when a throat clears behind Thomas. Standing directly behind him is Logan.

I feel the smile on my face falter, but not enough that anyone would notice. I stuff my hands in the pockets of my jeans to avoid nervously fidgeting with them. Being around Logan makes me feel on edge, especially with how he's staring at me with such intensity.

I hate that he has to look so damn good.

He's dressed casually, but I swear he can make a paper bag look good. His tousled dark brown hair matches the color of his eyes boring into mine. He's clearly aggravated I'm here.

Trust me, I feel the same.

Peyton releases Thomas from a hug before she notices Logan standing beside him. "Oh. Hi, Logan."

He moves his gaze to her and a smile spreads on his face as he wasn't just staring at me annoyed. "Hey, Pey. How was your guys' dinner?"

"It was good. What are you doing here?"

"Logan and I grabbed a bite to eat while we waited for you, babe," Thomas answers for him. "Old Jose was on the way to his truck, so we just picked you up first."

"That makes sense," she says as she wraps her arms around

Thomas' neck again and presses up to her toes before kissing him.

"Damn. I missed you too, baby." My brother laughs.

"I'm going to head out," I say, grabbing my purse on the chair.

"Do you want a ride?" Thomas asks.

"No," I answer way too quickly, shaking my head. "No, thank you. I'll be fine."

"But it's freezing out," Thomas argues. "And all you have on is that long-sleeved shirt."

I glance in Logan's direction and see amusement on his face because this entire conversation is strangely similar to our coffee shop run-in last week.

"I'll be fine," I say.

"Hold on." Thomas stops me before I can walk away, and then he looks at Logan. "Don't you have that extra sweatshirt in the back of my car?"

Logan snaps his head in his direction but doesn't move. Almost like he's shocked that my brother just offered me his sweatshirt.

"You want me to give her my hoodie?" Logan confirms, making sure he heard him correctly.

"Yeah?" He furrows his brows. "She can't walk back to her apartment in this weather. I know it's March, but it's record breaking cold out there. The weather doesn't know what it wants to do." He rolls his eyes.

"It's only two blocks, Thomas," I tell him.

"Nonsense." My brother waves his hands.

Logan pauses for a moment longer, eyes flashing to mine with hesitation for a brief moment before he retreats out the front door to grab his sweatshirt.

I stand there feeling like all eyes are on me. The last thing I want is to borrow this from him and be forced to see him again to give it back.

And I don't want to be consumed by Logan's scent.

"Tommy," I say now that Logan is out of sight. "I'm pretty sure your friend can't stand me. Now you're forcing him to give me his clothes."

Thomas swats a hand in my direction. "Oh, stop that. Logan loves you. You're like a little sister to him."

I say nothing back.

In fact, I can *feel* my heart rate pick up from that statement alone.

There isn't an ounce of 'love' toward me in that man's body.

For years, he's always been so kind to me. Granted we've never hung out or spent much time together. But the times that I did see Logan, he was always nice. He would say hi, have quick playful banter with me about putting up with three older brothers, but lately that's not the Logan I get in passing.

I'd be lying if I say it doesn't hurt. I miss the way he was friendly with me, or used to smile at me, or hell, even talk to me.

Now I just get the cold version of him.

I try not to let these things get to me, but the only thing that replays in my head right now is that I'm like a little sister to Logan. I know that's all I'll ever be to him, even if there was a time a few years back when I wished it was more.

When my all-consuming crush made me want him more than my next breath, but I remind myself I was young when I thought about things like that.

I was naïve, and he was just my brother's hot friend.

As that last thought crosses my mind, Logan walks back in with his hoodie and passes me the same royal blue one he had on when I saw him in the coffee shop. Our fingers graze and every nerve in my body spikes. The electric feeling from such a small move forces me to feel off, as if I'm going to tumble to the ground. We both stand there, staring into each other's eyes for a moment too long before he pulls away. It was so fast, one would think the contact burned his skin. I keep watching as he clenches the muscle in his jaw, looking angry over whatever that just was between us.

"Thank you," I say reluctantly, taking it from him, looking down at the soft fabric in my hands.

"Anytime, Emmy," Logan replies flatly. His tone leading me to believe he's definitely annoyed with this entire thing.

I'm equally aggravated because I hate that he calls me that. It makes me feel young. No one but Logan calls me that, and I'm convinced he does it just to piss me off.

I want to smile and show him he doesn't affect me, but I can't.

I can't because I keep replaying Tommy's words in my head.

He loves you like a little sister.

CHAPTER FIVE
Emiline

MOST OF THE students in my cohort have spent their spring break in some tropical paradise or visiting family. I've spent mine attempting to get ahead on assignments. I know myself enough to know that if I took a break from the books, it would only increase my stress and anxiety.

Except today.

Today, I forced myself to put *everything* to the side.

I can't remember the last time I had a day where I did absolutely nothing and bummed it on the couch watching reruns of reality television shows.

My issue is I don't know how to sit still and relax.

I ended up cleaning my apartment while the TV played in the background. Then, I went to the gym to use the Stairmaster, which was oddly therapeutic.

Now, I'm standing in the middle of my small living room, staring at my surroundings, wondering what the hell to do with myself.

Do I clean some more?

I could organize my kitchen cabinets. Avery would be proud.

Do I go over all my notes?

No. The whole point of today is to step away.

Do I open my textbook and read over material we haven't covered in class yet?

Emiline, stop.

Every thought is cut short when I hear a knock on my door. I check the peephole and find Brooke standing in the hallway. My eyes narrow in question because she never shows up unannounced.

"Are you okay?" I question, swinging the door open. My eyes scan her, and she's wearing a tight mini dress and a pair of heels as if she's ready for a night in town.

"Something has to be wrong for me to show up at my best friend's house on a Friday night and drag her out because I know she's sitting here contemplating studying things we haven't even touched in class yet." She raises an eyebrow from the doorway.

I chew on the inside of my cheek. "Well…"

"That's what I thought," she says, entering my apartment.

"You cut me off," I defend with my hands on my hips. "I was contemplating reorganizing my kitchen cabinets."

"And then you were thinking about studying some more," she finishes for me, hitting the nail on the head. But I keep my face passive so she doesn't catch on to the fact that she's right. "Get your head out of the books. We're going out before classes start back up again on Monday. I know you've been reading about gastrointestinal disorders the last few days, and it stops right now."

I avert my gaze to the floor. She's caught me.

"Ha! I knew it." She laughs as she plops on the couch. "Go get dressed."

I don't move from where I stand as I watch her grab the remote from where it's stashed in the end table drawer. I glance down at myself and note my oversized sweatpants that look like they've been through one hundred loads of laundry and

Logan's sweatshirt that, to my dismay, I have refused to take off.

I keep telling myself it's because of the comfort, not because of the person who owns it.

"I'm not even remotely ready to go out," I exclaim.

"I know," she says with her eyes fixed on the TV as she flips through the channels before landing on the one that plays all the old *Grey's Anatomy* reruns. "I'll wait for you. Ditch the Adam Sandler from *Big Daddy* outfit choice and put something hot on."

I bark out a laugh and shake my head at her antics before retreating to my room. That's when I notice my desk full of study material that I left open, and my stomach sinks, realizing that this might be a bad idea.

Aside from feeling guilty for not studying tonight, I'm also not the type of girl who goes out to a party or has these crazy nights out. I enjoy a drink or two with the girls if we go to dinner, but the bar or club scene is not for me.

But this is what I wanted today.

A day to do absolutely nothing school related.

I take a few calming breaths before I curl some of my hair and browse my closet for something to wear. I find an old dress I forgot I even had. Even the price tag is still attached. It's a solid bright red, form-fitting dress that sits mid-thigh and has a decent-sized slit up the left side.

It's actually kind of hot. Exactly what Brooke told me to wear.

"Almost ready?" she bellows from the living room.

"Just about," I shout back.

I slip on the dress, throw on some perfume, and put on my favorite pair of nude comfort heels, which have red on the bottom to match the dress.

I finally step out into the living room, and Brooke immediately turns her head.

"Hell yeah," She smiles and nods repeatedly as she gets up from the couch. "That's the outfit. That looks hot." She turns off the TV and grabs her purse while I grab mine and the key to my apartment. "I'm in the mood to dance. Let's let loose before the second half of the semester. What do you say?"

I pause for a moment because the idea of letting loose makes me uneasy. I force a smile in her direction despite feeling like this is a bad idea.

"Let's do it."

———

We settle on a bar that's only two blocks from my apartment. I use the term bar loosely because the atmosphere of this place feels more like a club. They have a live DJ tonight, packed with people on spring break.

"This place is the best," Brooke shouts over the music.

I take a sip of my vodka club and give her a nod.

I'm so thankful to have a friend like Brooke, who understands me enough to know I needed this more than I thought. I needed to leave my tiny apartment and feel this energy for a while.

I needed to get out of my head.

The music is pumping, and I feel the vibrations through every part of me. I can't help but sway from side to side as I sip my drink. It's kind of a freeing feeling to not have to worry about anything outside of these walls.

I've already decided that I will not be letting my anxiety get the best of me tonight.

"Oh, look." Brooke points to the other side of the bar. "It's Mason."

I look toward where she's pointing and notice Mason is, in fact, standing at a high-top table with a few other guys.

Brooke and I mostly know him from work, but my stomach does a somersault when I remember that Mason is one of Logan's coworkers.

In fact, the entire table is full of police officers.

Is Logan working tonight?

Is he going to be here? Is he already here?

No. Please, no. I don't want another run in with him. I was just starting to feel the effects of the vodka kicking in, and I don't want him bringing me down from my high.

Okay, I'm exaggerating a bit.

It's not that seeing him would bring me down from my high. Being around him makes me more nervous than not lately, especially when I don't know what version of Logan I'll get when I come face-to-face with him.

Will I get the Logan who sees me and scowls?

Or will I finally get a glimpse of the old Logan who used to smile at me.

The Logan I had a crush on years ago.

It's a mystery every time.

Mason turns his head as if he can feel Brooke pointing at him. His smile grows wide as he waves us over to them.

She grabs my wrist without another word, holding it tight, and weaves us through the crowd until we get to their table. I down the last of my drink in one gulp before we reach their table. Brooke comes to a complete stop without warning, and I practically collide with her back.

Two drinks in, and I'm already unsteady on my feet.

A downfall for not being a heavy drinker.

My eyes sweep the table, and I realize Logan is not here. His partner, Silas, however, stands in the corner, texting on his phone.

"Em, did you hear me?" Brooke says, snapping my attention back to her. "Did you want another drink? Mason is going to grab us a round."

I'm not sure I like this at all. Everything about being at this table with these guys feels off. I stuff down my urge to leave and finally offer Mason a tight nod. "I'd love a vodka club."

"You got it, ladies." He winks toward Brooke before heading for the bar.

I roll my eyes at how cringy his attempt at flirting is.

"Hey, Emiline." I hear from my side. My head snaps toward the voice, and I notice Silas smiling. He's got to be about seven feet tall as he towers over me.

"Hey, Silas," I say, but it comes out all nervous and jittery.

"How's school going?"

"It's been good." I sigh, realizing I don't need to feel anxious right now. Thankfully, it's still loud enough that no one would even notice. "It's going a little too fast for my liking, though," I add.

"I bet." He nods.

I'm just about to ask him how he got the night off when I *feel* someone come to a stop at my side. Turning my head to see, I'm met with deep, brown eyes that look downright annoyed I'm here.

Annoyed, but damn… why does Logan have to be so hot?

This has to be the alcohol talking.

My eyes trail down his body. I've never seen Logan dressed up like this before. He's wearing his signature pair of dark-wash jeans and a button-down shirt with rolled sleeves. He must have tailored that because there's no way a shirt off the rack in a department store would fit around those biceps.

I should ask him if he has a permit to carry those around.

Oh my god. No more drinking, Emiline.

I move my gaze back up to his and fight the urge to smile up at him when I see his annoyed expression falter. He doesn't tower over me like Silas, but he has a good few inches on me, even with my heels.

What would it be like to climb this man like a tree?

No. Stop.

Or to trail my fingers along that angry jawline?

Shut up. Shut up. SHUT UP.

"Shouldn't you be studying," Logan says flatly.

I usually ignore him, but something inside me snaps at his comment. Maybe it's the alcohol or the fact that I feel like he's bringing up my weakness right now despite not knowing anything about the anxiety that I deal with.

"What is with you and patronizing me every time I see you? First, you're on my case about not wearing a jacket. And now—on a Friday night, might I remind you—you're here telling me I need to be studying instead of enjoying my night. This is getting really old, Logan."

I see Silas hide his laugh from the corner of my eye, but Logan keeps the scowl on his face.

I guess I'm getting Logan with a scowl tonight. Lucky me.

He doesn't answer, so I continue. "It's spring break. I'm allowed a break from studying every once in a while."

His features soften as if he knows I'm right. But it's not enough for anyone else to notice.

"Well." He takes half a step closer to me. The slight movement causes the hairs on my neck to stand and my shoulders to stiffen.

I didn't know it was possible to feel a shiver run through my body while simultaneously feeling like every inch of me is on fire. But here we are.

He leans in close enough that I can smell peppermint on his breath. "Enjoy your night then, Emmy."

I roll my eyes and open my mouth to retort, but Mason returns to the table with our orders.

"Drinks for the ladies," he says, holding them up in both hands.

I chose not to give Logan any more of my energy and turn to face Mason. I muster up my best fake smile before grabbing the vodka club and gulping it down in one sip.

I'll probably regret it later, but I don't have it in me to care right now.

"Want to dance?" I ask Brooke.

"Hell yeah," she says, grabbing my hand before throwing it in the air as she shakes her ass.

I follow her without a single look back at Logan.

CHAPTER SIX
Logan

MY MOLARS GRIND together as I watch Emiline saunter off with her friend to the middle of the dance floor. I can't tell if I'm irritated that she's here while trying to enjoy one of my rare nights off or that she looks insanely attractive in her dress.

In all the years I've known her, I've never seen Emiline in a dress or even look like she does tonight. Granted, the times I did see her were few and far between. But this dress she has on hugs every curve of her body, especially her perfectly round ass. I can't help but watch how it sways back and forth as she walks away.

She's the most beautiful woman in this place tonight.

She's lethal in that color.

The moment I laid eyes on her talking with Silas, I instantly knew my night was fucked.

"Relax, Bennett," Silas whispers into my ear. "The vein on your forehead looks like it's about to explode any minute now."

I give him a sharp side-eye and avert my gaze from Emiline.

"I can't believe we're all off on the same night for the first time in months," Mason announces before I can say anything back to Silas. "It's wild in here tonight."

"Spring break will do that," Silas deadpans behind the rim of his draft beer. He then looks over at me, and I don't miss how the corners of his lips tip up in a smirk.

We both can't stand the guy.

Mason is one of the newer guys in the department. He's twenty-two years old and a total party animal when he's not working. He's one of those rookies who uses the badge in an attempt to get some ass. I know his type because that used to be me before I learned to respect the job and the badge I hold.

I keep hoping he will get to that point someday, but his actions make that hard to believe.

"I didn't realize they were having a massive party here tonight," I say to the guys, scanning the room and looking anywhere but the dance floor. Silas and I are regulars here, but I can't remember being here on a Friday or Saturday night. I had no idea that they converted this place into a club.

"Well, it's a club," Mason says matter-of-factly. "And it's spring break."

"I said that already," Silas grumbles. "And this isn't a club. It's a bar, or at least, it's always been on any other night we come here."

"They do this on the weekends." Mason shrugs casually as if he knows more than anyone else in the room. He's always like that. Young and thinks he knows everything there is to know about life. That type of attitude annoys the shit out of me.

I watch intently as Mason takes a sip of his drink and looks over my shoulder toward the dance floor, doing a total double take.

"Goddamn," he draws out, keeping his tone low, but it's just loud enough I hear it clear as day.

I turn my head to where he's looking and see Emiline dancing with Brooke like they're the only two women on the dance floor. It's as if there isn't a soul in the building, and it's just a random night in their apartment with blasting music.

I can't take my eyes off her as they belt the song's lyrics to each other.

Emiline bounces around. Her loose curls don't look like they have a single strand out of place despite how much they're tossing around with every move she makes.

Something about her relaxed posture and broad smile sends me into a bubble where all the surrounding noise vanishes.

The only thing I hear is the pounding of my heartbeat in my chest.

All I see is her.

Fucking perfect.

Her presence here tonight reminds me of the turmoil within me, a struggle I battle with every time I see her. The moment I saw her standing at the table with the guys I work with, a nervous energy rang through my body and I fought the urge to walk away.

My plan tonight was to finally take someone back to my place and get over this dry spell. If she was anyone else in the world right now, I'd be pulling all my cards to take *her* home with me.

But she's off-limits, I remind myself.

Why does she have to be this distracting?

"All I see is red," Mason says beside me. "And I'd love to fucking see it on my bedroom floor tonight."

My head snaps in his direction, and a protective rage bubbles deep inside me, threatening to come to the surface. Now *I'm* seeing red, and it's not from her dress. I don't allow myself to respond, and he doesn't acknowledge the reaction written all over my face.

She's not mine, I keep repeating to myself.

I have no right.

It's not my job to protect her.

And I'm supposed to be fucking avoiding her.

"Be right back," Mason announces, placing his glass on the high-top table before scurrying off to the dance floor where the girls are.

"Ready to head out?" Silas offers, knowing exactly where my

head is.

I shake my head in response to his question but keep my sight set on Mason as he approaches Emiline. He whispers something in her ear, and whatever it is makes her smile.

Her eyes briefly flicker to mine before she pulls her attention back to him. It was so quick that if I blinked, I might have missed it, but it was just enough for my body to react in a way I'm not familiar with. My heart rate picks up, and chills skate across my skin.

All it took was just one smile and one look.

But what did he just say to her?

What is she thinking right now?

Her body sways to the music while Mason moves effortlessly with her. I can't tell if their bodies are connected from where I'm standing, but they might as well be.

Her tight red dress rides up, and suddenly, my blood boils.

When his hands find her waist, I snap.

My feet move before my brain can react. I drop my drink on the table and walk toward them, ready to tell Mason to fuck off and bring Emiline home. Maybe not home with me, but away from him.

Except this time, I stop myself short.

I want to break his hands for even thinking of touching her, but I can't.

She's not fucking mine.

Why am I this fired up?

I shouldn't be. I really fucking shouldn't be.

I groan and turn around, returning to where Silas stands and refusing to look at him. If I do, he'll want me to explain what the hell that was, and I don't even know myself.

Is this what it feels like to be… jealous?

This is a wildly new feeling for me. Just the idea of Emiline being with someone else makes me possessive. But I can't let the anger consume me, even if I want it to be my hands on her.

I want to be the one holding her.

I want my body to be pressed against hers.

My plan tonight was to get out with the guys from work, have a few drinks, and hopefully end this everlasting relationship I've been having with my right hand each night. There's no way I can take anyone else home tonight because she'll be the center of every thought I have until I close my eyes and haunt my dreams.

I should be ashamed of that.

I should hate myself for thinking about her this way.

But I don't.

Instead, I'm standing here, staring at the one woman I can't have.

"You are *so* fucked." Silas laughs to my side as if I'm saying all of my thoughts out loud for everyone to hear.

Yes, yes, I am.

———

For the last half hour, Silas and I hung out at the table while the rest of the guys with us went off to hang by the bar.

The place got even more packed in just a matter of minutes after I left the dance floor and forced myself in any other direction but there. I didn't want to see what Emiline was doing. I didn't want to watch his hands all over her for another second or even the way her body would react to it.

But even without looking, I know she's still here.

"Ready to head out?" Silas asks.

I nod. "I'm gonna hit the restroom first."

I take the long way, rounding the dance floor to avoid sightings.

Whether I want to or not.

After washing my hands, I walk out of the bathroom and nearly collide with someone barreling down the hallway past me. I have to do a double-take as the person continues to run without even stopping.

Emiline.

"Emmy," I call her name.

She doesn't stop as she turns into the women's restroom at the other end of the dark hallway.

What the hell is that all about?

I turn to walk away, but alarm bells ring in my head, forcing my body to stop moving.

What if she's not okay?

Can I live with myself if I walk away only to find out something happened to her?

I immediately turn around and approach the door she just entered.

I push it open, realizing it's a multi-stall bathroom, unlike the men's bathroom.

"Emmy," I call out louder this time.

"Go away," she shouts, her tone clipped and irritated.

"You can't be in here," another girl says, standing at the sink and applying lipstick.

"Get out," I order.

She stares at me with her lips slightly parted from my tone before she realizes I'm serious. She stuffs her lipstick back in her purse and pushes past me to leave.

When she's gone, I find the stall where the sound of Emiline's voice just came from.

"Are you okay?" I ask.

"Why do you even care?"

I wish I had an answer for you, Emiline. I really do.

"Why are you crying? Are you hurt?"

She swings the stall door open, and despite looking like a complete mess, she's still stunning. Sweat glistens on her forehead, and her glassy eyes stare me down. I can't tell if she wants to fight me or—

"I'm fine," she snaps before a hiccup erupts from her chest. She tries to push past me, but I lift my arms to hold each side of the stall to cage her in.

"Can we not pretend like you care about me?" she scoffs. "Not even an hour ago, you wanted me gone."

"No, I didn't."

Emiline laughs, and it causes her to hiccup again. "You did. I saw you watching me while I was dancing, and you looked like you wanted me dead."

She doesn't break eye contact, and I get lost in those glassy eyes. Clearly masked from the alcohol of the night, almost causing me to forget why I'm here.

But I know why I'm here. It's because she was visibly upset, and whether she believes it or not, I care about her. I don't want to admit it while she's in this state.

I shake myself out of the trance.

"It wasn't you I wanted gone," I tell her honestly.

Her eyebrows knit together in confusion. I should really walk away. I'm taking this too far and allowing myself to get too close to her.

"Your dancing partner."

"Brooke?"

I shake my head. "The one with his hands all over you. Dancing with you all night and being close to you." I pause to allow my words to register.

"Why?" she questions without missing a beat.

"Because he doesn't deserve you."

Emiline rolls her eyes and hiccups again. "Here we go with the protective bullshit again." She lifts her pointer finger in the air, stabbing it into my chest. "I'm sick and tired of this, Logan. Let me live. If I want to dance with him, I will. If I want to go home with him, I will. If I want to fuck him, I will." She says the last one with a louder voice, emphasizing it so I hear her clearly.

The anger I felt earlier comes back in full force. My blood runs hot, and I can feel my knuckles turning white as I hold the sides of the stalls.

"So go."

"Maybe I will."

"I doubt that."

"Stop doing that," she grits out. She stares at me like she's waiting for me to move, but I don't. Finally she shoves at my chest, the contact of her hands on me causes my vision to blur as if I've been the one drinking all night. When, in reality, I've been too buzzed on my jealousy to take another sip. "Oh my god. Will you move? My Uber is waiting for me," she says.

There's no way I'm letting her out of my sight with the state she's in.

"Over my dead fucking body, are you leaving in a stranger's car."

"What did I just tell you about that?"

Leaving one hand still caging her in, the other leaves the stall frame, and my fingers grip her chin, forcing her to keep eye contact with me while I level with her.

My skin burns at the initial contact, but I do my best to ignore it.

"You are not getting in the car with a random person like this. If it means I'm a protective asshole, then so be it. But when I lay my head down to sleep tonight, I want it to be in good conscience that you're home safe."

Emiline's eyes widen, and she gasps. She didn't expect me to say that, and truthfully, neither did I. But standing in front of her and seeing the state she's in, I just can't let her out of my sight.

I reluctantly release my hold on her and let my arms fall to the side. I then gesture toward the door with a nod. "Let's go. I'm taking you home."

"I—Uh. Okay," she stutters. "Yeah. I mean, thank you."

"No need to thank me, Emmy."

"You just had to ruin it by calling me that," she groans, pushing past me.

I don't say anything back as she washes her hands and doesn't give me a passing look again before heading out the door with me on her heels.

So much for trying to avoid her.

CHAPTER SEVEN
Emiline

THE LIGHT SHINING through my blinds causes me to groan. I'm not even sure I can open my eyes with the pounding headache feeling like a rock band concert behind them.

After a few minutes, I reluctantly open my eyes and notice it has to be at least mid-morning. *Fuck.* I shoot upright in bed and assess my surroundings. I find Brooke lying in my bed next to me, utterly dead to the world. I have no idea what time we got home last night.

She must hear me wake up because she stirs next to me.

"My head," she groans. "Why is it so loud?"

I huff out a light laugh that causes the pounding in my head to intensify. I bring my fingers to my temples to massage them. "Yeah, mine too."

"I need coffee. I need sustenance. I need a greasy as hell Taylor ham, egg, and cheese on a roll," she moans.

"You're never allowed to eat one again if you call it that," I say, smacking her upper arm. "It's a pork roll."

"I'm too tired to argue semantics with you, Em." Brooke rolls over in bed, her eyes half open to shield them from the sunlight pouring in. "Don't you have fucking blinds?"

"I do. I must have been so out of it last night that I forgot to close them before bed. I don't even remember getting back here, if I'm being honest. Even you lying next to me is a surprise."

I should be able to remember getting home.

Brooke laughs. Soft at first, before she buries her face into the pillow as her laugh intensifies.

I toss a pillow at her head. "This isn't funny. That was so dangerous. We could have died or been kidnapped."

She finally sits upright in bed, and I can't help but notice that she's wearing my sweatpants and an oversized T-shirt from my closet. Since we didn't make plans for after the night, I'm relieved she's here and we got back safely.

"That's impossible when New York City's finest police officers are the ones that brought us home," she says.

My jaw falls open. "What? Who?"

"Before I get into the details about what happened, I need food."

Standing on my side of the bed, I watch her grab her phone from her purse, which she left on the floor next to my bed last night. I remain still as I see her texting, probably ordering breakfast sandwiches and coffee for delivery to my apartment. Without asking any more questions, I leave my room to brush my teeth, my mind filled with thoughts as I try to remember the details of us leaving the bar.

Who the hell brought us home?

Maybe Mason did.

I remember Mason asking me to dance before the night became a blur. I said yes, even though I don't really care for him if I'm being honest. From the little interaction I had with him last night, he seems like a cocky boy.

I say 'boy' because that's how he sounded when any word left his mouth. He dared to say, and I quote, *"This dress is smoking hot, but would look hotter if it was on my bedroom floor."*

My skin is crawling just thinking about it.

Because he doesn't even know me. Hell, *I* don't even know him.

I also remember him walking us to the bar to get another round of drinks on top of a shot of tequila. Pretty sure that's what did me in.

When we got there, he started asking me about myself. I mentioned I was in school for nursing, and he made an innocent comment about a friend of his who went through it but didn't make it.

That's when I started spiraling. My breathing got erratic, and I had to excuse myself to the bathroom to catch my breath and avoid a full-blown panic attack at the bar.

The events of the night replayed in my mind as I tried to remember what happened after that.

Oh my god.

That's when I ran into—

The doorbell rings, and Brooke runs to grab our breakfast and bring it to the table. She sets down an iced peppermint mocha latte in front of me and a breakfast sandwich.

"Can you spill now, please?" I ask her as I unwrap my sandwich.

She takes a long sip of her iced coffee, her eyes rolling behind her head in pleasure from the caffeine hitting her system. "God, I needed that." She sighs before fixing her gaze on me. "Now I can."

She's so dramatic.

"Logan and Silas walked us home last night." She pauses as if she's trying to assess my reaction to that. "And... Logan tucked us in."

"He what?" I practically shout.

"Relax. We were so out of it. He brought us back here because he says he lives close by."

"Why would he do that?" I ask, not realizing I haven't eaten my food and instead pacing around my tiny kitchen. "He can't stand me, and here he is being nice."

"You're exaggerating a little bit, don't you think?"

I shake my head. "I wish I was. He's not the same Logan I used to know."

"Explain," she says with a mouthful of food.

I groan, letting my head fall back. "In the few years I've known Logan, he's always been so nice to me. Remember that trip I took during first semester break to my brother beach house?" Brooke nods. "He was there, and I can't pinpoint what changed since then, but now he's kind of a jerk to me. I caught him staring at me at work a few months ago with nothing but rage plastered on his face."

"See?" She winks. "The man can't keep his eyes off of you."

My lips part in shock. It's like she didn't hear a thing I just said. "Maybe it's time for you to go home and go back to sleep. I think you might still be drunk."

Brooke laughs. "I'm so serious. Last night, I don't think he had eyes for anyone other than you the entire time we danced. From the looks on his face, he was absolutely seething. I thought he was going to commit a crime."

"I—" My thoughts stop as my brain remembers conversations with him.

This is the biggest downfall to being a lightweight when it comes to alcohol. If I have over two or three drinks, I have trouble remembering things.

It's why I don't party or overdo it.

I should have stopped last night, but running into Logan made me so on edge that I had to try to combat the nerves. Looking back, it was a bad idea—a terrible idea, actually.

But I remember seeing Logan in the women's restroom now that I've had time to process all of this. He told me right to my face that he wanted to get rid of Mason for having his hands all over me.

Was that his way of being nice?

I shake my head at the thought.

"He was probably mad I was in his presence. Why would he look at me any other way?" I shrug.

She scoffs. "No, ma'am. His eyes were downright murderous, and I'd bet money that it was because you were dancing with Mason."

I shouldn't care.

I *really* shouldn't care.

But I do.

I thought about Logan in the past, more than I would like to admit. I wanted to flirt with him and have him flirt back. I used to dream about how his lips would taste on mine or how his arms would feel wrapped around me. However, at that time, I was just an eighteen-year-old girl with a mind full of fantasies about a man eight years older than me that I had no business fantasizing over.

"You'd probably lose that bet." I smirk.

"No way. I think he has feelings for you." She waggles her eyebrows at me.

"You truly have the most delusional mind I've ever had the pleasure of knowing," I deadpan.

"Sometimes being delusional keeps me sane." Brooke laughs. "But if I'm being rational here, I'd tell you Logan probably has a giant stick up his ass. You should ask him why he's so angry with you all the time. And then you can tell him to get the fuck over it."

I chuckle as I take a bite of my breakfast sandwich.

"Or *you* can fuck him," she says so casually with a shrug.

I toss my crumpled-up napkin at her. "Brooke!"

"See? Delusional. Also, maybe I'm still drunk. Not sure. But..." She draws out the word before pausing to sip her coffee. "As a witness to the incident in the coffee shop and at the bar last night, something has definitely changed with him. But I don't know him well enough to know for sure."

She's not wrong. Something *has* changed.

And just like her, I'm struggling to figure out what that is. When I'm alone with my thoughts at night, I often think about that, but no solid reasoning ever comes up.

Yet, what if she's right? What if he *does* have feelings for me? Would I want to pursue something with Logan? Would I want to open myself up to potential heartbreak?

"I see your brain spinning. Talk to me," Brooke says.

"Want the truth?"

"Duh."

"I used to have the biggest crush on Logan."

She gasps and nearly chokes on her sandwich. "What! How am I just learning about this now?" She stands from the chair and rounds the kitchen island. "This is huge. This changes everything."

"It changes nothing."

"Does he know?"

I shake my head. "Hell no. Could you imagine what my brothers would think or say about it? I never told anyone until right now. Until you."

She stands still before me, and now it's my turn to see the wheels in her head spinning. But this could be a terrible thing when it comes to how Brooke thinks.

"I think you need to tell him."

Like I said, it's a terrible thing.

I aggressively shake my head from side to side. "Nope. No. Never happening." I turn to walk away from her.

"Em," Brooke says, walking over to me and placing two hands on my shoulders. "After seeing the way he is with you, there's definitely something buzzing in the air around you two. Call it sexual chemistry, attraction, whatever."

"We need to get you some water."

"Think about it!"

"Brooke, even if he was interested in me, it would be so awkward with him being my brother's best friend. Not just one of them. All three of them. He's completely off limits."

"So… sex?" She winks.

"I can't stand you right now."

"I know. I can't stand me either. But seriously, think about it.

This is one of those instances in which you will never know if you two are truly meant to be if you don't try. Maybe Logan is your soulmate. Or maybe he's the type of guy that's not meant to be in your life for a long time, just a good time. Are you picking up what I'm putting down?"

My lips parted in shock as I stand there, blinking at her.

"Good, you blinked. I can't sit back and watch you deny yourself the chemistry that floats in the air when you two are around each other."

"You're too drunk to have this conversation."

"No. I absolutely felt it at the coffee shop but didn't want to bring it up. His face got all twisty and nervous when you called him daddy. So hot." Brooke laughs at herself.

My body stiffens, and even though she's absolutely insane, she makes really valid points. I thought my past feelings clouded my judgment, and I thought something was there when there wasn't.

"I don't know, Brooke."

"I don't either." She shrugs and goes back to her iced coffee. "I'm just saying, don't throw any of this completely off the table. Wait it out, and if something comes up, it's fate. Even if you two keep it a secret for a bit."

I don't love the idea of keeping another secret from my brothers.

It's bad enough they don't know the extent of the panic attacks I have regularly.

This is a dangerous game she's suggesting I play.

Because all secrets kept in the dark eventually come to light.

CHAPTER EIGHT
Logan

May

MARC RAISES his glass in my direction. "Happy birthday, brother."

"Cheers to joining the thirty club," Thomas adds.

They clink their glasses of whiskey against my glass of water, and we settle into our boys' night at Moore's, a ritual that binds us together.

I lucked out this year, having my birthday fall on a Wednesday and being off work to get together with these guys. For years, we've been coming to this bar on Wednesday nights for drinks and to let off some steam in the middle of the week.

Initially, we picked this day because it was 'hump day,' and we'd all end up leaving with someone at the end of the night. However, it became more about catching up over small talk and a drink after Thomas started dating Peyton.

"What's with the water?" Marc asks after taking a sip of his whiskey.

"You know I don't drink and drive. And tonight, I have my motorcycle. I know none of you are going to ride that home for me."

"You got that right," Thomas says with an aggressive head nod.

"You won't ever catch me on that two-wheel death trap." Marc laughs.

He's not wrong, the thing is a death trap. I've had my motorcycle for a few years now. It's something I've always wanted growing up. Some men collect cars or sports memorabilia as a hobby. Having my motorcycle is my hobby. It's easier to maneuver New York streets with, and I love the thrill of the wind hitting my face. I'd ride this thing all year if I could. Hell, I do most of the time thanks to my cold weather riding jacket.

"How's work been?" Marc continues, directing his question toward me.

"Busy. You know how it gets this time of year. College kids are finishing school, so for whatever reason, the concrete jungle is an appealing place to travel and barhop. I think Silas and I have given out more DUIs this week than we have all year long."

"Ouch." Thomas shakes his head. "When will people learn that drinking and driving is *not* cool?"

"Agreed," Marc says. "It's dangerous as shit."

"You're preaching to the choir." I laugh. "They also have to know about Uber. It's on their phone, so don't ask me why they can't use it. On a more positive note, the talk of the precinct is that I'm up for promotion soon. One last step to get me closer to a fancy desk job."

Or one step closer to following in my dad's footsteps. But I don't say that out loud. Bringing up my dead dad is not a conversation I want to have on my birthday.

The job never leaves my head, though.

This job is my entire life and always will be.

I'm lucky to have nights like these with the guys to escape that pressure I put on myself to be the best at what I do. It's a weird juxtaposition: loving what I do but also wanting to get off the streets.

"I think it will be good for you," Marc says. "You would make an excellent chief. This next promotion will be a big step in that direction for you."

"Thank you." I offer him a smile. "Hopefully sooner than later."

Over the next hour, we discuss what Marc and Thomas have been up to over the last two weeks. They tell me Oliver has been traveling non-stop lately and insanely busy with business trips for his blog.

Thomas fills us in on his brand new place outside the city with Peyton and how much he loves it. He can't stand the commute to and from work, but it makes her happy. He's such a sappy shit now that he has a fiancée.

Then Marc opens up about how he's been on edge since he took Avery, his assistant, and Peyton's best friend, to the holiday gala as his fake fiancée this past December. His boss still hasn't said a word about who he's deciding to hand the real estate agency down to when he retires.

I feel bad for him because I know how much he wants this and the feeling of wanting something more than your next breath. It doesn't help that he's been swamped with work since Avery took time off to help her mom in Vermont after she had to have surgery.

"Fuck. My phone must have died at some point," Thomas says, trying to turn on his phone. "I should probably head back before Peyton worries."

"I can't help you because mine's been dead since before I got here," Marc scoffs.

"When has she ever been worried?" I laugh. "She knows she has you wrapped around her finger."

"Shut up," Thomas says with a smile. "When you stop fucking around and find the woman of your dreams, you will feel the same way."

"I still don't get how Thomas found a future wife before me,"

Marc adds, shaking his head. "I'm the brother who wants that in the future."

"That's because you can't stop looking for a wife. You have to date before you walk to the altar, Marc," I scoff.

"We've had this discussion before. I vividly remember those words coming out of your mouth that first night Thomas met Peyton." Marc scowls.

I chuckle against my glass of water. "I like to remind you every once in a while."

"Whatever." Marc rolls his eyes. "I'm out of here too. I have a long day tomorrow."

We all throw cash down on the table the same way we do every time we visit Moore's. "I'm meeting up with Silas, anyway. I have to drop the bike off first, and then I promised him birthday drinks."

"Remember, you're thirty now," Thomas jokes.

I give him an evil eye and ignore the comment because I'm not the party animal he thinks I am. "I'm hitting the restroom before I head out. Get home safe, guys," I say, my concern for their safety evident in my voice.

It's the same thing I always say when I part ways with them. I'll always be protective of my friends like this ever since losing my father the way I did. I worry about anyone close to me when they get behind the wheel. And not because I don't trust them. I don't trust others on the road. It's a responsibility I take seriously.

"Happy birthday, brother," Thomas says before bringing me in for a hug.

My chest tightens when any of them call me that. They don't use it in terms of friendship; it's used to remind me we're like family.

"Thanks," I say, returning the embrace.

"Yeah, happy birthday. We love you," Marc singsongs.

I glare at him. "Don't you start getting sappy on me now too," I joke.

They both laugh as we part ways, and I fire off a text to Silas.

> Want to hit up Callahan's for some birthday drinks in twenty minutes?

SILAS

I'm in.

Once I reach my bike outside, my phone buzzes in my pocket. Taking it out, I notice Emiline's name. I can't remember a single time she's ever called me before. We've had each other's numbers for a while now, but only because of a large group chat the girls started a few months ago.

I'll never understand what it is with girls and group chats.

"Hello?" I answer.

"Hey, Logan." Her voice is so soft in my ear. "Are you still with my brothers by chance?"

"No. They left about five minutes ago. What's up?"

There's a brief pause on the other end before I hear her whisper, "shit," under her breath.

"Is everything okay?"

Another pause. "No, but I'll figure it out," Emiline says quickly before hanging up the phone.

I don't know what this feeling is that builds so fast inside of me, but the sense of panic takes over. What if something is wrong with her? Thomas and Marc's cell phones are dead, and Oliver is still out of town.

I decide to call her back, but she doesn't answer this time.

"Fuck," I hiss under my breath.

> Answer your phone.

EMILINE

It's okay. I'm fine. I'm good.

> I may not be an expert, but when a woman says she's fine, she's not.

My phone buzzes with an incoming call from her, and I answer immediately. "Where are you?"

She sighs on the other end. "I'm at the library. But like I said, I'm fine. I just…"

I wait for her to respond, but her voice trails off.

"What's going on?" I ask, trying to keep my voice calm when everything inside me screams for her to tell me what's happening.

"It's stupid, and you wouldn't understand. I just wanted to see if my brothers were around to take me home."

"You don't have your car with you?" I ask, my anger subsiding with how worried she sounds.

"I don't have a car. I walked here."

I suddenly find myself ready to beeline to wherever she is because there's no way she's walking home this late at night *or* catching a taxi with a stranger driving her. I've witnessed too much shit for that to be a safe option for her in my head.

If anything happened to her, I'd never forgive myself.

"Send me your location. I'm on my way," I say before I hang up on her.

I strap on my helmet and swing my leg over to straddle my bike. Once settled in my seat, I pull my phone out of my pocket to place it on the dock I have set up between my handlebars. When I turn the key, the engine roars to life, and as soon as I do so, her location comes through on my phone.

Good girl.

Before I take off, I send a quick text to Silas.

> Raincheck. Something's come up.

———

I make it to the library in less than five minutes, not bothering to drop the bike off at my apartment to grab my truck.

One thing about me is that I always follow the rules of

driving and speed limits. However, I allowed myself this one exception to get to her as fast as I could.

As soon as I park, Emiline stands from the library's front steps with her backpack on. Her arms wrapped around her waist, hugging herself as if she's cold. But the weather here in early May is just the right temperature so she shouldn't be.

Everything around her is dark, including the street light over the steps, which looks as if it closed hours ago. I pull off my helmet but don't get off my bike, willing her to come to me.

"Happy birthday, Logan," she says in almost a whisper as she approaches the bike. "I'm sorry for causing you such trouble on your special day." She tucks a strand of blonde hair behind her ear as her gaze falls to the concrete sidewalk. She's too fucking perfect for her own good.

I scan her from top to bottom to make sure she's okay and in one piece. Once my eyes land on her face, I see a tint of red in her cheeks and a puff under her eyes. Either Emiline hasn't slept in days, or she's been crying.

I can tell her calling me was more than just needing a ride.

I slightly lean back on my bike, crossing my arms over my chest. "Tell me what's going on, Emmy."

She rolls her eyes, and I fight a smile because I know she can't stand that nickname.

"If I tell you, can you not tell my brothers? I don't want them freaking out over me more than they already do."

My mind travels to the worst-case scenario. Was Emiline on a date at the library, and he hurt her? If that's the case, I'll end up losing the job I worked so hard for because I'm going to fucking murder him.

I swallow before I speak. "I'm not going to say anything."

Her eyes meet mine. No doubt she's trying to see if I'm telling her the truth. She's right to not trust me. I've given her no reason to put an ounce of trust in me the last few time I've seen her, acting like an asshole to her.

I give Emiline a slight nod, assuring her I will keep this

between us. No matter what it is, I will help protect her with this.

As if she can sense my reassurance, she brings her bottom lip between her teeth once before finally speaking. "I had a panic attack."

Relief floods my body, and I can feel my shoulders release the tension I didn't even realize I was holding.

"They don't know," Emiline continues, her voice laced with panic. "I don't want them to worry about me. Please, Logan."

"I'm not great at keeping secrets," I admit.

She groans, and it sounds pained like her world will fall apart if this ever gets out.

"But I'll keep this one," I add to reassure and calm her. "I'll keep your secret. But you'll have to keep a secret of your own."

Her eyes lock with mine. Her blue eyes are stormy with uncertainty as if she's holding the world's weight on her shoulders, and the idea of adding one more secret will cause her to combust at any minute.

It makes every part of me feel on edge because the last thing I want is for her to carry any more weight.

But she eventually nods.

"You can't tell them I picked you up on the motorcycle or that you've ever been on the back of it. They are going to be more worried about *that* more than anything else."

"You didn't need to come get me."

"Yes, I did."

Her eyebrows pinch together. "Why?"

"Because I wouldn't be able to live with myself if something happened to you, Emmy. Grab the helmet strapped to the back and get on the bike. I'm taking you home."

My body lights up from her stare as she looks me up and down, assessing the bike as if she has a choice in the matter right now. There's no chance in hell that she's not leaving here on the back of my bike.

"Is it safe?" she asks.
"No," I shake my head. "But you're safe with me."
I don't know if I believe that myself.
But I'll do whatever I need to do to keep her safe.
That includes this secret.

69

CHAPTER NINE
Emiline

BUT YOU'RE *safe with me*.

His words reverberate in my mind as I scan the bike, humming under him as he sits perfectly on top of it like a knight in shining armor.

Feeling safe is a new and unfamiliar thing for me. With my family and even my past relationships, I struggled to feel comfortable enough and secure enough to open up about the demons I struggle with.

This feels different.

Without him knowing every detail, hearing it from Logan holds so much power.

It's embarrassing to stand in the dark outside of the library after I just had a panic attack over the material I was studying. The stress of upcoming exams still weighs heavily on my chest with each breath I take.

And now, the idea of having to sit on the back of his bike to get home might put me back into that same panic.

I'm afraid of letting him see me like this, in this vulnerable state.

I don't want *anyone* to see me like this.

The last couple of ones I've had have been during broad

daylight or at home in the comfort of my own space. I did really well managing them during my first semester. Still, this current semester has really taken a toll on me.

I have a major exam coming up next week, and I want to say I feel confident in the material I have worked tirelessly to understand, but nursing school exams are no joke.

The questions are insane and make you second-guess everything you've been studying. When you are presented with all the options, every one of them sounds good, but they only want to know which is the most correct.

For example, the patient has no pulse. A. He's dead. B. He's deceased. C. He has no heartbeat. D. He's fine.

Okay, maybe that's not the best example, but you get the point. The answers make no sense whatsoever.

Although I've experienced plenty of panic attacks before, there was something about the one I had tonight that left me on edge. I was clearly not in the comfort of my apartment, and I wasn't sure how I would make it home in the dark streets without having another one.

I love this city, but it's scary sometimes.

"Talk to me," Logan says. "Tell me what you're thinking, Em."

His tone is much softer than when I first talked to him on the phone. And hearing him call me anything other than that damn childish nickname has my heart pounding wildly inside my chest.

Looking at Logan, I can tell he's frustrated, and I want to crawl out of my skin. I hate putting people out of their way because of me. I hate feeling like a burden to someone. Yet here I am, wasting his time.

"I'm sorry, Logan." My voice trembles as I say the words. "I didn't mean to ruin your birthday."

"You didn't."

"But—"

"You didn't," Logan repeats, his voice a little firmer this time. "I wouldn't ever lie to you about something like that."

The hairs on my arms stand at the way he carries his words. It reminds me of my conversation with Brooke after spring break. I haven't been able to get it out of my head, but I haven't seen him at work or run into him with my brothers.

I finally talked myself into thinking she was crazy for suggesting pursuing something. But I'm not going to read too much into this. This isn't Logan having feelings for me. He's just helping me out because my brothers aren't available.

"While in the library, I was doing some practice questions and kept getting them all wrong." I blink, trying to keep my emotions at bay. "And I guess I just lost it. Panic took over because I'm trying hard to do well on these finals. I… I couldn't breathe, and my chest felt like an elephant was sitting on it. I just wanted to go home, but I was scared I'd send myself spiraling if I walked alone."

None of that is a lie, but I keep out the part about me being downright exhausted from working nights and studying so much. The content seems to get harder and harder as we move on, and I've also barely slept the last two weeks. I know I should have stopped studying hours ago because of that. I'm smart enough to know my limits and that the brain can't work without sleep.

It's just… my brain wouldn't let me stop.

"Put the helmet on," Logan tells me, holding it out for me to grab.

"You just carry an extra around with you at all times?" I ask. "Who's this for? I'm not wearing another girl's helmet."

I zip my lips together and wish I could take back the words as soon as I say them because I sound like a jealous teenager.

"No one has ever worn that helmet, Emiline," Logan responds with a smirk playing on his lips.

I really want to ask why, but I think better of it and stop myself from embarrassing myself any further tonight. Besides, seeing a hint of a smile on his face makes me want to get on the back with him.

Especially when he looks like this.

Logan on top of a motorcycle is lethal.

I can barely see any skin since he's wearing a long-sleeved black shirt, but it hugs every muscular curve of his body as if he painted it on before he left the house tonight. And since when have I found jeans so attractive?

I shouldn't *want* this.

Why is Logan breaking down all my walls?

Before I can overthink that question, he adds, "As a matter of fact, I've never had a girl on the back of my bike before."

The revelation jolts me back, but my feet remain grounded where they are. A part of me feels excitement over the fact that I'm the first. A small part also wishes I'd be the only girl ever on the back of *his* bike, but that's not what this is.

My brother's words from a few months ago replay in my mind and I quickly remind myself that I'm like a little sister to Logan.

That's all I'll ever be.

"Right," I choke out, barely able to swallow down the lump in my throat. I finally grab the helmet from him with trembling hands, placing it on my head.

It fits perfectly as if it was made for me.

Brain, can we please stop thinking this is more than it is?

I lift the front visor, and my eyes meet his through its opening. I can't see his lips since he also put his helmet back on. But a slight crinkle around his eyes tells me he's smiling under his helmet.

I reach up to buckle the straps, but my attempt fails quickly, and I can't hide my shaky hands this time.

Logan dismounts the bike for the first time since he arrived. He stands almost a head taller than me as he brings himself right into my personal space.

"Let me," he says.

Why is every single word out of this man's mouth so hot?

Logan's so close that his scent overpowers whatever weird smell is inside the helmet. He smells like a mix of cedar, soap, and gasoline, as if he's been on his bike all day.

Even with the helmet masking so much of the light from his face, his eyes stand out more than ever before. He keeps them locked on mine, blindly buckling the straps under my chin. His knuckles brush my skin, and my body erupts from the feather-like touch. As if he can sense it, he averts his gaze to where he works under my chin.

I close my eyes and steady my breathing. Every inch of me feels like I'm sitting in the sun with him being so close.

This really is a terrible idea. Horrible. Worst idea ever.

His hands stop moving under my chin, but he doesn't step away as he looks me directly in the eyes again. He's burning every fucking inch of me, and I swear I'm going to explode any second now.

I want to ask him what *he's* thinking. The same way he asked me before.

Is he feeling the same way I am right now?

Something's swirling around his head right now, and while I'd love to know, I'm also terrified of knowing the truth. I can't allow my heart to fall for him.

Logan suddenly clears his throat as if he's caught himself. "Done," he says before patting the top of my helmet and turning toward his bike.

Terror for mounting his death trap takes over the feelings I just had. Before I know what's happening, Logan reaches as far as his hands allow while sitting on the bike and hooks a finger in the belt loop of my jeans, pulling me toward him with a single finger.

Well... that was kind of hot.

His large hand grips the left side of my waist, and he urges me to look at him again, away from the bike. "You're safe with me," he repeats. "Hop on. Let's get you home."

His demeanor toward me has changed so much. It's softer than it was on the phone and exponentially different from the last few months of interactions with him.

But this feels different.

He *wants* to do this for me.

I slide down the visor on my helmet before throwing a leg over the seat and sitting as far back as possible. My hands rest on his broad shoulders before I grip them tight and hope like hell that I don't fall.

I watch Logan intently over his shoulder as he slides his riding gloves on one at a time before her turns the key and the engine roars to life.

Holy. Shit.

I grip Logan's shoulders to hold on for dear life. Just when I think we're about to take off, he jerks the bike forward and the apex of my thighs crash into his back as my hands instinctively move to grip the sides of his waist.

I thank the lords above that he's facing forward and we're both hiding behind the visor of our helmets. Because the way *I know* my cheeks are fire engine red right now is embarrassing.

To make matters worse, he reaches for my wrist to bring my hands around his torso and rest against his stomach. I saw the curves of his muscles through his fitted shirt. I felt them on his shoulders, but every ridge across his stomach under my hand makes me feel butterflies in my gut. Feelings I've worked really hard to stuff down deep.

"I need you to hold on," Logan orders over his shoulder before reaching for my hands again to give them the same three-pulse squeeze. "And don't fucking let go."

I tighten my arms, and at the same time, he revs the engine.

He doesn't even give any notice when he pulls into the street. I squeeze him and hold on like he's my lifeline. Like if I let go for even a second, I'll fall to my death.

After a series of turns, Logan lands on the one street that's our longest stretch before my apartment. He sits up on the bike just the slightest bit, with one hand on the throttle and bringing the other to my thigh as he cruises at a safe speed.

I can feel the brush of his fingers against my inner thigh that's nestled against his thick legs.

I know this means nothing.

I know that this is his way of ensuring I'm safe.

But it feels like more. Logan pulls his hand away as if he feels it too and doesn't realize what he's doing. He returns his hands to the handlebars, but not before giving my own resting on his stomach, another three-pulse squeeze before we pull into my parking garage.

I wish I knew what he meant by that small gesture.

Also, why is he pulling in here when he can drop me off at the front door?

After he pulls into a spot, he cuts the engine and I jump off as if the bike is in flames.

It might as well be after that.

I pull off my helmet, hand it to him, and force myself to step away from the bike—away from *him*.

"Thank you for the ride home," I stammer. "You could have just dropped me off at the front."

The corner of his lips tips up. "But this is where I usually park."

My gaze bounces from him to the bike and back to him as the realization hits me. "Wait."

"I didn't know we live in the same complex either. Not until I brought you home that night after your spring break rendezvous." Logan shrugs.

My cheeks heat again, remembering that night. "I never got to thank you for that. For you know… bringing us home and all."

He nods but doesn't say anything else.

"Well, thank you for this ride, too," I say in rushed words as I spin around and walk toward the residence entrance. Feeling every bit embarrassed that Logan is constantly saving me.

"Can I ask you something?" he almost shouts, forcing me to stop walking.

I turn around and notice him walking toward me, and I nod.

"Do you get them often? Your panic attacks?" he asks.

I nod again. Unable to form a proper sentence, I stare at his messy brown hair from the helmet and those eyes boring into me, illuminated by the parking garage lights.

Logan crowds my space more before he brushes the hair away from my eyes. "If you get them again, you can call me."

"I'll be fine." I brush him off, trying to hide any feelings. "Besides, why would you want to come to the rescue for someone you can't stand?"

Something darkens in Logan's features, but he doesn't say another word before turning around to hook the extra helmet on the back of the bike, completely ignoring my question.

I want to beg him to answer me, but the last thing I want to do is push him.

"Get inside, Emmy," he grumbles over his shoulder, without even turning to look in my direction.

I stand there, shocked and unable to say anything else.

When I finally move my feet to walk to my apartment, I promise myself that this will never happen again.

No matter what Brooke says. She's wrong.

CHAPTER TEN
Emiline

June

THE GIRLS ARE FINALLY ALL BACK TOGETHER again.

I need to study for my finals approaching next week, but I need this more.

My girls are the best type of escape when school or life gets too hard. Even if they don't know what I battle with alone, being in their presence makes me feel at ease.

Because that's who Peyton, Avery, and Kali are.

Tonight, Kali and I are helping Avery prepare for her first *official* fake date with Marc.

I call it official because the first one they went on was supposed to be a one and done thing. Now they have to drag on the fake engagement for the summer to help convince his boss that he's established enough to take over the agency.

They're going out tonight to lay the groundwork for how they will approach this and sell the relationship. The problem we're facing is the guy Avery was casually seeing, because she doesn't do relationships, who is currently texting her.

"It's funny if you think about it. I have no filter and give no shit what comes out of my mouth. But I can't break up with a guy to save my life," Avery says.

"That's normal." Kali shrugs. "You don't like the cry-baby shit. I've only met Dean a couple of times, but I can tell that he would be the whiny type of guy who doesn't want things to end."

"*That* would make you uncomfortable," I add. "For the sake of argument here, I never saw that going anywhere to begin with."

"How come?" Avery asks.

"You need someone who matches your attitude and gives it right back to you," I tell her.

"I don't have an attitude," Avery snaps.

"Attitude is the wrong word," Kali cuts in. "You're strong-willed. You're not afraid to share those wild thoughts in your head, regardless of what others think. You respect yourself enough to stand up for yourself. Which you definitely learned from your mom growing up."

"You don't like to be coddled either." I laugh. "That's why my brother couldn't be a more perfect fake fiancé for you."

"Right," she scoffs. "I have no doubt that Marc can handle my shit. He does every day at work. But I can also read him like a book. Deep down, he wants romance and a happy ending."

"You're good at the happy ending." Kali winks in her seat.

"We are *not* fucking going there," Avery says adamantly.

"Stooppp it," Kali drawls. "You've already had his dick inside of you, and you've been weird around him ever since."

"First of all." My face wrinkles in disgust at the idea of my brother's sex life. "I don't want to know who, what, or where my brother sticks his dick. Seriously gross." I shiver in my seat. "Secondly, you both certainly have been odd around each other. I have to agree with Kali here."

I've noticed how they were after the Christmas gala before she left. Something was off between them, and Marc has been acting weird ever since. I've been trying to tell myself that he's just anxious about work and waiting to hear what his boss has to say and to whom he's giving the company, but I've never been entirely convinced.

Marc and Avery are complete opposites. Still, everyone around them has picked up on their chemistry.

Everyone but them, of course.

"Is it really that obvious?" Avery says, throwing herself back on the couch.

"Yes," Kali and I say in unison.

"Dammit. This is exactly why this won't work out in his favor. Em, cover your ears," Avery tells me before returning to Kali. "You have no idea how hot that night was. He's the exact kind of dominant and dirty man that I like."

"You gave me no time to cover my ears, and now this might be my cue to go," I hiss.

"Don't leave me," Avery pleads, throwing her hands into a prayer motion. "You can't leave your fake future sister-in-law hanging like this. Besides, we know you're into kinky shit. You basically admitted during that card game on our trip to the shore that you want to be tied up."

Shit. I was hoping this would never be brought up again. Not only do the girls now think I'm into kinky shit, but that was also the trip where Logan started acting so differently around me.

Things are different now, but I'm not the kind of person these girls think I am.

Well, actually, that may be a lie. I *have* thought about kinky stuff more often than I can count. I've just never had a partner or sexual encounter where I felt comfortable and saw the opportunity to have more than just uncomplicated sex with someone.

"Now that you bring that up," Kali chimes in, directing her attention to me. "Was it just me, or was I feeling some sort of sexual tension between you and Logan?"

"I felt that shit." Avery nods repeatedly. "Isn't he old?"

"God, no. He just turned thirty. That's only eight years older than me," I say, but I wish I could take the words back as soon as they leave my mouth. It almost sounds like I'm defending something existing between us when nothing is happening.

"So, is this you admitting *something*?"

"No. Absolutely not." I shake my head rapidly because... shit. "He's my brother's best friend. Not just any brother... my oldest brother. We grew up together, so I have known him for like, ever. Besides, he's a cop. You know what they say about cops."

"That they like handcuffing in the bedroom?" Avery wiggles her eyebrows.

My thighs clench together at the idea of having him do that to me. But I quickly scold myself because that's never happening in this lifetime.

I wrinkle my face. "Ew. No. It's that they all cheat!" I lie.

"Not all cops cheat on their spouse, Em," Kali says. "Totally an inaccurate stereotype."

"I agree." Avery nods. "The small town I grew up in, everyone knew everyone. I knew dozens and dozens of cops there. Not a single one ever cheated on their wife or girlfriend. That shit would have been the talk of the town if any of them had."

"And Logan doesn't seem like the type," Kali adds.

I've replayed our interaction after he brought me home after my panic attack in the library repeatedly.

For many reasons.

The look on his face after I told him he didn't have to rescue someone he couldn't stand was indifferent. I couldn't figure out for my life if it was because I was wrong or right. He's so hot and cold with me.

One minute, he's showing up and making sure I'm okay.

Then he's asking me to call him if I have them again.

Then he's storming off without another word.

To add to the juxtaposition I'm facing, I can't rid myself of the idea of having my arms around him on the back of his motorcycle. It was hot, intense, and intimate—especially knowing I'm the only female who has ever been on the back of it.

I can't help but want to be in that position with him again, even if the motorcycle scares the hell out of me. Logan scares me just the same.

"You two clearly don't know him the way I know him," I snort. "Logan is the biggest playboy there is. I don't think I have ever seen him with the same girl more than once. Tommy will tell you the same thing. Even *he* thinks his friend is a playboy."

Only some of what I said is a lie. In the past, Logan was the biggest playboy in school. I remember it vividly as I listened to him talk with my brothers in the kitchen when he would come over to hang out.

It's one of the biggest reasons they told Logan I was off-limits.

But lately, I can't stop wondering… what if he wasn't.

CHAPTER ELEVEN
Logan

"DID you go out last night to celebrate your promotion?" Silas asks between bites of his sandwich.

"No, I didn't have it in me. I was beat," I answer, which isn't a lie.

Yesterday morning, I got promoted to captain, which is just another step closer to becoming chief. I'm not naïve to believe that it will happen overnight, and that role comes with hard work and sacrifices.

But the path to this promotion has demanded significant sacrifices from my personal life. I've often had to put my own needs on hold to pursue this goal, and I want nothing more than to make my father proud.

When I got the news, I was overcome with emotion, but I kept it all deep under the surface, hidden under the shell that I keep up around everyone.

A surge of pride washed over me as I looked out at the room filled with my fellow officers. I was chosen for this, a moment I wished my father could witness with a proud smile on his face.

But he wasn't. He couldn't be.

Even when I finally land the chief position, whether next year or five years from now, he still won't be standing there, and that thought alone guts me.

Despite that, I was deeply grateful Thomas showed up for me. His presence and that of my other friends in the department were a powerful reminder that I am not alone in this journey. I couldn't have asked for a better group of friends to be there when my dad can't be. Right before I was called up, I watched a fellow officer get his promotion, and his wife and young son were beaming with pride.

For a split second, I thought about how incredible it must feel to have someone who loves you with their whole chest standing there, supporting and cheering you on. But it was only for a split second because I was quickly reminded that that's not what I want.

If something were to happen to me, I wouldn't want my wife or, hell… even my children, to have to suffer the rest of their lives without me.

"Damn." He shakes his head. "You haven't been out since your birthday last month. You know… the night you ditched me. Which we have yet to discuss."

Yeah, no shit, I haven't talked about it.

I haven't talked to anyone about it, and I've been harboring my feelings for the last month. It's not because I think Silas would say anything to the Ford brothers since he's only met them a handful of times, but saying anything about it out loud makes it feel real. I don't want it to feel real.

I can't ever allow myself to get close to her like that again or I might definitely change my mind about my future plans.

Not that any of this matters much. When Emiline made a comment about me hating her, I didn't deny it. I couldn't even look at her after she asked. I didn't have an answer because the first thought it my head was that it would be better this way. It's better if she thinks I can't stand her so I don't feel inclined to give into temptation.

"Nothing happened," I lie. "I went home and went to bed. I was exhausted from working a couple of nights before that."

"Right," Silas says with a nod.

He doesn't believe me, and I don't blame him.

I throw my head back on the headrest of my driver's seat and close my eyes, trying to think of how I'm going to say this. Since that night, things have taken a strange turn with Emiline. It started a turmoil of emotions inside me, making avoiding her harder and harder.

She trusted me with a secret she hasn't even told her brothers, or the girls, for that matter. Then, I had her on the back of my bike. We already know how much I think about that feeling repeatedly.

To top it off, I can't get the thought of another man's hands on her out of my head. The idea of Mason's hands all over her over spring break made me only want it to be my hands all over her. My head was flooded with the irrational thought of not wanting *any* man to touch her again.

She's not mine to be protective of. She's not mine to rage in jealousy over. Yet I can't help but groan in frustration because it's actually pissing me off that I'm still thinking about these things.

That I'm still thinking about *her*.

"I know I'm just your work partner, but you can talk to me about shit, you know," Silas says. "Don't hold that all in."

I glance over at him in the passenger seat, and from the look on his face, I can tell he means that.

"You're more than just a work partner," I reassure him. "I consider you one of my good friends."

"Aww, I feel the same way, Bennett," he says, making a heart with his hand over his chest.

That forces a smile out of me. "Fine. I need to get it out anyway," I pause before turning my face in his direction. "That night—" I start to say, but I'm cut off when the dispatcher's voice cuts through the radio speakers.

"All units on hand to City General Emergency Room. The patient is armed and dangerous."

My stomach bottoms out, and I'm ready to vomit all the pieces of the hoagie I just ate.

"Lockdown in progress," dispatch continues.

"We're two minutes out," Silas says to me, buckling his seatbelt.

I can feel his eyes on me while I continue looking straight ahead through the window with my hands white knuckling the steering wheel because my mind is swirling with a million thoughts.

Is she working tonight?

Is she okay?

Is she… alive?

I snap myself out of it. "Forty en route," I respond through my radio as I throw the car in drive. I floor it as fast as I can to the hospital in hopes there are no victims.

Especially none named Emiline Ford.

———

"All clear." I hear Silas say into the radio on his shoulder, letting dispatch know everything is under control.

When we showed up here, security had successfully apprehended the suspect for us and had him pinned to the ground with his arms behind his back, a pocketknife lying a few feet from him.

He got violent with the nurses because they were busy tonight, and his girlfriend wasn't getting the attention she needed from the staff. These are typical frustrations nurses have to deal with in the Emergency room. Still, this man took it to a whole new level when he came out of their room swinging a pocketknife in the air and threatening to stab someone if they didn't figure out what was wrong with her.

I found myself worrying about Emiline the entire situation.

Even if my eyes didn't find her once.

The quick report given to us when we arrived said there were no victims. Yet, I still couldn't help but think Emiline was here somewhere, maybe keeping a safe distance to protect herself.

"Talk about a two in the morning wake-up call." Brooke laughs as she walks up to Silas and me standing by the nurses' station.

"Right? Guess we can skip the coffee," Silas jokes with her.

I furrow my brow because I'm not in the mood for jokes right now. The adrenaline crash from something like this always hits hard. I've quickly learned tonight that the adrenaline crash after thinking Emiline was in danger is even worse.

I hate myself even more for caring about her so much that I risked my life and my partner's life driving here as recklessly as I did. Then, I barged in here like it was my first day on the job without a care in the world other than to find her.

"Wrong. I always need coffee," Brooke jokes. They both laugh together, but I don't. She turns to face me. "You all right, Officer?"

"I'm fine," I snap before turning on my heel to get the hell out of here, but Brooke's words that follow stop me in my tracks.

"She was supposed to be here tonight."

I suck in a sharp breath and hope like hell no one around me noticed.

"She called out," Brooke continues, and I turn around to face her. "We had our final exam for the semester today. Well" —she looks down at her watch—"yesterday now, I guess. Night shift life." She laughs lightly, but my face remains flat and emotionless. "Anyway, she had a raging headache from lack of sleep and waiting for our grades to go up, so she called out."

I swallow past the lump in my throat because what Brooke is saying doesn't make me worry any less. I don't want to go there, but I can't help but wonder if the 'headache' was a cover-up for her friend to hide the panic attacks she struggles with.

I give her a tight nod. I didn't mask my emotions all that well if she picked up on the fact that I was thinking about Emiline.

Is it really so obviously written all over my face?

Silas places a hand on my shoulder, giving me a tight squeeze. "I think we should finish that conversation we were having before this call came in."

I nod again as we make our way to the SUV parked outside.

Once we're inside the car, I unload everything that's been on my mind.

CHAPTER TWELVE
Emiline

I FAINTLY HEAR a dull pounding that pulls me out of my deep sleep. I can't help but groan, assuming it's my neighbor.

For the last few months I've had to deal with a new, sex-crazed neighbor. All hours of the night I can hear the headboard pounding against my wall, sometimes it goes until morning. Or maybe not and he's just waking up for more.

Either way, there's no way someone has that much stamina.

Except, now, the pounding only gets louder. I think I even hear someone say, "Open up."

Oh my god, is my neighbor in trouble with the cops?

"Emmy?"

My eyes fly open, and I sit up in bed on full alert because I recognize that voice. Yes, it's a cop, but not just any cop.

And he's definitely not out there for my neighbor.

I throw off my blankets, and my eyes land on my clock, which reads a quarter after six.

What the hell is he doing here this early?

I don't even bother stopping to look at myself in the mirror before I run for the door, unlocking it and swinging it open. It takes me less than a second to realize I don't have a bra on because I can feel my body betray me as my nipples pebble under my tank top.

I really should have stopped to look in the mirror.

Logan stands there with a forearm resting on the door frame, his head down, and his other hand resting on his hip. My eyes trail his body, and I see he's still in his uniform. He looks… a mess, like he's been through hell during his shift, and the look on his face tells me he's in agony over it.

"What are you doing here? Are you okay?" I ask.

His eyes meet mine for the first time since I opened the door. "I came to ask you the same question."

"Well, I live here. I was sleeping like a normal human being."

He smirks. "That's not the question I was looking to have answered."

I pause and remember what I asked him. Goosebumps skate across my bare skin once I realize he's here because he's wondering if I'm okay.

I step back, allowing him into my apartment and closing the door behind him. When he crosses the threshold, I feel his presence everywhere.

Logan Bennett is in my space.

This isn't the first time, because I know he took Brooke and me home after the bar, but I don't remember that. This time, my body is *fully* aware of him being here. The old me who had a massive crush on him would be so giddy right now.

But I can't bring myself to think about it for too long because I'm downright annoyed that he's here before the sun is even up.

"Why are you here, Logan?" I ask to his back, crossing my arms over my chest.

"I had a call last night…" He pauses before he turns around to look at me. "It was the hospital."

"That happens often."

"No." He shakes his head, and the look on his face looks almost… pained. "The call was *to* the hospital. There was a man armed with a knife in the emergency room."

My eyes go wide, and I can feel the blood drain from my face. I rush past him into my kitchen to grab my cell phone to call Brooke and make sure she's okay.

I was supposed to be working last night.

"She's okay," he says before I can even unlock my phone, like he knows exactly what I'm thinking. "Everyone is fine. The guy's in custody."

"Okay," I say, swallowing past the feeling of my throat closing on me. I feel like I'm on the verge of another panic attack, but I can't allow it to come to the surface.

Not with Logan standing right here.

I was supposed to be there.

What if it didn't end well?

What if something worse happened?

What if I didn't call out?

I was supposed to be there!

I feel like I'm going to spiral despite Logan telling me that everyone is okay.

This is how my episodes start. I think of the worst possible scenarios that could happen, which forces uncontrollable thoughts to enter my mind, and then I just can't stop them.

I take a deep breath, thankful that he doesn't pick up on the change in my breathing pattern before he speaks again.

"I talked to Brooke after everything, and she said you called out for a headache. She mentioned something about having your final exam and that you were stressed waiting for your grade." Logan pauses again, taking a few steps to meet me in the kitchen. He stands across from me, and I'm thankful the kitchen island is separating us right now. If it wasn't, I don't think I could stop myself from wrapping my arms around him for the comfort I've craved for so long. "I wanted to make sure you were good."

I hear what he's saying without him having to say it.

He's the only one who knows what I've been struggling with, and Logan being here right now in my apartment tells me he probably thinks that the headache was an excuse to hide more.

"You weren't good," he says before I can speak. Not a question but a statement.

I shake my head reluctantly, knowing I'm admitting defeat if I tell him. "But I'm good now," I say to defend myself.

I hate feeling like this.

Especially in front of him.

"Em." He sighs.

This isn't the first time I've heard him say my name like that. It's always been 'Emmy' or my full name. Everyone calls me 'Em,' but something about how Logan says it causes a shiver to race through my body.

"Logan"—I round the kitchen island—"please stop. I'm fine. I'm used to this because I've dealt with it for long enough on my own."

"I…" Logan starts but stops himself. Instead, he just nods in response.

A few heartbeats pass as his gaze bores into mine like he's assessing the situation to determine if I'm lying.

He opens his mouth to finally speak, but my neighbor decides now he's ready to wake up for his morning routine. The gentle bang of the headboard hitting the wall causes Logan's head to turn toward my bedroom, and he raises a brow.

My head looks toward my bedroom before I look back at him with wide eyes. "It's not me," I say defensively. "Well clearly, because I'm standing here." I laugh lightly to ease the tension.

The muscle in his jaw ticks. "I'll see myself out," he says before he turns around to leave.

"Logan." I rush to stop him as if I need to explain myself. I know I don't need to, but I can't have him thinking that someone is in my bedroom. "That's my neighbor." I hike my thumb toward where the sound is coming from. "He does… that a lot in the mornings. He's a machine and doesn't seem to stop." I attempt to laugh and lighten the change in mood.

Logan turns around again to face me, his expression much lighter. "Stop doing what?"

My cheeks heat at the weight of his stare and what he's asking me. "You know," I answer, trying to avoid talking to my brother's best friend about sex.

He smirks so casually as if he already knows. "You can say it, Em."

I swear my cheeks turn crimson red just from the look on his face.

There goes my body betraying me again.

"He's having sex," I practically shout, throwing my arms out wide. Big mistake because I can feel the rush of air through my thin tank top. "Happy now?"

The smirk on Logan's face falls as his eyes trail over every inch of my body. I feel naked and exposed under the weight of his stare, knowing he can see my hard-as-stone nipples through this thin tank top. I quickly wrap my arms around myself, over my chest to avoid feeling completely exposed to him.

He doesn't say another word, turns around, and walks out the door.

What was that all about?

CHAPTER THIRTEEN
Logan

I LEFT her apartment feeling like the biggest asshole because all I could think about was getting out of there before I did something I would regret. One more smile or laugh from her—even if it was a nervous one to ease the tension—and my hands would have been all over her in a heartbeat.

But the rational part of my brain took over, and I left.

It's raining out, which makes for the perfect daytime sleeping weather for us night shifters. Except now that I'm here and changed out of my work uniform, I'm pacing my bedroom with my mind bouncing back and forth between climbing into bed for my six hours of sleep or going back down to her apartment.

I think there's a part of me that doesn't believe Emiline is actually okay. Maybe it's the desire in me to protect people. Or perhaps, it's because her response didn't convince me.

When I told her what had happened, I saw the wheels in her head spinning, and I left like a coward.

Is she sitting in her apartment right now thinking about it?

A desire to be there for her thrums inside of me, making it hard to even go to sleep if I tried right now. What if I went back to her place to make sure she's okay, to be a friend she needs.

I breathe out a sigh, and before I can second guess myself, I pull out my phone and order breakfast to be delivered to her apartment. Then I throw on a pair of sweatpants and make my way there.

I stare at her door for a minute looking for a reasonable excuse for being here before I finally muster the courage to knock.

I should turn around and go back to my place.

I shouldn't be here.

But the door swings open, and my scrambled thoughts are out the window when I take her in.

She changed in the twenty minutes I was gone and still looks just as perfect as she did before. Her messy hair is pulled into a bun on top of her head, her sweatpants look three sizes too big on her small frame, and her T-shirt is of the periodic table of elements.

The corner of my lip lifts before my eyes land on her face. That's when I notice she's been… crying.

"What are you doing here again? Is everything okay?" she asks.

I step into her apartment without an invitation. "I'm having déjà vu, Em," I say, hoping to bring a smile to her face. "I think that's the same thing you asked me a little bit ago when I showed up."

"And I'm asking again," Emiline says with a bite to her tone.

I should *not* find her sass as attractive as I do right now.

"Relax, Emmy," I joke in an attempt to ease the tension. "I wasn't convinced you were okay. So I ordered breakfast and coffee to be delivered here."

She releases a long, drawn-out sigh as she shakes her head and goes to the living room. She's clearly frustrated I'm here. I'm just as frustrated with myself for being here because I don't know what the hell I'm doing. It's why I find myself still standing in her entryway.

It's annoying how much I care, but I can't let it go.

"And what? We're just going to sit around and talk about my

weakness, Logan?" she asks, her tone laced with annoyance. "I regret ever telling you or having you pick me up that night. I was doing fine, not having anyone worry about me or wanting to talk about my feelings. Plus, you worked last night. Go home and go to bed."

I shake my head as I make my way to the living room, standing directly in front of her.

"That's not what this is," I tell her. "I figured you need a friend."

"I have plenty of them," Emiline retorts.

I cross my arms over my chest, and her eyes trail my movement. The way she looks at me with those eyes sets an inferno raging through my blood.

"How many of them do you have to talk to about this?"

She opens her mouth to speak, and I lean closer, pressing a finger to her lips.

This is getting more dangerous by the second.

Her soft pink lips against my finger are enough to tell me I should bolt. I should run out of here and get away from her. But I don't. Instead, I just pull my hand away like I just touched fire.

"Don't say another word. But back to what you said before… This is not a weakness, Emiline. You are not weak, and there is no part of me that thinks that about you. Let me keep you company and enjoy breakfast on the first day of your summer break."

Her lips part in uncertainty as she scans my face, looking for an ulterior motive or something.

She nods in agreement before she makes her way to her couch. It's small, likely because it's really only for her. I can't help but watch intently as she sits closest to the armrest, tucking her legs under her, pulling the blanket off the back, and draping it over her thighs.

"Want to watch a movie or something?" she asks. "Although, I don't know how you're awake right now. When I get home from work, I immediately crash."

I shrug a shoulder and sit beside her, my elbows resting on my thighs. She's a little too close for comfort, and I'm afraid if I sit back or she moves even an inch, her thigh will graze mine.

"Sometimes..." I pause, trying to figure out what to say. But immediately, I feel a comfort in her I don't usually have when I get home. "Sometimes our shifts are intense, and I have trouble falling asleep right away."

Emiline nods in understanding. "And last night was a lot."

"It was," I tell her honestly. But it wasn't being called to at the hospital that's causing me this turmoil. It was worrying about *her*.

"I called Brooke after you left before. She told me she talked to you."

"Yeah, we talked briefly," I say as I relax back in my seat. My body instantly feels heavy from the lack of sleep and the comfort of this couch. I turn my head to face Emiline, and she's already looking at me. "Is she okay?"

"Yeah, she was actually worried about you."

"Me?" I ask, furrowing my brow. "She was the one that had to witness the man pull a pocketknife on the nurses."

"Brooke is a hard-ass." She laughs. *My god, that laugh.* "Nothing like that bothers her. She's the type of girl who will come in guns blazing to a knife fight. That guy didn't stand a chance with her on shift."

That forces a laugh out of me.

Being with Emiline is so carefree despite the heavy topic of conversation.

"She said she couldn't read you like she can normally read people. Like something more was bothering you. She said..." Emiline stops herself, pressing her lips together before shaking her head. "Forget it."

"Em." I give her a sympathetic smile. "You can continue. You should know by now you can tell me anything."

"Do I?" She wrinkles her eyes.

I poke at the sensitive spot between her ribs and under her arms, which causes her to jump and squirm with laughter.

"What's that supposed to mean?" I ask.

Emiline stands from the couch, the serious mask back on her face as she paces back and forth. "It's just that... you're so hot and cold with me. I don't know what to think or believe. Brooke says one thing. You act another way. One day you're spilling coffee down my shirt and looking at me like I'm the scum on the bottom of your shoe, and then you're coming to my rescue at the library." She stops walking back and forth and brings her arms out wide. "And now, here you are. In my apartment, sitting on my couch, and being exceptionally nice to me."

A smile plays on my lips, and she looks down at me when I don't answer. Her smile matches mine, but she picks up a pillow and throws it at me.

I bark out a laugh. "You did not just throw a pillow at my head."

"I did!" she practically screams. "Now you're being hot again."

I raise a brow and smirk. "Is that so?"

This girl is my greatest temptation, and she's only making it worse with every word that comes out of her mouth. I'm genuinely hanging by a thread, and I feel that thread slowly fraying away.

She groans. "Oh my god, Logan. That is not what I meant."

I can't help but grin from ear to ear. "Can we get back to the basics of this conversation?"

"Which are?"

"What Brooke was saying when you talked to her."

Her cheeks turn blushing pink as she looks down at her hands. "Brooke thinks you care about me."

"I do," I say, quicker than I intended to.

"As... more than just your best friend's little sister," Emiline continues, her light blue eyes lifting to meet mine while she keeps her head toward the ground. "She thinks you are the way you are because a part of you wants me."

I stand from the couch as her words send a light shiver down my spine.

Suddenly, it feels boiling in here, and I can't breathe. I can hear my heart pounding in my head as I take a step closer to her. She lifts her head, eyes widening as I loom over her.

I hear her suck in a sharp breath, and what I would give to have her exhale it against my lips.

"Interesting," I tell her, tucking a tendril of hair that's fallen out of her bun behind her ear.

Emiline's eyes fall shut, and she releases that breath. My knuckle burns when it grazes the skin of her neck. Even with just that small touch, I felt her pulse pounding against my skin.

There's a knock on the door, and I pull away quickly, before my hands explore more of her body. I can already feel myself craving that burning sensation over every part of me, and it's a good breakfast that came at the right time.

Emilline takes a step back and opens her eyes again. "Sometimes, she can be a little out there with the theories that float around in her head. I should have never said anything," she says, making her way to the door.

I don't reply but stay where my feet are planted as I watch her grab the breakfast sandwiches from the delivery driver and place them on the kitchen counter.

"Still hungry?" she asks, her voice laced with nerves like she's embarrassed over saying what she just did.

I'm hungry all right, but not for food.

I've never had intimate thoughts this strong about Emiline before, but right now, I would give anything to throw her on top of the kitchen island and devour *her* for breakfast.

Have the taste of her on my tongue for the rest of the day.

I shake away the thoughts and offer her a nod as I take my place on the stool she has set on the kitchen counter. The energy has shifted in the room, and the only sound is the wrapper from the sandwiches.

I want to tell her Brooke is right—that I do care about her, and that I do want her. She's not just some girl to me, and she will *never* be just some girl to me.

I've tried to deny this.

I've tried to fight this off.

But I keep finding myself right here, with her.

"You look exhausted," she tells me, clearly mistaking my silence for being tired. "You should get some sleep."

"Are you trying to kick me out before we even watch a movie?" I joke, fighting through a yawn. *Dammit.*

"Go to bed, Logan."

I nod because she's right. I really should go home and rest.

I shouldn't be here in the first place.

I take the last bite of my sandwich and stand from the chair before I toss my wrapper into the trash. I think eating such a heavy sandwich just caused me to crash that much quicker than I thought I would.

"You owe me a movie," I tell her, pulling her in for a hug.

I'm usually pretty good at learning from my mistakes.

Except right now, I guess I didn't learn from the first time Emiline had her arms around me behind my bike, because now I most definitely don't want to leave this apartment with the way she's holding me.

I want to stay here with her in my arms.

I tilt my head into the delicate curve of her neck, and the smell of honey and vanilla takes over my senses yet again.

"Your friend isn't wrong," I whisper into the shell of her ear, and I feel her body become stiff under my arms. "I can't have you, but that doesn't mean I don't want you."

I release myself from her and turn around without giving her a chance to reply or give her another glance.

Because I know if I look at her, into those eyes…

I would never leave her side.

CHAPTER FOURTEEN
Emiline

PEYTON

Fourth of July party at our house!

AVERY

I am so there.

I can't wait to see James!

PEYTON

He can't wait to show you the additions to his dinosaur collection.

AVERY

Is this girls only? Or is my fake fiancé coming too?

PEYTON

Oh stop it. You know he's coming. Everyone will be here.

Everyone?

AVERY

Don't worry, Em. We will tell Logan to leave the handcuffs at home.

That's not what…

AVERY

You were thinking? Sureeeeee.

PEYTON

Leave her alone, Ave. There's nothing going on there.

What she said.

AVERY

I'll believe it when I see it.

Are you making your famous macaroni salad?

AVERY

You're the best at deflection.

PEYTON

Yes, Em. Ignore her.

CHAPTER FIFTEEN

Emiline

July

ONE THING I've learned to never take for granted is a break from school.

I'm not talking about the time off I had for spring break, where I still ended up studying. This is one where I'm forced to do nothing because the previous content is behind us, and we have no idea what's coming next because we don't get the syllabus until the first day of school.

Yesterday, I borrowed Oliver's truck and took a trip to the beach with Brooke. We laughed all day, soaked up the sun, and drank frozen margaritas until we crashed at Tommy's beach house for the night.

It was the first day neither of us had other priorities, like school work or a job, but to relax.

We needed it more than we thought we did.

After dropping Brooke off in the city, I headed straight for Tommy's house for a Fourth of July barbecue Peyton's putting together.

I hate that I don't get out here as much as I can anymore. Earlier this year, the two of them and my nephew James moved out of the penthouse and into this beautiful home in the suburbs. They now have a massive property with a white picket fence, something I never saw my brother having, but Peyton changed him.

I spent the ride giddy with excitement about seeing my nephew. Before starting my degree, I was the one who would always watch James while my brother worked. I hated giving that up and missing all that time with him, but on the other hand, Thomas would have never met Peyton.

I finally arrive and park the car. Marc and Avery are sitting on the front porch rocking chairs with Avery's mom. At least, that's who I assume it is because they look so much alike. A couple of days ago, through a group chat with my brothers, I learned that they were surprising Avery by flying her in from Vermont for the weekend.

"Ahh, Em!" Avery shrieks as she jumps from the chair to greet me. "I feel like I haven't seen you in years."

I can't help but laugh as she pulls me in for a hug. "Don't be dramatic. It hasn't been that long."

"Glad you could make it," Marc says from behind her before wrapping his arms around me. "And I hear a major congratulation is in order?"

"Yup." I beam, knowing he's talking about me passing my last class.

"I'm so proud of you, Emiline," he says, tightening his hold on me.

Pride washes over me. Nothing makes me feel better than my brothers being proud of me. With their success in their careers, just knowing they're there and supporting my journey means everything to me.

"Thank you, Marc." I release his hold and smile up at him.

They introduce me to Avery's mom and we chat for the next few minutes before I head inside. I make a pit stop for James and find him in his room playing with his dinosaurs and watching some shows about science and space before I see Peyton in the kitchen.

"I'm so happy you could make it out here," Peyton says.

"Me too. I missed you guys so much. It's not even funny. You more than my brother, but don't tell him that." I laugh.

Peyton makes a move to zip her lips shut. "My lips are sealed. How long are you on break this time?"

I sit on the bar stool across from her on the oversized island Thomas had built. "I get to enjoy a month of summer before the summer block starts. But don't you worry. It's only for one class, and it's a short one that's not an actual nursing class. It's a requirement they have us take before the fall block. So I'm here for allllll the last-minute wedding planning you need."

She laughs. "We totally still have a lot to do. But don't let it impede classes. I will be mad at you if you do."

"Noted." I nod through a laugh.

"Emiline," Thomas says as he opens the back sliding door and approaches me. "You made it."

"I wouldn't miss it." I smile from ear to ear as he greets me. "I missed you guys so much."

"We missed you too. Today really is going to be the best day. The weather is perfect, and Oliver is back from his trip, so everyone will be together again and able to relax and enjoy good food," he says.

My stomach does a somersault thinking about *everyone* being together again. When Peyton sent the group chat about this party happening, she didn't confirm or deny who *everyone* meant.

It's only been a week since I last saw Logan when he left my apartment.

I can't have you, but that doesn't mean I don't want you.

I haven't stopped replaying those words repeatedly like a song stuck in my head. But it's not a song.

Logan flat-out confessed he wants me. Everything Brooke suspected was right there before me, and the truth that came out has thrown me into a whirlwind of emotions. I won't deny that a part of me wanted it to be true, even though I keep telling myself I can't go down this road with him. But he feels the same way. We both know we shouldn't do this.

Besides, I've spent far too long getting over my crush on him to go back down that road only to end up disappointed or, worse, heartbroken.

I clear my throat to hide my nervousness. "Everyone?"

"Duh." Peyton laughs. "Except Logan will miss dinner."

Relief engulfs me, but I watch Thomas turn to Peyton. "But we're making extra for him, right?" he asks. "He's coming by after his overtime shift, and knowing him, he will be starving."

"You know it." She laughs. "I doubled everything because every time Logan steps in this house, he turns into a toddler who eats everything in sight."

I join her in her laughter as she talks about him. I know my laugh is all nervous and jittery, but neither of them picks up on it.

"What are the next steps for wedding planning?" I ask them to steer the conversation to anything but Logan.

"I just have to narrow down what I want you girls to wear so we can order them," Peyton says, not even noticing the rapid change of subject. "And we should talk about doing a little bachelor and bachelorette party."

Thomas groans. "I told you I don't want to do that."

"And *I* told you"—Peyton pokes his chest—"that we're doing it whether you like it or not," she tells him, then turns back to me. "We're not going to do the typical type, though. My idea is to head back down to the beach house for a night and hang out together. I don't need a bachelorette party either, but it would be fun to all hang out before the big day."

Oh no, I cannot go back to the beach house with Logan.

"Sounds good," I lie, forcing a smile.

For the next twenty minutes, while Peyton continues talking

about catering for the wedding and a DJ selection, I sit and hope my brother talks her out of the party idea.

After all, I'm fairly certain the beach house is what started this whole mess.

I stare blankly into the fire crackling under the moonlit sky in the backyard that Thomas and Peyton had built. It feels like a true oasis outside of city life, a place that forces you to decompress and relax.

There's been a shift in energy since Logan showed up an hour ago.

Not a bad one, but my body is very aware of his presence.

I expected things to be weird between us, but really, they're the complete opposite of that. Long gone is the man who, *I thought*, hated me for the last few months. Logan has done nothing but smile and laugh since he got here. And every time I chance a look in his direction, his gaze is already locked on me.

I don't know what to make of it, but I don't hate it either.

I opened up to him about how I thought he hated me and how it was driving me insane, so maybe he's just trying to be nicer now.

The two glasses of sangria I've already had don't help the fact that his laugh makes me want to laugh. Pair that with how he's been smiling at me, and it's a deadly combination.

Logan stands on the opposite side of the fire, and my eyes move from the fire to him occasionally. I can't help but check him out. He's wearing a pair of khaki shorts with a solid black tee that hugs the muscles on his arm.

"Do we have any more cheeseburgers left?" Logan asks.

My jaw hangs partly open, but I laugh. "Logan, you ate three already! How can you possibly fit anymore?"

He looks at me, and I swear his features soften, his smile growing wider the moment his eyes land on mine. This isn't him looking at me like I'm his best friend's little sister anymore. This is him looking at me like he has a soft spot for me.

"I'm a growing boy, Shortcake," he says with a wink before walking off to get more food.

Did he just?

If we ignore that god-awful nickname, did he just flirt with me?

The conversation continues around me as I stay seated, my mind wandering. I think back to all the things Brooke has said to me about Logan.

Would it be so bad if I tried to pursue something?

If Logan wants it, and he can't have me because of my brothers, what if we kept it a secret?

Now I know I have to be drunk from the sangria because of these insane thoughts.

I internally laugh to myself at how ridiculous that sounds. At the same time, Logan takes the seat next to me instead of his previous one.

I ignore the humming in my body as everything swirling around in my head only intensifies with him being so close. A part of me thinks this also isn't the craziest thing I've ever thought of doing. I mean… I decided to go to nursing school. That's pretty damn crazy.

I don't believe he's the relationship type, and I can't get into one with my crazy schedule anyway. But I want that. I can't deny it anymore. I fucking want it. I want to share the craziness of this life. Someone to talk to about my day and shift at work and vent about when I'm stressed.

I want that with Logan.

I've always wanted something with him, and it seems to become more prevalent every time I cross his path.

Thomas and Peyton pull me from my thoughts when I see how my brother looks at her.

That's the kind of love I crave in my life.

Someone who looks at me the way my brother does at Peyton

—full of love, want, and devotion. It happens every single time I witness them together, and I always think the same thing…

Everyone deserves their type of love.

"Can we, for once, not be a witness to this?" Logan throws his head back in the chair next to me. "There's too much love here today."

"Leave them alone, Lincoln Log," I say as I swat his arm with the back of my hand. "They're the only ones here oozing all the love. Get over it."

"Nah." He shakes his head before turning to look at me. "We got these two over here too." He hikes his thumb toward Marc and Avery.

"Oh no. No. No," Avery says, waving her hands in the air in defense. "You know this isn't real over here. Get the idea of *love* out of your head."

Marc says nothing back. They've been putting on a great show of being an engaged couple. It's actually a little too good of an act. I can feel his resolve cracking with Avery, and I know with full conviction that he will fall head over heels in love with her.

Logan looks over at Marc and Avery. "You two are…" He pauses in thought. "Really good at your act. That's for damn sure."

"Man." Oliver shakes his head from the other side of the fire. "I've been gone for way too long. I miss out on all the fun. I mean, I know you guys are doing the whole thing to impress the boss, but damn… I'm with Logan here. I can feel whatever you two have going on from over here."

"I'm glad someone said it." Thomas laughs over his glass of whiskey.

"Have you all bumped your heads?" Avery laughs, but I can tell it's an uncomfortable one. She doesn't want to show that side of her, and I don't blame her. She is *not* the relationship type.

"Leave them alone," I say, standing from my chair. "Let them worry about them. Let's play a game of cornhole."

"I'm down with that." Marc jumps up quickly. Our eyes meet, and I can see he's thankful I ended that conversation as quickly as it started.

"Girls against guys?" I say.

"I'm so down for that," Marc says as Logan stands up and follows him to the open grass. "Me and Logan against Emiline and Ave."

My steps falter, not because of the sangria coursing through my body, but because of the realization that girls against guys in a game of cornhole puts Logan or Marc on the same side of the game with me. Knowing Marc and what he has going on with Avery, he's going to take whatever side she's standing on.

Which leaves me in close proximity to Logan.

"You're going down, Lincoln Log," I say, playing off the nerves.

"You wish I was, Shortcake." He winks before he starts off toward the cornhole setup.

I freeze in place, and my jaw falls open.

Everyone around me also stands frozen, and my brothers look downright murderous over the words that just came out of his mouth.

He did not just say that out loud.

Logan turns around and makes eye contact with everyone in the group. "Oh please," he rebuts. "That's not what I meant. I meant, like… she wishes we were going down. Not." He stops his rambling and groans. "You all have dirty fucking minds."

"Do we?" Thomas says.

"I didn't take it the way you are saying it was meant to be taken," Marc adds.

"This is gold." Oliver laughs from behind the fire to break the tension.

"Let's just fucking play," Logan huffs, taking his spot on the side of the game.

This is going to be one interesting game.

CHAPTER SIXTEEN
Logan

SHIT. Shit. Shit.

I repeat that over and over in my head as I move to my side of the cornhole game with Emiline trailing right behind me.

"What the hell was that?" she whisper-shouts as soon as she catches up to me.

I turn to look at her, those fucking light blue eyes sparkling in the moonlight from her sangria-induced haze. "What was what?" I ask as if I don't know what she's talking about.

"Don't play dumb." She keeps her voice low so only I can hear. "You with that awful pet name and that comment…" Her cheeks turn a rosy shade of pink, and I can tell she doesn't want to repeat it. "You know."

I smirk down at her. "I don't know what you're talking about. Entertain me, Emmy." I take a small step toward her, and my body rumbles with energy from being this close to her. I'm playing a dangerous game, but I can't find a part of me that wants to stop. "What comment?"

"The going down… uh… comment." She fumbles with her words.

This isn't the first time Emiline has gotten shy with me when talking about sex. I remember watching how cute she was when she got all flustered talking about her neighbors' sexcapades that morning I showed up after work to check on her.

"Are you telling me you took it another way than how I meant it?" I grin.

Her lips part in shock and embarrassment, but Avery screaming that it's her turn, pulls Emiline from her thoughts. When I look across the game, I see Avery giving me a suspicious look. Her eyebrows pinch together as she stares at me, trying to figure out my motives.

I don't have a motive. At least I don't think I do.

I've just been coasting by, trying not to let intrusive thoughts of touching my best friend's little sister actually happen. I've been trying to keep my hands to myself, but I'm unsure how much more I can take. I've already admitted to her face that I want her, which is more than I should have ever said.

Emiline swings the bag across the lawn and misses. I follow when it's my turn, and then my gaze immediately finds her again.

This time, she breaks the silence. "They are going to think something's going on between us," she says with a nervous tone in her voice.

"No, they won't."

"This isn't funny," she groans. "My brothers…"

That's when I break.

"You think I don't know?" I cut her off but keep my words low only for her to hear. "You think it's easy for me to suddenly want to touch you in ways you've probably never been touched before? You think it's easy for me to keep my distance and force myself to hate you?"

She sucks in a sharp breath as her eyes bounce between mine. "I…"

"Yeah, I get it's your brothers, but those are also my best friends. I made a promise to them years ago that I'd never come near their little sister. To top it off, I'm not a relationship guy. And now…" My eyes trail her up and down as my tongue darts across my bottom lip instinctively. "Now you're killing me every time I look at you."

Emiline doesn't answer and remains silent as we take turns throwing the sandbags across the yard. I don't push it either because it could only hurt her in the long run.

It's bad enough she already knows I want her.

———

Emiline didn't say a word for the rest of the game, only intensifying the tension.

"Logan," Thomas says. "Can I ask you a favor?"

"Anytime." I nod.

"Marc and Avery are staying here tonight. Can Emiline catch a ride back to the city with you? She doesn't want to stay outside of the city and would rather get back to her apartment."

That was not what I expected him to ask me. Then again, I've been on edge since Emiline left me with nothing but silence.

I also feel a guilty conscience buzzing in my body that I'm going behind his back.

I am… but not in the way anyone would think.

I just happen to know something about Emiline that he doesn't know.

"Yeah," I say, clearing my throat and sounding more nervous than I intended to. "It's no problem at all."

In all the years I've been friends with the Ford brothers, they've never once visited my apartment. This sounds weird since they are my best friends, but we've always done everything at Tommy or Marc's place.

Besides, she *lives* in the same building as me, and I *am* going back that way.

Fuck my life.

I can't deny that I want to be close to her. I want her in the passenger seat of my truck, on back of my bike, taking over every space she can. But the words exchanged during the game and being as close as I was to her stirred something inside of me, something that's been building for months now that I've fought like hell to shake off.

Yet again, I try to remind myself I can't go down that road with her, but my mind doesn't seem to want to cooperate.

I finally turn around to find Emiline sitting by the fire on her phone. Her eyes are glassy, her cheeks flush.

"Ready to go, Emmy?" I ask her.

She lifts her eyes but not her head. The look is downright murderous, and rightfully so. She hates it when I call her that. "Yup," she says, popping the p. "I'm just waiting for my Uber."

"Logan is giving you a ride back," Thomas says before I can. "You're not getting an Uber this late."

Her head snaps up and her eyes dart between Thomas and I. "I'm fine, Tommy."

"I have no doubt." He nods in agreement. "But I'd feel a lot better if Logan took you back."

She turns her head to look at me and I can't tell what she's thinking right now. I'd like to believe the thoughts running through her head are good thoughts of being around me—close to me. But she might also be thinking to murder me.

"Fine," Emiline says with an argumentative tone as she gets up from the chair. Her body sways just the slightest bit as she clicks through her phone to cancel the ride and makes her rounds.

I don't take my eyes off her for a single second as she says goodbye to the girls and her brothers.

Once we get in the truck, tension fills every nook and cranny. Not even the sharpest knife could slice through the thickness of it all. It's not like I haven't given Emiline a ride before, and my motorcycle is much more personal as far as proximity goes, for fuck's sake. I'm making this way more awkward than it needs to be, but the quiet in this small space is just too much.

Relax, Logan.

"Thanks for the ride," she says flatly.

I nod, keeping my eyes fixed on the highway and not on the long, tan, and exposed legs on the passenger seat in denim shorts. I remind myself I can't stare and put us at risk of crashing this car.

We ride in silence for the next five minutes, and I expect this to be the case for the rest of our short trip home.

"Can I ask you a favor?" Emiline says, breaking the silence.

"Sure."

"Can you stop calling me Emmy?"

That's the last thing I expected her to ask for.

"I think I can do that." I smile and glance her way quickly to notice her eyes on the road ahead of us.

Emiline gives a tight nod. "It makes me feel like a little girl," she admits.

I stay silent because I'm not sure how to respond.

"And I'm not a kid anymore."

"You're not."

I can feel her eyes on me now without even having to look in her direction.

"You're not, Emiline," I repeat. My teeth clench together just a little more as the words come out of me like realization hitting me all over again.

"Thank you," she breathes out.

I feel myself relax a little in my seat as if that just relieved some of the tension.

"Listen," I start to say, but something flashes across my eyes, and I slam the brakes.

Emiline lets out a pained scream like I've never heard before and brings her knees to her chest and braces for contact.

"Fuck," I scream out, slamming harder on the brakes and swerving to the side of the road. My right hand leaves the wheel and moves across her chest to block any impact.

I look over to see what we just avoided and notice it's a fucking deer.

I park the car and rest my head back on the headrest to take a calming breath. My hands feel shaky from that near accident, and my head is spinning.

I hear Emiline's erratic breathing, and turn to face her, leaning across the center console to scan her from head to toe. "Are you okay?"

"Yeah," she says. But then, to my surprise, she laughs. Nervously at first, before it breaks into a complete fit of hysterics as if she just can't control it. This was not the reaction I was expecting. "I can't believe we almost died."

"We didn't almost die. Not even close. Even if we hit the damn thing, we'd still be alive."

"Could you imagine if we did?" She laughs harder.

Now I can't help but laugh with her.

But it doesn't last long.

Her laughter turns to tears in almost the blink of an eye.

As if she feels embarrassed, she climbs out of the passenger door and stands in the grass in front of the truck. I jump out and round the truck to take my place next to her.

"Are you okay?" I ask again.

"I…" Emiline pauses, allowing her laughter to die down. "I'm not sure why I'm laughing so hard. And I'm not even sure why I'm crying right now." She points to me before she paces the grass on the side of the road, keeping her gaze locked on where she's walking. "Today was the most fun I've had in months. Everyone together again and the break from school reminded me of how stressful and messy my life is. And then you had to flirt with me in front of all three of my brothers," she says, her tone growing in volume with her last sentence.

I can't help but grin at her. "Maybe I was."

She stops dead in her tracks and snaps her head toward me. "I…" Her voice trails off as she looks back down at the ground, and I hear her mutter, "*well*," under her breath.

A laugh bubbles out of me. It's cute how outspoken she is with a few drinks in her. But I also am not about to have this conversation when she's slightly under the influence. I want her to remember every word I tell her.

"Now you're laughing at me," she says with her hands propped on her hips.

"Never." I shake my head, my lips drawing a flat line. "But this isn't a conversation we should have right now."

"I'm not drunk, if that's what you think."

"I know." I nod. "But when I tell you I was, in fact, flirting with you, I want you to be one hundred percent able to remember every single detail."

Emiline's mouth hangs open, and her eyes widen, almost as wide as the deer in my headlights we nearly ran over.

I take a few steps through the grass until I stand in front of her. The look on her face stays there like a picture frozen in time. My eyes scan her briefly, and I can see everything, with the headlights of my truck being our spotlight.

The goosebumps that pebble across her tanned skin, and how her breath hitches when I get close tells me she feels everything I feel when I'm this close to her.

"I'd remember, Logan," she says with confidence, but her voice remains soft. "It's kind of hard to..." Emiline pauses as if she's trying to figure out what to say or because she doesn't want to say too much. "Forget."

The last word is so low that I would have missed it if I hadn't been paying attention to every detail about her.

"So you will remember when I tell you that you make it impossibly hard *not* to flirt with you, Em. It's damn near impossible to hide it from everyone around me too. If you're in the room, I want my eyes on you. If you're close to me, I want to touch you. And if you're near me, I fight every fucking urge in my body not to do something I'd regret."

She presses her lips together, and my eyes travel to them. Big mistake because all the blood rushes to my cock when she brings her bottom lip between her teeth and fights back a smile.

I groan as I throw my head back.

Emiline Ford is going to unravel everything I've worked so hard to keep buried deep inside, whether I want her to or not.

"I wouldn't regret it," she finally says.

"That might have been the wrong word because I wouldn't regret it either. But I don't want to make things complicated for either of us. It's a bad idea for us to go down that road."

She nods, remaining silent, but the disappointment written across her face is so loud.

"Let's get you home," I finally say despite wanting to say and do so much more.

It's best to leave it at this.

For now.

CHAPTER SEVENTEEN
Emiline

"HOW COME I haven't worked with or seen you in two whole weeks since our beach date over Fourth of July weekend?" Brooke asks as the server drops our salads in front of us.

We thank them, and I take a sip of water, mostly because I want to avoid this topic and why I haven't seen her. I don't have a reason for it other than I used some paid time off for two weeks to spend time with my nephew.

For the first time in a while, I actually took time off of work for me, and it felt weird. But I welcomed it because I knew I couldn't hold back with Brooke if I saw her at work.

I knew I would spill every single detail like a babbling brook the moment we had a second.

It's not that I don't want to tell her all the things Logan told me. It's just that I haven't been able to make sense of it all.

"I've just been really busy with the gym and visiting James," I finally say. Only some of it is a lie, but neither excuse takes up every minute of my time.

After my trip to Thomas' house, I realized I needed to spend more time with my nephew. He's growing up right before our eyes, and I don't want to regret missing anything.

"You're looking hella fine, girl." She wiggles her eyebrows.

"Not that you didn't before, but I can tell you've been lifting weights. It's a good look on you."

"Thanks." I offer her a smile. "With all this free time we have during the break and this summer class not being intense, I really have more time to focus on myself. My mental health has never been better. I'm not sure what I'm going to do when fall classes start. I don't want to give this up."

"And you don't have to," she reassures me. "You're so smart, Em. You can put aside an hour of your day to go to the gym. Or just listen to those supplemental videos we find online while you're on the treadmill," she suggests, her tone comforting before diving into her salad.

"Hmm, that's actually a really good idea."

"I'm full of them." She beams. "Speaking of good ideas, have you seen or talked to Logan more? I haven't seen him bring anyone in lately."

I take one more bite of my salad before placing my fork down and wiping my mouth in an attempt to gather my thoughts.

I remain silent when I nod.

"Ohhhh." Brooke sits up taller in her chair. "Tell me everything."

I laugh. "There isn't *a lot* to tell. But he was at my brother's house for his Fourth of July party. Then he drove me home. That's all."

She sits there, her mouth agape like she can't believe I didn't tell her.

I kind of feel like a shitty friend for it.

"But nothing happened," I continue.

Brooke's face morphs into disappointment that the tea isn't better.

Despite the amount of sangria I drank, I remember every single detail of that drive home. How embarrassed I felt, laughing so hard and then crying. Who the hell cries on the side of the road? Just thinking about it makes me cringe.

What I didn't anticipate was that Logan would spill more

than I ever expected him to spill. One day, he admits he wants me but can't have me. Then he admits to flirting with me and how it's impossible not to. I haven't seen him since, but my resolve around him is slowly cracking.

Everything I've felt for him in the past is creeping back to the surface slowly but surely as I fight to keep it down.

"So he didn't come into your apartment or anything when he dropped you off?"

I shake my head. "He was a true gentleman." I laugh lightly. "But I won't lie to you. Ever since you put the idea in my head, I almost want him to do very non-gentlemanly things to me. When he dropped me off at my door, I invited him in, but he declined and said it's best for the both of us if he went home."

"Best for the both of us?! Is he joking?" Brooke practically shouts.

"I know. I know. I haven't been able to stop thinking about it," I admit. "I'm constantly back and forth in my head about how I need to keep it the way it is, but there's no denying it anymore. I want him."

My body shivers the moment the words leave my lips.

I want him.

But to what extent do I want him?

I can't get involved in a relationship right now, with school starting up again, or in a friends-with-benefits situation because I know my heart enough to know it will end up broken.

"I love this for you," Brooke says.

"I don't," I scoff. "I can't stand these feelings and thoughts running through my brain. You know I'm a chronic over-thinker and a total people pleaser. All of this makes a bad combination of trying to figure out what he's thinking and what he wants."

Brooke's lips curve up in almost a sinister smile. "You know... you could always ask Logan himself."

"Are you insane?"

"You already know I am," she says casually. "Stop worrying about pleasing your brothers for two seconds and worry about yourself. If your brothers finding out is the biggest issue you face, then you two can do the secret hookup thing. This is your life, Emiline. Not theirs. They can't fault you for who you fall in love with and who you choose to spend your time with."

"Whoa, whoa, I said nothing about falling in love with him," I defend.

"Okay, I might have taken it too far with that. But all the other stuff. Listen, babe, I know you're the type of person who wants to please everyone around you. I love you for that, but it's time you worry about you. It's time you focus on what makes *you* happy, not what makes me, your friends, or your brothers happy. Although, you doing the dirty with Logan would make me *very* happy." Brooke winks.

"You're unreal, you know that, right?"

"And that's one of the many reasons you love me," she says with conviction.

With that, we both fall into a bout of laughter and continue our lunch date where we talk about our schedule and the next few assignments we have for our summer class.

Throughout the whole conversation, I can't seem to get Logan off my mind because Brooke is right.

It's about time I put myself first.

CHAPTER EIGHTEEN
Logan

"IN THE WORDS of the Jonas Brothers, it's been a hell of a week, but we made it." Silas sighs from the passenger seat.

"Your obsession with the Jonas Brothers is concerning. And you know it's only Tuesday, right?"

"Semantics." He shrugs.

He's right. It really has been a hell of a week. Even though it's only our second shift out of three.

Yesterday, we had at least seven calls before midnight even hit. Between drunk drivers, bar fights, and even an attempted robbery at the corner store, it was a mess. But this always happens in the middle of July.

It doesn't help that Silas and I worked more overtime than we could handle since Mason randomly moved out of state. It's not that he worked that hard to begin with, but having him gone forced more than half the department to cover shifts.

With Silas being single and me wanting the promotion to chief more than my next breath, it benefited us to take most of them.

The money in the bank is a nice bonus too.

"We need a unit to respond to the 110th Street apartment

complex," dispatch says through our radios. *"Suspected cardiac arrest."*

"We're only about two minutes from there," Silas tells me.

"Forty en route," I respond to dispatch and put the car in drive.

Silas flips a switch on the center console as I turn left, and the lights flash to life on top of the SUV. The sirens echo through the night as we race to the location. Calls like this always put me on edge since we don't get all the details until we show up on location.

The best thing I can do is take a few calming breaths and get my head on straight before we get to the scene. I've become pretty damn good at pushing any nerves I have to the side so I can do my job the best I can.

We arrive in two minutes and I don't see an ambulance anywhere in sight yet. In cases like this, with a medical emergency, the paramedics would handle most of it. Still, we are usually the first ones on the scene after the call comes through.

"ETA on the ambulance," Silas asks through his radio as we exit the SUV.

"Two minutes," dispatch replies.

We leave the SUV and enter the apartment to find a man, who looks to be about fifty years old, unconscious on the ground.

"I don't know what to do," the woman in the room sobs.

"Ma'am, I'm Officer Bennett. Can you tell me what happened?" I ask her, keeping my voice calm and comforting as Silas and I close the distance.

"He collapsed. He has a heart condition," the woman cries louder. "Please help my husband."

Silas checks for a pulse as I situate myself over him.

"He's not breathing, and I can't find a pulse," Silas tells me.

"I'm going to start compressions."

I position my hands one on top of the other and drown out

every sound around me to focus on counting the number of compressions and keeping my pace even.

After two rounds of compressions, the paramedics show up, and we seamlessly transition, working together to stabilize the man. I watch intently as they continue the care before we have to bring him to the hospital.

As per protocol, we have to escort the ambulance to the hospital. It's a busy night in the city, and the extra sirens can help us get him there faster.

"City General," Silas says from the passenger seat. He says it like he knows where my mind goes when I think of that particular hospital.

For the last half hour, I successfully focused on my job, and now we're going to the place where I risk running into her.

Instead of dwelling on that, I nod as we spend the next few minutes flying through the city streets to get the man there as fast as possible. Once we arrive, the paramedics unload the patient from the back of the ambulance and bring him inside.

Silas and I follow as an extra precaution since we were first at the scene. Both of us are also the type of people who want to see situations like this through and confirm he's okay.

As we walk to the room, I scan the area and a few surrounding rooms, looking for someone, only to find her not there.

For the first time, I'm disappointed that she isn't here.

It's probably for the best.

Right?

———

"He'll be just fine. Good job getting him here as fast as you did." The nurse smiles.

"That was all the paramedics," I say.

"Whatever you say." She laughs as she exits the room.

"Ready to head out?" Silas asks.

Just as I'm about to answer, I see Emiline sitting at the nurses' station, practically falling asleep. Exhaustion is written all over her face, and I know the feeling all too well. I briefly scan the rest of her and notice she's wearing my sweatshirt Thomas made me give her.

I was hoping she'd wear it, but I didn't expect to see it on her at work.

I almost never want it back because of how good it looks on her. It's almost like it was made for her, like I bought it with her in mind, even though I certainly didn't.

"Are you good for a minute?" I ask Silas, nodding toward Emiline.

He glances in her direction before looking back at me and giving me a smile like he's onto me. "Take all the time you need, Bennett."

Smug.

Just as I'm about to make my way to the nurses' station, a nurse stops me.

"Hey, you got a minute?" she coos.

Andrea.

Fuck, I don't have time for this right now, nor do I want to engage in conversation with the one nurse who doesn't stop flirting with me.

Letting out a sigh, I look from her to where Emiline sits, finding her staring with an expression that stirs something unwelcoming in my gut. Gone are the tired eyes I just saw.

I quickly look back at Andrea. "Sure, what's up?" Sounding more annoyed than I intended to.

"A couple of us are heading out Friday night for some drinks. From what I hear, a few guys from your unit are coming too." She grins. "I was wondering if you'd wanna go."

Andrea's a pretty girl, and if my thoughts weren't consumed by a certain blonde just a few feet away, I would flirt right back and take her up on her invitation.

Besides, I can still feel Emiline's eyes on me without even looking over Andrea's shoulders to confirm.

And damn, I want to look at her.

Only her.

I just need Andrea to stop talking to me.

"I'll see what Silas is doing," I finally answer back.

"I was sort of hoping it would be just you and me." Andrea flutters her lashes at me.

My body betrays me when my eyes trail from hers to just over her shoulder. Emiline is now aggressively typing on the desktop computer, her exhaustion long gone. I realize she can hear our conversation.

Andrea looks over her shoulder to see what I'm looking at before looking back at me. "She won't be there if that's what you're worried about," she whispers, leaning closer. The small move should affect me, and I should be interested in a woman flirting with me the way she is, but I feel nothing. "I know you don't care for her. Besides, she has assignments to do for her summer class."

I swallow and give her a tight nod. I didn't realize how much I'd shown my disdain for her. Or, has Emiline talked about how much I've avoided her?

This used to be what I wanted.

Is it still what I want?

"Although the answer will probably be no, I'll let you know, Andrea."

"Yeah, no worries." She shakes her head in embarrassment. "Just let me know." She pulls out an alcohol swab from her pocket before writing something on it. She pockets her pen before slipping the swab into the uniform pocket on my chest. "You have my number now. Hope to see you there, *officer.*"

There's one thing I hate more than how much I think about Emiline, and it's when women use my job title in a suggestive tone. It makes me feel like they're only after one thing.

I make a mental note to trash her number as soon as possible.

"Have a good rest of your night," I say as I slip past her and make my way to the nurses' station.

I stand on the other side of the desk, leaning on my elbows over the surface that separates us to look at Emiline over the computer screen. She keeps her eyes fixed on the desktop, typing away. When she realizes I'm not moving, her blue eyes meet mine, and her stark beauty hits me right in the chest. Something about her wearing that royal blue color makes her eyes shine much brighter up close.

"Can I help you?" Emiline asks in a very professional tone.

A smile plays on my lips. "Just checking on you," I lie because, quite frankly, I have no idea why I'm standing here. I should have left after that conversation with Andrea. I should have left with Silas when I had the chance.

She scoffs. "That's unnecessary. But if you *must* know how I'm doing, I'm tired as hell, and I still have seven hours left. I truly will never make it."

"That's a bit dramatic."

Emiline's expression remains blank as she stares at me, but she averts her gaze from mine and back to her computer screen and goes back to typing as if I'm not even standing here anymore.

Is she… jealous?

After watching my interaction with Andrea, that has to be what this is.

"You know; you could get some coffee." I smile down at her. I don't know why I'm smiling, but for some odd reason, I can't help it. It's like it's happening on instinct. Especially when I see her sitting there in *my* clothes. "The stuff that's filled with caffeine. That helps people stay awake."

"Hilarious." She shoots me a cheeky grin as she crosses her arms over her chest, leaning back in the chair. "Did you come here to make jokes?"

I lift a shoulder. "I'm just saying hi."

It's Emiline's turn to smile. The way she does sends my heart rate into overdrive, because it's fucking stunning when she does.

"That's not what you said. You said you were checking in on me."

"Isn't that the same thing?"

"No."

"Fine." I smack the counter lightly and turn on my heel. "Grab some coffee, will ya?" I tell her over my shoulder as I retreat away.

"Okay, Daddy. Whatever you say," she says in a smug tone.

My steps falter, and I pause momentarily before shaking myself out of them and walking away. I refuse to acknowledge what Emiline just called me because if I do, I will say something I should definitely not be saying right now.

An hour after we leave, Silas and I grab a coffee at the place outside of the hospital.

"Are you good if I run home and let the dogs out?" Silas asks as we're about to leave the coffee shop. He always leaves at some point each night shift to let his two dogs out.

"Yeah, no problem." I nod. "Keep your radio on."

"You got it, boss."

I sip my all-black coffee, watching Silas walk out and head toward his apartment. Once he's out of sight, I look at the menu on the wall behind me with the different types of caffeinated beverages available. My eyes land on the word peppermint.

I can't believe it's on the menu in the heat of summer.

I must be losing it because I find myself returning to the counter and placing another order. Before I know it, I'm back in the emergency room with a large, iced peppermint mocha latte in hand.

Emiline's eyes widen when I approach the nurses' desk. She scans her surroundings before looking back at me. "What are you doing back here?"

I raise the iced latte toward her, trying my best to keep my face void of emotion. "This is for you."

Her jaw hangs open as she looks from me to the cup. "Why?"

"I know how these overnight shifts are. I wanted to get you something to help you get through your shift."

She offers me a soft smile.

What I would give to press my lips to hers.

She reaches across the counter between us and takes the drink from my hands. "Thank you," she says before taking a sip. "Peppermint mocha?"

I nod.

"How did you… this is my favorite drink."

I nod again. "Yeah, I remember you getting it."

I remember every fucking thing about her it seems.

Emiline's smile grows and something in me flutters to life. Seeing her smile and being the reason she smiles, sparks a fire inside of me, making me want to be the reason she does more and more.

"Thank you, Logan," she says. "This means a lot."

"Don't mention it," I reply, smiling down at her because I can't help it. "Have a good rest of your night."

And with that I turn to leave.

Because this feeling racing in my chest for her is dangerous.

Thomas would kill me if he ever found out.

CHAPTER NINETEEN
Emiline

I FIND myself standing in front of the full-length mirror of the guest room at Thomas' beach house, adjusting the hem of my dress for the hundredth time. My heart is beating so fast in my chest, and I can't seem to calm my nerves.

The light blue fabric sits mid-thigh, and the thin strap leaves my shoulders exposed.

It's hot here on the shore.

But that's not why I chose this dress for tonight.

I release a sigh as I continue to stare at myself, running my hands through my hair. Reluctantly, I decided to keep it down and straight. The humidity is only going to cause it to frizz.

Tonight, we're going out for a conjoined bachelor and bachelorette party for Thomas and Peyton to celebrate the love they've found for each other before the big day next month.

Yet, I can't get my brain to focus on anything other than Logan being here too.

It's been a few weeks since he showed up at my work to bring someone in for a cardiac arrest, only to leave and come back an hour later with my favorite latte in hand.

Him remembering my order altered my brain chemistry that day.

Not to be dramatic or anything.

But something so small, means a lot to an overthinker like me who has always felt like he couldn't stand me.

Things are shifting between us though.

"Em, you ready?" Avery shouts from the hallway, snapping me out of my thoughts.

"Yeah, just a second," I reply, giving myself one last look in the mirror before grabbing my purse.

When I open the door, I find Avery standing against the wall with her arms crossed over her chest. A smile spreads across her face as she takes in my outfit.

"Leaving little to the imagination I see." She winks.

"Don't start, Ave," I scold, not wanting her to make this any more awkward for me than it already is.

She rolls her eyes. "Whatever you say, girlfriend. Let's go. The limo is waiting for us."

"A limo?"

"You know these Ford brothers," she scoffs. "We might only be going out to dinner and some drinks, but they want to roll up in the best form of transportation."

I laugh as we descend the stairs to meet everyone waiting for us.

Once I step outside, the humid air smacks me right in the face. Long Beach Island in August feels like the armpit of summer. Not that New York City is much different, but there's nothing I hate more than moisture in the air and feeling sweaty.

My anxiety flared to life the moment my eyes land on Logan standing outside the limo talking with Oliver. I have no idea what they are going on about, but they're both laughing.

I feel like I don't see Logan laugh nearly enough.

Avery closes the door behind me with a bang and it forces everyone to look in our direction. Heat rises to my cheeks when

Logan's eyes land directly on mine. This time it's not because of the weather.

Except the way his eyes trail my body, makes it feel cold out here.

"We're going to be late for our reservation," Peyton says, opening the back door to the limo. Everyone starts to move behind her, piling in one by one.

But Logan doesn't move.

I don't move.

We stare at each other as if there's no one else around us while my heartbeat thrums in my chest like a beating drum, faster and faster the longer we keep eye contact.

But that only lasts a few seconds before he breaks the stare and piles in behind Oliver. My hands feel shaky and I will the thoughts down of spiraling into a panic attack. Every part of me is dreading this evening.

But I want to do this for Thomas and Peyton.

I just didn't want to do it here.

The beach house brings up so many feelings for me. Mostly, I don't want this night to be over and Logan goes back to hating me the way he did the last time we left here.

I inhale and exhale a calming breath before getting into the limo behind him.

Thankfully he took the seat on the opposite side.

Distance is best.

———

Dinner went better than I thought it would.

We all engaged in conversation as if everything was the way it used to be.

Avery, Kali, and Peyton all discussed some last-minute things we need to do next week before the wedding, while Marc filled us in on all the renovations he plans to do to his new house he bought in the mountains and the guys asked about him taking over the real estate business from his boss.

It makes sense that he bought the house in the mountains after his trip there.

It's where I think he officially fell in love with Avery.

Those two had heart eyes all of dinner.

Now that dinner's over, we walked down the street to a small restaurant that sits on the second floor of the building and over-looks the bay. The music is upbeat, and the area is packed with plush seating and a small dance floor in the middle. The sun has just crossed the horizon, but the hue of orange still lingers in the sky.

I find myself staring at the colors changing in the sky on the balcony when Logan comes up beside me, close enough that our forearms graze when he rests himself on the ledge. The heat from his body seeps into me, suddenly making it hard to concentrate.

"Having fun?" he asks.

I nod, turning to meet his gaze. "Yeah. It's so beautiful out here."

"Yeah," Logan says, keeping his eyes on me. "It is."

I avert my gaze to the horizon, my brain wondering if he meant the sky or me. And because I'm a glutton for bringing heartbreak on myself, my head wanders to the idea of him calling Andrea after she gave him her number.

Did he call her?

Did they hang out?

I'm irrationally jealous of my coworker.

We both stand there for a few minutes in silence, until we hear a loud crash of glass hitting the ground. Both of our heads snap in the direction of the dance floor to find Avery and Peyton laughing in hysterics over spilling their drink all over the floor.

"We hit that move way too hard," Avery breathes out through her laugh.

"I haven't danced this hard in years," Peyton shouts over the music. "Now I have to pee."

"Oh, me too. Me too." Avery says.

"I should probably follow and make sure she doesn't fall down the stairs on her way." I hear Thomas tell Marc.

"Right behind you," Marc nods through a laugh.

I watch as everyone filters through the doors, including Oliver and Kali who said he needed another drink.

Logan doesn't move from beside me.

I half expected him to follow for another drink too.

But instead, he turns to face me, forcing me to do the same.

"Em," he exhales. "You look…. tonight... shit. I don't have the words."

My cheeks pink from the way he's so flustered right now, and I can't help but smile through the conflicting thoughts I have about him.

For the life of me, I can't figure out what the hell is happening here.

Except right now, Logan is looking at me like he wants me.

I can't have you… but that doesn't mean I don't want you.

The words ring in my ear, bringing me back to the time he said it, how I felt with his arms wrapped around me, and his face in my neck whispering them to me.

I take a step into him, willing him to let whatever is going on between us just happen.

Logan's hand reaches up to the side of my face, brushing a loose strand of hair away from my eyes and tucking it behind my ear. The softness of his touch sends goosebumps down my spine.

Kiss me. A silent plea.

His eyes bounce between mine as if he's considering it. His eyes drop to my lips as his body sways closer as if a breeze just forced him into me.

Only for Logan to pull his hand back, taking a step away from me. His eyes bounce between mine one more time before shaking his head and retreating through the doors that everyone just left through only moments ago.

I've been reading this all wrong.

Logan doesn't want me. Is there attraction? Sure. But I'm always going to be like a sister to him, aren't I?

I feel my breathing pick up, and my brain spiraling into anxiety.

I need to stop thinking this is more than it is.

Logan Bennett will never see me as more.

CHAPTER TWENTY
Logan

EVERY PART of my body screams to skip the gym today, especially after spending the last three nights wide awake and staring at my ceiling, willing the thoughts of Emiline from the weekend out of my head.

I almost kissed her on the balcony of the restaurant.

I almost fucking kissed her.

And I can't help but wonder if I made the biggest mistake by *not* kissing her.

I immediately shake those thoughts from my head because this is not what I want. I can't let myself get wrapped up in a relationship and risk someone, anyone, falling in love with me. It's not who I am.

My focus needs to be on my job and the reason I stayed in New York City all those years ago in the first place—to make my dad proud.

When I was eighteen, I had a choice. My mom sold our home and moved south to a small town in Georgia to start a new life. She wanted a fresh place where every corner in the city didn't remind her of my father. She suggested I either move with her or move out to San Francisco and try to get a job there to be close to my two cousins, the only other family I had. Still, it had been years since we were in contact with them. It didn't feel right to move near people who felt like strangers despite having a family tie.

Even with my immense loss and challenges, I refused to give up on my dream of working in the Big Apple. If anything, losing my father only strengthened my resolve and shaped the person I am today, the person who hides behind a double-layered brick wall to keep people from getting too close in fear of losing someone else the way I lost one of the most influential people in my life.

Or someone losing *me* and being responsible for the heartbreak my mom and I went through.

With a long sigh, I finally manage to get out of bed. I brush my teeth and head to the living room to grab my gym bag. Standing in front of my key rack, I debate between the motorcycle and my truck before deciding on the motorcycle. I lock the front door, the click of the lock echoing in the hallway, and head for the staircase. As I descend the first flight of stairs, the door to the second floor opens, and there's Emiline.

I practically fall down the last step but get myself together quickly.

Since finding out she's lived in the same building as me, we've only run into each other a few more times. But it hasn't knocked me off kilter the way it does today.

Probably because I haven't been able to get her out of my head for the last three days.

"Hi," Emiline says, stopping her steps at the same time mine stops.

"Hi," I say back.

She smiles, and I can't help it when my mind instantly travels back to having her on the back of my bike. I don't understand why my mind went *there*. Likely because I'm holding my bike keys in my hand ready to go for a ride on the way to the gym.

I never let anyone on the back of my bike.

It might seem like a small thing, but it felt huge to me.

"Don't you think it's a little odd that we keep running into each other more and more now that we know we both live in the same building?" She laughs.

God, that laugh. It's beautiful.

I hold up my hands and smile. "I'm not doing it on purpose, I swear."

"Relax, Logan. I'm only messing with you."

I laugh with her to ease the tension. I can't tell if it's real tension or if I'm making it up in my head. But either way, it's there.

It's maddening how she manages to make me feel so nervous all of a sudden.

No woman has ever stirred up these feelings in me.

I've gone from actively trying to avoid her, to jealous over seeing her with another man, to being nice and bringing her coffee at work, to almost fucking kissing her. I'm struggling to comprehend the turn of events.

I take a moment to trail my gaze over her frame when I notice the duffle bag around her arm. She's also wearing biker shorts that reach just above her knees, showing off her toned legs, and a thin, oversized crewneck, which is a little much for this August heat.

"You still can't seem to dress appropriately for the weather, I see," I joke.

"Ha ha, hilarious," she deadpans. "I'm heading to the gym and ready to sweat out my frustration over studying. I need to leave my apartment and take a break before I lose it."

"Everything okay?" I ask, clearing my throat.

Emiline smiles, and it's genuine for the first time in a while. "I'm good. This summer class is a lot more than I thought it would be. I promise it's not bad. I'm almost done with it. But I don't really want to talk about the whole panic attack thing today, if that's okay."

I give her a slight nod of understanding. I know the feeling of not wanting anyone to see what you're battling inside. People tend to look at you differently and treat you like a glass vase that may break.

I don't want her to feel like that with me.

"After you," I say, waving my hand at her to continue down the stairs.

"Where are you headed?" she asks.

"I'm also heading to the gym." I shrug my shoulder, which is holding the gym bag over it. "Don't tell me we also go to the same gym and never knew."

I open the door to the stairwell, allowing Emiline to cross first. "Park South Fitness?" she says before looking back to me for an answer. I nod. "I love it there," she continues. "They have more than two Stairmasters and a great selection of weights. I don't feel lost when I'm there. I noticed recently that they have boxing classes, too. One day, I'll overcome my fear and try it."

I laugh and shake my head at her rambling. It's weird how normal this feels with each other now. We aren't bantering annoyance back and forth. This feels… good.

"I've been going there for a while now since Silas introduced me because of those classes you're a tad bit scared of." I playfully bump her shoulder with my side.

"Hey, don't start mocking me for being a *tad bit* scared of getting punched in the face," Emiline says matter-of-factly.

"You're cute." I laugh, but quickly stop when I realize what I just said.

The playful banter with her had the words flying out of my mouth before I could stop them, even if they weren't a lie.

"I mean, it's cute that you're scared of getting punched in the face at a boxing class," I say in a flustered tone, trying to right my previous statement. "You know those classes aren't punching other people, right? You punch bags or a partner holding mitts."

"Yeah." She nods repeatedly, but her tone is hushed. "I know."

We both keep walking, but I can't help but feel like I've

offended her with that little flustered ramble trying to save myself.

Although I *had* to save myself, she's too young to be corrupted by me, and I can't have her think I see her in any other light than just a friend.

Maybe that's why I didn't kiss her when I had the chance.

Are we friends now though? It's safe to assume we are after the way this entire conversation is going down.

Once we exit the building, I continue walking down the sidewalk with her instead of making my way into the parking garage for my bike or truck like I normally would. The gym is only about four blocks away anyway.

Besides, something in my head says I need this walk with her more.

"It's beautiful out," I break the silence.

Emiline inhales and exhales slowly as she faces the sun, allowing it to brighten every inch of her face. "It really is considering it's almost the end of summer. Usually it's disgustingly hot this time of year."

A man on roller skates zips by us on her side and causes her to stumble slightly, but she catches herself. I can't stand the ignorance of some people when others are clearly walking where they're supposed to be walking.

I place my hand on the small of her back and guide her to the inside of the sidewalk, putting her between me and the building.

She adjusts the strap of her gym bag, looks down at the ground, and smiles.

"You just did the sidewalk move," she says.

"Excuse me?" I say, looking over to her.

She looks up at me, her smile still in place. "You know, keeping the girl on the inside to protect her from runaway cars. Except, this one was a runaway skater boy."

"That guy was being a jackass on those skates and could have run you over," I say, defending my motives.

"Right," she draws out.

And with that, I have nothing left to say.

———

During our walk to the gym, Emiline told me a story about a time she fell off her rollerblades when she was younger and never touched them again. It felt good to just laugh with her.

Once we made it to the gym, she thanked me for escorting her as a joke. I laughed it off, but it only made me want to be the one to walk her to the gym anytime she wanted to go. Those thoughts coursed through my brain my entire session with the trainer. Silas had to take his dogs to the vet, so it was just me and my brain consumed by Emiline.

Once I step foot back into the main gym space, I take a moment to scan the area to see if Emiline is still here. I don't even know why I allow myself to do this. I'm clearly a glutton for punishment.

My eyes land on her as she steps off the Stairmaster. Sweat glistens on her forehead, and her hair is pulled up in a messy bun. I suck in a deep breath when I notice she's now wearing nothing but biker shorts and a strappy sports bra that shows off the perfect curvature of her breasts.

Fuck. Even a sweaty mess at the gym, Emiline looks like a goddess.

All of my nerve endings are buzzing right now.

I decide to stay a little longer and ditch my bag in the locker room before heading for the weight room, where I spot her in the corner with a few dumbbells scattered around her legs. I most *definitely* don't miss the eyes on her, and right now, looking at her and seeing how good she looks, I don't blame them.

The moment I cross the large room to greet Emiline, I'm immediately stopped in my tracks when I notice a man walk up to her first. She takes her headphones out of her ear and offers him a polite smile. I can't hear what they are saying, but she has a smile on her face.

My stomach churns in… jealousy?

Stuff it down, Bennett.

After the incident with Mason at the bar over spring break, I haven't allowed jealousy to roar its ugly head inside of me. But all bets are off when it comes to her. Besides, she's probably just being nice because that's who she is.

I should turn around and just go home. My energy is depleted, and my arms are toast anyway, but my body is betraying me. Wanting to keep a close distance and not interrupt the conversation, I take a seat on the leg extension machine.

Muscle man picks up a set of dumbbells and Emiline does the same. I watch intently as they both do bicep curls simultaneously while I do rep after rep on the machine, completely losing count of how many I've done until I start feeling an intense burn in my thighs.

The second they are done, he reaches out and squeezes Emiline's bicep. She laughs at something he says before turning to pick up the dumbbells again. When she leans down, he cranes his neck to give her ass a long glance.

That's when I snap.

I'm not even thinking when I hop off the machine, making my way over to them.

Emiline spots me through the mirror and turns around. Her smile is the same as it was earlier when she says, "Hi."

"Hi." I smile down at her, wrapping my arms around her and pulling her body flush with mine for a quick embrace.

Big. Fucking. Mistake.

I clearly haven't learned my lesson from the last time I had my arms around her.

I didn't want to let her go then, and I don't want to now.

So yeah, a sweaty, hot, and big mistake embrace.

"What are you doing?" she whispers, looking up at me with beautiful wide eyes.

"I just finished my session with the trainer and wanted to see how you were doing."

My eyes bounce from hers to the muscle man standing behind us now and then back to her. Her silence tells me she understands precisely what I'm doing here, and, to my surprise, she goes with it.

"How did it go?" she asks, taking a small step into me.

"My arms are dead," I say to her before turning my head to give the muscle man one last look. "But don't worry… I can still pick you up and swing you around later."

Emiline gasps and her cheeks turn the perfect shade of pink. I wink at her before I extend my hand to greet the man who was checking her out before. "I'm Logan."

"I—Uh, I'm Jim," he says, returning the handshake.

"Jim," I scoff. "A man named Jim at the gym checking out my girlfriend's ass? Iconic. Really."

"I'm sorry, man." He holds his hands up in defense. "I didn't know she was with anyone."

I nod in understanding. "No harm done. But keep your eyes off her next time you see her in here, understood?"

With a quick nod, he retreats to the other side of the gym to finish his workout.

"What the hell was that, Logan?" Emiline smacks my arm with a very serious look on her face.

The truth is, *I* don't even know what that was.

I fucking promised myself I wouldn't allow myself to get this close. I went from acting like a complete asshole to being unable to control myself.

There has never been a moment in my life where I wanted a girlfriend or saw a future where I had a wife. Not a single girl has ever been someone I saw something long-term with.

Emiline is the first and only woman who has ever taken over every thought in my head.

Who makes me irrationally insane.

"That was me keeping you safe," I finally answer before I turn around and leave.

Because that's all I can ever be to her despite wanting quite the opposite.

CHAPTER TWENTY-ONE
Emiline

September

I WILL NOT HAVE *a panic attack tonight.*

I repeat the words over in my head as the night progresses. Even though the drinks are flowing and my brother just married the love of his life, my brain is everywhere but here.

I hate that my thoughts have the power to take over my head like this.

I started a new semester two weeks ago, and there has been a lot of information to process. I promised Thomas and Peyton I would be here and present for their big day, including the days leading up to it.

Although I had to lose a lot of sleep to keep up with studying and be here, I knew it would be worth it. But the idea of missing a lecture yesterday has me wondering what I'll need to play catch up to this week.

Then there's the other major issue present today.

Logan Bennett.

He's not meant to be an issue, but I nearly fainted on the spot when I first saw him today. The tux he's wearing matches the rest of the groomsmen, but there's something about how he wears it that lights something inside me.

I can't even deny I've fantasized about how he would look tonight. It doesn't do my thoughts justice. The man looks good in everything, but I can't keep my eyes off him.

The worst part is he came without a date.

I was hoping he would bring someone so I wouldn't have to drool over him and would have a reason to dance with whomever I wanted. I'm only lying to myself, , because if Logan had brought someone, my body would reek of jealousy, and the entire room would know how I feel about him.

I'm surprised the whole emergency department didn't pick up on it a few weeks ago when he brought me coffee. I felt my insides boil when I saw Andrea flirting with him. I know Logan used to be a massive flirt, but I've never seen it in action.

All I saw was her slipping him her number and everything in me went dark.

I wanted to rage.

But then, when we went out for Thomas and Peyton's conjoined party, he almost kissed me. So if he brought a date tonight, I would absolutely not be able to control my jealousy.

As if the thoughts in my head summoned Logan, my eyes land on his as he walks across the dance floor in my direction.

My stomach dances with nervous butterflies as the corner of his lip turns up. His eyes trail over my body as he takes in my bridesmaid dress that Peyton let us pick out ourselves. My skin pebbles with goosebumps as he stops directly in front of me, and I feel my cheeks heat.

"Hey, stranger." Logan grins.

I smile back at him and almost forget how anxious I was just a few minutes ago. He has this power over me that no matter what emotions I'm feeling when he's close, he's all I can think about. It's like he drowns everything else out. "It's been a while, hasn't it?"

"A little too long if you ask me."

It's only been two weeks?

My breath catches, and I hope like hell he didn't notice. "Yeah?" I choke out.

"Yeah, Em."

My insides crumble at his soft tone when he says my name. I'll never get over the way he calls me *Em*. It seems so small and like it shouldn't matter because everyone calls me that.

But I want to hear it repeatedly from him.

I've only had one freakin' drink. What is wrong with me?

My smile grows wider. "Yeah, I agree. It's been too long." I feel off kilter with Logan, standing here while simultaneously feeling on cloud nine. Just as he opens his mouth to say more, the music changes from upbeat dance music to a slow song. "I'll let you get to your date for this," I state with a forced smile.

I immediately hate myself for trying to get a rise out of him knowing damn well he didn't bring one. I turn to walk away, but Logan stops me when he grabs my wrist. My head snaps in his direction, and his smirk tells me he knows he caught my bluff.

"You know I didn't bring a date," he says, stepping forward. Our bodies are so close that if a gust of wind were to blow, I would collide with his chest. He leans his head over my shoulder. "But I've been wanting a dance with you all night," he whispers only for me to hear.

I think back to Brooke's words about putting myself first for once. I need to stop giving a shit about what my brothers have to say, but I also don't want them to believe this is something it's not.

"Are you asking me to dance with you?" I pull my head back and raise an eyebrow at him. "Do you think that's a good idea tonight?"

Logan's eyes scan my face, but he remains silent, looking deep in thought. The moment he brings his bottom lip between his teeth, my thighs clench together with want and desire. Even with the most minor moves, this man has the power to make me melt into a puddle at his feet.

"I don't give a fuck anymore," he whispers, the smile on his face growing wider. "I'll handle your brothers later, but right now… I want to dance with you."

Logan extends his hand, urging me to take it and follow him to the dance floor. I place my hand in his without a second thought and instantly feel my skin burn from the touch. We look down at where we're connected before our eyes meet again.

There's no way what I just felt is one-sided.

Logan guides me out to the middle of the dance floor. He stops, standing still momentarily and never taking his eyes off me. I never thought I would ever experience being consumed by another person to the point where everything around me would fade out, but that's how it feels standing in front of Logan.

His arms skate around my waist before he places a palm across my lower back. I feel the same burn right through the thin silk of my dress, but despite the heat, I shiver at the touch.

"Is this okay?" he whispers, clasping his other hand with mine.

I nod, unable to form even a single word, let alone a whole sentence.

The moment Logan steps into me, forcing our bodies together as we sway to the song's slow tempo, I think I completely stop breathing. All the air becomes trapped in my lungs as I live in the moment of dancing with him.

"You look beautiful tonight, Em," he says on a long, drawn-out exhale.

"You don't look so bad yourself, Logan."

"I'm going to ask you a question now," he says almost instantly.

I nod, nervous over what he's about to ask.

"Why didn't *you* bring a date tonight? There's no way you couldn't find one."

I laugh lightly. "I could ask you the same question."

"Oh." He raises his eyebrows. "We're playing this game, huh?"

"Maybe." I shrug.

Logan pulls me tighter as if he can't be close enough. His eyes scan around us, whether to search for someone or to make sure no one saw what he just did. I can't be too sure.

I decide to do the same and notice Avery staring with her jaw on the floor, but she quickly averts her gaze when she catches me looking at her.

"You know why I didn't bring one tonight," Logan whispers.

I snap my head in his direction and swallow past the lump in my throat.

"Because it wouldn't be fair to her…" Logan pauses, collecting his thoughts. "It wouldn't be fair because my eyes would only be on you. You make it impossible not to look at you."

"Logan," I breathe out.

"Now tell me why *you* didn't bring a date," he says. At the same time, his fingertips dig deeper into my back.

"For the same reason," I admit without a second thought.

His head falls back. He slowly takes a deep breath before releasing all the air and looking back at me. "I'm slowly losing all restraint with you, Em. I'm trying really fucking hard here to be respectful toward you and keep my word to your brothers, but there's only so much a man can take."

My hand that was resting on his shoulder moves to his chest. His heart pounds under my palm and I know now the two of us are on the same page with how we feel.

My lips curve into a grin, and I watch as a concerned look fills his face.

"Think you would be able to keep another secret?"

I don't know if it's the one drink I've had or the feelings building inside me that makes me so bold, but I think it's safe to assume that I surprise both of us when I say that.

The look on Logan's face causes my heart rate to rev faster. He looks concerned, and my eyes land on the way his throat bobs when he swallows.

I press up on my toes and wrap both arms around his neck. In the middle of the dance floor where my brothers—or hell, even the girls—can see us right now, I press my body into him, and I swear his cock hardens against me.

I lean into his neck, and he twitches at the feel of my breath on his skin. "I didn't bring a date because I'm tired of fighting whatever the hell this is between us," I whisper. "I'm tired of avoiding it because my brothers might think it's wrong."

I thought admitting this to Logan would make him back away from me, but he tightens the hold around my waist, giving me three squeezes.

But he remains silent.

He doesn't tell me if he feels the same way or anything.

"Am I the only one who feels something?" I question, pulling my body away from him.

"I don't do relationships, Em," he replies.

I straighten under the weight of his stare. He's looking at me like he's waiting for my reaction. Maybe he thought that statement would disappoint me.

His eyebrows pinch together in confusion when the grin on my face widens.

"I can't do a relationship either." I shrug. "I'm swamped with school, and I can't commit to anyone or anything other than my studies right now."

None of that is a lie, but there will always be a small part of me that wonders about the future. When I finish school and graduate, will Logan still be in my life? Will we still have this insane chemistry between us that's undeniable? Or will he want to move on with someone else?

"Okay?" Logan says, but it comes out like a question.

"I was just thinking that maybe we can—" I'm cut off when Kali comes running to the dance floor.

"Em, we need you for a picture." She laughs through her words like she's had too much to drink. "Avery has the best idea for one with all of us girls. Sorry, Logy," Kali says, utterly oblivious to what's happening between us.

I smile sympathetically, and Logan nods in understanding. I want to tell him we can finish this conversation when I get back, but I don't get the chance to do that.

The same way I didn't get a chance to tell him I'm ready to just give in.

CHAPTER TWENTY-TWO
Logan

THE ENTIRE WEDDING feels like a blur.

I couldn't even find it in me to keep drinking after my dance with Emiline. It's the most sober I've ever been at the end of any wedding I've attended. I feel off kilter and should probably have my head examined.

This isn't fucking me. I'm usually five to six whiskeys deep and taking someone back to my room at the hotel and kicking them out before I fall asleep like the asshole I am.

I was.

Instead, I haven't been able to keep my goddamn eyes off Emiline.

I'm frustrated beyond belief.

The lights come on in the ballroom, and everyone says goodbye to Thomas and Peyton as they drive off in the getaway car. Marc and Avery follow in a separate car with Thomas' son, James, because he's staying with them for the night.

I find myself looking for Emiline, but I feel her before I see her. She comes to a stop next to me with a small rolling suitcase and stops where I wait for a taxi to take me to the hotel I booked for the night so I don't have to drive back into the city.

"Where are you staying tonight?" she asks.

"I'm just up the road at the Garden Plaza," I tell her, adjusting the backpack over my shoulder as I try to avoid looking at her. "How about you?"

"Same."

My head snaps in her direction and I grin. "Interesting."

Her shoulder bumps me with a laugh. "Don't be smug. I had no idea anyone else was staying there. It's a small hotel and the only one I could get at the last minute since I didn't book until last week."

"I'm starting to think you're following me." I smirk.

Something about being around her evaporates all the frustration I had *about* her throughout the night. I can't take these feelings back and forth with her.

One minute, I'm telling myself to run away because she's off limits, and the next, I'm craving and wanting her more than I need to breathe.

"You?" Emiline raises an eyebrow. The sass in her tone right now is so hot. "Never. But I'd be happy to share a taxi with you since we're going to the same place."

"I'll have to think about it," I joke, tapping my pointer finger on my chin.

The taxi pulls up, and I jump in first while Emiline stands on the curb with her arms crossed over her chest. The smile on my face grows the longer I look at her. I can't even blame the alcohol right now because I barely had any.

This is all her.

"Are you going to get in?" I ask with a raised eyebrow.

"I was letting you think about it," she mocks.

"You're going to be the death of me."

"I can say the same for you," she concedes. "I'm only taking this ride with you because I don't feel like getting in one alone."

Emiline climbs in the backseat with me, and I can't help but stare. Even after a night of dancing, she doesn't look like she even broke a sweat. I want to touch every inch of the exposed skin she has while wearing that dress, too.

When she finally settles in her seat, the slit on the side of her dress shows more skin and I fight myself not to grip her thigh and pull her closer.

"Is that the only reason?" I ask curiously.

Emiline nods but remains silent.

It stays that way for the rest of the five-minute drive to the hotel, only increasing the tension floating in the air between us.

We exit the taxi and check in individually at the front desk. Once inside the elevator, I hit the button for the tenth floor.

"Look at that." She laughs. "How the hell did we end up on the same floor when only a quarter of the hotel was booked?"

"How do you even know that?"

"I asked." She shrugs when the elevator door closes.

Being in this confined space with her makes me want to claim her right here.

Slide that dress up and confirm she wants it as bad as I do.

It feels like she wants to say something. Hell, *I* want to say something, but I don't even know where to start.

All I know is that it's taking everything in me not to touch her how I want.

The elevator chimes, and we both exit.

"I'm 1002," she says as we make our way down the hall.

I look down at my little envelope that holds the key card to my room. "I'm 1004."

Emiline doesn't reply but smiles down at her card. We continue walking down the hallway until we reach our rooms. She stands in front of her door, and I stand in front of mine.

Fuck, I want to reach out and drag her into my room, but my head is saying don't do it.

She pauses, staring at the handle as if she's going through the same conflicting feelings. My eyes trail to the card held between her fingers, which she's tapping on her opposite hand, deep in thought.

She suddenly snaps out of her daze and unlocks her room.

"Good night, Logan," she whispers before pushing the door

open and allowing it to close behind her, not even allowing me a chance to respond.

I enter my room feeling more frustrated than ever, ripping off my suit jacket and tie before tossing it on the bed. The feeling intensifies when I unbutton the first few buttons of my dress shirt and continue pacing the small room.

Emiline was right when she told me a while ago that I'm so hot and so cold with her. I can feel exactly what she's talking about.

What if we both gave in to this feeling between us?

Just as the idea enters my mind, I hear a knock on the door that separates our two rooms. I stare at it for a few beats before taking a few steps, pausing only for a moment before finally opening it.

Emiline stands there, still in her bridesmaid dress, with her hands resting on the door frame. Her face is hard to read, but I can see her chest rising and falling as if she's been doing the same thing I've been doing over here.

Pacing the room in turmoil over these feelings.

"Logan," she whispers, her eyes still glued to the ground. The way she just said my name feels like it took everything in her just to say it.

I take tentative steps toward her, but she still doesn't look up to meet my gaze. So I take her chin between my pointer finger and thumb, urging her to look at me and tell me what's wrong, to let my eyes transpire the words I'm too afraid to say.

The moment her doe eyes finally look up at me, all the restraint I've been holding on to breaks.

My fingers still grip her chin as I lean in without another thought and finally, *fucking* finally press my lips to hers.

Her hands immediately leave the door frame, and she grips the sides of my dress shirt to bring me closer like this kiss is a lifeline for her. The feel of her soft lips on mine erases every single thought in my mind other than the way it feels to kiss her.

It feels like the sweetest sin, but one I would gladly repeat over and over again. It feels like I've been waiting forever for this moment with her.

Emiline's body melts into me, and all the space that was just between us becomes non-existent. My hands move to grip the sides of her neck as I kiss her like *she's* my lifeline now.

Her hands travel up my body and around my neck before they tangle in my hair as she rises on her tiptoes, intensifying our kiss.

She's needy for me. For more.

My hands grip her hips, and before I can overthink it, I hike her dress up enough so I can lift her in my arms. She wraps her legs around my waist, and I turn my body toward the wall to hold her against it.

Our lips remain glued together, and I take that moment to swipe a tongue across her bottom lip, urging her to open for me. And she does. She welcomes me in, angling her head to the side for a deeper kiss.

This doesn't feel like a normal kiss.

This is filled with pent-up feelings we've been fighting for far too long.

Her hips grind into my already growing erection, and I groan into her mouth before I break the seal on our lips.

"Em," I breathe out, but she doesn't stop moving her hips on me.

Emiline's lips part as she tries to catch her breath, and I know she can feel how hard my cock is right now, just from having her in my arms and pressed against this wall. Not to mention how fucking good it feels to have her move the way she does.

The urge to take everything she's willing to give me is so strong, but a small voice in my head tells me that I maybe should stop this.

"Logan," Emiline practically moans. "Just… don't stop."

The noises coming out of her mouth when she says my name

doesn't make those urges go anywhere. Instead, it only makes me want to do this that much more.

It makes me want to rip this dress off and fuck her here against this wall. It takes everything in me to hold back for just a few more moments. If she wants this, I want to hear her explicitly say it.

I grip her chin between my finger and thumb again, forcing her to look at me. "I didn't hear you say please."

Her eyes widen like she didn't expect me to say that, but I'll do whatever she wants me to do at this point.

"Please, don't stop," Emiline says, grinding her hips up and down my cock. Harder and faster with each second that passes. Even with her panties on and my dress pants, I can feel how wet she is right through the layers. "Please."

"So pretty when you beg," I grit out. "But we need to make one thing clear. This is a one-time thing. We're just getting this out of our system, right? So this can't happen again, and no one can find out about this."

She nods, and I know she understands. I doubt she wants to deal with the repercussions of someone finding out just as much as I do.

"Use me, Emiline."

"Oh. My. Fuck," she pants as she continues rubbing herself against me.

There's a good chance I might come just like this. Looking at the way her face morphs with pleasure right now.

"Are you going to come for me?" I ask, digging my fingers into her hips. "Just like this? Against this wall and riding my cock?"

"I-I think. I don't know, but it feels so good," she says with a breathy moan.

A growl comes from deep in my chest at the idea of her coming for me, with her little moans in my ear. I grip her hips, pushing her off me to stand on her feet, and her eyes look confused as the hem of her dress falls back to her ankles again.

My arms rise to the sides of Emiline's head, caging her in and keeping some space between us so my cock can breathe.

I lean down, staying a mere breath away from her lips.

"I'd love nothing more than to watch your face as you fall apart, grinding on me, but if you're going to come for me, I want to taste every drop of your orgasm."

"Logan—"

I eat her words when I seal my lips on hers. I move my lips down and pepper kisses across her cheek and down her neck along the pulse that beats wildly *for* me.

I lower myself to my knees, bunching the bottom of her dress in my hands. "Tell me to stop," I urge, looking up at her. "Tell me this isn't what you want and I'll stop."

"It's just… I don't know if I can come like that." I raise a brow at that. She must pick up on my confusion because she bends down to put her dress back in place and tries to move away. "This was a bad idea."

I stop Emiline before she can walk away by grabbing her wrist and standing to face her. "It isn't, and that's not what I meant. I just want to understand what *you* meant."

She releases a long sigh. "I don't always get off, okay? I can't remember the last time I had my needs met. No one has ever done this before. I don't know why you stopped me before. I was this close." She emphasizes words by holding her fingers up close together.

I can't help but smile because all I hear is *challenge accepted*.

"Wanna make a bet?" I ask.

She rolls her eyes. "What kind of bet?"

"I can have you coming with my name on your lips in less than two minutes flat," I say with complete confidence because I know I won't be able to stop until she's dripping for me.

"Cocky, much?"

"Confident. Big difference," I grin. "And since this is a one-time thing for us, I plan to fully get my taste of you so when you leave, and I lay in bed gripping my cock to the thought of your wet pussy on my lips, *I* can come in less than two minutes too." I wink.

Emiline's lips part as she stares at me.

She's absolutely not used to being talked to like this.

I bring myself to my knees again and lift her dress up to expose her panties. Her back falls against the wall, and she presses her hips forward for me, giving me access. I hook a finger in the band of her lace panties, bringing them down, and my eyes greedily drink in the view of how her body responds to me.

I want to memorize every single one of her reactions.

I let her panties fall to her ankles, and she gasps when I press my lips to her pubic bone.

I finally look at her glistening pussy when I reach between her thighs. I feel my cock throbs against my dress pants, wanting to feel the wetness coat my length, but I ignore it.

Emiline opens up easily, and I can hear her breathing pick up when I haven't even touched her in her most sensitive spot. I finally dip a single finger in, and she instantly coats me.

I groan as I spread her wider, and she lifts a leg for me and rests her foot on my shoulder, giving me easier access.

I'm not one for rushing this sort of thing because it's my favorite thing to do, but I'm on the clock to make Emiline come.

A bet is a bet, even though I have no clue what's at stake here.

I dip my head down and disappear between her legs, my tongue swiping against her pussy. Emiline's back arches off the wall, and her hand tangles itself in my hair.

A part of me knows this is the worst idea. There's no way that, with the way she tastes, I'll be able to make this a one fucking time thing.

Not a chance.

I swipe slow, languid strokes. I then find her clit, giving it a long suck before flicking my tongue over it repeatedly. Her legs tremble around me, and her body shudders.

"Oh my god. Oh my god," she repeats. "What the hell are you doing to me? Th-this feels too good, Logan. So good."

I grin into her pussy. The hold she has on my hair tightens, and I'm going to come in my pants if she continues like this. There's no way I'll last more than one minute when she goes back into her hotel room before I jerk myself off. If I even make it that far.

As I sense she's about to go over the edge, I slide a finger into her entrance and feel her clench around me. I hook it just the right amount to find the spot I doubt anyone has ever touched on her.

Her pussy throbs around my finger, and now I know she's ready. I add in a second finger and suck her clit harder and faster, making her hips buck into my face.

"I. I. I'm coming," she screams. "Logan. Oh my god, Logan." She continuously repeats my name as she comes.

And I do too.

I can't fucking believe I just came in my pants like a teenager.

Emiline's orgasm crashes through her to the point she can barely stand, but I hold her upright with both hands as I taste every drop of her. I know I can never let this happen again, so I focus on remembering how she tastes on my tongue during this moment.

So fucking sweet. The kind that's too good for someone like me.

I don't allow doubts to creep into my head as I stand and come face to face with her. She's flushed and out of breath but still looks just as beautiful as she did at the start of the night.

"That was…" she starts.

"Beautiful." I cut her off. That's not quite the word I was going for, but it was on the tip of my tongue. I raise the two fingers coated with her arousal and lick them clean as she watches intently with wide eyes.

"Watching you come for me. Hearing you scream my name when I made you come… fucking exquisite."

I'm not about to tell her it's the reason I came in my pants too, so I turn around and adjust myself. Making a woman come like that has never had that much of an effect on me. I face her again, reaching up to scratch my head and wondering how to handle this now that it's done.

I don't want her to leave but if she stays, all bets are off.

"It's getting late," I say at the same time she says, "Thank you."

I quirk an eyebrow at her. "Thank you?"

"You know…" Emiline waves her hands in the air, unsure of what to say. She's nervous, and it's so cute. "For all of that. I'm glad we both got some of that out of our system, you know?"

"I do."

She picks her panties up from the ground and turns toward the doorway leading to her hotel room. "Good night, Logan."

She closes the door behind her before I can say anything.

I didn't get to say it back *again*.

Now, all I can think about is how much I want this again, yet at the same time, how I should never let it happen.

CHAPTER TWENTY-THREE
Logan

THOMAS

You never made it to the after party.

MARC

I was wondering the same thing. I thought you and Oliver would be the first to show up.

I know.

THOMAS

What happened? Of all people I thought you would totally be there.

OLIVER

Wondering the same. You left me hanging, wingman.

I wasn't feeling it.

MARC

Has hell froze over?

OLIVER

Tell me you at least took someone back to your room. Because I sure as hell didn't.

No…

OLIVER

Oh a man of mystery.

THOMAS

MARC

Yup. Hell has frozen over.

Yeah. I guess it has.

CHAPTER TWENTY-FOUR
Emiline

November

ASIDE FROM THE wedding two months ago, today is the first time most of us have been together since Thomas and Peyton's Fourth of July party.

We're at Marc and Avery's penthouse, where they're hosting their first Thanksgiving as a real couple. The smell of turkey wafts through their place, and my stomach growls.

"Everything smells so good," I tell Avery as I sit on the kitchen island's barstool.

"Thanks. I didn't cook a single thing." She smiles proudly. "I absolutely paid someone to prepare all of this for us since Kali couldn't come today to help."

We all laugh because that's such an Avery thing to do.

Kali skipped dinner tonight. In our group chat yesterday, she told us it's been a week from hell for her, and she just wants to sit around the apartment today and sulk.

We tried to convince her to come, but sometimes a girl just needs a day.

"You all laugh, but if I cooked dinner tonight, the building would be up in flames, and the turkey would be burned to a crisp. We all know this," Avery says with certainty.

"It's for the best," Marc adds, popping the cork off a bottle of wine.

"At least we know it's edible," Oliver says, sitting beside me.

"You hush." Avery points the tongs she's using to mix the salad in his direction. "I didn't hear you complaining last week when you ate more than half of my apple crisp."

"Because that apple crisp is the greatest thing I've ever had in my life," Oliver says. "If you didn't make it for dessert today, I'm leaving now."

"Bye." Avery wiggles her fingers in his direction before pointing off to the right. "Door's that way."

"She's got jokes." Oliver laughs.

"Don't let her fool you. The apple crisp is already made, and we just have to pop it in the oven after dinner," Marc says.

"Ha." Oliver points toward Avery. "I know you wouldn't let this day go by without making that for us."

"You two are nuts," I tell them both before Marc passes me a glass of red wine and I quickly thank him.

"Are you enjoying your short break?" Marc asks.

"I am." I nod. "I'm taking a break this semester for the first time and haven't opened any of my books this week. I'm a little nervous I'll get behind or forget everything." I force a small laugh. "But I keep telling myself I'm almost done."

Only some of that is a lie.

I'm actually very nervous. Missing that lecture right before the wedding sent me into a spiral where I locked myself in my apartment for weeks. I called out of work a few times, skipped the gym and Tuesday dinners with the girls to get caught up on the material and study harder than ever before.

"You're so close, Em," Oliver chimes in. "You have what? One more semester after this?"

I nod. "I can't believe how fast it's going."

"My baby sister." Oliver beams with pride as he leans over

and wraps an arm around my neck, pulling me into his chest. "She's going to be the most badass Registered Nurse."

"I'm not a *baby* anymore, Ollie." I laugh.

"I know. I know. But you'll always be my baby sister." Oliver kisses the top of my head before releasing me.

"Dinner's ready," Avery says, placing the turkey on the kitchen island in the middle of the already laid-out side dishes. "Grab a plate and dig in."

Thomas and Peyton stand from the couch, where they were doing a Thanksgiving turkey puzzle with James on the coffee table. James doesn't leave his spot on the floor. His tongue sticks out in concentration as he places a few more puzzle pieces into spots before rushing toward the kitchen for food.

Avery's dinner is set up buffet style. I love it when dinner hosts do this because it avoids the annoying interruption of asking someone to pass a dish when they are trying to enjoy their meal.

"Wait, where's Logan?" Oliver asks Thomas.

My stomach does a somersault at the mention of his name. I've been wondering the same thing but didn't want to be the one to ask.

When my head isn't consumed by schoolwork, it replays that night after the wedding repeatedly, like a movie. A movie I really need to stop watching, but can't find it in me to turn off.

Logan Bennett kissed me.

Not only did he kiss me, he gave me the most epic orgasm I've ever had. One that I didn't think I could ever get from someone going down on me.

I want it again.

I want it with *him* again.

Logan was adamant that getting it out of our system was a one-time thing. But how the hell do you get a man like *that* out of your system?

"He usually works." Thomas shrugs.

"We put a chair out for him in case he makes it," Marc adds. "I left the invitation open for him."

"I'm *sure* he'll be here," Avery says flatly, but her eyes are fixed on me.

She's looking at me like I'm the reason he'll be here. Like she knows something I don't. Avery has always thought something was happening between us, but aside from the wedding, I never thought she was this suspicious.

The front door to the penthouse opens as soon as the words leave her lips, and Logan walks in, wearing his signature smile.

And he's looking directly at me.

He's dressed in dark wash jeans and a long-sleeved Henley shirt. The shirt's dark green color makes his eyes look almost like dark whiskey tonight.

Neither of us can take our eyes off of each other.

The tension in the surrounding air thickens, and I find it hard to breathe suddenly.

Logan's presence brings me back to that night in the hotel.

"Hey, he made it," Oliver says, dropping his plate at the table and heading to Logan for a man hug.

"Just in time for dinner, Logan," Avery tells him.

"Glad I could make it," Logan says to the room, but he's still looking at me.

I avert my gaze and focus on putting food on my plate.

Everyone takes a moment to greet Logan before he enters the kitchen and makes his own plate. Everyone does the same before taking their seats at the table.

Marc sits on one head of the table while Thomas sits at the other. No seating arrangements were planned, but weirdly enough, all the girls took their place on one side of the table while James, Oliver, and Logan sat on the other.

With Logan directly across from me.

Dammit.

"I almost forgot to tell you guys!" Peyton starts. "We got our wedding pictures back last week. You guys, I am so obsessed with them. They came out so good."

"I can't wait to see them," Avery squeals in excitement. "Especially the ones of us girls jumping up and down on the bed in our robes while we got ready that morning."

"You mean before you fell off the bed?" I raise a brow in her direction.

"Listen"—she points her fork in my direction—"I was able to contain the extent of my bruises to just my legs. Which stayed hidden under my bridesmaid dress, thank you very much."

Peyton and I laugh at the memory while Marc shakes his head.

"They all came out amazing," Peyton continues, pulling out her phone to show us. "I have some fantastic ones of you all during the slow dancing songs too."

I keep my head down toward my plate but lift my eyes to find Logan looking in my direction.

It makes me wonder if he's thinking the same thing I am.

She passes the phone to Avery and me. "Have a look," Peyton says.

Avery swipes to a picture of Peyton and Thomas dancing, and I can't help but smile. How they look at each other with such unmistakable affection reflects how much they really love each other.

She swipes again, and it's a photo of her and Marc. Avery has her arms wrapped around his neck and looks like she is singing the lyrics of the song, while Marc looks at her like she put the stars in the sky.

Avery swipes one more and lands on a photo of Logan and me.

My stomach falls to the floor.

Logan's hands are resting on my hips. I don't think it's something the girls, or even my brothers, could pick up on by simply looking at the image, but he was gripping me tight like he needed me closer. Our bodies are only inches apart, and I continue to scan the photo before I land on our faces.

We're smiling at each other, our eyes locked as if the rest of the dance floor was empty, and it's just us.

"Interesting," Avery whispers before closing out of the image and handing the phone back to Peyton. "I can't *wait* to see the rest now," she says louder this time.

My breathing picks up, but I do my best to hide it.

"I can't wait either," I say, using the most excited tone I can muster up. "I'm going to run to the restroom quickly."

I don't wait for an answer and avoid looking at anyone when I get up and walk away. As soon as I enter the bathroom, I close the door behind me and press my back to it as I work on controlling my breathing.

In for three, out for three.

There's no way anyone other than Avery could pick up on that. She's always just assumed something was going on. That's definitely why she said that like that.

This guilty consciousness I have over nothing is making my head spin.

There's a light knock on the door, and I immediately assume it's Avery coming to tell me she thinks something is up.

"Open the door, Em," Logan whispers.

No, no, no. This is even worse.

I swing the door open and come face to face with Logan, who's got one hand resting on the doorframe. With one look at him, all the panic coursing through my head is gone.

"Are you okay?" he asks.

"What are you doing?" I hiss, keeping my voice low. "You can't be in here."

"I'm not in here." He smirks before taking a small step back, pointing toward the bathroom floor. "You're in there, and I'm standing out here." He points at the hallway floor.

"Don't mock me right now," I say, placing both hands on my hips.

Logan pauses, his eyes scanning me up and down. My body heats almost instantly under the weight of his stare. As if he can sense it, he averts his gaze down the hall.

"I saw the picture," he says, facing away from me. "It's fine, Em. Don't read too much into it."

I take a step back as if I've been punched in the gut.

"Are you serious right now?" I ask.

Logan turns to look at me again before stepping into the bathroom and closing the door behind him. The scent of his cologne fills my senses, making breathing harder.

The thought of my brothers walking by at any second and finding us in this compromising situation makes me want to pass out.

"Logan," I barely breathe out.

"I'm so serious right now," he says, finally answering my question.

His body crowds my space, and I take another step back.

"I can't believe you." I shake my head with my back against the wall now. "Did we even see the same picture? There's no way they will not see the same thing I just saw. Hell"—I throw my arms in the air—"there's no way they won't see how you were looking at me."

"The way I was looking at you?" He pauses and takes a deep breath.

I swallow and remain silent because I don't know if he's mad at me or the situation.

"The way I was looking at you," Logan repeats. This time without question. "I'm positive that right before that photo was taken, I told you the same thing I'm going to tell you now. You make it impossible *not* to look at you. I didn't even want to show up tonight," he continues, running his hands through his already-tousled hair. "I only did because I knew you would be here."

My mouth opens in shock. "You told me that night was a one-time thing."

"I did…" He pauses as he stares at me. "So I need you to stop looking at me before I go back on my words."

Logan turns to walk away, and the moment his hands land on the door handle, unexpected anger fills me. I know I also agreed to one night, but I'm tired of this push-and-pull.

"Logan," I call out.

He doesn't turn around to look at me, instead lifting his head to the ceiling, and I can see the turmoil racing through his head.

"What was that night for you?" I say, and my tone causes him to turn and face me again. "Just another night where you can say you got a girl off? Huh? Everything you said to me before that picture was taken, was that just a way to get me right to where you wanted me before I broke my barriers down and begged you to get me off?"

Something in Logan snaps. He takes a heavy step toward me, and both of his hands cup the side of my face, angling my head so my gaze meets his. I lose my breath with his touch and how close his face is to mine.

"Is that what you think, Emiline?"

"I don't know what to think anymore," I reply, closing my eyes to avoid his harsh stare. "I don't know," I say, the last words barely above a whisper.

Laughing from the kitchen breaks us from our bubble, and we both remember we're in Marc and Avery's bathroom.

"You should go," I tell him. "Please."

He turns around to leave but stops himself. "Everything I've ever said to you was the truth, Em." His voice is soft and sincere this time. "You weren't just another woman to me that night."

And with those final words, he exits the bathroom.

I'm left alone with his words coursing through my head a mile a minute. I don't know what to make of this thing between us anymore. I've told him once that I'm tired of fighting it.

Isn't *he* tired of this fight, too?

I allow myself another minute before leaving the bathroom to avoid looking suspicious. As soon as I enter the kitchen, Logan is nowhere to be found.

"You just missed Logan leaving," Marc said.

Did he leave because of me?

"He said his stomach was all messed up from some bad lunch meat he ate for lunch," Oliver adds, shaking his head. "Who the hell eats lunch on Thanksgiving knowing that we have a turkey and side dish buffet just a few hours later?"

"Yeah, very weird," Avery adds, her eyes glued to me.

I offer her a flat smile and return to my seat at the table. I force myself to eat the rest of the food on my plate before heading home early.

Only to later lie in bed, staring at the ceiling while thoughts of Logan take over every square inch of my brain.

CHAPTER TWENTY-FIVE
Logan

I'VE NEVER NEEDED a boxing session more than I do today. And it's not because of the Thanksgiving dinner I ate yesterday.

It has everything to do with the woman who's owned my thoughts over the last few months.

As usual, I enter through the doors to Park South Fitness, and Silas stands there waiting for me at the desk. He taps his fingers on the counter the way he always does like he's been waiting for hours, when, in reality, it's only about five minutes.

"Always late, Bennett," Silas jokes.

"No. I'm on time. You're the one who's always five minutes early, O'Connor." I laugh back. "Let me get changed quickly so I don't keep you waiting any longer, Princess."

He laughs, and I make my way to the locker room.

Once I change into my gym shorts and T-shirt, I stifle a yawn, and my body screams for me to leave and go back to bed. My body battery feels completely empty, but I need this session to release my pent-up frustration over the last twenty-four hours.

Hell, over the last few months.

"Ready?" Silas asks when I step out the door.

"No," I answer honestly. "But let's do it."

We make our way to the back room, where the boxing room

is. One reason I love this gym is that it's convenient and has everything in it. Most gyms don't have a room like this, but the owner is a huge boxing fan and put it in about a year after they opened.

"You first this time," he says, securing the velcro on his mitts.

I put on my gloves and take my place in front of Silas, bringing my hands to my face and mustering up any energy I can find to give it my all.

I throw a few jabs and right hooks, but it feels like I'm moving in slow motion. I stand in position and take a deep breath before trying again, but my body just doesn't want to follow through, no matter how much I try.

"Fuck," I scream.

Silas drops his hands to his waist. "All right. You know I never pry, but what's going on with you today? This isn't like you. I usually struggle to keep up with you."

My hands fall to the side, and I take a few steps back, letting my back fall against the brick wall that lines the room.

"Maybe I'm getting the flu," I say.

"No," Silas scoffs. "I've seen you sick before, and you still put in more effort than you are now."

I don't answer him immediately because honestly, I don't know what to say. I barely slept last night after that little interaction with Emiline at dinner. I can't stand the thought of her sitting at home and thinking that what happened after the wedding was simply because I found pleasure in getting a woman off.

Of course, I got pleasure from it because it was *her*.

I let my body slide down the wall until I sit, bringing my knees to my chest. I rest my forearms on my knees and throw my head back before I say, "I didn't sleep well last night."

"Okay?"

I sigh before admitting why. "It's Emiline."

Silas stares down at me, unmoving, like he's waiting for more.

"Remember how I told you she's the Ford brothers' little sister?"

"Oh no." His eyes widen. "You fucked your best friend's little sister. Damn."

I throw my glove at him, and it catches him off guard. "I didn't fuck her."

Silas laughs, throwing his arms up in defense. "Okay."

"I swear, I didn't. But that day, something happened that made me… look at her differently. Now I look at her like—"

"Like not your best friend's kid sister anymore," he finishes for me.

I nod. "I've tried so damn hard over the last year to stop thinking about her."

"But you can't shake it off," Silas continues.

I shake my head. "This isn't who I am, and it's driving me absolutely nuts," I admit. "And after Thomas' wedding, things got a little out of hand back at the hotel."

"Oh, so you *did* fuck her?" he asks, shocked.

"Not really." I shake my head. "God, I knew I shouldn't have done anything. I already couldn't stop thinking about her, and now it's even fucking worse. She's completely taken over my life. And before you ask, yes, I know I'm being dramatic."

He holds up his hands. "I wasn't going to say it."

I throw my other glove at him. This time, he's ready for it. "I can't avoid her. I've tried so hard, and it's damn near impossible. When I'm out with the guys, the first thing I think about is her. I tell myself it's because she's related to them, but I don't even know if that's the real reason anymore. There's this part of me that doesn't want to stay away, but I know I need to keep my distance."

Silas shrugs. "For what it's worth, you're doing the right thing."

My head tilts to the side. "I am?"

"Yeah." He nods. "I think if you got involved with Emiline, it could end up *very* messy for all parties involved. What if you fall in love with her, but something happens between you two and you end things? Then you can't hang out with your friends when she's around because it has the potential to be awkward as hell."

I scoff. "Good thing I don't fall in love."

He lifts a shoulder and averts his gaze. "Everyone falls in love at one point in their life."

I always had a feeling that Silas has been through some shit himself, but I never asked him about it. I respect our working relationship enough to not pry.

"Not me," I say back, standing up from my place on the ground. "You know me well enough to know that I'm not that type of guy. My job comes first, and it will *always* come first."

He nods in understanding but says nothing back. I can tell by the look on his face that he wants to say more.

"You can say it," I urge him.

"It's just…" Silas pauses as if trying to find the right words to say. His eyes meet mine. "This job isn't everything, Bennett. I know it means a lot to you, and you want to make it to the top and land that chief position. Believe me, I already know it's yours. But when you're at the end of your life and everything flashes before you, will you be happy knowing all you had was your job?"

I avert my gaze because he makes a good point.

Nobody knows why I always put my job first. I've never really talked about it, and I plan to keep it that way. The only way for him to understand where I'm coming from is to get it off my chest.

"I've been here long enough, O'Connor," I finally say. "I've seen more shit than I want to see. I lost my dad after I begged him to bring home pizza after work when I was a kid." I swallow back the emotions from that statement alone. "It's not that I don't want that kind of life of being in love and having a wife in the future. It's that I can't allow it to happen. I can't have something happen to me. God forbid I have kids!" I can feel my voice rising with more emotions than I care to show right now. "And they… lose their dad. Or my wife ends up losing her husband. I've knocked on too many doors to give people the news that they've lost the love of their life. I've watched husbands and wives crumble to the ground, unable to breathe, knowing they would never speak to their spouses again, that they'll never have another normal family dinner together again. That does something to you I can't explain."

Silas quietly nods in understanding but, again, says nothing more.

Because he knows what it's like, he's had to do it too.

The energy I didn't have ten minutes ago now flows through my body after letting out the emotions I have kept locked in a vault.

"Ready for another round?" I ask, changing the subject before he can say anything else.

Silas raises a skeptical brow. "Only if you're ready to give me everything you got."

I nod. "I'm ready," I tell him, even though every part of my body screams I'm not.

I need this.

I need to let everything out right here, right now, through these punches.

CHAPTER TWENTY-SIX
Emiline

December

> **BROOKE**
>
> Are you sure you don't want to go to the library?

> I'm positive. It's getting late.

> **BROOKE**
>
> I can come over and we can go over the material together?

> I'm going to run through the study guides once more and try to get a good night's sleep.

> **BROOKE**
>
> Ok babe. We got this, ok? We didn't come this far just to come this far. You know the material. You know you're going to pass this.

She's right. I know this material because I've studied it like the back of my hand. Repeatedly, until I can recite the words from the textbook out loud without even having to look.

But it doesn't stop my mind from going into overdrive before exams.

This isn't just any exam. It's the *final* exam that will determine whether I finish this entire program.

One more semester to go.

One more semester to go.

I've been repeating it to myself tonight and over the last few nights when I feel myself drowning in the weight of the pressure from this decisive exam.

I'm expected to graduate in June. That's only six months away.

You can do anything for six months.

I let out an audible groan, even though no one is here to listen. My head pounds from staring at the small text inside my book while simultaneously reading study guides on my laptop.

My phone rings and I see Oliver's name flash on the screen.

"I do not have time for this right now," I say to myself, frustrated.

I want to ignore the call but can't because it's my brother. Not that he's the one who would worry the most if I didn't answer, but if he tells Marc or Thomas I didn't pick up, they will be here within three seconds with an army to break down my door and make sure I'm okay.

"Hey," I finally answer.

"Hey, baby sis." I can practically hear the smile on his face. If that's even a thing. "How's it going?"

"It's going," I say flatly. "Just studying for my final exam tomorrow."

"Tomorrow? Already? I can't believe how fast this semester is going for you."

"I can't either." I muster up a laugh. "A little too fast for the amount we're expected to know."

"You're a smart cookie," he says. "You're going to get an A plus-*plus-plus*." He laughs, emphasizing each plus he says, which makes me laugh at how carefree he is about life.

"When is your trip?" I ask, trying to change the subject.

"I leave the day after Christmas. So in a few days," he confirms. "I'm excited to see Marc's new place up in Roxbury. Maybe I'll get some good shots for a blog post too."

"That sounds great," I say, staring down at my textbook. "Listen, Ollie. I hate to cut this short but I have to study so I can pass this tomorrow."

"Of course, Em," Oliver says. "You'll pass with flying colors in case I need to remind you again. I love you."

"I love you too, Ollie," I reply and hang up the phone before I get emotional with him.

I love that everyone has confidence in me, but what if I don't pass?

I can feel my pulse race and my breathing get shallow, and after that short conversation, I know my mind is diving into the dreaded panic.

I don't know why I'm this way.

I don't know why I can't believe in myself the way everyone else does.

The pressure feels like an elephant sitting on my chest, and I want to scream, but I can't. *This* is the reason I avoided the library tonight. I knew this would happen because it happens before every exam or when I'm extremely stressed.

I stand up and bring myself to my living room and away from the sight of my books. I need to ground myself, but it's so hard. I want to pick up the phone and call the girls or my brothers to let them calm me down, but I can't let them know.

My breaths come out fast and erratic now. I sit on the edge of the couch, with my hands squeezing the cushion on each side of my thigh as I work hard to control my breathing before I pass out.

A knock at the door causes me to jump from my seat.

I say nothing and don't move to open the door but cover my mouth with my hand. Maybe if I'm quiet enough, they'll leave.

The person on the other end is silent, and tears form in my

eyes. This is when someone discovers what I've been trying to keep to myself.

This is when everyone will look at me like a fragile doll.

"Emiline, are you there?"

No. Why is Logan here right now? This can't be happening.

With how fast my heart is racing, I really think I might pass out.

"I know you're in there," he says from the other side of the door. "I just ran into Brooke at the coffee shop."

Shit.

My only saving grace is that he already knows.

"It's open," I shout through ragged breaths.

The door flies open, and Logan's eyes land on mine as he steps into the apartment. The tears fall faster, and my breathing becomes more frantic than before as we both stare at each other from across the room.

"I"—pause—"can't"—pause—"breathe."

He rushes to sit next to me, worry etched in his face. He's the *only one* who knows my secret, but there's nothing worse than him actually witnessing it.

And I hate him knowing this part of me.

"You're having a panic attack," Logan says without question.

I nod my head repeatedly.

He scans my body up and down like he's unsure what to do to help me. Then he places both hands on my shoulders, keeping his eyes level with mine and silently begging me to keep my gaze set on his.

"Breathe for me, Em," he urges. "Slow and steady."

I suck in one deep breath, but it catches in my throat, and Logan wipes a tear that falls down my cheek.

"Name three things you can touch," he says.

"T-the couch." I inhale and exhale. "The pillow." Another inhale and exhale. "You."

I force myself not to look away from him, watching intently as Logan swallows before speaking again.

"Name three things you can hear."

"I hear…" I pause. "The dishwasher is going." I can feel my breathing slowing. It's still irregular but not as rapid as it was before. "The television is on in my bedroom." Another quick breath. "You."

"Now, name three things you can see," he says.

"You," I say without missing a beat. My heart is still racing, but my breathing is steadier now. A sob breaks free, and tears pour out of my eyes. "I see you. You're all I see."

With his hands still on my shoulders, Logan gives me three quick squeezes before he pulls my head into his chest for a hug. For the first time in a while, Logan just holds me.

Something about how he does it tells me he's willing to carry my deepest secret with me. Which sounds so silly, but it's always been mine.

It's the one I've fought so hard to keep just to myself because I didn't want to burden anyone else with it. But now… now it feels easier, lighter to carry when someone is there.

I wrap my arms around his waist and embrace this moment with him before it ends.

I know it's going to because good things always seem to end.

He releases his hold on me and stands from the couch. "Fuck," I hear him mutter under his breath as he walks away from me, running his hands through his hair as he paces back and forth in my living room.

The little energy that was left in my body is now gone, which is what usually happens after a panic attack. I always need to go right to bed because my body crashes hard.

Except Logan being here has me on edge.

"I told you to call me if this ever happened again," he says, worried, still pacing around the room. "Have you still been dealing with this on your own? All this time?"

"You're not my dad," I bite back, standing up from the couch. I feel lightheaded at the sudden move after such an intense moment, but I ignore it. "I've been doing just fine handling it on my own. I was before you found out, and I am now."

"That didn't look like it, Emiline."

I feel so small under the weight of his words. They hit me like a dagger in the chest. I shouldn't care what he thinks. He's made it very clear there's nothing there between us.

"Why are you even here, Logan?"

"I was getting ready for work and thought I'd get a coffee before I head to the station," he pauses as if collecting his thoughts. "I ran into Brooke, and she said you had your final exam tomorrow. She told me jokingly that you were at your apartment freaking out. Then I show up here and you're in the middle of a panic attack, Emiline."

"Well, I'm fine now," I say, making my way to the door to show him the way out. "You checked on me. You just saw me at my weakest moment, the way no one ever has, so you can head to work now."

I open the door and wave my hand as if to shoo him out.

Except, he doesn't move from where he stands in the middle of my living room with his hands in his pockets and his eyes fixed on mine. His feet might as well be concrete blocks because the way he's standing right now tells me—

"I'm not leaving," Logan says, cutting off my thoughts as he crosses his arms over his chest.

"What about work?"

"I called out sick on my way here," he says matter-of-factly.

"I..." I try to say something, but my words fall short. "I'm tired, Logan. I have to try to get some sleep. Like Brooke said, I have a final exam tomorrow. You truly don't need to be here and take care of me. I can handle myself. I always have."

Logan looks at me almost as if my words hurt him. I didn't intend for them to, but I can't have him pitying me.

"You don't have to do this alone."

Before my mind reels with thoughts, I watch Logan make his

way to the kitchen, opening cabinets and the refrigerator like he's looking for something.

"What are you doing?" I ask as I relent and close the front door.

"I'm hungry and I'm sure you haven't eaten either. So I'm looking for ingredients to make something for dinner," he says, still shuffling through all the drawers. "How do you survive with nothing here?"

I shrug. "I haven't had much time to go shopping because of class."

He pulls out some defrosted chicken. "Is this still good?"

"It's questionable." I laugh, and his head snaps in my direction as if my laughter was something he didn't expect to hear. I didn't expect it either, but the way he moves around my apartment makes me feel more at ease, and my previous annoyance is gone. "I maybe have twenty-four more hours left before it needs to be tossed."

His lips twist into a smile, and I swear I melt right there in front of him.

It's been so long since I've seen that smile on his face, and I've been dying to witness that again since the wedding. There's something about it that sparks a sense of comfort in me.

I'm not even surprised I could recover from that panic attack so quickly, with him guiding me back to reality.

Even if he hadn't said anything, I believe I would have felt better with Logan just being there.

I'm too tired tonight to convince him to get out of my apartment. So, I'll embrace this part of Logan that I don't get too often. I don't think anyone gets this part of him often, either.

He reaches into one of the lower cabinets and pulls out a frying pan. "Did I see Captain Crunch in the cabinet over there?" he asks, spraying some oil he found on the pan and placing it on the stovetop.

"Yeah?" I furrow my brows as I make my way to grab it for

him. "What in the world are you planning to make with chicken that's on its last leg and Captain Crunch?"

His head falls back as he groans. "Emiline Ford. You've never had Captain Crunch chicken?"

I chuckle and cover my face while shaking my head.

"You live under a rock, don't you?"

"No?" I draw out the word, but it comes out with a mix of giggles because he's being so serious about this chicken thing right now. "I just have never heard of this combination before."

"Just wait," he says, pouring some of the cereal into a Ziploc bag. "Your mind is about to be blown."

I take a seat and watch him work his way around my kitchen as if he's used it one hundred times before. In a way, I guess Logan has since he lives in the same apartment complex and probably has the same kitchen layout I do.

I totally stare at his body as he moves freely in my space. His forearms flex when he shakes the bag of crushed cereal. He cracks an egg in a bowl before coating the chicken and then putting it into the bag of crushed cereal as if it was breadcrumbs. My mouth feels dry, and I forget for a moment that he's my brother's best friend. He's so much more than that right now, and I think we both know that.

"Do you have a way to manage these panic attacks?" he asks, returning to the earlier conversation while placing the prepared chicken in the frying pan.

"I try to just focus on my breathing." I shrug. "Thankfully, I'm almost always home when it happens. I usually take a hot shower when it passes and then go right to bed."

He nods. "Are you still going to the gym?"

"I haven't been able to go in a few weeks."

Logan nods his head again but says nothing back. He flips the chicken in the pan as if he's thinking about something. Logan is one of the few people I can't get a read on to determine his mood or feelings about something. It makes me uneasy every time I try.

"You really should try boxing," he says before I can ask anything more. "It works for me, at least."

I shake my head. "I don't think I can. I'm terrified of embarrassing myself in front of everyone."

He looks over his shoulder and offers me a smile. "You could come with me."

"Logan."

"I'm serious. I don't know enough about what you deal with to understand the cause of your panic attacks. For me, boxing has always been an outlet, a release to let go of everything in my head. I think if I don't let it out in some way, shape, or form, then I might actually go insane," Logan says with a light laugh.

I nod in understanding.

"Or I could take you to therapy," he continues.

My heart skips a quick beat at his final words, but he's unfazed by them. He just continues moving the chicken around the pan to ensure all sides have the perfect golden crisp.

I stare at him in shock. "Why would you do that?"

"Why wouldn't I?" Logan speaks so casually like it's something he would do so easily for me.

"Let me get this straight," I start. "You're offering to take me to therapy? I'm baffled by this entire night. It feels like I'm in an alternate universe."

He uses the tongs to remove the chicken from the pan and put it on a glass plate. Then he turns around and places it between us on the kitchen island. I look from the plate and up to him to notice he has a smile on his face.

Not just any smile, a sincere one.

He really means what he's saying.

"I told you I'd never lie to you, Em. I recall I also told you that your secret is safe with me. I've kept my word, and I'm going to continue to keep it as long as you keep one for me, too."

I swallow, goosebumps skating across my skin at what he's going to share while nerves dance around in my gut. I tilt my head to the side and give him a questioning glare.

"You can't tell your brothers I can cook," he says with a wink.

My lips part because I was *not* expecting that. After a few seconds, I burst into laughter, and Logan does the same.

"I can't tell them anything about you, including that, so you don't have to worry," I say very matter-of-factly.

"Because they would know we were spending time together."

As the words roll off his tongue, our laughter subsides, and we stare directly into each other's eyes.

We both swallow simultaneously, averting our gaze and once again, we fight this feeling that's so very clear between us. There's no questioning this. It's as plain as black and white written in ink.

"Dig in," he says, passing me a fork and taking a seat right next to me on the island.

There's nothing fancy about this.

There's no fun side dish.

Just two people digging into the—

"Most delicious chicken I've ever had," I finish my sentence out loud with a mouthful of food. "Is this recipe legal?"

"It's very legal." He smirks.

"I hope you know you'll have to make this for me weekly now."

I want to regret the words as soon as I say them, but I also want to spend more time with him. Only if he says—

"That works for me," he replies without hesitation.

"Really?"

"I've been lying to myself long enough. I've been avoiding you because I've been terrified to let these feelings grow into more."

"I'm so tired of fighting it," I confess.

"I am, too," Logan says, looking down. "But I told you I can't do relationships, and that hasn't changed. I just... can't." He shakes his head as if he's trying to gather his thoughts.

The way Logan just told me that leads me to believe there

is more to him under the surface that he doesn't show every-one. There's a deeper meaning to why he can't do rela-tionships.

I want to ask him, but it's already been a charged night.

"I'm also nowhere near ready to tell your brothers that I'll be spending more time with you," he adds.

"Yeah, they can't find out." I nod. "That would be a recipe for disaster."

"But…" Logan finally lifts his head to look at me. "I can't ask you to carry another secret. Us hanging out would be a pretty big one. I fear what any of your brothers would do to me if they found out. I think they might actually murder me and make it look like an accident." He laughs. "So if it's too much, tell me now."

I offer him a smile, turning my hand over until he places his hand in mine. "I didn't ask you to carry *my* secret with you, and you're doing it willingly for me."

"What do you want this to be then, Em?"

"Whatever you want it to be, Logan." I shrug. "I told you I can't do the whole relationship thing either. At least not right now with school. So, good friends?" I ask.

Logan looks at me intently. His tongue rolls across his lower lip as his eyes trail my body once before meeting my eyes again. He still doesn't offer an agreement, picking up the now empty plate from the counter and putting it in the sink.

Then he rounds the island to where I'm sitting and stands over me.

"The *best* of friends, Emiline." He grins wickedly.

The way he says it sends chills through every single nerve in my body. If I don't walk away now, I'm going to do something very *unfriendly* to him, and I don't have time for that.

I have an exam in the morning.

That should be my only focus.

"Well." I stand from the barstool. "I'm going to head to bed. Big day tomorrow and all. Lock up on your way out, *bestie*," I shout nervously before going down the hallway to my room without a passing glance.

I close the door behind me and let myself fall to the floor.

In for three. Out for three.

This will be one interesting *friendship*.

CHAPTER TWENTY-SEVEN
Emiline

MY ALARM WAKES me at six, the way it always does the morning of an exam. I like to give myself some time to have coffee and a good breakfast and review the material one more time.

Instead of making coffee first, I decide to sit at my small desk and flip through my study guides. I don't know if it was the conversation with Logan last night or the panic attack knocking me out, but I slept like a rock.

I slept better than I have in months if I'm being honest.

With each page flip of the review book, my confidence grows. With each line I read over, I knew the answer and felt good about it. Once I'm done, I go back to the pages I flagged to review those again, just to be sure.

Just as I'm about to close up my books to get a shower and some coffee, I hear a toilet flush, and my fight-or-flight kicks into high gear.

My nervous system acts without thinking when I grab a notebook from my desk and slowly leave my bedroom. I creep down the hall to where the light shines under the bathroom door.

I'm halfway down the hall when the light turns off. I hold my breath and watch as the door swings open. That's when I lunge for the attack. My notebook makes contact repeatedly, and every ounce of energy I have is coming out with every swing.

"Emiline," Logan shouts.

I stop what I'm doing, stammering backward until my back hits the wall. "Logan, what the hell are you doing here?" I snap.

"I never left." He shrugs casually. "And what the hell kind of help would that flimsy little notebook be if I was an actual intruder?"

I lift the beaten notebook. "It is *not* flimsy."

Logan rips it from my hand and shakes it like a soft, floppy paperback book. "See?"

I cross my arms over my chest. "Fine. I didn't know what to grab, and that was the first thing my eyes landed on before I came out here to murder my intruder."

"You weren't going to murder me with that." He smirks.

"I could have."

"No, you wouldn't have," he states firmly. "But now that I've witnessed whatever the hell that was, we really need to get you into the boxing ring. Stat."

"I don't need any more classes," I say before turning to walk away. "School, boxing, cooking, I don't want any of it."

"You need cooking lessons, too?" Logan gasps, following me down the hall. "My lord, Em."

"I don't, for your information," I tell him over my shoulder as I enter the kitchen and make a beeline for the coffee pot. "I'm a great cook."

"Buttered pasta doesn't count."

"How do you know that's my go-to meal?" I ask him, putting a pod into the machine and pressing start.

"Based on the way your pantry and refrigerator are stocked."

I turn around to give him my best version of scolding eyes, but everything I wanted to say is completely gone.

How did I not notice Logan was shirtless when he walked out of the bathroom?

I have to blink back the look on my face, because there's no doubt he noticed me gaping at him.

"What time is your exam?" he asks casually, pulling his shirt over his head.

"I… uh—what?" I stutter.

"Your exam, Emiline," he repeats. "What time do you have to be there?"

I glance over at the clock on my microwave, relieved I have some time before I need to leave. "I don't have to be there until nine."

Logan looks from me to my coffee pot and back to me before covering his mouth with his hand. The crinkle around his eyes tells me he's laughing.

"Is my hair that messy?" I ask, reaching for the bun on my head to feel how out of place it is.

He shakes his head. "What is it with you and making a mess with coffee?"

Crossing my arms over my chest. "Excuse me?"

He gestures to the machine sitting on the counter behind me. I turn to look and that's when I see my coffee spilled all over the counter because I didn't remember to put an actual mug there.

Dammit, Logan and his abs.

"Oh my god," I shout, reaching for a roll of paper towels that is nearly empty, attempting to wipe up the disaster I just created. "Of course, this would happen when I use my last peppermint mocha pod."

Logan comes up behind me with a dish rag, bumping his shoulder with mine before helping clean up some of the mess. "Lucky for you, it's the holiday season. You have an endless supply at your fingertips."

I pause, facing him and resting my hip against the counter while I cross my arms. "Are you making fun of my addiction to iced peppermint mocha lattes?"

"Me?" Logan asks, hand flying to his chest as if pretending to be shocked. "Never."

I gently snatch the dish rag from his hand and swat it across his arm. He laughs, backing away from me, holding his hands up in defense as I continue. "You think you're so funny, huh?"

"I'm a hoot." He laughs.

I roll my eyes. "I can't help that I like what I like. What about you? Don't you have something you can't live without?"

Logan brings his fingers to his chin as if deep in thought. "You've put me on the spot here, Emiline. That's a tough question to answer. It's like asking me if I was stranded on a deserted island, what would be the number one thing I'd bring."

I can't help but smile because, for a brief moment, I forgot I had a final exam this morning. I forgot that I'm usually studying last minute before I leave my house.

It feels so good to laugh like this the morning of.

It feels so good to laugh *with him*.

"I guess you make a very valid point." I nod in agreement with him. "But I'm going to jump in the shower since this mess has delayed my caffeine intake, and I'll need to stop and get one on my way in."

Smirking in my direction, Logan asks, "Do you want to tell me which one you plan to stop at so I can avoid it? You know, so I don't *run* into you again?" He winks.

I point a finger in his direction, attempting to narrow my eyes, but it's hard with how cheesy my grin is. "If I didn't need this shower and caffeine, I would pick up that rag again and use it to its full extent. You'd end up with a bruise or bloodshed."

"From a dishrag?" he jokes.

I nod confidently before turning on my heel and making my way down the hall toward the bathroom. "You've been warned. I'm sure I'll see you at the coffee shop in about an hour."

I hear him laugh from the kitchen before I hear the jingle of keys. I wait for my front door to close before releasing a sigh from the other side of my bathroom door.

Unable to wipe the smile off my face, I glance at myself in the mirror. Holy hell, I truly look like a hot mess. Hair flies out of my bun in every single direction, and there's absolutely a pizza sauce stain on my shirt.

How embarrassing.

But then my gaze falls on my own reflection in the mirror.

Even feeling embarrassed by how Logan just saw me, I'm more relaxed than ever.

I jump in the shower quickly so I can get in and out with enough time to look over my study guide one more time and then grab a coffee on the way to campus. I know I don't have enough time to dry it, so I pull it into a side braid in before getting dressed in black leggings and my university sweatshirt.

This sounds insane, but I always wear this to exams.

Call it a superstition, but I passed the first time I wore it. So my mind tells me I have to wear it for every test.

Grabbing my purse off the chain in my bedroom, I make my way to the living room to find Logan sitting on my couch.

"I thought you left," I say, crossing the room to stand directly in front of him.

Logan stands from the couch. "I did. But only to get you your iced latte." He gestures toward the kitchen, where I see a medium latte sitting alone on the island.

I look back at him, lips slightly parted. "You went and got me caffeine?"

He nods.

"Why?"

"I didn't want you to be rushing this morning." He shrugs. "Besides, what if you ran into someone else in the coffee shop?"

My lips twist in a grin, but I roll my eyes as I walk into the kitchen to grab my drink.

"Also," he continues from behind me. "I'm taking you to class." My head snaps around in his direction, and he's already walking toward me. "I had planned to take you all along. It's why I stayed."

"You really don't have to do that, Logan," I tell him.

"I know I don't, but I want to." He lifts his hands, fingers trailing along the braid draped over my shoulder before he smirks. "Besides, what if a skater boy tries to take you out? Can't have you missing this test because you got run over."

I give him a light shove on the chest, and he barks out a laugh.

"Would Skater Boy even be out when it's this cold out?"

Logan lifts a shoulder. "You never know, Emiline."

I scan his features and realize he's serious. His protective nature is showing, and I'm not mad about it. "Fine. You can take me if it will make you feel better."

"It would," he replies quickly.

I don't understand what's happening, but I like this. Being with Logan feels good. Even if we have to hide this 'friendship' from the world. Even if it means staying in our own little bubble.

This feels really fucking good.

———

Logan, true to his word, surprised me by getting me to class on time.

I thought we would walk because that's what I always do, and with the skater-boy comments, it just seemed like that would happen.

Instead, we took his truck. The short drive was filled with a random conversation about our favorite snacks and candy, keeping me laughing the entire time.

Logan likes Twizzlers. I pegged him as more of a Kit-Kat type guy or any kind of chocolate. But he actually hates it, which we playfully argued over because who hates chocolate?

When we pulled up to the curb, Brooke was waiting for me on the stairs. A smile stretched across her face, seeing that I was with Logan. She looked proud of the fact that she had been right about him the whole time.

Logan didn't wish me good luck on my test or tell me to break a leg.

He told me, *"You got this, Emiline. You're going to ace it with flying colors."* His confidence in me is why I walked in with my head held high and ready to finish the final.

It's the first time I've walked into the classroom without doubting myself.

Leaving the exam, I find Brooke in the hall waiting for me.

"We did it." Brooke shimmies. "One more semester to go. Can you even believe it?"

"It feels surreal," I say honestly as we make our way down the hall and out the front doors to walk home. "How did this fly by while simultaneously taking forever?"

"Beats me. But can we move on to more pressing matters?"

I narrow my eyes.

"Logan dropped you off?"

I shrug. "It was nothing."

It was everything.

"It wasn't nothing! What was he even doing with you this early in the morning? When I saw him at the coffee shop last night, he was heading to work."

"He was."

"So he just skipped sleep to bring you to class?"

I shake my head.

"You're killing me with these vague answers," Brooke groans.

I stop walking, turning to face her. I couldn't even hide my smile if I tried.

"Oh my god." Her hand covers her face. "What is happening?"

"Logan showed up last night—" I stop myself because I realize I'm about to spill my secret to her. I don't want her to know, but this isn't the time and place to do it. "And we just talked."

"You just talked?"

Nodding, I continue, "Then we had dinner together. It was nothing. Except, I went to sleep and woke up to him still in my apartment. Brooke, he stayed the night. He wanted to make sure I got to my exam on time."

Brooke stands there, mouth agape. Shock is written all over her features.

Then she breaks out into a happy dance right there on the sidewalk.

"Yes. Yes. *Yes*. I knew it. I knew Logan liked you and cared about you. This is so amazing, Em. Eek!"

"Whoa, whoa, don't get ahead of yourself. We agreed to a friendship."

"Friendship, my ass," she scoffs.

"I'm serious. We're going to just see where it goes for now, but I won't lie to you. I really like him, and I'm enjoying seeing where this goes."

"Do your brothers know?"

I shake my head rapidly. "And they won't for a while. At least until we're ready. I can't have them bursting this little bubble of happiness."

Brooke wraps her arms around me, holding me tightly. "You're happy." She says it as a statement. "No one deserves this more than you," she whispers.

My heart fills with hope and fear at the same time.

Because I am the happiest I've ever been.

But what if this all crashes and burns?

CHAPTER TWENTY-EIGHT
Logan

January

WHY AM I so nervous all of a sudden?

Emiline and I have fallen into a routine where we swap places for movie nights and dinner between her place and mine. Obviously I do most of the cooking.

We've grown comfortable together.

I'd be lying if I said it's been impossible not to have my hands all over her.

But I'm trying because I want to be there for her. I want to be the friend that she needs. I want to be a small source of comfort in her life when she needs someone.

It shouldn't be this complicated, but Emiline still makes me nervous even after the last few weeks spending time together. I don't want to fuck this up.

The knock on my door only intensifies my nerves. I make my way there, taking a deep breath before opening it. I find Emiline standing with a smile on her face and a bag in her hand. She looks casual and relaxed, wearing a pair of leggings and an over-sized T-shirt.

Something about the way she feels comfortable enough around me to not get dressed up makes me feel relaxed.

"I come bearing snacks for movie night," she says, lifting up the bag.

I widen my stance, crossing my arms over my chest. "Your choice of snacks will determine if you can cross this threshold."

Emiline rolls her eyes. "Don't worry, I got you your Twizzlers."

"You may enter." I laugh as I step aside, allowing her in. "Did you decide what movie you want to watch?"

She walks toward my kitchen to place the bag down before unloading the contents. "I have a few in mind."

I meet her at the table and notice she has the entire candy aisle on my kitchen counter. "Did you raid the local convenience store?"

"I can't answer that. You'll have me arrested."

I bark out a laugh. "Don't worry. You're safe with me."

Emiline's laughter dies down while she stares at me. She's still smiling, but I see the wheels in her head spinning like she's deep in thought.

I hope she knows I mean it when I tell her that.

"Tell me your movie ideas," I urge, hoping to steer the conversation away from something more serious.

"I was thinking we could watch *10 Things I Hate About You*. It's one of my favorites," she exaggerates.

I give her a knowing glare. "Are you trying to tell me something?"

"Me." Emiline feigns shock. "Never."

"Yeah." I shake my head. "I see what you did there."

We both laugh as she maneuvers around my kitchen, finding little bowls to put the snacks in. I grab a throw blanket from my hallway closet and return to see her settled on the couch. The candy bowls scattered around the table with two glasses of soda poured for us.

I watch from behind her as she clicks through my channels.

Seeing Emiline in my space when I never bring girls back here feels so different. She looks like she belongs here, and that revelation hits me square in the chest.

"Hurry up," she shouts. "It's starting."

"I'm right here," I say calmly. She turns around, not realizing I spent the last few moments staring at her and taking this all in. I place the blanket on the back of the couch before plopping down next to her. "What's this movie about?"

"You're kidding me, right?"

"I don't watch movies."

"You don't watch movies but invited me to a movie night with you?"

Shit.

"I wanted to spend time with you, Emiline," I tell her honestly. "I like spending time with you."

She stares at me from the spot next to me on the couch, blinking and mouth slightly parted like she didn't expect me to admit that.

Seems like she has that effect on me.

I can't control the words out of my mouth and how I respond to her.

But a visible shiver runs through her body before she turns to face the TV.

"I grabbed a blanket," I say, reaching behind us and draping it over her legs.

My knuckles graze her forearm, and heat skates across my skin when I do. The urge to run my hands all over her to feel more of that only intensifies. It's not the first time I've felt this way when I touched her.

Emiline looks down at the place I just touched before looking up at me.

The burning desire in her eyes makes me want to lean in and kiss her.

I promised we could be whatever she wanted us to be. I promised that our last time would be our only time.

I'm usually a man of my word, but I'm losing all restraint.

"Logan," she whispers.

My hand reaches up, brushing the loose strands of hair out of her face before wrapping my hand around the back of her neck. I keep my eyes locked on hers while my heartbeat thunders in my chest.

"I want to kiss you, Emiline."

"Why?"

"Because it's all I can think about doing every time I look at you."

She moves first, closing the gap between us and pressing her lips to mine. She sits up on her knees, and my other hand comes up to cup the side of her face, keeping her in place. I never want this kiss to end.

She moans into my lips before angling her head to allow a deeper kiss.

Kissing Emiline is heaven and hell.

I shouldn't be doing it, but damn, it feels right.

I pull myself back from her, and our eyes lock. "I didn't invite you over for this, Em. I don't want you to think that."

"I know you didn't."

"But the movie."

"Fuck the movie," she breathes out before gripping my face and locking her lips on mine again.

My hands move on their own accord as they reach for her waist. She lifts herself off the couch to straddle my legs, hovering a safe space above me. I tilt my head up, hands gripping her waist as she kisses me with such intensity that my head feels like it's spinning.

She pulls away, panting as she stares down at me.

Lips perfectly swollen, and a tint of pink across her cheeks.

Fucking perfect.

Emiline's fingers tangle in my hair, eyes bouncing between mine as if she's trying to silently figure out the next step.

My hands find the hem of her T-shirt. She sits up enough for me to lift it over her head, leaving her in only a black lace bra, the swell of her breasts directly in my line of sight.

I lean forward, pressing a kiss to her chest right above her heart.

She relaxes on top of me, no doubt feeling what kissing her is doing to my cock between her legs. She moans, and her head falls back, allowing me access to her neck, where I trail kisses along her pounding pulse.

"Beautiful," I whisper against her skin.

Her hips move ever so slowly against me. Just enough for me to realize that we both lied when we said the last time would be the only time.

"Touch me, Logan."

I pull the strap of her bra to the side, kissing her collarbone. "Where do you want to be touched?"

"Everywhere," she pants.

"I need you to be more specific."

I pull the other strap down, pressing a kiss to that collarbone. Emiline reaches behind her, unclasping her bra and tossing it to the side. Her breasts are on full display for me. I lean forward, taking the hardened nipple between my teeth before sucking it.

"Fuck," she moans, eyes fluttering closed.

"Is this where you want to be touched?"

She nods in approval. I bring my hands up and cup both breasts in my hands, teasing her nipples between my fingertips. Her hips move faster against me as if she's craving the friction her body so desperately needs to feel.

But there's no way she's getting off on me again by dry-humping my cock.

With one hand still teasing a nipple, my other reaches for the waistband of Emiline's leggings. Her eyes snap open, looking down at where my hand is.

She lifts herself off my lap until she's hovering over me, giving me access to reach my hand inside and feel how wet she is right now.

As soon as I do, a guttural groan leaves my body.

"You didn't tell me how wet you were." A smirk forms on her lips. "If grinding against my cock got you this wet, I can't wait to feel how wet you are once I do this."

Two fingers slide inside of her with ease, my palm making contact with her clit. Her head falls back in pleasure. I lean forward, keeping my lips on the pounding pulse of her neck while I fuck with my hand as best I can with her pants still on. Her hips grind against me, and I swear, there is nothing sexier than the way Emiline feels pleasure.

It only makes me want to be the only one to ever be able to do this.

"That's it, Em. Ride my hand. Take what you need from me and grip my fingers with your pussy. I want to feel every single thing."

"Oh my god, Logan," she says breathlessly.

"Yes. Say my name when you get yourself off. Remind me who gets you off like this. Who makes you feel this good?"

"Logan," she shouts, reaching the breaking point of her orgasm.

I can feel she's close. Her arousal coats the palm of my hand as it rubs against her clit, back and forth with each buck of her hips.

I want more.

I want to feel her lose control with me inside of her, but know that I can't push this.

"I'm coming. Oh my god, I'm comi—" she shouts, but I cut her off by reaching behind her neck, and pulling her face to mine, eating her moans with my lips as she rides out her orgasm on top of me. Everything around my fingers tightens, her body stills, and she struggles to even kiss me back.

I don't relent, holding her lips to mine. I realize immediately there's no turning back after this.

Emiline's body finally relaxes as she releases our kiss. I pull my hand from her leggings, and at the same time, she climbs off my lap. She sits next to me like she's spent. Like her body just went through a marathon of feelings.

I stand and lean down to kiss her lips quickly before going to the kitchen to clean up. My cock is screaming for attention, but I don't want her to think this is about me. I want to give *her* pleasure. Before going back to the living room, I run to my bedroom and grab an old pair of sweatpants to give her because I know her pants are probably a mess after that.

When I leave my room, I find her in the hallway.

"Sorry, I was grabbing you a pair of sweatpants to change into," I say, handing them to her.

"Thank you," she says shyly, taking them from my hands.

Gripping the back of her head, I lean in to kiss her forehead. "No need to thank me. Go get changed. We have a movie to watch and snacks to eat."

Emiline smiles widely before sidestepping me for the bathroom.

When she returns, we watch the entire movie together, lying on the couch with my arms around her and her head on my chest.

That's where we stay the entire night before we both fall asleep.

Emiline Ford has changed me.

I can't tell if that scares me or excites me.

Either way, I don't want this to end.

CHAPTER TWENTY-NINE
Logan

I'M MENTALLY DRAINED from the rollercoaster of emotions I've already been through today.

The chief brought me in earlier because he said he had to talk to me about something. He prefaced it by saying it was nothing serious and I wasn't in trouble. I gathered, considering I haven't done much in the last few weeks since I took some paid time off over Christmas and spent the holidays relaxing.

Thomas and Peyton invited me to their place with everyone, but I declined because I had picked up an overtime shift. A few days later, I spent the entire night with Emiline in my arms after an intense movie night.

I don't regret it. Not even for a minute.

In fact, I've never wanted more of something in my life.

The issue I'm facing is dreading being in Thomas, Marc, and Oliver's presence. Mostly because I'm afraid I'll slip and tell them what's happened between us before Emiline and I agree to do so. Besides, she and I haven't even talked about if we would, when we would, or what the hell this truly is between us.

I want her to take control of this situation because the last thing I want to do is to cause her any more stress than she's already under. Yet here I am, sitting at our usual spot in Moore's and having a drink with the guys while doing everything I can not to bring her up in conversation.

I slap my hand on the table. "For the first Wednesday in forever, I finally have some news for everyone and something exciting to share."

"You finally got to sleep with your one and only celebrity crush?" Oliver jokes.

"Why do you have to keep bringing that up?" I fake pout. "You and I both know that will never happen."

Besides, I totally have a thing for your sister.

"Continue with the news, Logan," Marc urges.

"I had a meeting with the chief today. We discussed the possibility of a promotion for me this upcoming summer. If all goes well, you're looking at the next Chief of Police."

"No way," Thomas says first.

"Good for you, brother!" Marc slaps my shoulder from my side.

"I'm not sure I'm ready for it, but I'm excited."

And that's the truth.

It's been a long-time dream of mine, but that doesn't mean I'm ready to lead the entire department. I've been here long enough and grew up around this line of work to know what I need to do and how to take on the job, but the anxiety will always be there.

It doesn't matter how tough you are on the outside. Change can be scary for anyone.

The conversation shifts to Oliver as he tells us about his recent trip to Marc's new house, in Roxbury, A nice, quiet, mountain home he picked out as the family getaway to escape the hustle and bustle of the city.

"Are you still in contact with the bartender?" I ask Oliver.

His face twists into something I've never really seen on him before. Sure, I've seen him smile before. The guy never stops smiling, but this one is different.

"She has a name, you know," he says.

"Eww. Fix your face." I wrinkle my nose in disgust. "Why are you smiling like that?"

"Here we go," Thomas says, leaning forward on the table.

"Should I tell you now or later that she's here in the city?" Oliver says.

"I thought she lived there?" Marc questions.

"She did. But…" Oliver pauses. "I may have kinda-sorta… brought her home with me."

I extend my fist across the table for a fist bump. "My brother."

I find my mind wandering as Marc asks him more questions about his situation with the bartender. I can't stop thinking about how things are so different now.

Thomas, Marc and Oliver are all moving forward with their lives.

It doesn't make me want to join them in the happy bliss of love.

But it makes me wish I could tell them about Emiline.

Not that what's transpiring between us is love, but we have such a good time when we're together. There's no denying the intense chemistry.

I feel this pounding in my chest whenever I look at her. There's this insane need to kiss her and touch her whenever she's near.

Something sat dormant for a long time, and it took me until recently to allow myself to accept the feeling for what it is. There's something about a woman like her that you just can't let go of.

Sitting at this table and looking at the guys makes me see that.

But it also makes me think back on my conversation with Silas.

This deep part of me can't let her love me, and that won't *allow* me to love her.

What if, one day, she asks me to pick up a pizza on the way home from work?

No. No, I can't allow my thoughts to go in that direction.

I dull my deepest inner turmoil by taking a long pull of my drink.

Just as I'm about to bring myself back to the conversation, I hear the end of Oliver saying, "Her and her daughter."

My drink sprays out of my mouth across the table. "Come the fuck again?"

Admitting this is a big deal for him. It's his way of telling us that there's something there, and he could potentially see a future with the woman.

I glance around the table at my friends whose lives are all changing. Should I make some changes myself?

I told Emiline I didn't want to fight this anymore.

It's time I stopped denying it to myself and actually did it.

———

I kept to myself the rest of the night as my head continued to go haywire. Once I walk through the parking garage, I try to decide on whether I should just knock on her door and talk this through with her.

Then, I remember Emiline told me she didn't want a relationship.

Hell, *I* told her I didn't want one.

I groan out loud, and my fists clench at my sides with each step I take. This is irritating the fuck out of me. My desire to be with Emiline invades every square inch of my brain, even when I try to push it away.

As if I conjured her up with my mind, I open the door to the stairs leading up to the apartment and see her standing a few steps up on the first landing.

I wait for her to move, but she doesn't. Her body faces the steps, but her head is tipped back as she stares at the ceiling.

"Emiline?" I say, taking the steps two at a time to reach her.

She snaps out of whatever daze she was in, and her eyes widen when she spots me. I swear I hear her mumble "shit" under her breath.

"What are you doing?" I ask, worried.

She lifts the books in her arms. "Just coming back from the library. I had my first lecture for this semester today."

Emiline has that look in her eyes that tells me everything I need to know. Her eyes are glistening as if she's been crying and on the verge of crying again.

"There was a lot of information today," I state.

She nods.

"And you went to the library alone."

She nods again.

A wave of disappointment fills me when I realize she felt overwhelmed and didn't call me. I don't want her to deal with this alone when I want to be there for her, but I push my feelings aside because it isn't about me right now.

She looks up at me and blinks once before a single tear falls down her cheek. I don't hesitate to brush it away with the back of my finger.

I tuck a stray strand of hair behind her ear when she finally says, "I'm trying really hard here."

"What are you talking about?"

"I'm trying to be strong and hold it together, Logan. I don't want to burden you with my issues when I can't control what happens." Emiline's voice quivers with each word out of her mouth.

My hands move to cup her cheeks, lifting her head slightly so she's looking at me. "I want you to let me be there for you, Em."

"Why?"

I wait to answer, hoping the right words come to me, but I say what instantly comes to my mind. "I don't want you to feel like you have to do this alone."

Emiline closes her eyes, and I can feel her body relax beneath my hands even though I'm only holding her face. She sinks into me and rests her head on my chest as she wraps around my waist, the other still clutching her books.

"I'm so tired, Logan," she cries.

One of my hands cups the back of her head, holding her to my chest, while the other hand moves to her upper back.

"I know, Em."

I let my chin rest on top of her head, and my eyes fall closed. In my head, we aren't standing in a stairwell where anyone could walk in at any moment.

It's just the two of us.

"Let's get you home," I tell her.

She eventually pulls away from me and nods.

There's no way I'm leaving her alone in this state.

We take the steps one at a time. I don't take my eyes off Emiline the entire time she fidgets with her purse to grab her keys out. Unlocking the door, I don't say a single word before filtering in behind her.

She pauses, looking up at me as if she's assessing my next move.

I lean in to press a kiss to her forehead before guiding her towards her bedroom.

She quickly gets changed, brushes her teeth and climbs into bed.

Silence stretches between us.

Reaching for the hem of my shirt, I lift it over my head before I climb into bed behind her. I pull her back into me and hold her tight. Honey and vanilla fill my scenes as I inhale and exhale a relaxing breath behind her. Emiline in my arms has never felt more right than it does at this moment.

"I got you, Em," I whisper in her ear.

Her hands grip my forearms with a three pulse squeeze before her body relaxes into mine.

I never realized she picked up on all the times I've done it to her.

I got you.

Three pulses for three words.

And we both drift off to sleep.

CHAPTER THIRTY
Emiline

"IT'S bullshit that we have an exam the second week of classes," Brooke groans through the phone speaker sitting on my desk.

"You didn't think they'd make our last semester easy for us, did you?"

"Well, no. But they could have followed the same plan for the last few classes we took. The first test happening in week three is a much smarter idea, not week two."

I laugh as I flip through the pages of our study guide. Our one saving grace is that each exam this semester is only on one body system, instead of having to learn multiple and then figure out what will be on each exam.

"Did you remember to eat?" she asks me.

I roll my eyes even though she can't see me. "Yes, Mom."

Little does she know, Logan has been making sure I'm constantly eating. Whether it's him showing up at my place to cook something or he's having something delivered when I tell him I'm studying. The small gesture means so much to me.

"I'm just making sure. I know how you get when you go into study mode. Normally, the only thing in your stomach is peppermint mocha. Just partying away down there," Brooke jokes.

"You're hysterical," I deadpan. "I actually feel okay. I understand all of this content on the nervous system. But I mean, I'm definitely still nervous."

"Girl, *all* my systems are nervous about this."

The shit that comes out of her mouth.

"On that note, I'm going to get off the phone to study some more. I'm already annoyed I'm missing Taco Tuesday tonight."

"You always have next week. Isn't that like a standing thing you have, anyway?" Brooke asks.

"It is, but it was at my brother's house this time. Remember, I told you Oliver has that new roommate?"

"Don't remind me," she says, annoyed. "Oliver is probably falling madly in love with her, and I lost my shot at being with the hot blond brother."

"First, ew." I wrinkle my face in disgust. "Second, I doubt it. She has a daughter and is trying to become a chef in the city. He's just helping her out. You know Oliver will never settle down. Anyway, that's all beside the point. I was excited to meet her tonight, and *she* was cooking all of us dinner."

"You totally should have gone. One or two hours away from the books wouldn't have damaged your studying that much."

Oh, if you only knew.

"Yeah, I guess you're right. But let me get back to studying. Love you."

"Love you too. See you tomorrow," Brooke says before we both hang up.

I spend the next fifteen minutes reviewing the study guides when a text comes through my phone.

LOGAN

What are you doing?

I stare at the message on my screen because Logan never texts me. The proof being there isn't a single message between us before this one.

I'm just finishing up studying for the night and planning to relax on the couch for a bit.

It isn't a lie. I was just wrapping up reviewing the final pages and wanted to wind down with a trashy TV show so I could actually sleep tonight.

LOGAN

No, you're not.

Just as I read his text, there's a knock on my door.

I jump from my chair and rush to the entrance of my apartment. I open it to find Logan standing there wearing gray sweatpants and a sweatshirt, his legs spread apart and his arms crossed over his chest.

He looks… mad.

"Are you okay?"

"I'd be a hell of a lot better if your door was actually locked," he scoffs.

"It was," I lie, hoping he doesn't notice.

"No, it wasn't." He shakes his head. "You didn't even hear me open the door a few minutes ago, did you?"

"Well…"

"That's what I thought," Logan cuts me off before stepping into my apartment. "I know you're planning to watch TV, but you have to get chan—"

His words fall short when he notices what I'm wearing. I immediately feel shy under the weight of his stare. I've stood in front of the man in panties and a bra, but being caught wearing his sweatshirt I never returned feels *very* different.

"I keep meaning to return it."

The corner of his lips twist up into a grin. "Keep it. It looks better on you."

Heat pricks my cheeks, and I feel shy all over again.

"Besides, you're going to need it tonight," he adds.

"You don't want me to get a jacket?" I smirk, remembering a

similar conversation from the past. "You know, *Daddy*, since it's so cold outside?"

"Emiline, don't start something we won't have time to finish," Logan warns, clearing his throat. "Keep the sweatshirt on but put a jacket on too."

I cross my arms over my chest. "Fine. But where are we going? I need to finish this review packet."

"And I know you enough to know you'll keep going and spiral if you don't step away. So I have the perfect spot for us to go, but it's going to be chilly there."

I stare at him for a few moments before finally agreeing to whatever he has up his sleeve. I change into a pair of black leggings and a sports bra and put his sweatshirt back on, remembering to grab a jacket on my way out of my bedroom.

"Let's go," Logan says as soon as I enter the living room again.

We make our way outside, and I think he's going to guide me toward his truck and the parking garage. Instead, he walks right to the sidewalk, ushering me to the inside, away from the street.

Wait.

"Where are we going?" I ask again.

"The gym."

"It's late. Aren't they closed? Besides, I'm not sure I want to work out right now," I tell him honestly.

"We aren't working out, and yes, they are closed to the public."

"Do you have a key for twenty-four-hour access or some-thing?" I ask jokingly.

"Tonight I do."

My steps falter, but I keep up with him until we reach the gym. It's pitch-black inside. Logan pulls a key from his pocket to unlock the door. Once he does, he places a hand on my lower back to guide me inside, and just the small touch makes me want him to keep his hands on me.

He locks the door behind us before walking through the dark building, bringing me into the back where the box—

"No," I tell him when I realize what he's got planned. "I told you I can't box."

Logan smiles. "I know the owner, and he owes me a favor. So tonight, you're boxing with me. I know you said it made you nervous, but it's just me here. No cameras either." He flips the light switch in the private room, and a soft yellow glow illuminates the room.

It's intimidating being here, but knowing that it's just Logan makes me less nervous about this.

"Listen," he says, moving his body so he's standing directly in front of me. His hands land on my shoulders as he leans down to look at me. "I know you've never done this before and that's okay." Logan releases his hold on my shoulders and walks into the open room. "Silas introduced me to this place after we had a bad night at work. This is where we come to release everything we're holding in. Most of the time, we don't say a word to each other, but we both know that it's us letting everything we're feeling out of our bodies the only way we know how. There's just something so…"

"Therapeutic," I answer for him.

Logan turns to face me, standing in the middle of the ring. "Yes. I thought that maybe this might be something you can do, too. If you don't love it, we never have to do it again, but I've been thinking about this a lot. I thought about you the last few times I came here with Silas."

"Me?"

He nods. "You drive me insane. In a way I never saw coming, and it frustrated me to no end."

I spent so long truly believing that Logan couldn't stand me, and here he is, standing in front of me again and asking me to let him in.

"I told you I didn't want you to keep doing this alone, and I meant every word," he continues.

I nod quickly in response because I want to let him in completely.

So I step into the ring to join him. "Tell me what to do."

Logan smiles, and everything in my body lights up as I watch him pick up two large red gloves. He slowly walks toward me before lifting my hands and putting them on for me. They feel heavy at first, but once he straps them around my wrist, I adjust to them and immediately feel a strength wash over me that I didn't know I had.

Logan dons two gloves himself, but his are flat, unlike mine. Then, he takes his place in front of me and holds both of his hands up. "You're going to aim for these when you throw your punches."

I nod and throw my first one. "Like that?" I ask, unsure if I did it right.

He smirks over at me and tilts his head. "Come on, Emmy. I know you have some power in you. Show me."

I inhale and exhale a deep breath, and this time, I punch a little harder.

"That's it, Emmy. Keep going," Logan says, maintaining his position in front of me.

He's trying to get a rise out of me, using that nickname repeatedly to make me punch harder. This time, I try throwing two punches back to back. When the second punch connects with his mitt, something I've never felt before surges through me. A feeling I can't quite describe with words.

Then, I keep going, and like Logan told me, I feel like I'm releasing everything I've been holding back.

I've fought for so long to make everyone proud of me.

Being the youngest and *only* sister, I've fought hard to live up to the expectations I felt I needed to rise to. Not a soul told me I had to be great, but my brothers are. It only felt right that I tried to fit the mold of the Ford family.

But I kept getting this overwhelming feeling that I'll never be good enough.

And no matter what my brothers told me, I always felt like I'd never make them proud enough.

That's when the panic sets in, and I question if they say those things because they have to, because I'm their baby sister and it's their job, or because they actually mean it.

Couple that with the anxiety about whether I'll be a good nurse or not. This profession is challenging, and I always wonder if I can handle it. Am I smart enough to care for patients in the real world?

I throw punch after punch, hoping to quiet my thoughts.

Logan doesn't stop me once. He doesn't tell me to slow down or to take it easy. He just stands there and allows me to release everything holding me back.

When I eventually stop, my gloved hands fall to my sides as I try to control my breathing to avoid completely breaking down in front of him.

"How did that feel?"

"A lot," I admit. "Does your mind always go to weird places when you do this?"

He nods.

"I think I get why this works now."

I raise my gloved hands again. "I need more." I start throwing punches, even though Logan's not ready. "I hate that I put so much pressure on myself."

I finally say the words I've been burying inside for so long. I want to let Logan into the deeper parts of my mind. I know I can trust him, and being so busy with hitting makes sharing much easier.

"My brothers are so successful."

I throw two more jabs at the mitts he holds up.

"What if I'm not?"

I don't allow Logan a chance to answer because I get brave and start throwing hooks in his direction. I have no clue what I'm doing, but I've watched people box here and there to know what some punches are.

"I just."

Another jab.

"Want."

Right hook.

"To fucking."

A jab.

"Be enough."

With one last cross jab, I fall to my knees on the floor, holding myself up with my gloved hands.

"I just want to be enough," I say quieter this time.

I close my eyes, willing the tears away because this doesn't seem like the sport that allows tears on the mat. I feel spent from punching as hard as I did, but inside, I'm the strongest I've ever felt.

With my emotions this high, a panic attack would normally set in.

But it doesn't.

My breathing is fast but controlled.

"Emiline," Logan whispers, crouching down to my level. "Look at me."

He rests his knuckles under my chin, urging me to do so. Reluctantly, I open my eyes and sit back on my heels. A tear forms in the corner of my eye, and I will do everything in my power not to let more fall.

"You are enough, Em. You're more than enough. You're Emiline Ford, and there's no one out there like you."

I deeply inhale and allow my eyes to close again, my lone tear escaping. I can't help my wandering mind when I think about what's happening here. More specifically, what's happening between Logan and me.

I finally open my eyes again to find him still looking at me. "Logan, what are we doing?"

"We're talking."

I shake my head. "No. Us. Here. What's this between us?"

I watch as he swallows before he speaks, "We're doing whatever you want to be doing. I know this is uncharted territory, but I find myself wanting to be your person more and more."

"You want to be my person?"

Logan nods. "Out in the open. In secret. Behind closed doors." He shrugs. "Whatever you want it to be. I just know I don't want to stay away from you."

I lift myself up and launch myself into his arms. He catches me effortlessly as he falls back to his heels. I hold Logan tighter than ever before, and he does the same.

A wave of emotions rushes through me. Happiness mixed with fear, because there's a chance this could end terribly.

There's a chance I'm putting my heart on the line to be broken.

But it's a chance I'm willing to take.

CHAPTER THIRTY-ONE
Logan

EMILINE OPENED up to me and showed me what was going on in her head, which is all I've ever wanted.

She slightly pulls away from my embrace but keeps her arms wrapped around my neck.

"I feel like so much between us has been a secret," she says. "I hate to make you keep this thing between us from everyone."

I shake my head. "I'm okay with it if that's what you want. I don't want us rushing to tell everyone anything if we aren't ready."

She nods and continues to stare at me. I can tell by the look in her eyes she's thinking about it.

Emiline opens her mouth to say something, but I cut her off. "I don't want this to be overwhelming, so how about you get through this semester first? If by June, when you graduate, we both want to keep this up and tell your brothers about us, I'll be there right next to you, holding your hand."

This smile is real and genuine and because of *me*.

"Now, let's go home."

I stand and outstretch my hand down to help lift her up. After that, I clean up the mitts while she removes her gloves and does the same. Just as we're about to leave, she stops me.

"Logan," she says from behind me. I turn around to face her. "Do you… want to come back to my place?"

I smirk in her direction before taking two steps toward her. "What did you have in mind?"

Emiline shrugs and walks past me, heading for the front door. "Well, I *was* going to catch up on my drama-filled TV show. It's about this badass lawyer in Washington, DC who solves everyone's problems. Oh, and she's got a thing on the side with the president. It's so good. You can join me."

I bark out a laugh as I unlock the door and guide her outside before locking up behind me. "It's cute you think we're going to actually watch it."

Her lips part and I walk us back to her place, silence stretching between us the entire walk there. There's a tension in the air that neither of us wants to acknowledge.

As soon as she unlocks the door and crosses the threshold, I kick the door closed behind us and pin her against the back of the door. I cage her in with both hands and press my body into her, so she feels the effect she has on me.

"Logan," she breathes out.

"I've wanted to kiss you again since I saw you in my sweatshirt," I say against her lips. "Tell me, why didn't you give it back?"

"Because." She places two hands on my chest and pushes me away from her. She slowly reaches for the hem of my sweatshirt and lifts it over her head, tossing it on the floor beside her and leaving her only in her sports bra. "I was hoping at some point you'd get to see me take it off."

A growl vibrates through my chest.

"Now you can kiss me," she says.

I don't waste another second and claim her lips as mine. I don't know what she'll choose in the end, but as long as Emiline allows it, these lips will be mine and no one else's.

Her body presses into mine, and I lift her up, holding her against the door again. She wraps her arms around my neck, and

I kiss her wildly while my hands roam every exposed part of her I can touch. She opens up for me and lifts her head to deepen the kiss.

I've never wanted anyone the way I want Emiline Ford right now.

I meant everything I told her in the gym.

She is enough.

She's *more than* enough.

She's everything.

"Logan," she pants breathlessly against my lips. "Take me to my room."

I hold her tight in my arms as I walk us to her room with her legs still wrapped tightly around mine.

I'm fully prepared to toss her on the bed and claim her in every way, but she wiggles free from my hold to stand in front of me. Her hands on my shoulders roam from my chest and down my stomach until she reaches the hem of my shirt and lifts it over my head.

A grin forms on her lips as she finds the waistband of my sweatpants next.

She reaches under it, and the moment her hands grip my cock, I just about lose it. I should get a medal for holding it together and not throwing her on the bed to fuck her right here and now.

"Jesus," she whispers, barely loud enough for anyone to hear.

I bite my bottom lip because it's so hot.

"What are you planning to do here, Em?"

"I'm not really sure anymore." She laughs shyly. "Your cock feels like a weapon. Do you have a permit to carry this around with you?"

I laugh, but it comes out strained because her hand is still wrapped around me. "You can handle it."

Her laughter dies down, and her lips part. Those perfect fucking soft pink lips I want wrapped around my cock right now.

Emiline tugs at the waistband of my sweatpants with her free hand, pushing them and my boxer briefs to the floor.

My cock springs free, and she lowers herself to the ground in front of me while keeping her eyes locked on mine. A devilish smirk plays on her lips until she settles herself on her heels, my aching cock only inches away from her face, before looking back at me.

"What are you doing?" I ask her, cupping her chin between my fingers.

Her cheeks turn pink, and I can't help but grin.

"I'm not sure I know how to do this very well, but I want to…" Her words trail off, reminding me that she gets nervous when talking about things like this.

"What do you want to do, Em?"

She looks from my cock, and back up at me, not wanting to say the words out loud.

"Use your words for me."

"Your cock," Emiline finally says. Her tone is laced with urgency like she's eager to have me in her mouth. She shifts against her heels before saying, "I want to suck your cock, Logan. I want to make you feel good."

I don't move.

I *can't* move.

Doesn't she know she's made me feel good from the moment things changed between us? I've felt lighter, free, and, dare I say, happier.

This also shows me that she trusts me.

I know most people I know do, but having her trust me feels different.

Better.

I gently run my hand over the top of her head before letting my fingers tangle in her hair as I hold her in place.

"Suck," I order her.

The corner of her lip tips up as she grips my shaft. I hiss at the contact. She slides her hand up and down my length from root to tip before she leans in and licks the drop of pre-cum off there.

"Fuck," I draw out.

My head falls back the moment she wraps her lips around the head and takes me into her mouth. With her hand still wrapped around me, she moves it up and down in unison with her mouth.

I'm afraid to look back down at her.

I know if I do, I won't last much longer but screw it. I want to see her make me come undone.

When my eyes fly open, she's already looking up at me. Her lashes fluttering and her mouth filled with my cock.

"Look at you on your knees for me with your mouth filled with my cock."

I watch her move her hips every once in a while, as she continues sucking me. She's turned on, which only makes me closer to the edge.

I have to hold it together.

I need to hold it together because this feels too good for it to end so soon.

She pauses her movements, removing my cock from her mouth with a pop to take a break to get a breath of air. I look down at where her eyes are staring at my length, glistening from her ministrations.

She grips it with a little more force this time and moves her hand up and down again, twisting with each move.

"Hmm. That feels so good, Emiline. You're doing so good."

"Yeah?"

I nod. "You take me so well in that pretty little mouth of yours. I can only imagine how well your pussy would take me if I were to fuck you right now."

She wiggles below me, stroking faster and harder before she licks my cock from root to tip.

"That turns you on, doesn't it? The idea of me sliding my

cock inside of you." She squirms some more. "Fucking that perfect pussy of yours?"

She moans as she takes me in her mouth again. I hit the back of her throat, and I nearly combust right there.

"Fuck," I growl, my body vibrating from the pleasure. My hand cups the back of her head, keeping her still as I work my hips, fucking her face.

Her eyes flutter closed, and tears form in the corner of her eyes.

My jaw flexes as my looming orgasm only intensifies.

Her hands roam over my thighs before she grips my hips to keep herself steady and take everything I give her. When I feel myself closer, I pull out of her mouth.

"Are you going to be a good girl and let me come down your throat?"

She nods repeatedly.

"I need your words, Emiline."

"Yes. Come down my throat."

I grin down at her, using my thumb to stroke the side of her cheek. "I didn't hear you say please. You know I love hearing you beg for me."

"Please, Logan."

I grip my cock in my free hand and angle it toward her mouth. She opens for me so eagerly, ready for more. When her tongue darts out, I glide myself in. Her eyes flutter closed instantly as she hums in approval around my length.

I let go as she takes over, and I move both of my hands to the back of her head while I thrust in and out in a steady rhythm.

I keep my eyes on hers the same way she does me.

"I'm going to come," I tell her, barely able to get the words out.

Her free hand grips my ass to give herself more hold. My cock hits the back of her throat, and I feel it constrict right before I come.

Stars dance in my vision as I shout her name.

"Em, fuck."

She moans, looking up at me while I release everything inside of her mouth.

I tilt my head back, willing the feeling to come down, but it doesn't. It would be impossible for this feeling to go away when it comes to her.

She pulls me out of her mouth, and when I look down at her, I watch intently as she swallows. Her hand comes up, and she wipes the mess we just made from the corner of her mouth.

"That was…" she begins, but I cut her off by pulling her up and lifting her up into my arms.

My lips meet hers in a desperate kiss. If she wasn't mine before this, she sure as fuck is now.

With her legs wrapped around my waist and the feeling of her body connected with mine this way, my cock stirs to life again. There's no need for a break with her because every single thing she does turns me on.

"I need you," she mutters against my lips.

"I'm at your mercy, Emiline. Whatever you need, whatever you want, it's fucking yours."

She laughs lightly. "Damn, I got an A+ for sucking cock then, huh?"

I don't join her in her laughter because I don't want her to think that's what it is.

My forehead falls to hers. "It's so much more than that. Being with you and having you in my arms… I want more of it. This time with you? I want more of it. So whatever you want, it's yours."

Emiline pauses for a second, pulling back before her eyes scan my face as if she's trying to figure out if I'm serious or if I'm just saying it in the heat of the moment.

And fuck, I wish I had said all of this sooner because I wasted so much time fighting what's really happening between us.

"I want you to fuck me, Logan."

"I…" My words fall short because hearing her so boldly tell me that after not being able to talk about it in front of me stirs something in me.

"If I do this, I won't be able to stop," I tell her seriously.

Emiline presses her forehead to mine, holding me tighter with her legs around my waist. "Then don't stop."

I lay her down on the bed and she scrambles on the sheets. She pulls down her leggings in a hurry and rips off her sports bra, leaving her in nothing but her panties. She settles herself in the middle of the bed, propped up on her elbows and looking at me with sultry eyes.

I don't move. I couldn't even if I tried.

Her breasts are perky and round. I want my hands all over them and to suck the hard nipple between my teeth and feel her wither under my touch.

My eyes trail her body, and I can visibly see the fucking wet spot on her lace panties. My lips turn up as I bring my eyes back to her face.

I raise a brow at her. "You wore lace panties to go boxing with me?"

"You didn't tell me where we were going. You just made sure I had a sweatshirt and a jacket. You know, doing your little protective daddy thing."

I growl at the use of that word as my cock stirs.

Her eyes trail down at the movement. "Got a daddy kink?" She smirks.

"No. But I do have an Emiline kink." I smile down at her as I grip my cock in my palm and pump it two times. "Take your panties off for me."

She lifts her hips and hooks a finger in the thin strap on her hips and slides them down her legs. So slowly that it physically hurts to watch. Then she tosses them to the side and spreads her legs open for me.

"So eager," I rasp. "Now, touch yourself. I want you to show me how wet you are. Show me how turned on you got by sucking on my cock."

Emiline's lips form the perfect O shape as the look in her eyes morphs into one that's heated with desire.

"I'm very eager," she says, taking her hands and cupping both of her breasts.

I grip my cock harder as I watch her every move.

She so delicately slides her hands down her stomach until she reaches the spot right above her pussy that clearly aches for contact. Her finger reaches lower, disappearing into her pussy right before she pulls it out and raises it in the air to show me.

I bring myself to the edge of the bed, and I lean down over her. My one hand stays around my cock, and my other wraps around her wrist as I guide her finger between my lips, sucking it clean.

She sucks in a breath, her mouth parted slightly.

"I knew you were turned on by that. You must be aching for me."

"I want you so bad right now. All of it. I want everything."

I walk away for a moment to reach into my wallet and grab a condom. I quickly roll it on before coming back to find her with her bottom lip between her teeth.

I climb on the bed and position myself between her legs. She opens wider for me, and I lean in just enough so the head of my cock rests just over her throbbing clit.

Despite how much she's dripping, I keep my eyes fixed down as I spit on her pussy. She gasps, and her eyes flutter closed for a moment before opening them to watch what I do next.

I run my cock through her wetness a few times. Her hips buck when I press it against her clit.

I angle my cock and slowly press into her.

"Holy shit," Emiline cries out with just the tip inside.

"You're so fucking wet for me," I hiss.

The feeling of her around me as I push in a little more is almost too much to bear. I thought coming down her throat would hold me off, but this feeling is unlike anything else.

"Fuck me, Logan," she says, already out of breath.

"I'm working really hard to hold it together right now. I need a minute."

I hold myself inside of her for one, two, three breaths before I pull out of her. When I push myself in this time, I move a little quicker until I reach full hilt.

I throw my head back and let my eyes fall closed at the sensation taking over my body. When I finally get it together, I thrust in and out of her, finding the perfect rhythm and ensuring she feels everything I'm feeling.

"Talk to me, Em."

"Oh my God," she cries out. "I feel… so full. I feel so good."

"You're taking my cock so well." I pause my movements, pressing fully into her until I completely disappear inside of her. I look down at where we're connected. "Jesus Christ, I think I may need another minute."

"No, don't stop," she begs.

A smile plays on my lips. "You have my cock deep inside of you right now, and you're still begging, Emiline? You're greedy, aren't you?"

"Yes," she cries out. "Yes. Please keep moving."

I pull out of her and thrust in as hard as I can, my movements quickening with each movement. Her pussy pulses around me, and I know she's close.

"Logan," she screams, throwing her arms over her head and clutching the surrounding sheets. "Fuck. Logan."

"That's it. Scream my name when you come for me. Because no one else will ever make you come like this again. Only me."

She shakes her head, hips bucking into me. "No one," she whimpers. "Only you. Oh my god. I'm… I'm going to come."

The way she confirms that only I can do this for her makes me feral, forcing me to drive into her harder and faster.

I lean over her, caging her head with my hands because I don't want to miss a minute of her face when she does. With one more thrust, she falls apart under me.

My name is on her lips as her back arches off the bed, and she squirms under me, her body trembling from her orgasm.

Just watching her come for me sends me over the edge with her.

"Emiline," I whisper her name repeatedly, although I'm not sure she can hear it through her daze.

I've seen her come, but being inside of her and feeling it is a whole new feeling that I want more of.

I don't bother pulling out of her when I bring my face to hers, resting my forehead against hers. "Emiline," I whisper again. "Fuck." I kiss her before I say anything more.

Because the truth is, I don't know what to say. There are no words to fully describe how I feel right now.

Our kiss is slow and tentative this time.

It's a seal on what we just did.

Her phone starts ringing incessantly in the other room, forcing her back to reality. I slowly pull out of her and roll to her side until I'm on my back.

"Someone's desperate to get a hold of me." She laughs, reaching for a T-shirt to slip on before heading to grab her phone.

I watch as she walks away, but don't move off the bed. My body is drained, and my brain swirls over everything we have done.

Her brothers would murder me if they ever found out about this, and truthfully, I don't have it in me to care.

Being with her lights something up in my life that I didn't know was missing. I swore I'd never allow my heart to get involved, and a piece of me wants to preserve that and keep the wall up.

But a piece of me wants Emiline to break it down.

When she comes back, she has a worried look on her face.

I sit up on my elbows. "Everything okay?"

"Do you have any missed calls?"

I pull myself off the bed and reach for my sweatpants, tugging them on before finding my phone. "I have two missed calls from Thomas."

"Shit." Her hand flies to the top of her head as she paces the room. "There's a text in our girl gang group chat from Peyton and Avery about how my brothers questioned if I was studying tonight or with you."

I find my shirt and throw it on. "*Shit.* I should leave before they get here."

Her lips turn down into a frown. "Yeah. I don't think they would actually show up, but you never know."

"You never know," I repeat, not wanting to leave but not wanting them to find out like this.

She reaches for the nape of my neck and kisses me again. It's not a goodbye kiss, just acknowledging the situation for what it is and knowing we're both on the same page.

She finally walks me to the door. I stand in the hallway, staring at her while she looks back at me.

"Good night, Logan," she says, closing the door on me.

I throw out my arm to stop the door from closing on my face because I won't let this be another time she tells me good night and I, stupidly, don't say it back.

She looks at me, confused.

"Good night, Emiline," I say, pressing my lips to her for a short kiss.

She smiles up at me as if I just hung the moon for her.

"And happy birthday."

She looks back at me, shocked that I even remembered. Even though it's another few hours before it's actually her birthday, I wanted to be the first to tell her.

"Thank you," she replies. "I can't believe you remembered."

I wink and press one more quick kiss to her lips. "I remember everything when it comes to you."

Once she closes the door—I make sure she locks it too—I stand at her front door for a few moments before I bring myself to walk away.

And the only thought that runs through my mind is that I'm completely and utterly ruined by Emiline Ford.

CHAPTER THIRTY-TWO
Emiline

February

IT'S BEEN two weeks since Logan and I decided we were going to see where things go between us.

He suggested we wait until after I graduate to tell my brothers or anyone anything, giving us a few months to explore where this *could* go.

I won't lie and say the idea of being something more with him doesn't scare me. I'm scared to let myself fall for him and end up heartbroken. I'm afraid to lose him if this ends up not working.

But despite all of my fears, everything about Logan just makes me want him that much more.

He's also been so good at letting me put school first.

Brooke and I have been studying nonstop, switching between doing so at the library or in my apartment.

Every time we have an exam coming up, Logan checks in on both of us to see if we need anything. He's taken me boxing twice since our first time.

And he was right, those sessions truly help me release anything negative I have floating around in my head.

Over the last weeks, I've also finally met Oliver's roommate, Macey, and her daughter, Mackenzie. She's the sweetest little girl I've ever come across, and she reminds me of an older version of James.

Smart with just the right amount of sass.

Oliver told me he was falling hard for Macey and mentioned he wanted to take her on a proper date. I offered to have Mackenzie come hang out at my place because I love kids so much and actually have a lull in studying this week.

I'm not sure if kids will ever be in the cards for me especially now that I'm entering a career I've been working so hard for, but I love spending time with them.

"Emiline, can we watch *Harry Potter*?" Mackenzie asks.

My hand flies to my chest. "A girl after my own heart. Of course we can."

"Yes!" She fist pumps the air before hustling toward the couch and grabbing a blanket to cover herself. "Can we make popcorn, too?"

"Normally, I'd say heck yes. But I think we should eat dinner first."

"You're right." She nods. "What do you have in mind? Do you want me to make my famous French toast?"

I laugh at her. "How about we make a deal? I'll cook dinner tonight, and tomorrow morning you can make me your famous French toast I've heard *amazing* things about."

"You've heard of it? Is it really that famous?"

I nod. "Oliver loves it."

She smiles from ear to ear. "I love Ollie. He's the best."

"He really is. But listen, I'm not the best cook like your mom. I can make a mean buttered pasta, though. Does that work?"

"I love buttered noodles!"

Just as I'm about to make my way to the kitchen, my phone buzzes with a text message.

LOGAN

What are you up to?

Just hanging out with Mackenzie. You?

LOGAN

Great. I'm on my way over.

What? Why?

Three bubbles dance around my screen, but then they disappear. Two minutes later, there's a knock on the door.

I know without even looking that it's Logan.

I open the door to find him standing there with two grocery bags in his hand. He smiles and lifts them up to show that he brought dinner with him. I'm kind of thankful because after experiencing his chicken, my pasta now sounds so boring.

"I come bearing gifts in the form of dinner," he says. "I figured you probably had nothing," he adds, his voice lower so Mackenzie doesn't hear.

"Thank you."

Logan scans the apartment as he steps in and notices Mackenzie deep into the start of her Harry Potter movie. Then he leans in and gives me a quick kiss on the lips. Almost as if we do it every single day.

I can't allow myself to think about that right now.

So instead, I focus on Logan's backside as he enters the kitchen to unpack the groceries.

"It's Captain Crunch chicken night," he exclaims.

"What is that?" Mackenzie asks before turning her head toward the kitchen. "Oh, hi, Logan."

"Hey there, Mackenzie," Logan says with a welcoming smile.

"You two know each other already?" I ask.

"We met briefly one night when I stopped by Oliver's place," he says to me before directing his attention back to Mackenzie. "But to answer your question, it's the best kind of chicken. You know how your mom makes chicken coated in breadcrumbs?"

Mackenzie nods. "Yes. It's my favorite."

"This is about to be your new favorite." He laughs. "It's the same thing, but the breadcrumbs are replaced with crushed Captain Crunch cereal."

"*Get out!*" She leaps from the couch. "Can I help?"

"Think you can crush up some cereal for me?" Logan asks her.

She nods and goes next to Logan to do exactly that.

The entire interaction makes my stomach flutter with butterflies. I have only ever seen Logan interact with James when all of us are together. He's always been so good with him, but James is much younger.

Watching the way he talks to Mackenzie feels different.

He would make an amazing girl dad.

I shake off my thoughts because why is my mind traveling there now? We aren't even officially in a relationship, and here I am, picturing him with our child.

Our child? Oh my god, my brain needs to shut up.

"You good over there?" Logan asks.

"Perfect," I answer quickly.

Logan just smiles as he opens the pack of chicken and gets to work with Mackenzie.

Out of nowhere, the butterflies in my gut turn into dread as I watch them interact. She's so excited about this recipe and making it with Logan.

What if she goes home and tells Oliver?

What if she tells everyone at James' birthday party tomorrow?

I can't ask a young girl to lie to her mom and everyone around her for us.

I excuse myself to the bathroom while the two of them do their thing. I feel like a panic attack is coming over me, but I also feel in control, unlike in the past.

I remind myself the situation is out of my hands, but what I can control is my reaction. I'm not sure if it's because I know

Logan is in the other room or because I don't want to scare Mackenzie into thinking something is wrong with me. Still, I sit on the toilet seat lid with my hands resting on my upper thigh as I work on my breathing.

In for three, out for three.

In for three, out for three.

If it gets out, it gets out, right?

If they find out, that saves us the need to keep things a secret.

In for three, out for three.

A knock on the bathroom door startles me out of my breathing exercises.

"Yeah?"

"I'm coming in," Logan announces from the other side of the door before swinging it open. He takes one look at me and closes the door behind him.

"Where's Mackenzie?" I ask.

"A good part of *Harry Potter* was coming on."

I nod in response, unable to form words.

Logan crouches in front of where I sit on the toilet lid. "Talk to me."

"My brain just went a little crazy."

"School?" he asks.

I shake my head. "You with Mackenzie. What if she tells her mom? Or Oliver? Or she mentions it at James' birthday party tomorrow? Not a soul knows we hang out."

Understanding crosses his features, but he doesn't look concerned. "Then we'll deal with it," he simply says.

"Just like that?" I bark out a laugh.

He smiles. "Just like that."

He takes both of my hands that were resting on my thighs in his. Then he lightly squeezes my hand three times. I never understood why he does it, but for me it's his silent way of reassuring me that everything will be ok.

"I'm not going anywhere, you know that, right?"

I don't move and don't respond because how can I know

that? Things could get ugly fast if this gets out before either of us are ready.

"I'm in it," he says, releasing the hold on one of my hands to take my chin between his fingers. "I'm in it *with you*."

I nod again, and he leans in to kiss me.

"Now…" He stands, extending his hand for me to take it. "Let's eat dinner and finish this movie."

I take his hand in mine and everything feels right.

No matter how this turns out… it just feels right.

"And one more thing." He stops before opening the door. "Don't try to object, but I'm staying the night. No funny business." He winks. "But after all of this, I just want to make sure you're okay before we go to the party tomorrow."

I smile and nod. A feeling of comfort washes over me, knowing he's going to be here.

"Now let's eat. I'm starving," he says before guiding me to the kitchen.

———

Logan stayed true to his word. There was no funny business.

He slept on the couch, which made me irrationally angry at first because there was nothing more I would have loved than to fall asleep in his arms.

But I didn't want to sound needy.

Instead, I laid in my bed, staring at the ceiling, thinking over everything and anything that has involved Logan in the last year. It's wild to believe it's been a year since he spilled coffee down my shirt, and I swore he hated me.

It's been a year of juggling school and overcoming everything I thought I couldn't, and that thought alone had me smiling to myself in the dark.

Not only has so much changed in my life, but I've changed too.

Lately, on days when I feel my anxiety setting in, I remind myself that I've overcome so much.

I remind myself that Logan is there.

That he's asked—no, demanded—to be there with me through it all.

When I came to that realization last night, I wanted to jump out of bed and tell him how much he really means to me. How I don't want to wait until I graduate. How we can figure this out together, just the two of us.

Because I want that.

I want a future with him, regardless of any consequences it might bring.

I hear dishes clink together in the kitchen, pulling me from my thoughts. I quickly get dressed, brush my teeth and make my way in there, only to find Logan standing over the coffee maker making two cups.

My heart nearly beats out of my chest when I see he has the peppermint mocha syrup out. The fact that he knows my absolutely favorite coffee flavor is enough to make me want to scream about us from the rooftops.

"Good morning," Logan says with a smile.

The deep gravel of his morning voice makes my stomach flip around. All I can think about is him lifting me onto the counter, spreading my legs enough so he can step between them to give me the best good morning kiss I've ever had.

My guest bedroom door opening pushes those thoughts away.

Mackenzie comes out, rubbing her eyes. "Morning."

"Morning, Mackenzie. Did you sleep okay?" I ask her.

She nods. "Very. That bed was so so comfy."

"I'm glad." I smile at her.

"I'm glad you're still here, Logan," she says, walking over to him and taking a spot next to him in the kitchen. "I'm hoping I can make my famous French toast this morning." She looks over at me. "Pretty please?"

"Of course. I'm excited to try it," I tell her.

"Excellent. Do you want some Logan?" she asks him.

"Well, if it's *your* famous French toast, count me in," He laughs. "Anything I can do to help?"

She shakes her head. "Nope, but I need supervision when the stove is on."

"You got it." He salutes her. "Consider it supervised."

They both laugh as Logan shows her where everything is, moving around my kitchen like he knows it better than me.

My phone buzzes, and I see a text from Macey.

MACEY

How's Mackenzie doing? Did she sleep ok?

She slept like a rock. LOL. She actually just woke up a few minutes ago and is begging us to let her make her famous French toast.

MACEY

It's her favorite meal to make.

wait... Emiline...

Yeah?

MACEY

What do you mean by 'us'?

Oh. My. God. I spent all of last night worried that Mackenzie would be the one to tell her mom or Oliver about us, and here I am, nearly spilling the beans.

Me and the dog.

I cringe as I send that message because I clearly do not have a dog, and the last thing I want to do is start lying to my friends.

I put my phone face down because I don't want to see what she says.

When my focus comes back to Logan and Mackenzie in the kitchen, my heart soars all over again.

"Are you two coming to the party today?" Mackenzie asks us.

"Yup. You know James is my nephew, right?" I ask her.

She looks shocked. "You're his aunt? That's so cool! I don't have any aunts," she says, but her facial expressions don't change. She's still smiling as she waits for the French toast to turn golden. "One day, I will, and it will be epic."

I chuckle with her despite feeling a piece of my heart break for her.

I know a bit about Macey's story, but I never got a chance to really learn more with how chaotic my schedule is. I just know that Macey is the best addition to our girl gang.

"I'm actually going to go get ready. We have to head out soon," I tell her. "Your mom and Oliver are going to meet us at the party."

"Perfect." She flips the French toast over. "These will be ready for you when you get back."

I look at Logan and find him already staring at me with a smile.

The way he looks at me causes my stomach to flutter.

I know one thing for sure, today is going to be a long day of hiding my attraction for him in front of everyone.

CHAPTER THIRTY-THREE
Logan

How are you feeling after the party today?

EMILINE

Better

Relieved that Macey didn't bring anything up.

I knew everything would be okay, Em. You should really start trusting that I know what I'm talking about.

EMILINE

Oh yeah?

Yup. Everyone was so wrapped up in the news about the gender reveal, no one ever gave it a second thought.

EMILINE

It wasn't them I was worried about. I was afraid Mackenzie was going to spill the beans that you were at my place.

And she was having a blast with James and the other kids.

EMILINE

Yeah, I guess you're right.

Say that again…

EMILINE

Absolutely not.

Shouldn't you be working?

I should.

But I was thinking of you.

YEAH?

Don't sound so shocked. It's starting to become impossible not to think about you.

CHAPTER THIRTY-FOUR
Emiline

BROOKE

don't study too hard tonight.

I'm not. I actually just finished up and waiting for Logan so we can have dinner.

BROOKE

Oh, yes. "Dinner." I love it.

💀 It's actually dinner.

BROOKE

I know it is. The best part about this one is you don't have to cook for him.

Ditch the panties too. Just my suggestion.

You're unreal.

BROOKE

You love me.

But really... ditch the panties.

LOGAN'S PLANNING TO come over for dinner tonight. Which is really nothing new since we've fallen into a routine with each other. Except I'm nervous for *this* dinner for some reason.

I want Logan Bennett so badly, and I can't stop thinking about the last time we had sex, which was after my first boxing lesson.

And that was almost a month ago.

After successfully making it through our first gathering with my brothers and the girls for James' birthday, I wanted him to come back to my place.

Watching him with the kids during the party and how his eyes never left mine made me want to be closer to him that night.

Being forced to keep my hands to myself all day made him irresistible by the evening.

Except he got called into work after another officer called off.

He didn't miss the opportunity to text me to make sure I was okay after the day though.

Lately, our work schedules have been opposite each other, too. I hate to even admit this at the stage we're in, but I actually miss him.

Which doesn't tamp down the anticipation of seeing him tonight.

After coming back home, I decided to take a long 'everything' shower where I wash my hair, exfoliate and shave.

Just as I finally get situated in the living room to fold some laundry to pass the time while I wait for him, a knock sounds on my door. A smile so big stretches across my face as I rush to open in. As soon as I open the door, he takes me in, scanning my body from top to bottom.

I ditched the sweatpants and oversized T-shirt tonight and went with a loose-fitting pair of shorts and a tiny tank top. I already feel my nipples harden at the weight of his stare on my body.

"Come in," I say, opening my arms to let him pass me.

He crosses the door frame but doesn't take his eyes off me. There's something so insanely hot about the way he looks at me.

I close the door behind us. "I was just folding some laund—"

My sentence is cut off when Logan grips my waist and pulls me flush against him, crashing his lips to mine as he wastes no time.

He backs me into the door, and my body molds to his like we belong together. Fused so tightly it would take some powerful outside force to pull us apart.

He removes one hand from my waist and brings it to the side of my face, angling my head just right to deepen the kiss. I moan into his mouth, and I swear I feel his chest vibrate at the same time his tongue swipes across my bottom lip.

I open up for him, allowing his tongue to tangle with mine.

Kissing Logan Bennett feels euphoric, and I never want it to end.

To my dismay, he pulls away.

"I miss you too." I laugh against his lips.

"You don't listen very well, do you?" he says in a low, husky voice.

The tone sends shivers down my spine and right to the sensitive spot between my legs. I fight the urge to rub my legs together and cock my head to the side in confusion.

"I thought I told you I wanted you spread out on the kitchen counter for me?"

I absolutely remember the text he sent me earlier this afternoon, but he's just too fun to tease.

I raise a brow as a smirk forms on my lips and playfully push him away from me. "Hmm, I don't recall."

I sidestep him and make my way to the kitchen, feeling Logan's presence behind me. I stop and turn when I reach the counter, gripping the hem of my tank top to toss to the ground. "This counter? Oh, that's right. You said this is what you wanted for dinner."

His Adam's apple bobs with a swallow as he nods.

I keep my eyes fixed on his as I hook a finger in the waistband of my shorts, letting them fall to my ankles with my panties. As soon as I kick them away, I lift myself up on the counter.

The cold granite against my skin is quickly replaced with warmth when Logan positions himself between my legs and wraps his arms around me to pull me into him.

He looks me deep in the eyes like he wants to say something but can't find the words.

"I missed you, Logan."

He presses his lips to mine again in response, silently saying it back to me. I don't regret saying how I feel, but I've also learned that Logan has difficulty with feelings and words. The few times he's spoken up about things, it felt like it took everything out of him.

I kiss him back, wrapping my arms around his neck and tangling my hands in his hair. I can already feel his growing erection between my legs, and it lights an even bigger fire inside of me.

His hand trails up my back until I feel his palm along the side of my neck, his thumb resting over my pounding pulse. Another moan escapes my lips and into his mouth. He eats every sound as if he's starved for it.

He grinds into me the same way I do him, causing friction between my legs and an urge to take his cock out.

"Fuck, Em." He breathes against my lips. "You're driving me insane."

"Me?" I scoff.

"Yes, you. You answer the door in those tempting shorts, wearing nothing but a tank top and expecting me to exchange pleasantries. When all I can think about is fucking you against this counter."

My heart rate spikes at his admission, and I feel my breaths coming out quicker. As if he senses it, a smile crosses his lips, and his hands move to grip my thighs as he spreads them open wider before taking a step back.

I'm completely open and on display for him.

"Is this what you wanted?" he asks.

I nod eagerly in response.

"I like hearing your words, Em. Tell me exactly what it was you wanted when you asked me to come over tonight."

I swallow past the lump lodged in my throat. Talking about sex has always been hard for me. Yet, with Logan it comes so easily.

"I really want to feel you inside of me again."

A growl vibrates through his chest.

"Unfortunately, you'll have to wait." He lowers himself between my legs, taking in the sight before him before he peppers kisses along my inner thigh. Then he repeats the move on the other leg. "I *need* to have a taste of this. It's been too fucking long."

Then he kisses me right where I have been aching for him to kiss me again. The contact causes me to sit back on my hands, spreading my legs as wide as they can go.

His tongue swipes through, reaching my clit, and my back completely arches. My head falls back, and I moan at the intense pleasure I feel while he circles my clit in a rhythmic pattern. My hips move on their own accord, chasing his mouth.

I'd like to think this is all related to missing him and the buildup in anticipation of seeing him tonight.

But it's most certainly not.

This is all Logan. He makes me feel alive.

"Down here," his raspy voice says between my legs. "I need your eyes on me while I eat your pussy."

Oh my god.

I open my eyes and look down at him, propping myself on my elbows for a better view. His eyes are looking up at me, and just seeing him between my legs does something to me.

My legs already feel weak, but I lift them and rest my feet on his shoulders. He uses his hands to cup my inner thighs, spreading me even wider so I can get a good look.

He smirks up at me while one hand leaves my thigh before he drives two fingers inside of me. Hard and fast while he latches his lips over my clit.

"Fuck, Logan," I cry out, my body lifting off of the counter. "Oh my god."

"Tell me how you feel. Keep using your words for me."

"So good. So, *so* good," I moan, my voice rising as the pleasure only intensifies.

"You're dripping down my hand already. You're so nice and wet for me," Logan groans. "I can't wait to slide my cock in you and fuck you hard and fast."

"Logan," I scream through my pants. I dig my fingers into his hair, keeping my eyes fixed on him. "Keep talking."

He looks up at me again but not lifting his head an inch away from my pussy.

"I didn't hear you say please."

"Please," I beg. "You… you're going to make me come. I want to come."

"That's the goal. I'll make you come so hard that you'll see stars. And when you're done, I'll make you come again around my cock. You think you'll be able to do that for me?"

I'm barely able to get a nod out because his tongue flicks over my clit faster and with more pressure, moving at the same speed his fingers fuck me. He curves them slightly and I do exactly what he said I was going to do.

I come fast and hard.

My vision blurs at the intensity of this orgasm as my legs quiver around him, my head falls back, and I scream out his name repeatedly as he removes his fingers and drives his tongue into me. Tasting every drop of my orgasm.

I barely have a moment to breathe before he lifts himself up, hovering over me and claiming my mouth with his.

I melt into the kiss, tasting myself on him as he kisses me

with more desire than he ever has before. This kiss is wildly different from the others. It's laced with need and urgency.

It's one that tells me he wants every single part of me.

I reach down and hook a finger into the waistband of his shorts to push them down to free his cock, not releasing myself from his kiss.

"I need you inside of me," I moan against his lips.

He kisses me again and backs away. "Hold on. I need a condom."

I grab his backside so he doesn't move far away. "No. I need you inside of me now."

"Em." He says my name with pain in his voice. He presses his hips into me, and the head of his cock lines up with my entrance. He puts the smallest amount of pressure, letting the tip graze my pussy. "That's dangerous. I've never been with anyone without a condom before."

"Neither have I," I pant. "I'm safe. I've been tested recently."

"Me too." He scans my features. "Are you absolutely sure?"

I nod, pulling him into me, the tip grazing me again. "I need you, Logan."

The statement is more than just needing him inside me for sex. It means so much more than that. Logan has become my safe space. The calm to the raging storm in my head.

He doesn't say another word and slowly presses into me. Inch by inch, until he's completely seated inside of me. But he doesn't move or pull out. He stays right where he is, pressed into me with his eyes locked on mine.

"Are you ok?" I ask.

He shakes his head. "If I move right now, I'm going to come in three seconds."

I can't help but chuckle.

"Stop. Don't laugh, and don't move. I'm not joking."

I bite my bottom lip and buck my hips up into him because there's nothing more I want than to see him come undone.

For me.

He grips my hips hard as his eyes flutter closed.

His brown eyes are replaced with a storm cloud when he opens them again. A feral beast I just unleashed with one small move of my hips.

He moves his hand to my chest and pushes me down until my back is flat against the counter. His fingertips trail the spot between my breast, down to my naval, until he reaches the spot where my panties usually rest.

He replaces his fingers with his palm as he presses down and slowly pulls himself out of me and thrusts hard into me.

I let out a scream filled with pleasure.

"Your pussy was made for me, Emiline. Every single inch of you was made for me."

His thumb moves down and he presses it against my clit, forcing my back to fly off the counter. But he's quick to press me back down.

"Oh my god," I moan.

He picks up speed with every thrust. Fucking me hard and fast, like he promised he would. I bring my hands over my head, gripping the opposite edge of the counter. It's almost too much to bear.

"Tell me how you feel," he asks again.

"I feel so full. Your cock feels so good."

He growls and picks up speed. My words unleash more of a beast than before. His hands grip my waist so hard, I'm sure I'll see bruises there tomorrow and don't even have it in me to care.

"Harder," I pant.

"Beg for it. I want to hear you begging for my cock."

"Fuck me harder, Logan. Please. You feel so good. I need more."

He lifts himself up higher on his feet, reaching over my body to grip my shoulders. I look up at him, and he brings his bottom lip between his teeth. He slowly pulls out and drives his cock full hilt into me.

"Yes," I scream.

He repeats the move, slowly pulling out before thrusting hard inside of me.

"I'm going to come," I say between ragged breaths.

"Not. Yet."

"I don't think I can hold back," I tell him honestly. The pleasure is so intense right now if he repeats that move one more time, I'm a goner.

"You can. And you will. You will not come until I tell you to come. Understood?"

I nod my head in understanding, but my body and brain are not connected right now.

He's completely taken control here.

It turns me on so much that I don't think any part of me is listening to what he's demanding.

He closes his eyes and grips my shoulders tighter. The move forces me to stay in place as he picks up speed and simply fucks me to oblivion. The look on his face tells me he's trying to hold back himself.

"Logan." I bring his attention back to me, and his eyes snap open. "Come with me."

He groans under his breath, and for once, it's my words that send him over the edge. His abs contract, and we both fall into our orgasm together. A mix of moaning and screaming as I say his name, and he screams mine.

I've obviously had my share of orgasms with Logan before. Still, there's something about this one that solidifies everything between us. This wasn't just a quick fuck for either of us, this was explosive chemistry.

This was our bodies coming together figuratively and literally.

After a minute, we both come down from our highs. He slowly pulls out of me and rounds the counter to grab a rag from the cabinet where he knows I keep the clean ones. I hear the water turn on, but I can't find the energy to lift myself off the counter to see what he's doing.

"I have zero energy left in me," I tell him from where I still lay on the counter.

He laughs. "Here."

I open my eyes and find his hand there for me to take as he lifts me off the counter. Then he does something that I never expected him to do. He lifts me bridal style in his arms and walks me into my bathroom.

Neither of us say a word to each other.

He sits me down on the bathroom counter and turns on the bath for me. My lips part in a mix of shock and admiration for this man. I wasn't sure Logan was this type of man. But watching him draw a bath for me, checking to make sure the water is warm, and using my favorite bubbles on the edge makes my heart burst.

I could love this man if he let me.

He lifts me off the counter and places me in the tub, kneeling beside me as he uses my scrub brush to wash my body.

"I'm sorry if I was too rough with you," he says, breaking the silence.

"Don't be." I smile at him.

"Did I hurt you? I'm afraid I left bruises on your hips or your shoulders."

I shake my head. "I'm already a little sore, but the good kind."

He doesn't answer back, just continues to wash me.

This whole night and this little interaction with him only makes me want more with him. I knew this would happen from the start. I knew that if I opened up my heart for him, that there's a chance it might break.

But there's a part of me that believes he won't do that.

There's no way he didn't feel what I felt tonight.

It was more than just sex.

"I missed you too," Logan says. "You told me earlier that you missed me. I just wanted you to know I missed you too."

My hand finds the back of his neck, and my fingers tangle in his messy hair.

"Will you stay the night?" I ask.

He nods.

After my bath is over. I pull out an extra toothbrush I had in a drawer and give it to Logan. Then we both get ready for bed, and I hate my mind thinks about wanting to do this every day for the rest of our lives.

Once in bed, he wraps his arms, pulling me closer, and I fall asleep feeling like this is all I've ever wanted.

I fall asleep realizing we never actually ate dinner.

I fall asleep thinking about a future with him.

And for the first time in months, I sleep like a baby.

CHAPTER THIRTY-FIVE
Logan

"COME IN." I hear from the other side of the door.

I take a long, deep breath before I find the courage to open the door, knowing the current chief of police is standing on the other side, and I don't know what he's calling me here for.

"Good morning, Bennett," he says. "Have a seat. I know you're just getting off shift and the last place you want to be is my office, so I'll keep this short and sweet."

He's got that right.

I take a seat in the chair across from his desk. "What can I do for you, sir?"

"You can take this office from me and this job." He laughs.

I laugh with him, knowing he's joking, but then his face morphs into a serious expression. I haven't even been captain long enough, so he can't mean this right now.

"I know I just laughed, but I was being serious," he says, taking a seat across from me. "I know I've left you hanging since January, and it's now"—he flips through his desk calendar—"Lord, it's already March. Anyway, I want to offer you the position of Chief of Police. It would be effective at the end of June."

My eyes go wide. "You can't be serious. Sir. I mean, you can't be serious, sir."

"None of that. I've known you since you were in diapers, Bennett."

"I'd love to set up an interview date for it," I tell him.

He shakes his head. "Unnecessary. You were our only candidate up to take my position. Either you're the only one stupid enough to want this kind of work, or no one is reading their emails about deadlines. Either way, it's yours if you want it."

My brain swirls a mile a minute with this new information. I walked into his office, ready to go home and go to bed for the day, and now my heart's racing, and adrenaline is pumping through my body.

I have worked so hard to achieve this position.

I never thought about how it would make me feel to actually get it.

"I see the wheels in your head spinning," he jokes. "You don't have to give me an answer right now, but I'd love to retire by the end of June. You know I'm not an emotional guy, and I don't do the sappy shit, but Logan…"

My heart stops at his use of my first name.

Chief has known me my whole life, and he's only ever addressed me by my last name. It makes this feel entirely too personal.

"You've worked your way up the ladder and earned everything you've been given because you worked hard for it. I've never known an officer in any of my units to put their job before anything else."

I give him a curt nod because he's right.

No one on the force cares more about their job than I do.

That's because I don't have what they have. They have families, wives, and things to go home to. They have lives outside of work when I've made my job my entire life.

That immediately makes me think about Emiline. Do I now

have someone to go home to? Is she my person? Is there a future there?

"Can I let you know soon?" I ask him.

"Of course. Go home, sleep, and we can talk about it later."

I offer him a quick goodbye and make my way out the door.

My brain's running faster than my feet can walk me to my truck.

I think about this new offer. About Emiline and what's truly going on between us. I think about what my future might look like if I say yes to this job and make things official with her. I also think about what her brothers will think about all of this.

I pull my phone from my pocket and text the one person who I know can talk me through this mess in my head.

> I need a boxing session later tonight.

SILAS

> See you there at 6pm.

———

"Did you get any sleep today?" Silas asks. "You seem more sluggish than usual during our warm-up."

"No," I answer honestly, unscrewing the cap to my water bottle and taking a long swig. "I couldn't sleep."

"Did you get in that much trouble meeting with the chief this morning?" he jokes.

I look him dead in the eyes with a blank look on my face.

"Oh shit." His expression turns serious. "Is this a conversation we should have had over drinks?"

"No. I needed this. I needed to just think about things. You know, talk things through with you."

"Aww, you love me."

"Shut up."

I sit down on the edge of the boxing ring, and Silas joins me.

A few moments pass before I finally have the courage to say something.

"He offered me his position."

"No way. That's amazing, Bennett. You should be so proud of yourself."

"I am," I answer, but my tone lacks emotion.

"Now tell me why you don't seem happy about it."

"A lot has changed."

"You mean what you have going on with Emiline?" he asks.

I nod.

Silas is the only person in the world who knows about what's been going on with Emiline. While I don't see her nearly as much as I'd like to, the thought that I miss her when I'm not with her scares the daylights out of me.

I was adamant about not wanting a relationship.

She didn't either.

But when things shifted around us, and I realized I couldn't be without her, we ended up in this situation, with me falling for her harder than I intended to.

"I don't know what I want anymore," I admit. "One day, I'm dead set on making my job my entire life. The next, I'm…"

"Falling for your best friend's little sister."

I cringe. The way he says it sounds so wrong. He makes it sound like committing a sin.

But I won't lie to myself. I can't lie to myself.

I've fallen for her. I wouldn't call it love. But it's there.

"Logan," he says with a sigh. "You know it's okay to change paths, right? It's okay to want something different and change your mind. The future is not black and white. It can change in an instant."

I feel a mix of emotions building inside of me.

If anyone knows that, it's me.

"I just don't know how to handle the—" I'm cut off when the door of the boxing room creaks open.

As if I thought her into existence, Emiline stands there looking around the room before her eyes land on us. She smiles and lifts her hand in a wave before walking over.

Neither one of us moves from where we sit.

"Hi, guys," she says. "Sorry to bother, I was just finishing a workout and thought I'd swing in to see if you were here," she says, looking at me.

"I was just heading out," Silas says.

"Oh no." She waves her hands in the air. "Don't leave because of me. I was just saying hi before I left. I'll head out."

Silas looks from me to her before looking back at me and giving me a tight nod.

Emiline watches as he silently grabs his bag and leaves the room. My head falls and I look down at the ground. My body is drained of any energy to stand up and greet her.

On top of it, my brain is a mess of emotion right now, and the last thing I want is for her to see me like this.

She doesn't say anything and crouches down in front of me. She rests both hands on my thigh, begging me to look at her. I can't. Not right now. Not when my head is not in the right place.

"What's going on, Logan?" Her voice is so soft and comforting. Like she can wrap me up in her words and hold me there, getting rid of every negative thought in my head.

"I'm good."

She stands, taking a step between my legs. Her hand gripping my jaw forces me to look up at her. "What's. Going. On."

My eyes fall closed, and my hands come up to wrap around her. I press my head into her stomach and just breathe her in.

She's here.

In my arms and asking me to tell her what's happening in my head.

"I'm a mess," I exhale against her shirt. "I don't need you to see me like this."

"I think it's only right since you've seen me at my worst," she says.

I look up at her, my chin resting against her. She's smiling and everything in me calms down just by seeing the look on her face.

"Talk to me, Logan."

I shake my head. "I can't."

"Why?"

I swallow. "I'm supposed to be strong for *you*. I'm supposed to be your rock and who you run to when in need. I'm supposed to be the person who carries whatever you need with me on my shoulders."

"And who is that person for you?"

I fight to keep my emotions stuffed down.

No sleep.

A meeting with the chief.

Life changing before my eyes.

My future changing.

"I… I don't know," I admit.

"Let me be your person then." She takes her hand in my jaw again until I look up at her. She brings her other hand up so that now both cups my cheeks. She offers me a soft smile. "Let me in."

It's the same thing I've said to her so many times.

I inhale slowly, and the scent of honey and vanilla engulfs me before I release an exhale. This is where Emiline learns *my* weaknesses.

"All my life, I've wanted to be like my dad. I wanted to follow in his footsteps and make him proud of the man I've become. I've made my job my life to get to the point of making that dream a reality."

She nods, lowering herself to eye level with me, intently listening to every word that rolls out of my mouth.

"I had a meeting with the chief this morning. He's offering me his position. He wants me to take over as chief of police."

"Logan, that's amazing."

I don't smile and don't acknowledge her words.

"But everything in my life has changed…" I pause, looking her deep in the eyes and hoping like hell she understands what I mean by that. "So much that I'm not sure it's what I want anymore. I'm left here wondering what I even want in life."

She stares at me with confusion written all over her face.

"You, Emiline. I want *you*."

She stands, taking a tentative step back as if my words kicked her in the stomach.

I reach up, taking both of her hands in mine as I stand before her. "In a good way."

"I don't understand."

"I lost my dad after he picked up an overtime shift to help the department. I was young and begged him to get pizza on the way home. Of course, he did because he would do anything for us."

All the emotions I fought so hard to keep down come to the surface. I blink them away, but it's no use. Saying them out loud to her only makes them that much more real.

"He was more than just a father to me; we was my hero and a role model. I was a twelve-year old boy begging his dad to stop and pick up a pizza on the way home from an extra shift he worked because the station was short-staffed. He was the type of man who would do anything to make his family happy. On his way back, he got stuck in traffic and decided to try a different route when another car ran a red light and slammed straight into him. He was pronounced dead at the scene."

She gasps, her hand flying to her chest.

"I-I'm so sorry."

"Losing him the way I did and being as young as I was changed me in a lot of ways I wasn't ready for. Growing up, I swore I would do whatever it took to follow in his footsteps and become a cop," I continue. "Putting my job first before anything and anyone. Mostly out of fear of putting someone I care so much about in the same situation my mom and I were left in."

Emiline only stares at me, void of expression on her face.

"Which is why I said I *can't* do relationships, Emiline. I'm fucking terrified of something happening to me. Leaving you the way my dad left us," I choke out the last words.

Her hands fly to my face. She pauses, scanning my features before she throws her arms around my neck, pulling me in for a hug. This feels good. Letting it out with her and feeling her comfort me the way she is.

I hate her knowing this.

I hate her seeing me like this.

"You don't have to be afraid with me," she whispers against the shell of my ear.

I finally wrap my arms around her, holding her tighter than I ever have before. Afraid that if I let go, she's going to slip through my fingers.

"Yes, I do."

She pulls her head back.

"You scare the shit out of me, Em. More than my job does. More than the future does. You were the curveball thrown into my life. You have derailed my plans and made me want new things to the point I question whether I even want this position anymore."

"You deserve that position."

"I do," I agree. "But I'm not so sure I deserve you."

She shakes her head, pulling away from me again, which only irritates me.

I fight her by pulling her back into me. "But I want to. I want to be good enough for you."

"You are. Logan, don't you see that? You've been the one to pull me out of my deepest days. You've been my person from the moment you learned all the weakest parts of me and you still stuck around."

My head falls to her shoulder. This time, I allow the tears to fall. I allow everything I've always held back to come to the surface.

"I'm not going anywhere," I say against her skin.
"Good. Neither am I."
For the first time in a long time, I let someone hold me.
And fuck, it feels good.

CHAPTER THIRTY-SIX
Emiline

I FINALLY MEET up with Avery and Macey for a late lunch.

Avery and I get a seat at the table while we wait for Macey because she worked the afternoon shift today.

"You look exhausted," Avery says to me.

"I am."

"You're on spring break, right?"

"Yes. God, not having to go to lectures this week is such a relief. I've never been more ready for graduation."

"Almost there, girlfriend. I can't wait to watch you cross that stage at graduation. I'll probably be the loudest one there screaming your name." She laughs.

She's not wrong. I know my brothers will be cheering me on, but Avery has a voice that will carry, and I can't wait for that moment.

From day one of school, my driving force to keep going has been the thought of crossing that stage to get my diploma as a graduate of the accelerated nursing program.

To some, it may not seem like something that big. But for me, it's not just about walking across the stage. It's about walking across that stage and seeing the look on my brothers' faces, showing me how proud they are of me. Showing them I can do it and that I made something of myself.

"I can't wait," I say instead of getting too deep with her.

"The plan I think is for all of us to be there," she continues. "I wonder if Oliver is going to bring Macey."

"I don't think it's that serious between them."

She gives me a knowing grin. "You forget that I know everything."

My stomach sinks with her admission. I've had a feeling she's been on to me for a while now with what's happening between me and Logan. She's good at picking up on things before anyone else does. If the two of us couldn't fight off the tension floating around us in the past, there's no doubt that she's picked up on it too.

"I'm willing to bet she walks in here all glowy and thoroughly fucked," she adds.

"Avery," I scold. "I don't want to know this about my brothers."

As she's about to say something back, Macey walks into the restaurant. And of course, Avery was right.

"Drink on you," Avery says.

I roll my eyes. "Fine."

"What's going on?" Macey asks.

"We took bets on how much you'd be glowing when you walked in here after your rendezvous with Oliver." Avery winks.

Macey's cheeks turn pink as she sits down. "That obvious, huh?"

"Yes. Now spill." Avery leans forward on both elbows with her hands clasped together under her chin.

I internally chuckle at her, but I focus my conversation on Macey and the details about her trip with my brother, hoping she avoids the intimate ones.

Avery calms her nerves by telling her the story about how she and Marc got together.

"Yeah." Avery laughs. "I didn't want to do it because I'd

never been in a relationship. I swore off all men because of some daddy issues, which is a story for another day. Still, the point is, I was in a similar situation and I was scared out of my mind because I never had feelings for a man before Marc."

"Her admitting that is a lot," I add. "Avery doesn't do feelings."

"Facts," Avery exclaims with a finger in the air.

"You two looked so in love when I met you that time in the mountains, though," Macey says.

Avery nods. "That was for show. But things were already escalating quickly at that point. I was trying to fight off the feelings I knew I had for him, but just didn't know how."

"How did you handle it?" Macey asks.

Avery holds up her hand to show off the diamond on her ring finger. "I fell anyway. I just had to let him catch me."

Just hearing Avery talk about how she fell in love when it was the last thing she wanted makes me wonder if that's what's happening between Logan and I.

Am I in love with him?

I mean, my feelings for him are so strong that I feel them deep to my core.

I want a life with him.

I want to keep this up after graduation.

"I guess I'm just nervous after hearing about his history with women," Macey continues. "I'm not as experienced as he is so I'm unsure how to process all of it. What if he gets bored with me? What if he ends up changing his mind in a month? I don't know how the male mind works."

"I'd never lie to you about things like this," I tell her honestly. "Oliver was kind of a playboy for a long time. He's always lived carefree and like every day is his last. But he hasn't talked to my brothers about that stuff since his birthday trip last year."

"How would you know what he talks to his brothers about?" Avery raises a brow in my direction. "Marc says he doesn't talk to you about those things."

Shit. Avery is about to call me out.

"I mean… I'm just assuming."

"Are you assuming? Or is Logan telling you about the conversations they have at the bar when they go out Wednesday nights?" Avery says with an accusing tone.

I feel my cheeks turn crimson red with how she's calling me out like this. I feel guilty, like I'm hiding something, but Logan and I have never talked about his nights out with my brothers.

I'm being honest in saying I'm assuming.

So why do I feel guilty?

"I fully plan to circle back to this new revelation after you continue with what you were saying about Oliver to Macey," Avery says. "Because I'm sick and tired of you two hiding whatever relationship you are having behind our backs."

"There's—" I start, but pause quickly as my lips close with a tight seal.

Would it be so bad if I told them?

Avery won't say anything and I doubt Macey will either.

I should really get this off my chest.

"Fine," I concede. "I'll tell you guys everything after, but if I find out it got back to my brothers, you're all fucking dead."

"Fine, continue," Avery encourages her.

I look back to Macey to continue even though the nerves in my stomach are at an all-time high. "Like I was saying, Oliver changed his ways after his birthday trip. He hasn't been with anyone since he met you. I'm not just talking about when he saw you again at the bar you worked at. I'm talking about that first flight you two took from Montana to New York."

My hands fall to my thighs and my breathing picks up.

I try to focus on the conversation in front of us, but I'm also terrified that Avery will 'circle back' to this.

"I think I'm really falling in love with him." Macey sighs.

"Oh, babe." Avery chuckles.

"You fell a long time ago," I finish for her.

Avery continues laughing while Macey sits there smiling. I know the look on my face is one Avery can read.

"You did too, Emiline." Avery winks.

"Huh?"

"I told you I was going to circle back. We solved Macey's problem, and now it's your turn."

"I don't have a problem," I say.

"Tell us about Logan," Avery urges.

I look from her to Macey and back at her.

"I won't tell Oliver if that's what you're worried about," Macey adds with a shrug. "You look kind of nervous. Call it mom instinct."

It's taken me a lot to fully trust someone.

I learned to trust Logan, so I know I can trust these two now.

"So, a little over a year ago—"

Avery spits out her drink. "Are you kidding me? It's been over a year?"

"Would you let me finish?"

"Proceed. I have to hear this." Avery sits forward more in her chair.

"It started when I thought he couldn't stand me. He started treating me differently, and I just felt so off around him. I don't know how to explain it. We had a very heated coffee shop run-in, and things always seemed so weird when he would show up in the ER."

"I hate that feeling," Macey says. "It's like something is wrong, but he can't communicate it."

"Yes," I emphasize. "Then one night I was in the library studying and…"

I didn't think this through. I didn't know how to tell this story without telling them about my panic attacks. I fall completely silent and still. My hands tremble under the table and I look down at them.

I'm going to have to lie to my friends.

I can't let them know just yet. I'm not ready.

"And?" Avery asks, eager to hear the story for the juicy details.

"And someone was creeping me out," I lie. "I called Thomas and Marc, but neither of them answered. It was a Wednesday, so I called Logan to see if he was with them so someone could come get me. He wasn't with them anymore but he showed up.

"He started getting slightly protective over me and ensured I was okay after class and studying. I thought it was because he saw me as his little sister or something, but—"

"It wasn't." Avery interrupts, grinning wildly. "I knew I saw something there. I suspected it for a while, but Peyton's wedding confirmed it. I wanted to fuck you both with how hot you looked on the dance floor."

"Avery," Macey scolds.

"Emiline knows this is who I am."

"I do." I chuckle behind my hand. "But yeah, things are definitely taking a turn now. We're seeing each other a lot more. And doing… things."

Avery rolls her eyes. "Just say the word. It won't bite."

I look around to make sure no one's listening. "Sex."

I cover my face with my hands while Avery laughs across the table. "I love you so much, Emiline."

"I love you too," I tell her.

"So you two are officially a thing?" Macey asks curiously.

I lift a shoulder. "Truthfully? I don't even know anymore. Our plan was to wait until after graduation to talk to my brothers. It's hard to hide or deny how we feel when we're around each other anymore."

"I get that." Macey nods. "Are you afraid of them finding out?"

I look her dead in the eyes. "Macey, I'm shaking in my seat just telling you two. Hell yeah, I'm scared. They are going to murder him. I'm their baby sister."

"I can hold Marc back." Avery grins. "I know exactly what to do that gets him to stop worrying about everyone else and focus only on me."

"Don't even tell me," I beg.

She extends an arm toward Macey. "Maybe Macey wants to know."

"She doesn't."

"I'm kind of curious." Macey giggles.

Avery turns to face her. "I usually drop to my knees first, and then I let him fuck me from behind."

"I'm begging you! Please stop."

"Well…" Macey's eyes go wide. "I was not expecting that. But back to your current dilemma"—she turns to face me again —"I think if you two feel the way you do about each other, you should see where it goes and stand together when everyone else finds out. It's just a bump in the road for you two that you can overcome together. It will only make you that much stronger in the end."

Macey's advice fills me with a sense of warmth and comfort.

I only have to make it till graduation hiding this secret from everyone else.

Three more months until the inevitable storm hits, and I'm bracing myself for it.

CHAPTER THIRTY-SEVEN

Logan

April

How's studying going?

EMILINE

Good. I think.

I don't know, the words are blurring together.

I'm going to the gym if you want to join me and take a break.

EMILINE

Boxing or lifting?

Boxing. I get my lifting workout tossing you around in the bedroom now 😏

EMILINE

I like that kind of workout

Come with me.

Please.

I showed up at her place thirty minutes after sending the text, even though she never responded.

I woke up this afternoon after working last night, and the first thought I had when I opened my eyes was Emiline. I'm still scared of where we'll end up and what will happen, but I don't care about my fears anymore.

I want it.

I want her.

Emiline opens the door and I drink her in like a glass of whiskey. She's wearing her black biker shorts and an oversized T-shirt with her hair pulled back in a ponytail.

"Ready for the gym?"

She rolls her eyes. "I guess I'm going to have to be. I don't feel like going, but you asked nicely." She takes a step toward me, wrapping her arms around my waist while I wrap mine around her head, pulling her face to my chest.

"Where's Silas?" she asks, knowing he's my go-to person for this.

"He had an emergency vet visit for his dog."

She nods and goes to grab her things for the gym. "Grab a sweatshirt," I call out.

"It's like 75 degrees out," she says, coming back to the living room.

"We're taking the bike."

Her eyes widen in fear. "Logan. I can't get on that thing again. It scared the hell out of me the last time I was on the back of it."

I smirk. "You trust me, Em?"

Her features soften as she reaches into her small closet behind her door and pulls out a sweatshirt.

Not just any sweatshirt… mine.

"I trust you," she confirms.

I take her hand in mine and don't let go as we walk down the stairwell to the garage where I park my bike.

I needed this today.

I needed her.

I had another meeting with the chief earlier. He asked if I'd decided because a month has passed since he first gave me the offer.

The old me would have given him an answer that day, but now, I can't make decisions about my future without seeing if what I have with Emiline is real.

It feels real.

I just need to make sure she feels the same.

But what if I say no to the opportunity I've worked so hard for, only for Emiline to decide to end things because the pressure from her brothers is too much? What if she graduates and wants to date other people?

I should focus on the present, but I'm the type of guy who worries about the future. I can't make a plan right now without knowing for sure.

Once we reach my bike, I hand her the helmet she wore the first day I picked her up. She puts it on effortlessly now as if she's practiced since that night.

Things are different this time because she's not coming down from a panic attack. She's stronger than she's ever been, if that's at all possible. She's always been strong. She just needed someone to tell her.

I remain silent as I throw my leg over the bike, taking my helmet from the handlebars and sliding it over my head.

I lift the visor and turn to face Emiline. I pat the small seat behind me, urging her to climb on.

Placing both hands on my shoulders to balance herself, she hikes a leg over the bike and situates herself behind me before she grabs my waist.

"Closer," I say over my shoulder. "I need you closer."

She scoots until she's flush with my back. I will myself to keep my breaths even and steady. Nerves spike inside of me because even though she trusts me and I asked her to, I don't trust people on the surrounding roads.

I turn the key in the ignition, and the bike rumbles under us. Loud enough that it echoes through the parking garage.

My hand finds Emiline's on my waist and I bring it to rest flat against my stomach. She does the same with her other hand without me even telling her.

Such a good girl.

"Ready?" I ask, putting on my riding gloves.

"I think so."

"Do not let go of me."

Her palms press into my stomach, telling me she understands what I'm asking, but she says the words I need anyway. "I won't."

I pull out of the parking garage and onto the street. The ride to the gym is only a couple of blocks and I wish it would last longer. The feeling of having her against me on the bike makes me want to never let her go.

When I turn onto the main street that leads to the gym, I keep one hand on the throttle and use my other hand to cover hers. I intertwine our fingers as she holds me tighter than before.

I want to turn this bike around, skip the gym and get her in bed, holding her the way I really want to hold her right now.

But the gym coming into view erases those thoughts.

I throw the bike in park and she leaps off it as if it's on fire.

I turn off the engine, remove my helmet and dismount before my hand grips her wrist, pulling her back to me. My other hand finds the small of her back, holding her flush to me.

She removes her helmet and her eyes bore into me with concern.

"I just needed to hold you again."

Her smile is soft and warm, like a blanket covering every part of me that needs comforting. I run my palm over the top of her head, smoothing her messy hair before finding the back of her head and pulling her for a kiss.

My lips meet hers, and everything around me blurs.

I've kissed people before, but kissing Emiline Ford feels like the world stops spinning on its axis. It awakens a part of me I never knew existed to the point where I'm ready to derail every-thing I've worked my entire life for.

It feels like giving up everything for her.

Reluctantly, I pull away from her.

"What was that?" she asks curiously.

"I've been wanting to kiss you all day, all week. I never thought I'd be the type of man to say this, but I'm starting to feel like being apart from you is slowly killing me. Like kissing you is the air I need to breathe each day."

A smile stretches across Emiline's face as her hand comes up to cup my jaw, and on instinct my face melts into it, feeling her warmth against my skin while her thumb strokes my cheekbone.

"Good thing I'm not going anywhere, and neither are you."

I nod before blindly gesturing behind us. "Let's get inside."

Once we're inside and settled, Emiline stands in the middle of the ring. The single spotlight overhead being the only thing illuminating her in the dark. I've always said she's too pure to corrupt with the darkness that lingers inside of me.

Her standing there only confirms that.

"Ready?" I ask.

Emiline nods, moving to pick up some gloves, and puts them on like she's been doing this for years. She hasn't, but we've been doing these sessions for a while now.

Both of us escape everything around us together.

She throws the first few punches into my mitts, and I see something change in her—anguish. It's like doing this is painful for her tonight.

I let her throw a few more before I wrap my hands around her forearms, stopping her in her tracks.

"Talk to me."

She shakes her head. "Keep going." She tries to throw a few more punches, but I don't let her. "Logan! Let's just do this." I toss my mitts to the side and work to remove the gloves from her hand.

She silently fights me, annoyed as hell that I'm stopping her.

"Not until you talk to me."

"I can't! Because I don't know what's wrong with me right now!" Her body sags as the tension in her evaporates. "I'm so tired. I'm so stressed. My head is a mess right now."

I throw my arms around her body, pulling her head to my chest and holding her there as tight as I can. She grips my T-shirt as she melts into my arms, and we stand like that for only a few minutes, but it feels like years.

She eventually pulls back, but I hold her shoulders so she can't go too far.

"What can I do to help?" I ask.

Emiline's hands find the side of my face again while she searches my features like she's memorizing them. I know that look because I do the same when I look at her.

Then she lifts on her toes and presses her lips to mine.

My hold on her upper arms tightens at the feel of her plush lips on me again. This is different from the kiss we had outside by my bike. This time, she's opening up for me. Wanting me. Craving me the way I always crave her.

"Emiline," I breathe out against her lips. "You can't kiss me like that here. I can't control how I respond to it."

A smirk plays on her lips.

"Emiline," I warn.

"I'm sorry." She chuckles. "When you kiss me like that, it kind of makes me go a little crazy."

A growl vibrates in my chest and straight to my cock.

I lean in, my lips grazing the shell of her ear. "When you kiss *me* like that, it makes me want to bend you over right here in the middle of the ring and spank you until my handprint marks that pretty little ass of yours red."

Emiline gasps, clearly not expecting me to say that. Then she does something *I* least expect.

She gives me a devilish grin before lifting herself on her toes to kiss me again. The same way she did before, but with more force. Her head moving to the side to deepen the kiss, arching her back into me in hopes of feeling my reaction to her.

I'm sure she does because my cock is on full alert from this.

"I warned you."

She pulls back, the grin on her face and less than an inch from my lips. "I know."

My resolve snaps and I no longer give a fuck where we are.

I spin her around, placing a palm on her stomach while my other hand grips the back of her neck to bring her back flush against my front. I force her to bend at the waist while I thrust my hips into her.

"This what you want, Em? To drive me so crazy my cock is begging to be inside of you?"

"I mean… we have the place to ourselves, right?"

We do. I have a key to the place because the owner knows me enough to trust me to take care of it even when he's not here. He trusts that Silas and I will come in to box and leave.

I hook my fingers into the waistband of her shorts and push them to the ground. There's no part of me that's thinking straight right now, but Emiline has this effect on me.

She keeps herself bent at the waist, allowing me the perfect view of her ass. I take a minute to memorize it in this light. "Fuck, Em. You should see yourself right now. Ass on full display for me like you want my cock out here in the open room."

"I want your cock," she admits without missing a beat.

I raise a brow. "You're turning into quite the dirty talker, Emiline. I'm not sure how I feel about that."

My hands find her ass as I run my palm over her cheeks before giving them a tight squeeze. She fits perfectly in my hands.

I lean down to press a quick kiss to the left cheek before moving to the right. I hear a slight moan escape her just from kissing her there.

My hand then reaches between her thighs, and my middle

finger finds her clit instantly. She's soaked and throbbing for me already. I rub slow circles repeatedly, just to drive her as crazy as she drives me.

"Mmm," she hums.

"You're drenched, Em. Tell me why you're so wet right now."

"I'm like this every time you're around."

Fuck. Me.

She's just unleashed my inner beast with her confession.

I take my hand away, spinning her around as fast as I can before picking her up. She squeals in my arms, and I swallow her sounds as I kiss her with every fucking thing I have in me.

I carry her to the side of the room, placing her down before spinning her around again. Her hands find the wall in front of her, and she arches her back immediately to give me the same display of her backside again.

I push my shorts to the ground and my cock springs free, screaming and leaking from the tip already. I lean in, lips crazing her pounding pulse. "I'm not going to spank you. But I will fuck you. Hard and fast. Just the way you like it."

"Please," she pants.

"My good girl."

My hands round the back of her neck, my thumb feeling how fast her heart is racing under my touch when I press her down further, giving me better access. I grip my cock with my other hand and guide it to her entrance.

In one quick thrust, I'm deep inside of her.

Disappearing completely inside of her.

"Ahh," she screams. "Yes!"

"Yes, Em. You take my cock so well," I hiss.

I drive in and out of her, keeping a steady rhythm because she feels so good. So tight. So wet.

I watch as she takes one hand off the wall and brings it between her legs. I feel the contact on my balls as she runs circles over her clit.

"That's my girl. Touch yourself. Make yourself come for me."

"Oh, Logan," she breathes out.

There's nothing better than the sound of my name on her lips when I'm inside of her feeling every muscle contract around me, feeling her lose control only for me. This isn't just sex anymore. It's wild and frenzied and everything we both need.

I pause my movements, driving in as far as I can go and holding myself there as I lean over her back. Close enough to her ear so she can hear me.

"I'm yours, Emiline. I'm all fucking yours. Now show me how your pretty pussy can mess up my cock."

"Fuck," she moans louder. She presses her ass into me as I drive in and out of her again, meeting my moves thrust for thrust. Her walls pulse around me, and I know she's close. She puts both hands back on the wall, and my hands grip her shoulders from behind.

"Yes, Em. That's it. Come for me."

"I'm coming." Her breaths come out ragged and harsh.

I pick up my pace, reveling in the feel of her around me. Then her body trembles under my hands. A mix of profanities and my name on her lips as her orgasm hits her like a tsunami wave.

Mine does the same.

My stomach contracts and I release everything I have inside of her.

Everything around me is a complete blur, except for her. I've never seen *her* more clearly than I do right now.

We might be keeping our relationship a secret, but she's mine in every sense of the word.

CHAPTER THIRTY-EIGHT
Emiline

May

MY ALARM GOES off at five and I shoot out of bed faster than I ever have. The anxiety of the day barely let me get a wink of sleep last night.

It's our final exam day, the culmination of years of hard work and dedication in our nursing program.

Not just any final exam, but our last one as a nursing student.

Lying in bed last night, I kept replaying disease processes in my head. But I also kept telling myself that I've made it this far, that I *can* and I *will* make it through.

It doesn't make me any less anxious though.

My negative thoughts creep in. My thoughts of self-doubt and not feeling good enough. The idea of making it this far, and this taking me out.

Imagine I fail it so severely I have to retake the last semester over again?

I tossed and turned every time that last idea crossed my mind.

I brush my teeth and get dressed before going to the kitchen to make two cups of coffee. As soon as it stops brewing, Brooke comes out of the guest bedroom.

"You're truly a sick individual for being up with the sun today of all days," Brooke groans as I slide the cup of iced coffee in front of her. "But I love you for filling me with caffeine."

"You know I'm up early on exam days."

"I didn't think it was *this* early."

"It's usually not." I laugh. "But I barely slept last night. I'm so nervous about this exam."

"We got this, Em. You know we do," she reassures me.

Brooke's soft tone makes me feel more at ease. She and I have the same brain. We study together, and tend to get similar grades, so hearing her say it really lessens the heavy weight sitting on my chest right now.

Brooke has no idea the power behind her words, either. I had no idea that she was spending the night, so I didn't spiral into a full-blown panic attack this morning since Logan had to work last night.

I asked her on a whim, claiming we can review together in the morning before we leave and without hesitation, she said yes.

I've said it before and it's worth saying again, I don't know what I'd do on this journey without her.

"Did you want to review the study guides before we leave in nine hundred hours?"

"Don't be dramatic. The exam is at eight."

Brooke looks at her wrist where there is no watch in sight. "And it's five."

I grin. "Just enough time."

"You're annoying as hell."

"And you love me for it."

We drink our coffee and spend the next hour reviewing practice questions in the back of our books. Then, we pull up the online resource the college provided us and do some more there together. We talked through the ones we got wrong, discussing the rationale behind each answer and reinforcing our understanding of the material.

I finally decide to take a shower and attempt to shut my mind off for the next twenty minutes.

I can do this.

I've made it this far. I can make it through this.

There's no need to panic.

I wonder if I should call Logan and just listen to his peace of mind. I know he's sleeping and wouldn't mind if I woke him up for this, but I decide against it.

I can do this.

I finally leave the bathroom and find Brooke in the living room, waiting for me.

"You got this," she tells me, as if she's heard all my thoughts.

I smile at her. "*We* got this."

And for the first time in a while, I believe it.

———

"I can't believe this is our last test ever," Brooke says next to me.

"Don't forget the boards."

"The big one that makes us officially nurses," she squeals. "I am so excited for this. We did it, Emiline. We made it to the end and are about to each live out our dream of being nurses."

I smile over at her as we walk the last block to class.

Just as we round the last corner, the campus comes into view, and I stop dead in my tracks. Brooke notices and looks from me to the front of the building and back to me, and a broad smile fills her face.

"You're one lucky girl," she whispers before walking ahead of me and leaving me behind.

I stand still. Frozen. My feet are cemented to the concrete.

Logan takes a few steps off the stairs and approaches me.

He's here.

He showed up… for me.

"W-What are you doing here? Shouldn't you be sleeping?"

He stops in front of me, brushing a stray strand of hair away from my face and behind my ear. "You didn't think I was going to miss you going into your last nursing school exam, did you?"

"I mean… yeah. You worked. You should be sleeping."

His hands reach up to hold my face, and his smile makes me want to melt. It's full of adoration and reassurance.

"I'm exactly where I want to be."

"Logan." I exhale under my breath.

"You got this," he says, then leans in to press his lips to mine. It's on the busy sidewalk of New York, out in the open for the world to see.

I sink into him, my hands gripping his T-shirt.

He showed up for me.

Logan pulls away, keeping his lips close to mine. "I couldn't let you walk in there without you knowing how proud of you I am. You've come so far. You've sacrificed so much. And you did it, Em. This is your last hill before you graduate."

I blink away the tear that fights to come to the surface.

"I've never met someone as driven as you. I know you worry about not being good enough or you're afraid that you will fail. But you didn't fail. And you're more than enough to be a successful nurse."

I close my eyes and listen to the words he continues to say.

"When you walk in there, I want you to tune the voices in your head out that tell you otherwise. Understood?"

I open my eyes and nod in agreement.

He kisses me again, and I hate that I have to leave him like this and go inside. I just want to be out here with him, kissing him like this.

"Now, go show them what an A+ looks like."

"Thank you, Logan," I tell him, lifting on my toes and wrapping my arms around him. He returns the embrace, holding me as tight as he can.

"After graduation," Logan whispers in my neck. "After graduation, we do this for real. Just a couple more weeks."

I pull back, scanning his face for any ounce of uncertainty, but I fall short. There is none. He's being serious.

He kisses me one more time before pulling away and letting me walk into the building.

I take a few steps before I turn around to face him again.

"You're always showing up for me on your birthday, huh?"

He smirks. "You remembered?"

"I always remember when it comes to you."

He shakes his head because he knows he's used those exact words with me before. We both turn to go our separate ways.

There are no longer any questioning feelings in my mind.

I'm in love with Logan Bennett.

CHAPTER THIRTY-NINE
Logan

EMILINE

I did it! I passed my exam. I'm officially a
nursing school graduate!

OLIVER

That's my sis!

AVERY

FUCK YEAH!

PEYTON

Oh my god, you can't do this to me with my
hormones! I'm crying! We're so proud of you!

THOMAS

I knew you could do it! I'm proud of you!

MARC

Our sister is a nurse!

KALI

We didn't have any doubt that this day would
come. Amazing news!

MACEY

I'm actually crying, too. You're going to be the
best nurse.

I'm so proud of you.

MY PALMS FEEL sweaty under the table after sending that text message.

Oliver, Marc and Thomas all have their eyes on the group chat Emiline started to tell us the good news. I sat there, having no idea how to respond. I couldn't *not* respond, because it would look weird.

Are they all reading too much into my text?

"Aww. You're nice to her," Oliver coos.

I raise a brow at his comment. "As opposed to?"

"She thinks you hate her," Thomas chimes in, and I tilt my head more in confusion. "Remember that night I forced you to give her your sweatshirt? She told me then she thought you hate her."

The words come out so casually.

As if it's no big deal.

That was over a year ago. I felt justified at the time because I thought I did hate her. I *wanted* to hate her because I started looking at her differently.

I shrug a shoulder at his comment. "I don't know," I say, which is my best response to keep my mouth shut and avoid spilling the truth about what's really happening.

"Either way, that was nice of you to say that to her. I know she's hard on herself," Thomas says.

"I'm glad she's done with school now so she can come around a little more," Marc adds. "I felt terrible for all the times she couldn't make it because she was studying."

"I agree. I hated when she missed Taco Tuesday the night Macey met everyone," Oliver says.

I swallow past the lump in my throat because it's the first night they've brought this up and now all three of them have their eyes on me.

"She was studying… right, Logan?" Thomas says with a bite to his tone.

No. I took her boxing and then when we got back to her house, I had the best sex of my life.

I raise my hands in defense. "Don't look at me. I have no clue what she was doing that night," I lie.

And fuck, I hate lying to them.

It's the first time I've been questioned and forced to lie. If I tell them everything now without her here, it's going to piss her off. It's going to piss *them* off.

"We're going to murder you, ya know?" Marc jokes.

This time, I don't have it in me to throw a joke back.

"I think I'll head out guys," I tell them, standing from the chair.

"What? It's your birthday. Have another drink with us," Oliver says.

"I worked last night and barely slept today."

Because I stayed up late to kiss your sister good luck before her exam.

"Okay, that's a valid excuse." Oliver laughs.

The three men who are like brothers to me stand and hug me for my birthday and to say goodbye.

After that, I head home with only one Ford family member on my mind and wanting to see before the end of the day.

I knock on her door before my feet even come to a stop.

She opens it immediately and jumps into my arms.

"Emiline," I say, inhaling her scent as I bring my face to her neck. I've missed her, and it's only been since this morning.

She pulls back from me, smiling from ear to ear.

"I did it, Logan." She jumps up and down, gripping my upper arms in pure joy. Seeing her like this is a side I want to see every single day.

I want to make it my mission to see it every day.

"I got you something to celebrate," I tell her, holding up the bag in my hand as we make our way to the couch.

Emiline tucks herself into the couch on her heels while I sit beside her. "You didn't have to get me anything," she blushes.

"Of course I did."

I hand her the bag, and she leans over to kiss me. It's quick, kind of like a habit. A habit I'd be more than happy if it stuck around.

She sits back, the smile never leaving her face. She rips out the tissue paper, reaching into the bag before looking up at me in shock. Tears already sting her eyes as she pulls out the box.

"You got me a stethoscope?"

I nod. "I know you have one for nursing school, but I wanted to upgrade it for you."

She opens the box and pulls out the new one. It's light blue, and her name is engraved on the neck.

She puts it in her ear as if she's going to use it. She lifts the bell of the stethoscope to assess it, and she's completely in shock. That's when she notices the engraved words on the silver piece of the bell.

Emiline Ford, RN.

"Logan," she whispers. "I—uh—I don't even know what to say."

"You don't have to say anything. You did it. You're so amazing, and I'm so proud of you."

She places the stethoscope down and moves the gift bag to the side, rising to sit on my lap. She straddles me, hugging my thighs with both legs while my hands wrap around her waist on their own.

"Thank you. I couldn't have done it without you."

I look up at her, staring with nothing to say.

Because it's at this exact moment I almost say three words I've never said to anyone before. I'm not wired for those kind of words. I'm not equipped to hear them back, either.

"When is graduation?" I settle on.

"Two weeks." Her eyes bounce between mine. "My brothers are planning a celebration dinner after the ceremony. Are you coming?"

I nod.

"Maybe we can tell th—"

I cut her off by reaching up, cupping both sides of her face, and pulling her down to me for a kiss. I don't want to think about the mess this could potentially become when everyone finds out.

At least not yet.

Her hands find the side of my face as her body falls on top of mine. Chest to chest, her legs straddling me. I open up for her, allowing her tongue to swipe across mine.

My hands find the small of her back to hold her to me, and it's just enough to release a moan out of her.

"That's not what I came here for tonight," I tell her against her lips.

"But I want it. I want you. I want…." Emiline pauses, pulling back away from me just enough to reach between us and palm my cock with her hand. "This."

"Fuck."

She uses that as her time to shimmy off me, bringing herself to her knees in front of me on the couch, urging my legs to open wider for her.

"No," I stop her. "This is your day. I should be dropping to my knees for you."

She smirks up at me, reaching for the belt of my jeans to unclasp it. "You seem to forget that it's also your day."

She undoes the belt, button, and zipper and attempts to tug them off of me. I try to protest, but she looks at me with a raised eyebrow. I roll my eyes and lift off the couch just enough so she can.

"Good boy."

"Emiline," I growl in warning, but don't have a second more to protest because she wraps her hand around my length. Sliding from root to tip dangerously slowly until her palm covers the head. Wiping the pre-cum from the tip and sliding it back down my cock.

My head falls back, and she taps the top of my thigh with her fingertip. My eyes snap to hers.

"Watch me, Logan."

My dirty fucking girl.

I meet her gaze and watch as she lowers her head and drags her tongue up the base of my cock. She swirls her tongue around the head before taking me entirely in her mouth.

"Jesus Christ," I groan.

Her head moves up and down at just the right speed, bobbing in a rhythmic rhythm. When her hair falls over her face, blocking my view, I reach up and take it between my hands. Holding it there like a hair tie, keeping her hair in place.

"I wish you could see yourself right now. You take me so well in that pretty mouth of yours."

Emiline hums around my length, and the vibration goes right to my balls. If this is supposed to be for me, there is *no way* I am coming down her throat.

I cup her face and pull her up to sit on my lap.

"Logan," she protests.

"While that was the hottest fucking thing I've ever seen… I refuse to come down your throat tonight." I run both of my hands through her hair, pulling her down to me. My lips grazing her ear. "I want to come inside *my* pussy."

Emiline grins at that, pushing to stand as she tugs her shorts off quickly. I move to stand with her, but she stops me when her hands push my chest, so I'm falling back on the couch.

She reaches for the hem of her T-shirt, lifting it over her head. Now she's completely naked and on full display for my eyes only.

Straddling my legs again, Emiline reaches between us to

guide my cock to her entrance before slowly sinking down on it. "Oh my god, Logan," she moans.

My hands find her hips, guiding her back and forth on my cock. Giving her the friction I know she needs to get off. She finds her speed, and her face morphs into nothing but pleasure as she rides me.

I cup her breasts in both hands, bringing the hardened nipple between my teeth before sucking on it, keeping my eyes locked on hers the whole time.

I don't want to miss a second of the pleasure she's getting from this.

"You like riding my cock, Em?"

"Yes. Oh, yes."

"I know what you like. I know that when I do this…" I buck my hips up, putting more pressure to hit that sensitive spot I know drives her crazy. "Your lips form that little O shape, telling me you like it."

"I do. Oh my god, I do."

"I know that when I do this…" I reach between us, pressing my thumb to her clit, and rubbing slow circles. "Your body trembles around me, telling me you're close."

"I am. I definitely am."

"I know that when I do this…" I grip her waist, holding her up just enough so she's hovering over my thighs, and I thrust up into her. Hard and fast. "I can make you come."

"Yes! I'm coming. *I'm coming.*"

I feel her pulsing around my cock. She holds herself up on my shoulders, allowing me to fuck her from below her. I don't stop until I feel her body shake.

And it does.

Her arms go weak. Her legs feel heavy.

Emiline moans my name on repeat as she buries her head in my neck. I don't let her pull off of me, and I don't move her away. I allow her this minute to catch her breath.

When she does, she lifts her head, looking me in the eyes.

I'm finding myself getting more and more lost in them with every glance she gives me.

Without me having to say a word, she moves her hips back and forth tentatively. I know she's sensitive right now. I know she's coming down from a high that's out of this world. She's ready for more, and fuck if that doesn't make me want to come again.

"Are you going to make me come, Emiline?"

She nods. "I want you to fill me up. I want your cum dripping down my legs when I'm done."

"Jesus Christ. Who are you, and what have you done with my girl?"

She giggles, cupping my jaw. "And I'm definitely your girl. I'm going to show you how much in about two minutes."

"Two minutes, huh?"

"Want to make a bet?"

There's no way I could even win this bet because I know I'm about sixty seconds from coming anyway.

"You're on."

Emiline picks up speed, rocking back and forth on my cock. I can feel how soaked we are, but the moment she bounces on my cock, I can *hear* how wet we are. Nothing but the sound of slapping skin fills the air. Her breasts bounce with each move.

"You win. I'm coming," I grunt.

My release pours into her harder than ever before. Truly, I'm surprised I lasted this long. She's a dream in every way possible.

Emiline has a heart of gold and the motivation to do anything she sets her mind to. Her stunning beauty is enough to make me fall to my knees and want to worship her.

The way she kisses me makes the world around me disappear.

It's the kind of kiss that makes me want to scream about us from all the rooftops of the city. It's the kind of kiss that makes me realize I've never been happier than I am with her.

If the job disappears tomorrow, I have her, and that's all I need.

She's all I need.

She's all I want.

I just hope it's enough in the end.

CHAPTER FORTY
Emiline

June

"I'D LIKE TO MAKE A TOAST," Thomas announces to the table, tapping the butter knife on the side of his glass.

We all direct our attention to him, and a smile stretches across my face.

"I want to start off by thanking everyone for coming out tonight to celebrate my one and only baby sister for her graduation. Although you're not a baby anymore, you will always be to me." He laughs. "I don't know what going through the accelerated program you went through was like, but from the outside looking in, I could tell it was a lot for you."

I do my best to fight off the frown my face wants to morph into.

Because he has no idea.

"I've always been so proud of you, Emiline. I've been lucky enough to watch you grow up and become the woman you are today. I was there when you took your first steps and remember it like it was yesterday. Today, I witnessed you take the most important steps of all. The ones where you cross a stage to accept your diploma as a nursing school graduate."

Thomas looks down at his glass, swirling the amber liquid around as he blinks back his emotions.

"It's so hard to talk about this without becoming emotional. And I'm not an emotional guy," he scoffs. "But I hope you know that if Dad was here today, he'd be so insanely proud of who you've become and your career choice. I know Mom couldn't make it because of the storms and her flights being canceled from overseas, but you know she's so proud of you, too."

I wipe the tear that falls down my cheek.

I scan the table, seeing that I'm surrounded by every single person I care about. The people who have made me who I am today. The people who stayed by my side through it all, even when I had to go missing just to study.

My eyes land on Logan, who's looking at me with a lopsided grin.

I'm not sure how to read that expression.

The man who has flipped my entire world upside down in the best way. From the moment he learned the deepest parts of me I hid from the world, he didn't leave. He stayed. He shouldered them with him.

Why does he look so off right now?

"So if everyone can raise a glass," Thomas continues, and I turn my attention to my brother. "A toast to Emiline. You did it. I can't wait to see all you do with this new career."

"Cheers," the group says in unison.

My eyes fall back on Logan, who places his glass down and leaves the table.

I don't have a chance to follow him because the girls start talking.

"Now you can come back to our weekly Taco Tuesday nights," Avery says first.

"I just have to study for another few days." I laugh. "I have my board exam coming up. Once I pass that, I'm *officially* a free girl."

Peyton waves her hand. "You're going to crush it."

Thomas, Marc, and Oliver all stand to follow Logan to wherever he went. I'm assuming the bar in the other room.

Avery watches them move before turning her head toward me. "Are you planning to tell your brothers tonight about you guys?"

"Keep your voice down," I whisper.

"Tonight would be a good night to do it," Macey adds.

I had the same thought. But the way he was looking at me before, and how he just got up and left the table after Thomas gave his speech, leaves me with an uneasy feeling in my gut.

Something is different with him.

"I was thinking about it. But tomorrow is Mackenzie's birthday party. I don't want it to be even more awkward tomorrow and have everyone fighting with each other over us. Plus, I'm not even going to be there. The guys will be up in arms with each other, and I can't even defend us."

"That's valid," Avery says.

"Understandable," Peyton adds.

"The plan was after graduation. I want to tell them. I want them to know and let this shit storm happen to get it over with. I don't know how they will respond, but I need to get it off my chest."

I'm tired of holding too many secrets from them.

After that speech he just gave, it physically pains me that I've been going behind their backs. Not telling them about my mental health struggles or that I've fallen head over heels for their best friend.

"You love him, don't you?" Macey asks.

I can't help but smile at that. The idea of loving him was never something I thought would happen. It's not something I believed was in the cards for me. To have a man like him treat me the way he does.

I nod in response. "I think I do."

"I love this so much," Peyton says all giddy.

"Have you told him?" Avery asks.

I shake my head aggressively. "No. God, no. At the beginning, he told me he didn't want a relationship. But over the last year, he wanted to see where this would lead us, and we would make a decision after I graduated. His actions show me that he wants this, but I'm terrified of finding out what he says back if I tell him."

"You don't want to rush him into anything." Peyton shrugs. "That's understandable."

"But I really do—"

My words are cut short when all the guys come back to the table. Thomas, Marc, and Oliver laughing, and Logan faking one. I know it's forced because I've seen him truly laugh before. I've seen him let himself go enough that the laughter is real.

"You really do what?" Oliver asks, coming down from whatever just had them in hysterics.

My eyes bounce to the girls and back to him. Silently looking for an excuse.

"She really doesn't want to go to work tomorrow," Macey answers to save me. "She doesn't want to miss Mackenzie's birthday party."

I offer Macey a thankful smile but hate myself for the way she just jumped in and lied for me.

"We'll save you some cake for the next day." Oliver walks over to me, wrapping an arm around my shoulder. "We know you wouldn't miss it otherwise."

I give him a curt nod, my lips sealed as I look toward Logan. Once again, he's not looking at me.

Two weeks ago, he showed up at my apartment with the most thoughtful graduation gift. Ending his birthday and the night with the best sex we've ever had. I don't know how it's possible for it to get better and better each time.

Since then, he's stayed over a few times.

Not once giving me any inclination that things were off between us.

Why now?

Why today?

I can't help but feel like he's acting totally different like he's pulling away from me.

My heart gallops behind my ribs while my mind runs rampant with doubts. Was I nothing more than a good time for him? Was I just something to help him pass the time?

On a date where we both talked about remaining hand in hand to tell my brothers the news, it seems like he's already giving up on me.

———

The uneasiness never leaves me the entire rest of the night.

After dinner, I just wanted the night to be over so I could bring Logan back to my place and talk about what's going on in his head. But the girls ordered drinks, shots, and dessert.

The night wasn't ending soon, it seemed.

A few hours later, I finally excuse myself to use the restroom. Once inside, I lock the door behind me in the single-stall room and take a minute to gather myself.

Resting my hands on the edge of the sink, I take a few deep breaths while I decide how to go about this.

A few options are laid out in front of me.

Walk out there and just announce I've been seeing Logan. I can tell the whole room I love him and I want a relationship with him. But it would be weird telling an entire room when I haven't said those words to him.

Scratch that.

I could also walk out there, drag Logan down the hall, and ask him what's happening between us. What has his head so wrapped up tonight? *Then,* ask him if he's ready to tell everyone.

No, that doesn't work either.

I don't want to pressure him.

"Ugh," I groan, at the same time a knock sounds on the door.

"Be out in a minute," I shout.

"It's me."

Logan.

I rush to unlock the door, swinging it open and finding the same uneasy, lopsided grin on his face.

He steps into the bathroom without an invitation, and I close the door behind us.

"Hey." I can barely get the word out.

"You didn't tell them," he says, without missing a beat and getting straight to the point.

"I—uh—I wasn't sure how you felt about it."

Logan pauses, staring at me, his eyes glossy and boring into mine.

The uneasiness creeps right back in full force.

"I want to. I do. But…" Logan starts.

My lips part to say something, but I clasp them shut.

"We can't tell them tonight. Not yet. We need a few more days," he continues.

I nod reluctantly because his tone is laced with hesitation.

Does he not want this anymore?

"Today is your special day, Emiline. It's your graduation. Everything Thomas said earlier today is the truth. We're so proud of you. I don't want telling them to ruin this for you. They're going to lose their minds. You and I both know that."

He's right.

I didn't even think about how this would ruin the best day for me.

"I thought you were mad at me," I admit.

He barks out a laugh. "I'm mad at the situation, Em. I'm fucking aggravated I can't hold you out in the open, kiss you the way I want, intertwine your fingers with mine while he told that speech. I wanted to scream."

He pauses, looking for a reaction from me, but I don't have one.

I read the entire situation wrong. As someone who's always afraid someone is mad at me, I just couldn't help it.

I need to learn to let that go with Logan.

"I'm sorry, Logan."

He reaches up to brush a strand of my curled hair away from my face. "There's nothing to be sorry about. It's just… better if we don't tell them yet."

I want to scream those three words right now.

I want to tell him I can't wait for everyone to know I love this man.

His heart.

His mind.

Who he is as a person.

"Do you want to stay at my place tonight?" I ask him.

"Like you even have to ask."

CHAPTER FORTY-ONE
Logan

THE RUMBLING thunder wakes me out of a dead sleep.

Even with Emiline's warm body connected with mine, I had trouble falling asleep replaying everything from last night in my head. I wanted her to tell her brother's. I wanted us to be out in the open. But at the same time, my head was filled with thoughts of the truth being out there. The damage it could cause for both of us.

I'm not ready for it yet.

I'm not ready for the commitment as much as I love waking up next to her.

My brain wouldn't stop thinking about what my future looks like as I laid there with her in my arms. I should want this. I should want to love her and be loved by her.

I fucking hate that I'm not wired for that.

I look at the clock on Emiline's nightstand and see it's already nine in the morning. I turn to find her sleeping soundly next to me. Her hair fanned across the pillow, her lips slightly parted, and the blankets curled under her neck.

I lean down and press a kiss on her forehead. She stirs under my touch, her sleepy eyes barely opening.

"Good morning," she says groggily.

"Good morning." I press a kiss to her lips. "I'm sorry to wake you up. The thunder woke me up, and you looked so peaceful. I need my lips on you."

Her hands come out from under the covers, and she wraps them around my neck, pulling me into her for a searing kiss.

"I want to stay here in bed all day." She smiles against my lips.

"You can and you should," I tell her. "You work tonight."

"I don't want to," she whines.

"You're almost done with your shifts as a patient care associate. You're almost ready to be a nurse."

"I'm not ready to become a grown-up in nursing."

I laugh at her. "Yes, you are."

I give her one more kiss before I throw the covers off and get out of bed.

"What are your plans for today?" she asks.

I find my shorts on the ground and put them on. "I'm going to meet up with Silas at the gym in a little bit. He's probably already there waiting for me knowing him."

"I think I might stay right here when you leave. This weather is the perfect sleeping weather and I, for once, don't have any anxiety about school work I need to be doing."

"You deserve it, Em."

This feels good—too good—the mindless morning banter after waking up to the most beautiful woman. I wish my head would stop fighting me in this relationship. I wish I could get out of my brain and let myself love her how she deserves to be loved.

My plan today is to talk to Silas about it. He's the best at understanding me and what I'm going through. If there's anyone who can make me feel better about this, it's him.

We never go to the gym early in the day, but today is the day —my deadline—the last day left to give my decision to the chief.

I don't tell Emiline that, though.

I don't want her to know I haven't decided yet.

She's going to tell me to do it. She's going to be the most perfect and supportive person, urging me to go after my dreams. That's just the type of person she is.

Needless to say, between yesterday's events, waking up next to her, and deciding the fate of my future... meeting with Silas at the gym is beyond necessary.

I grab the rest of my things, brush my teeth, and find her still lying in bed. She has a smile stretched across her face that causes mine to mirror it.

"Get some good sleep today," I tell her, leaning down to kiss her. I hold myself there longer than I want to. But not too long that I don't leave. She needs sleep, and I have a packed day of things to take care of.

"Have fun at the gym," she tells me before reaching for one more kiss. "Love you."

I hover over her in shock.

What did she just say?

Her hand comes up, smacking her over the mouth. Her eyes widen as if she didn't expect those words to come out.

She just...

"Oh my god." She covers her entire face with her hands. "I—uh—oh my god."

"What did you just say?"

She looks at me, her hand still covering her mouth.

"I love you," she repeats behind her hand before letting them fall to her sides. "It's not how I wanted to tell you, but it slipped."

"It just slipped?"

This isn't how it was supposed to happen.

She wasn't supposed to fall in love with me.

At least not yet.

She wasn't supposed to tell me she loves me.

At least not yet.

"You can't," I say before she can say anything more. "You weren't supposed to fall in love with me."

Emiline sits up in bed, positioning the covers over her and hiding herself from me.

I don't blame her.

My tone is anything but pleasing.

"You didn't tell me not to." Her tone is laced with pain.

I fucking hate myself for reacting this way, but I can't find it in me to stop.

She. Can't. Fucking. Love. Me.

I pace the room, wondering how the hell we got here. I mean, I know how we did, but the fact I allowed her to fall in love with me. After everything I've been through with my dad, she *can't* love me like this.

At. Least. Not. Yet.

"You didn't tell me not to!" This time, her voice is stronger and louder. "What did you expect to happen, Logan? We spend so much time together. You spend nights at my place. We have sex about every other day. You've been there for me in my darkest times."

I run my hands through my hair, pulling at the ends.

I could make this easy.

I could just tell her those three words that I know I feel toward her and this argument could be done.

But the walls around my heart are so tall.

My mind won't allow me to feel that way out of fear for the future, fear that she will fall madly and deeply in love with me and one day I'll pick up pizza for her on the way home and——

"I have to go."

"Logan," she begs. "Please."

"You weren't supposed to love me," I said much louder than I intend to. My irrational fears are creeping in and taking over. And I don't know how to make them stop from clouding my judgment.

She gasps and sits back in the bed as if my words just punched her.

"I'm not built for this. I'm not this kind of guy. I have a fucked up mind, and I can't allow you to get hurt."

"You don't really believe you could hurt me, do you?"

"I can. And I will."

Emiline's shoulders sag and she looks down at her hands in her lap.

I turn and walk out the door without another look.

I need to breathe and get my head on straight.

I need to talk this through with Silas.

I would never hurt her in the ways she thinks I would.

My crushing fear in my chest is leaving her the way my dad left me.

It would be too much of a devastating end to a beautiful beginning.

CHAPTER FORTY-TWO
Logan

"PUT THE GLOVES DOWN," Silas shouts.

My hands fall to my side in defeat while my chest rises and falls in quick, rapid movements.

"Put them down," he orders. "You're going to tell me what has you so worked up today. Because I can't keep up with you. You're going to break my hands right through the mitts if you keep throwing punches like that."

"No," I snap. "Keep going."

I throw punch after punch in his direction, letting out every ounce of frustration this day has built.

"Talk to me," Silas says out of breath.

I retake my stance, legs slightly parted, with my arms covering my face. "I have a meeting with the chief today." I throw one jab, followed by a right hook. "I have to give him my decision by the end of the day." I throw a jab with my left, then my right. "And Emiline told me she loves me."

He bounces away from me, not allowing me to get another punch in.

He stands there in shock.

"She told me she loves me, and I told her she wasn't supposed to fall in love with me and I walked out."

"Fuck," he mutters under his breath.

"Yeah." I sigh, feeling completely defeated.

I drop my gloves and keep my eyes fixed on the ground. I hate myself more than I ever have before for how I reacted.

"What are you planning to do with the chief?"

I shake my head. "I don't have an answer."

"And… Emiline?"

"I don't have an answer for that either."

"Do her brothers know about you two?"

"No."

He nods, his understanding of the situation evident in his eyes.

"You love her." It comes out as a statement.

I scoff. "Another thing I can't answer."

He steps closer, placing a hand on my shoulder. "You love her, Bennett. There's no doubt about it."

I raise a brow, and he levels his eyes with me.

"I've seen a change in you over the last year. From the first time you told me you saw Emiline differently until recently. You used to be a hardass, covering up whatever pain you kept hidden deep inside of you by being the way you are. There's nothing wrong with that. But I've seen you spending time with her, change you in good ways. You allowed yourself to be open and vulnerable with someone. You let some of those walls down for her. And most importantly, you cared for her when she needed you the most."

I raise the corner of my lips, but not enough for a complete smile.

"No wonder she fell in love with you," Silas continues. "But you need to know there's nothing wrong with loving her back. I know you worry heavily about the future and what's to come. But you can't. You fucking can't let that take away any ounce of happiness you have. Letting the future control your actions… hell, letting *fear* control your actions will not make you feel any happier. I've said it before, but when you're at the end of your life, lying there, and you see the bright lights when it's your time to go and your life flashes before your eyes… will you be happy with what you see? Or pissed off because you let the greatest thing that has ever happened to you slip between your fingers."

I blink back the tears, not even caring that my best friend is about to see me cry.

"Let it out, Bennett. Let the tears fall. Let yourself feel all the things."

"I don't know how to let myself love her," I choke out. "How do I let the crippling fear of an uncertain future go?"

"I wish I had an answer for that," he says, echoing my words. "But you just have to live in the moment, Bennett. That's all any of us can do."

I nod because he's right.

I have to just live in the moment with her, I can't let what happened to my dad hold me back from experiencing the greatest joy in my life.

"Now, go have your meeting with the chief," Silas says. "Call me later and let me know how it goes."

———

I pace my kitchen back and forth, thunder booming in the distance.

I didn't follow his instructions very well because I called the chief on my way out of the gym. I told him something had come up, and I needed one more day to let him know. I lucked out because he's always been very understanding and didn't ask any further questions.

The man *is* in a rush to retire, but he also doesn't want to rush to give the position to someone who's going to drag the department to shit.

So I ended up back at my apartment after the gym.

I took a long, hot shower—which did nothing for my racing mind.

I tried to watch Sports Center but couldn't focus.

I tried to fold laundry, but I only thought of Emiline.

I picked up the phone a hundred times to call her. I checked to see if she had reached out to me. I half expected her to send me a long text message telling me I'm a piece of shit. But it's been radio silence.

After another twenty minutes of pacing my kitchen, I pick up the phone to text her. But before I do, I throw the phone across the room, realizing this conversation needs to be had face-to-face.

If I sleep now, I can show up at her place when she gets off work.

But there's no way I'm sleeping.

What if I show up at her work, bring her a coffee, and see if she has five minutes to talk?

It's not the best idea, but also not the worst.

Deciding I won't be sleeping until I talk to her, I grab my truck keys. Thunder booms and lightning flashes across the sky as I reach my truck at record speed and pull out of the parking garage.

The roads are a mess.

My windshield wipers are set to the fastest speed, and it's still not enough. I want to speed to City General, but I can't do it in this weather. Frustration takes over as I slam my fist against the steering wheel.

Mother Nature really wants to test my patience right now.

I'm driving down the road, and the next thing I know, my head snaps toward the passenger seat.

Pain sears up my entire left side as my truck flips upside down.

I scream as it hurls itself repeatedly for who knows how many times.

My seatbelt crushes my chest.

The airbags deploy into my face, and I can't breathe.

The truck finally stops, and I realize I can't feel my legs.

My breathing is erratic as I try to see what's happening around me.

I'm upside down.

I can't fucking breathe.

Emiline's name is the last thing I remember…

Before everything around me goes black.

Part Two

NOW

CHAPTER FORTY-THREE
Emiline

I faintly hear someone calling my name, but I can't open my eyes to see who it is.

What the hell happened to me?

Why can't I move?

A light shining on my face causes me to squint and slowly open my eyes. When I see a doctor with a penlight and Brooke standing over my bed, the realization hits me and my eyes fly open.

I'm in the hospital.

"What happened?" I ask, feeling my heart rate pick up. "How long have I been asleep for?"

"You're in the hospital, Em. You passed out. You've been out for maybe a half hour," Brooke says. Her words are reassuring, but her tone leads me to believe something else is worse.

"Why am I here?" I ask, slowly pulling myself up in bed.

I scan the room and see it's just her and the doctor. She's still wearing scrubs and her hair is a mess. It almost looks like she was just part of…

A code.

My hand flies to my face, and my eyes widen as I stare at her.

"Brooke." Her name comes out like I'm gasping for air. Like I'm reaching for the truth of a terrible dream I remember having just moments ago before the light and her voice woke me up.

Then it hits me like a brick wall.

Logan.

Accident.

Flatline…

I snap my attention toward Brooke, but she looks at me with a void look, her lips sealed shut as if she doesn't want to tell me that my dream is real.

That it really happened.

That Logan is fucking dead.

A strangled sob escapes me, and the upper part of my body falls into her arms. She catches me as she sits on the edge of my bed. My shoulders shake, and I feel her rubbing my back to comfort me.

He's gone.

How the hell am I supposed to go forward after this?

"Emiline," the doctor says. "I'm so sorry you're going through this right now. But while you were unconscious, we ran some blood work to make sure there wasn't an underlying condition to you passing out."

I pull away from Brooke and use the hospital blanket in my lap to dry my cheeks. I need about a hundred more of these full-size blankets for what's coming, and this doctor here—who I've never met before—wants to discuss *me* right now. When all I want to know is what the hell happened to Logan?

I nod anyway so he can get this over with, and we can talk about more important things.

"When someone your age who is healthy passes out, we like to run a quantitative blood test."

"You mean a pregnancy test?" I ask, shocked. "There's no way."

"As I'm sure you know, the test measures the exact amount of

HCG in your blood and can even give an estimate of how far along you are," she says matter-of-factly.

"Yes." I nod repeatedly. "Why are you telling me all of this?"

"Because you're about six weeks pregnant, Emiline," she says without missing a beat.

As if saying her reveal isn't flipping my world upside down.

I don't move from where I sit.

I don't look at Brooke, but I *feel* her hands coming up to cover her face. Of course, she didn't know. Hell, *I* didn't even know.

And now…

"Oh my god." The realization hits me, and the tears flow uncontrollably. "I can't do this. I can't do this," I say over and over, my voice rising every time the words come out of me until eventually my voice breaks.

I can't catch my breath, and for the first time in months, I feel like I'm on the verge of a panic attack. The monitor attached to me beeps rapidly, and I look up to see my heart rate climbing.

I'm pregnant.

Logan's dead.

I'm supposed to be taking my boards next week.

The beeping grows louder before the doctor places both hands on my shoulders. "Emiline," she says sternly. "I need you to take a deep breath for me."

I look her in the eyes but can barely make her out through my tears.

I do as she says, but I feel myself breaking with every second that passes because it's not Logan looking back at me. She's not giving me a three-hand squeeze. In front of me is not the only person who can ground me and bring me back.

"I know this is a lot to take in," she says reassuringly as she rubs her thumb along my collarbone and keeps her eyes level with mine. "You've been through a lot today, and this news didn't help. I'm sorry, but we had to let you know as soon as possible."

I shake my head and work on controlling my breathing again.

"Good job, Emiline. Slow, deep breaths," the doctor says. "Talk to me and let me help you through this."

"I…" I start to speak, but the words fall short.

I can't even articulate words right now, let alone tell her how I'm feeling.

My day has been a roller coaster from start to finish.

I wanted to call out of work tonight, but something told me I shouldn't. My plan was to spend the day in bed. But after Logan left, I couldn't go back to sleep. My head just replayed our last year together like a film over and over again.

I tried so hard to force thoughts of him out of my head today.

Because I told him I loved him.

It was a slip of the tongue, but one I don't regret.

I truly thought we were on the same page. But we weren't.

He flat-out said I wasn't supposed to love him.

And now he's…

I don't even want to think about it right now, but he's gone.

I'm pregnant with his child, and he's just… gone.

Six weeks along? How is that even possible?

"I see the wheels spinning in your head, babe," Brooke says, taking a seat on the edge of my bed by my legs. She places a hand on my thigh and gives me a small squeeze. "I'm here for you. I clocked out and I'm not leaving your side. But just so you know, Logan is-"

"Do you have my phone?" I cut her off, not wanting to hear what she has to say.

She nods and pulls it from the pocket in her scrubs to hand it to me.

I shake my head while also waving my hand at the phone because I don't want to see it. I know I never got to change my lock screen image since he told me we couldn't do this anymore. It's a photo of Logan and me relaxing on my couch after one of our many movie nights.

"Can you just text the group chat I have pinned at the top and let my brothers know? I can't call them right now." The last words come out with a strangled voice as I wipe another tear from my cheeks. "Just tell them there's been an accident and they need to get here. Make sure you tell them I'm fine and that it's…" I can't even find it in me to say his name.

"Are you sure you want me to do that?" she asks, knowing I don't even need to say anything more.

I nod a few times. "Yes. I need them here."

As much as I know I need everyone here, I don't know how I'm going to tell them that their best friend is dead.

Or that I've been having a relationship with him being their back.

That I'm carrying his child now.

I lay down in bed and close my eyes before I send myself spiraling again while Brooke sends the text message. She takes a seat on the chair at the opposite end of the room, giving me some time to myself but being close enough if I need her.

My hands wrap around my stomach.

There's a life growing inside of me now.

A life that's made half of me and half of him. Tears flow again, and I can feel my pillow soak them all up.

I don't know how I'm going to survive this life without him.

But I know I need to do this for the baby.

I *have* to do this.

CHAPTER FORTY-FOUR
Thomas

ALL OUR PHONES chime and vibrate simultaneously on the kitchen counter. None of us move from our seats because we all probably have the same idea that the family group chat is going off since Emiline is at work.

Peyton is the only one to reach for hers.

"Guys." Her voice sounds pained.

My head whips in her direction, and I can't help but notice her face is ashen. A look of sheer terror engulfs her features, as if the words she just read have altered the course of our lives.

"Babe," I say as I jump from the couch, reaching for her. "What is it? Is everything okay?"

My hands grip her shoulders, forcing her to look me in the eyes.

No one around us moves as they wait for answers.

"It's… it's…" Her lips tremble as she looks up at me, blinking several times before finally speaking. "It's Logan."

Marc springs from his seat on the couch and Oliver circles the room. Each of them positioning themselves directly behind me, a silent show of solidarity.

"Em texted all of us in a group chat. Well, it's not her. It's her friend with her phone." She holds up her phone to show us.

EMILINE

This is Brooke. Emiline's friend. I saw this thread pinned to the top of her messages and wanted to let you know there's been… an accident. Emiline is ok, just shaken up. But she said to tell you that it's Logan.

I'm sorry to send this via text, but she told me to. He's been in a terrible car accident. You need to get here right away.

I can feel the blood drain from my face.

My best friend. Who's like a brother to me. He *is* a brother to me.

My chest feels tight. I bring my hand up to rub it to ease the ache that's building in my ribcage.

My best fucking friend.

"Let's go in the bounce house," I hear Macey say as she takes the kids back outside.

Once they are out of earshot, Marc loses it.

"Fuck," he screams. Pulling at the strands of his hair, he takes his place on the couch. His elbows rest on his knees, and he looks like he's going to vomit.

I don't blame him. I feel it too, but I can't move from where I stand.

"What do we do?" Oliver asks hoarsely. "Do we rush over there? We're not even in the city."

Peyton looks up at me, her face full of fear and sadness.

"We don't have all the details. Before we put ourselves into a full panic, we have to find out what's going on. But as your wife, I need to tell you something."

My insides crumble.

I feel dizzy as my stomach swirls with nerves.

"Your sister," she says, clearing her throat as she nervously wrings her hands together. "She's going to need you."

"What does she have to do with this?" Marc spits out as he stands quickly from where he was just seated.

"It's not my place to tell you the rest." Peyton shakes her head. "But she's going to need her big brothers. She's going to need support."

My eyes look over to Avery to try and read her face. Being in my line of work, I can read people like a book. I know when they are hiding something from me and are reluctant about taking the offer I put on the table. But Avery's face remains passive.

She knows too.

"My sister," I say flatly.

"And Logan," Marc adds, jaw clenched tight.

The silence in the room is so loud right now.

CHAPTER FORTY-FIVE
Marc

THE JOURNEY to the hospital felt like the longest drive back into the city. For now, it's just Thomas and me because the girls wanted to stay back and give both of us some space until we figure out what's going on.

Not knowing the fate of my best friend, *our* best friend, has left me a complete head case with nerves for many reasons, only to have to worry about my baby sister on top of that. Emilline is at the hospital now, and from the sounds of it, she's not taking this well.

And based on the girls' response at the house, there's way more to the story.

How long have they been going behind our back?

How long have the girls known about this and said nothing?

I want to be furious like Thomas right now. Honest to God, I think there's smoke coming out of his head. But I don't have the energy for it because two people I love are hurting in their own way.

I'm optimistic enough to know Logan will be fine.

I know Emiline well enough to say she's the strongest girl I've ever known.

"I'm looking for Emiline Ford," I tell the receptionist when I enter the hospital.

She clicks away on her computer for a moment. "And your relation?"

"I'm her brother. Marc Ford."

She nods. "She's still in room 18 in the emergency room."

"She's a… patient?" I ask, my voice getting stuck in my throat.

She nods.

"Logan Bennett," Thomas interrupts next to me. "Where is he?"

"And you are?" she asks, completely unfazed by his tone filled with rage.

"Thomas Ford. Not related. But all he has," he snaps.

She clicks away on her computer. "He's on the fourth floor in the intensive care unit. He's only allowed one visitor at a time because of the severity of his case."

Thomas goes sheet white before swallowing and giving her a curt nod.

"You go see him. I'll check on Emiline, and we can switch when you're ready."

Thomas nods. I can see the emotions building up inside of him.

"He's got this, Thomas. Believe that. We don't know what's going on yet. Take a deep breath. We're here now, and he's got us."

Thomas nods again before heading toward the elevator to the fourth floor. I turn toward the signs pointing to the emergency room.

I make it to Emiline's room and find a girl sitting in a chair across from her. I recognize her from the photos Emiline sends us of her drowning in study material. This must be Brooke, the one who messaged us.

She notices me standing in the doorway and jumps from the chair to meet me.

"Hey, I'm Marc." I extend my hand to her, working on keeping my voice calm.

"Oh good, you made it. I'm Brooke. I know we haven't met, but Emiline tells me a lot about you guys."

I acknowledge her but look over her shoulder into the room.

Emiline lays curled up with her knees to her chest on her side on a stretcher with two blankets draped over her.

"Listen, before you go in there..." Brooke starts. "She's not taking this well. Just to give you a quick rundown, Logan was brought into the ER with another victim of a car crash. We don't know what happened, but Emiline ended up in the room as I was performing chest compressions..." She pauses and attempts to swallow back emotions. "When someone took over for me two minutes later, I ran to find her, and she had passed out in the hallway. We brought her in here, and it looks like... it was a panic attack that caused it."

The way she paused before finishing that sentence leads me to believe something more is going on that she's not telling me.

"Is there more you want to say?"

Her eyes go wide, but she shakes her head. "No."

Before I can argue with her, my phone chimes with a text message.

THOMAS

Logan's in critical condition. He has a broken leg and a fractured collarbone. He also has some internal injuries that forced the doctors to put him in a medically induced coma.

My stomach flips, and I want to throw up right here in the hallway, but I don't have time because I hear Emiline call my name.

"Marc?"

I look over Brooke's shoulder and sidestep her into the room as I pocket my phone.

"Em." I sit right on the edge of the bed and wrap her in my

arms. She falls into me, her body shaking with sobs as she cries into my chest.

"Shh," I murmur in her ear. "I'm here. I got you."

"I'm so sorry, Marc," she says, but it's muffled against the fabric of my T-shirt.

I pull back, slightly angry that *she's* apologizing right now. I keep myself at eye level with her and my hands on her shoulders. "What are you sorry for?"

"They didn't tell you?"

"Tell me what?"

"About… Logan," Emiline chokes out his name as if this is the first time she's said it since she woke up.

I nod. "The girls stayed home until you're open for visitors, and Thomas and I are taking turns."

"Taking turns?" She tilts her head in confusion. "There's no reason for you two to take turns to see me. I'm not in some kind of isolation." She looks over to Brooke, standing off in the corner. "Why can't they all be here?"

"Not here, Em," I say. She looks back at me. "We're taking turns with Logan."

Now it's her turn for her face to go sheet white. She looks like I just broke her heart all over again by saying his name out loud.

"Is he? Oh my god. Is he alive?" Her breath catches in her throat like it's closing in on her. "Where is he?"

"He's in the intensive care unit. You didn't know?" I ask, confused.

"Is he alive?" she practically shouts as more tears form in her eyes.

"He's alive. But he's in critical condition," I answer honestly, leaving out the details for now.

I watch as Emiline crumbles right in front of me.

She brings her knees to her chest and covers her face as she sobs uncontrollably.

I've never felt so helpless for my sister in my life.

This was real.

Whatever she and Logan have going on is so fucking real.

CHAPTER FORTY-SIX
Emiline

I PRETEND to fall asleep so Marc and Brooke will leave me alone for more than fifteen minutes. Brooke hasn't left my side since I woke up, and don't get me wrong, I'm incredibly thankful for her.

But right now, I need some time to process what's happening.

Logan is alive.

He's alive.

The second the door to my hospital room closes behind them, I break down and let the tears fall. I use the layer of blankets over me to hide my shaking body and the pillow to mask the noises of my cries.

I don't even understand why I'm still a wreck over this.

I lied. I totally know why.

My body is changing by the minute, and hormones are racing in preparation for a growing baby. Right now, this little thing inside me might just be the size of a pea.

In another four weeks, and it will be the size of a strawberry.

I only remember this from when James' mom was around and going through her pregnancy. Each week, there was a different fruit and vegetable.

What would Logan think of all this?

Our last words to each other weren't good ones.

In my heart, I should've seen it coming. I just graduated and watched Logan's demeanor change at my graduation dinner.

He wanted a little more time before we told them.

This wasn't how I wanted them to find out.

Now, Logan is in a medically induced coma, and I'm left to deal with them on my own. The last thing I plan to tell them is that I'm having his baby right now.

I can't imagine the rage when I add that to the fire.

Nausea rises into my throat and I throw the covers off to run to the bathroom inside my room. Nothing but bile comes out because I haven't eaten since yesterday morning. My chest hurts from puking as hard as I am and I just let more tears fall right into the toilet.

How do I even have tears left to cry?

There's a soft knock on the door.

"It's me," Brooke says quietly.

"Come in," I choke out, my voice feeling drier than the Sahara Desert.

The door opens and she crouches down beside me. She places one hand on my back and wraps my hair in her other hand to keep it out of my face. She says nothing. She knows that just being there is enough for me.

I attempt to throw up again, but nothing comes out.

"I'm sorry," I cry between heaves.

"Shh. Don't be."

I shake my head. "I'm sorry for lying to you for so long."

"You didn't lie to me about anything. I knew what was going on with Logan."

I sit up and reach for a piece of toilet paper to wipe my face and blow my nose before tossing it in and flushing. I sit back against the wall, bring my knees to my chest, and look up at Brooke, still crouched beside me.

She offers me a sympathetic smile.

"Not about Logan."

She cocks her head to the side in confusion.

"I've been…" I pause, trying to figure out how to say this. "Dealing with panic attacks."

"Is that what it was when you saw… you know?"

I nod. "I've been dealing with them since school started. When I get overwhelmed or anxious about something, I just spiral. Before every exam, I'd get so lost in my head and let the thoughts take over."

Brooke sighs. "Oh, Em. I wish you would have told me."

"Trust me, I wish I did too. I just didn't want anyone to know. I didn't want you or anyone else to look at me differently. I was afraid those who knew would treat me like I was made of glass and might break at any second."

Shaking her head, Brooke stands up. She extends her hand for me to take it to get me off the floor, saying nothing as she guides me back to the bed, sitting on the edge beside me.

"Dealing with this doesn't make you weak, Emiline. It makes you the strongest person I know for facing the world and these feelings on your own every day. You've been too strong for too long. Let us help you now."

A tear trickles down my face again, and she reaches up and wipes it.

"You're not alone, Emiline," Peyton says from the door.

I turn my head and see Peyton and Avery standing there. Peyton has flowers in her hand, and Avery is… crying?

"Are you crying?" I ask her.

"Don't start with me right now," Avery scolds. "We heard every word of that whether or not you wanted us to. It hurts so bad to hear you've had to battle that alone."

They both enter the room and take a seat on the opposite end of the hospital bed, angling their bodies to face me as I sit higher in the bed, crossing my legs.

My head falls, and I feel an overwhelming sense of guilt for hiding this for so long. "You will never know how sorry I am for not saying anything."

"None of that," Peyton says, pulling my head down to her chest and wrapping her arms around me. "I've never had a panic attack, so I can't speak about what you went through, but I can only imagine it was hard for you to deal with. I'm sad I couldn't be there for you, but we're here now. We know now. And you're not alone ever again. Do you understand?"

I nod.

"This one I had last night was the first one I've had in a long time," I tell them honestly. "Logan has been helping me make them easier to deal with."

"We're just happy you had at least one person in your corner for this," Peyton says.

"I should've seen the signs." Brooke wipes a tear from her eyes. "You always got so distant the day before exams and even the morning of. Like your mind wasn't there. I should've known."

"I made it so no one would find out. Don't beat yourself up," I tell Brooke before looking at Avery and Peyton. "None of you should. And right now, I'm so happy you guys know. It's a massive weight lifted off my shoulder."

For now.

I'm telling them one secret only to hide another. Brooke is the only one in this room who knows, and that's how I'd like to keep it until Logan wakes up.

If he wakes up.

"Have you guys seen Logan?" I ask.

Peyton shakes her head. "We came to you first."

"Have you?" Avery asks.

My head falls again. I look down at my hands as I wring them together nervously. I want to see him more than I need to breathe, but I'm terrified to see him that way. I'm scared to death I'm going to walk into the room, and he'll choose that moment to stop breathing. I'm not ready to lose him. I can't lose him.

"I'm scared," I finally admit.

"We can go with you if you want," Peyton offers.

"That's a good idea," Brooke adds. "Better than your brothers." She looks at Peyton and Avery. "No offense to you guys."

"None taken." Avery holds her hands up in defense. "You are so right."

"Do you think I can go now?" I ask.

"As long as you're ready," Peyton says.

I nod.

Even though no part of me is ready for this.

CHAPTER FORTY-SEVEN
Emiline

I FEEL myself falling apart before I'm even in the room.

My palms are sweating, and I want to throw up again. But I hold it back. I know there's nothing left in me, anyway.

Standing outside his door, I take a deep breath before looking at Peyton. She gives me a silent nod and a single squeeze of my hand before she sits in the hallway chair outside the room.

Opening the door, my heart breaks more than I knew was possible.

The room is dark, and Logan is hooked up to so many machines I don't know where to look first.

My eyes land on the monitor lit up with a few colors showing his vital signs. The wires connected to it travel to the machine next to his bed that beeps for each breath it's giving him.

The machine that's keeping him alive.

Then I see the giant cast on his leg, lifted and elevated a few inches off the bed by a device hanging from the ceiling.

My gaze finally lands on his face. My hand flies up to cover my mouth as I suck in a sharp breath, still standing close to the door.

I want to run.

I want to cry.

I want to scream.

How did this happen? How did we get here? One minute, I'm telling him I love him, and the next, he's walking out my door without another word, only to end up in a hospital bed.

I take slow, tentative steps into Logan's room as I approach the side of his bed. My body tingles with nerves. Being here is the scariest thing I've ever seen. Which says a lot based on what I've seen working in the emergency room.

But no one prepares you for seeing the love of your life hooked to a machine keeping him alive.

"Logan," I breathe out.

He doesn't move. I don't expect him to.

But one thing I learned through school is that even in a coma, the person on the other side can still hear you, even if they can't respond.

"Logan," I say a little louder, hoping if I say it enough, he might just wake up for me.

Nothing.

There's a chair already on the edge of the bed, likely from one of my brothers visiting him. I round the bed, not taking my eyes off him because I don't want to miss even a single movement he might make.

I sit down, wrapping my arms around myself.

"Why you?" I whisper. "This isn't fair."

Looking down at his hand resting on his side, the urge to climb into bed with him and wrap my body around him is so strong.

I reach for his hand, taking it in mine. It's warm and soft like I remember it to be. It's the kind of warmth that, when you touch it, provides you with a type of comfort that nothing else can.

"It's me, Emiline," I tell him. Even though I'm sure he knows my voice. "There's a lot we have to talk about. I know you can't answer right now and I don't expect you to. The way we left things…" I swallow past the lump in my throat full of emotions.

"I know that's not the way it's supposed to be. This isn't the way we're supposed to end, Logan."

I let the tears fall and emotions emerge like a broken dam. I grip his hand with a three-pulse squeeze the way he's always done for me and let my forehead fall to the side of his bed.

"This isn't how we're supposed to end. Come back to me. Come back to us. I can't do this alone."

I let everything out right there on the edge of his bed.

To a man who can't say a single thing back.

"I meant what I said. I love you so much, Logan Bennett." I cry harder. "Fucking come back to me. I'm begging you."

I lift my head to look at his face.

Bruised and swollen to the point it doesn't even look like him. I stand up from the chair and cup his face, pressing my lips to his forehead. Keeping them there for one, two, three heartbeats.

No response.

I fall to the chair, sitting back and just stare at him. Shifting my eyes between him and the monitor. My tears quickly turn to anger. Rage for him being in this situation.

"Come back to us!" I shout before I fall apart again.

My upper body falling over his waist.

I hear the door open but don't lift my head to see who it is. I don't even care anymore because it's not Logan.

Multiple sets of hands are on each side of me, lifting me off the chair and bringing me to the couch at the other end of the room. I cry harder, refusing to open my eyes.

"Come back to us!" I shout again, a painful scream from deep in my lungs.

"Shh," Marc says in my ear. "I got you."

I grip his t-shirt as I lean into his chest, and I don't even know how to feel right now. I let out everything inside of me. The tears flow as I scream through my cries, and my body shakes as Marc holds me tighter in his lap.

The only thing that can stop this is hearing Logan's voice.

And I don't think I'll hear it anytime soon.

CHAPTER FORTY-EIGHT
Oliver

I'VE NEVER FELT SO much pain watching my little sister fall apart in Marc's arms. My heart is beating rapidly while simultaneously breaking with each second that passes.

I look at Thomas, standing beside them, hands in his pockets and looking down at Emiline. Likely thinking the same thing I am.

How in the world can we help her through this?

I don't think we can.

The only person who can is Logan.

When I first heard about these two, I didn't have the same reaction Thomas and Marc had. Thomas lost his marbles. He wanted to fight him, and I thought I saw smoke coming out of his head at one point.

Marc handled it a little better. He was hurt by them hiding it but was ready to talk about it and understand why.

Me? I had a different perspective that shifted theirs when I finally arrived at the hospital. Both of them now have totally new outlooks on the entire situation.

Because Logan is our best friend.

If he's such a good friend to us, then why wouldn't he be good enough for our only sister?

I understood where they were coming from based on his past, but people change when they fall in love. I used Macey and me as an example. Logan and I were the same person. We loved to go out and find random hookups.

I actually cringe thinking about that life now.

But then I met someone. I fell madly in love with her, and my outlook on life changed.

If Logan feels for my sister the way she feels for him, I know he's not the same guy anymore. There's no better person in the world I'd want loving and caring for Emiline than Logan.

I blink back the emotions coming to light because the situation we're in right now could prevent that from happening.

Logan might not wake up.

I'm *very* optimistic he will.

But that 'what if' still sits heavy in my head.

"I'm not going anywhere." Emiline stands from Marc's lap and walks over to the chair beside Logan's bed. Taking his hand in hers. "I'm not leaving him."

"We're not saying you have to leave for good," Marc starts.

"We're just suggesting you go home, shower, and maybe pack a bag for yourself," Thomas adds.

Her face falls. "What if Logan wakes up when I'm gone?"

"I don't think…" Thomas begins but stops himself. "Emiline, I'm not trying to hurt you more than you're already hurt. But he's in a medically induced coma. If you go home to shower and pack a bag, he'll still be here."

"I'm scared he won't be!" she raises her voice.

I bring myself to the other side of Logan's bed and look at Emiline. "What if they take you home to get your things together, and I stay here with him? This way, he's not alone."

Emiline shakes her head. "I'm so scared, Ollie."

I round the bed and bring myself to crouch in front of her. "I know you are. We all are. But you have to take care of yourself, too."

She doesn't say anything for a few minutes as she stares at our best friend lying there attached to so many tubes.

"I know you guys don't approve of this, and this wasn't how we wanted you to find out," she finally says, staring at him before turning to look at us. "But I love him. So much that it physically hurts to think about him not being here anymore or him waking up and I'm not here."

"We know," Thomas says first. "And we understand."

"You do?" She looks shocked.

"At first, I didn't want to accept it." Thomas shrugs. "Know that it's hard for me to accept any man. You're our little sister. I'm always going to be insanely protective of you."

"Whether you were falling in love with Logan or another man, we would have reacted the same way," Marc says.

Her features soften. "I'm sorry we didn't tell you sooner."

"Don't be," I say first. "We know now. No more secrets between us. We're family."

Something washes over Emiline that I can't quite pinpoint as she averts her gaze back toward Logan. I look at Thomas and Marc and they both have questioning looks on their faces, likely wondering exactly what I am.

But none of us have it in us to ask her about it.

Whatever it is, she will tell us when she's ready.

"Ollie, are you sure you won't leave him?" she asks me. "If I go home and shower? I'll be so fast."

I nod. "I won't leave him until you get back."

Emiline stands from her chair, leans over, and presses a kiss to Logan's forehead.

My heart breaks for her all over again.

Then I watch her walk out the door with Marc and Thomas.

And I hope like hell nothing happens while she's gone.

CHAPTER FORTY-NINE
Emiline

TRUE TO HIS WORD, Oliver never leaves Logan's side.

When I got back to my place, I felt myself crumbling all over again. I was in the comfort of my apartment while Logan sat here in a bed, unable to breathe on his own.

I cried in the shower.

I cried for him and what the future might look like.

I cried for me and our unborn baby that I have no clue how to handle. I'm still a baby myself. How in the world can I raise one?

I cried for my future and all the hard work I put in at school.

I graduated and accomplished something that few people can say they did. We didn't even graduate with half the class we started with, which is how complex and intense the program was.

And now I'm supposed to take my boards in two days.

The test that will give me my license to practice.

But I can't even focus on that when all this is happening.

I cried for the insane turn of events that life is throwing me right now.

I felt a sense of relief wash over me halfway through my

shower as my cries mixed with the water. I let the stream cascade down my back at a scorching hot temperature.

I've been through so much.

Life has tested me in ways I could have never imagined.

This is just another test, right?

Logan's going to come out fine in the end, right?

The only thing different this time is that I have the support of everyone around me. My struggles are out in the open. I don't need to do this alone anymore.

That's why I'm here now, sitting in Logan's hospital room and trying my best to focus on studying, even though I don't know if I can even go through with taking this test in a few days.

There has been no change in his condition. They also don't normally allow visitors to stay overnight. I'm thankful they made an exception for me, and Brooke pulled some strings to get me a small round table in the room so I could get stuff done while I wait.

There's a knock on the door, and I look up to see Brooke standing there. She's in her work uniform with her badge at the neck of her scrubs.

"Hey, you," she says in a low tone. "I wanted to come check on you while I had a break."

I lift the notebook in my hand. "I'm attempting this, but I'm struggling to focus right now."

"That's understandable," she says, sitting across from me at my small table in the corner of his room. She looks over at Logan in bed. "Any change?"

I shake my head.

"What do you want to do about the board exam in a few days?" she asks.

"I don't know, honestly. I'm not sure I'm in the right mindset to take it. Plus, I'm not sure I want to leave Logan for that long. You know it can take hours."

"Do you think you will change your test date?"

I shrug. "I don't want to. Mostly because I've heard of people putting it off once and then they end up putting it off again. Only to repeat it until they never take it."

Brooke lets out a soft laugh. "I've heard that too. Do you think one of your brothers could sit here while you go take it?"

"They might. I'm so scared to leave him and he'll wake up while I'm gone. I have so much I want to say to him and… tell him."

My hand instinctively covers my lower stomach.

There's so much to tell him.

Brooke sits up straighter in the chair, leaning on the table. "I'm going to be honest with you here. Do this, Em. Do this for you. Do this for him. Do this for your baby. Whatever reason you need, but you have to take this test. You've worked so damn hard, and I know that if Logan was awake right now, he would want you to take this test. I'm sure he would force you to take it the same way I am."

"You're right."

"I am?" she asks, shocked.

I nod. "You are. I have to stay focused on the future. Whether the outcome here is good or bad, I will need something for myself when it's done. Logan might wake up and hate me. Logan might wake up and decide he wants to be with me. He also might… not wake up." I swallow past the emotions in my throat. "I think studying will help me not think of every single bad outcome possible."

Even saying that out loud, I know it's a lie.

My brain is in complete chaos right now. I don't think the material I reviewed before Brooke came in here stuck anywhere. I haven't slept. I've been nauseous just about every hour. I can't keep food down. There's a human growing in my stomach. I'm sleeping on a couch that I'm pretty sure is made of wood and not cushion.

Everything around me is falling apart.

"How about this," Brooke starts. "Why don't I reschedule mine for the same day and time as you if a spot is available? This way, you don't have to go alone. And we can come back here as soon as it's done."

"You'd move your date up by two weeks, and take it in a few days, for me?"

She nods. "I'd do anything for you. That's what best friends are for."

I'll never know how I got so lucky to have Brooke as my best friend, but I will never take it for granted.

"Okay. Let's do this," I tell her before looking over at Logan.

He's turned into my biggest supporter. My crutch when I needed someone to hold me up. My anchor keeping me grounded in the darkest of waters.

I'm going to be strong. For you, Logan.

CHAPTER FIFTY
Emiline

THERE'S BEEN no change in Logan's condition over the last forty-eight hours.

It's a mix of fear, guilt, and uncertainty that grips me as I prepare to leave Logan for my boards today. The thought that he might take a turn for the worse while I'm away is a constant, nagging worry.

I rise from my chair in the corner of his room, the same spot I've occupied for countless hours, and approach his bed. "Come back to us," I whisper, my voice barely audible, just before the door creaks open and my three brothers enter.

"How's he doing?" Oliver asks first.

"No change."

He nods, and Thomas and Oliver make their way to his bed.

"You got this, Logan," Thomas tells him, barely above a whisper.

I feel myself getting emotional with his tone, but Marc coming to my side, grabs my attention. "Are you almost ready to go?" he asks.

"I'm going to leave here in about five minutes."

"I'm actually going to take you," Marc says. "I talked to Brooke already, and she's meeting us downstairs."

I offer him a weak smile. It's hard to even force myself to do that today. Now that I think about it, I can't remember the last time I did.

"You don't have to do that."

"Yes, I do. I'm going to drop you two off, and I'll be waiting around the corner at the little coffee shop whenever you're done. I have to do some work, anyway."

"Will you have your phone on you? In case the hospital calls?" I ask.

Marc holds it up. "It's fully charged, and I even brought my wall charger with me. This way, I'm available when you call me or when Thomas does if there is any change."

I nod.

I look down at Logan laying in the bed the way I always do.

He still looks so different to me, yet exactly the same.

"I'll be right back," I tell Logan before kissing his forehead.

Just as I'm about to walk out the door, Thomas stops me.

"Emiline," he says, and I turn to face him. "You got this, okay? You're going to do amazing. When you come out on the other end, you will officially be a Registered Nurse, and I couldn't be prouder of you."

Thomas walks over, wrapping his arms around me, and I melt into him.

He knows that's exactly what I needed to hear to calm my beating heart.

"I love you, Em," he whispers.

"I love you too, Tommy. Thank you."

And with that, I leave and hope like hell he's right.

It's done.

All the hard work I put in during classes and all the late nights studying are behind me. We graduated, and now the biggest exam of my life is done.

I felt an overwhelming sense of pride when I walked out of that building. Because I did it without letting my inner thoughts win. Before going in, Marc talked me down before he even knew I was on the verge of spiraling.

The support system surrounding me makes me feel guilty for not speaking up sooner about everything.

Now, I have to wait and see if I actually passed.

My issue right now is I'm sitting in this cold, dark hospital room, waiting for Logan to wake up, and I have nothing to keep my mind off this mess in front of me.

Because of that, my mind wanders.

What if Logan were to wake up right now and decide he doesn't want me in the room? Or that he tells me to get out?

I rise from the chair in the corner, only to sit down on the one next to Logan's bed. I know deep down he can hear what I have to say, and there are just some things I need to get out without fearing what he might say back.

"Hey, Logan." I take his hand in mine, looking from his face down to his limp hand before looking back up at him. "I took my boards today. I hated leaving you, but I wanted you to know I only left because I needed to get that out of the way. Marc drove me there. You would be proud to know I didn't have a panic attack before I walked in. I remained grounded and focused. I thought of you and everything you've always told me. I pictured you telling me I could do it. That I can pass the test and the voices in my head telling me I can't are just a bunch of liars. I don't know if those are the exact words you've said to me, but I pictured it anyway."

I look down at his hand, squeezing it and hoping he grips mine back.

"I miss you so much, Logan. You have no idea how much I wish I could hear your voice. There's so much I want to tell you, but I can't tell you like this. I thought I lost you that night they brought you in. The steady ring of your heart in a flatline is why I can't sleep. When I close my eyes, I'm right back in that room.

Standing in the doorway and watching my best friend do chest compressions while the man I love lay there without a pulse."

Tears form in my eyes as I bring myself back to that moment.

Right before the world around me went dark.

"I'm so tired, Logan. I feel like each minute that passes, the voices grow louder and louder. They tell me I should leave, that you wouldn't want me here. But *my* voice is telling me there's still a chance for us. You left my apartment without another word, but after this... after almost losing you this way... I can't lose you again. I don't understand why this is happening to you, and I don't think I ever will."

I continue to talk as if Logan is actually going to respond.

My heart breaks with each word out of my mouth, knowing he's not going to say anything back. Knowing he's not going to move in this bed.

"Do something," I whisper. "Say something. Please. Tell me you're here. Tell me you hear me. Give me some sort of sign."

Nothing.

I take his hand between both of mine as I lower my head and rest it on the edge of his bed. Letting the tears flow like a steady stream for the first time all day.

The door to his room flies open, and two nurses rush in.

My head snaps in their direction, and I stand up quickly because they look worried.

"Is everything okay?"

They both stop dead in their tracks and offer me a soft smile and nod. "Everything is great. We just saw some activity on Logan's heart monitor and wanted to make sure everything was okay."

I look up and see the heart on the monitor beeping and his pulse reading just over one hundred.

"We silenced it for you the other night so it didn't bother you while you were resting," one nurse said.

"Were you just talking to him?" the other nurse asks.

"I was."

They smile again. "Logan hears you, Emiline. His heart started beating a little quicker from whatever you were talking about."

My lips part in shock, and I wipe a tear from my cheek.

I asked for a sign and he just gave me a bit of hope in the darkness surrounding me.

For the first time in days, I smile.

A real smile filled with hope.

CHAPTER FIFTY-ONE
Logan

I HEAR YOU, *Emiline.*

Wait for me, please. I'm begging you.

I'm trying to come back to you, I promise.

The light is so bright, and I hear everything you're saying, but I can't move. I can't open my eyes.

I need you. Please, don't fucking leave me.

CHAPTER FIFTY-TWO
Emiline

TODAY'S the first day I've left his room since the board exam because the girls are forcing me to get out and eat a real meal. Truthfully, I haven't had the appetite for anything more than crackers.

I'm carrying around this new guilt of telling everyone one secret just to keep another. But this one is mine and Logan's secret to tell. The last thing I want is for him to wake up and learn he's the last to know.

The girls brought me to a little spot on the same block as City General. They know I want to stay close in the event something were to change.

"Any updates?" Peyton asks.

I shake my head.

"It has to be any day now. Thomas said the doctors mentioned how everything is looking good."

"It is. They took him off the ventilator, and now it's just a waiting game."

A waiting game I'm not handling very well, with nothing else to keep my brain occupied.

"I'm going to be the one to come out and ask," Avery says

next to me. "You haven't said anything, and I can speak for all of us when I ask… are you a registered nurse now?"

I smile as I look around the table. Peyton, Avery, Macey, and Kali look at me as they wait for my answer.

"I was hoping you would ask." My smile grows wider. "I wanted to wait until we were all together to tell you. But I passed. I'm officially a nurse."

It pained me to smile and celebrate as big as I did when I got the results because that day was the most draining for me. Still, I have never felt so proud of myself seeing the one-word 'pass' on the website.

That morning, I was puking nonstop, Logan had to go for multiple tests, and I hadn't gotten any sleep the night before because I couldn't get comfortable in the makeshift bed set up for me.

It was hard to smile and be happy.

But I logged in from his room, and even though I was alone, I didn't feel like I was.

Logan was there, and I knew deep down he had heard me.

The girls erupt in a fit of cheers and congratulations.

"We are so proud of you, Emiline," Macey says first. "You're going to be such an amazing nurse."

"I agree," Kali adds. "You freakin' did it!"

"I totally did." I laugh, and the table goes quiet. I look around, wondering if I said something wrong. "What?"

Peyton smiles first. "It's really good to see you laugh. I know this last week has been hard on you, and I'm proud of how well you've handled things. You took the biggest test of your life, lived in a hospital, your brothers found out about you two, and you're still smiling."

My smile falls.

"No, no. Go back. I don't want you to be upset." Peyton reached her hand across the table to take mine. "I just needed you to know we're proud."

"Thank you," I say honestly. "I truly think I'm just numb to everything still. But I woke up and felt this overwhelming feeling that today would be a good day. I think it's because I knew I was meeting with you guys. I don't know if you know this, but the four of you are good for the soul."

Avery does a fake bow over the table. "At your service."

Macey swats her upper arm. "I feel the same way about you all. I wouldn't have made it here in the city without you guys."

"There are a lot of emotions happening here," Avery says. "But also, I feel the same."

"Look at everything we've been through together," Peyton says, looking around the table. "Me getting a job on my first day in the city. Remember when I met you at the park, Emiline? I was so nervous."

"You definitely were."

"And then I fell in love with your brother, only for Avery to fall in love with your other brother." Peyton laughs.

"Listen, he totally fell for me first. I fought that shit hard," Avery defends.

"Riiiight," Peyton draws out. "And then we met Macey, who I'm pretty sure was the only woman in the world with the power to pull Oliver out of team single for life."

"He changed my life." Macey smiles, and I swear it reaches her eyes.

"We've all been through so much," I repeat Peyton's words. "I'd be lost without you guys."

With that, we all stand from our chairs for a group hug.

This weirdly feels like a goodbye.

Something about that thought makes me think of Logan again. And the moment I do, a cold breeze hits my forearm.

Alarm bells ring in my head.

My appetite is gone, and I want to run out the door.

Macey is the first to pick up on it. "Is everything okay?" she asks.

"I…" I stand and look at the door and back at them. "I think I need to get back to the hospital."

"Why don't you eat first," Peyton says. "Thomas said he would—"

Just as the words leave her lips, her phone rings.

"Speak of the devil." She answers her phone. "Hello?" Her smile falls. "Okay, I'll tell her."

Peyton hangs up and looks at where I stand. She doesn't have time to speak before I bolt out the door as fast as I can.

I'm coming, Logan.

———

My heart is racing, a frantic drumbeat in my chest, and I'm struggling to catch my breath. It's not just the sprint from the restaurant that's left me breathless.

I stand in the hallway, trying to gather my thoughts before I walk in.

On the other side of that door, my life could be transformed into a dream or a nightmare, the fear of regretting my decision to leave his side forever haunting me.

Thomas spots me through the tiny window on the door and comes to meet me. He opens the door and starts to say something, but I hold up a hand to stop him. I don't want to know. I need to find out for myself.

Instinctively, my hand covers my lower stomach.

Thomas might think I'm just nervous, holding my stomach. But it's more than that. It's a silent prayer for our baby, a plea for what's behind the door to be him coming back to us.

To us.

I release a long, deep breath, my anticipation reaching a fever pitch, before I finally turn the doorknob.

My eyes land on Logan in the bed.

I don't have time to react before my vision gets fuzzy from tears.

"Emmy."

CHAPTER FIFTY-THREE
Logan

I THOUGHT I knew the pain when I was laying here, not being able to move in bed while she sat there and talked to me for however long I've been out of it.

But nothing will ever compare to the look on her face as she stands in the doorway, seeing me awake for the first time. It will be an image that will remain burned into my brain for the rest of my life.

She looks like she hasn't slept in days.

She looks… weak and tired and so damn small.

"Emmy," I repeat, ensuring she heard me the first time. My throat feels raw, and my voice comes out hoarse.

"Logan."

My head falls back into the bed, and I close my eyes.

I've dreamed about hearing her say my name again.

Hearing her say it while I'm awake feels even better than I imagined. It makes it feel real that she's still here.

That she didn't leave me.

Even after I walked out on her.

"Please, come here." I pat the side of the bed, my arms still feeling so heavy and weak.

She looks behind her at Thomas, standing right outside the

door. He nods and closes the door behind her before she returns her gaze to me.

She takes one step in but doesn't come any further.

She almost looks... scared.

I don't blame her.

"Emmy." My voice is louder and more demanding this time, forcing me to choke. "Please."

She takes slow, tentative steps toward me.

And then she smiles. It's weak and barely noticeable, but it's a sign *my* Emiline is still there.

"I thought I told you to stop calling me that."

I laugh, causing me to choke again.

She makes her way to my bedside, looking me up and down as if she doesn't believe I'm here. That she doesn't believe that I'm awake and alive.

I reach up and grab her hand hanging at her side.

I give her three squeezes and she crumbles beside me. She releases a painful cry and falls to her knees in prayer at my bedside. It kills me that I can't sit upright now or that I'm unable to jump up from the bed and wrap her in my arms.

She rests her head on my bed, and my hand tangles in her hair because I need to touch her. I need her to know this isn't a dream.

"I'm so sorry, Logan," she cries out.

My hand moves under her head to lift it so she's now looking directly at me. My eyebrows pinch together as I cup her chin between my fingers. "What in the world are you sorry for?"

"I don't know. I don't know. I didn't know if you'd want me here with how we left things. But I couldn't leave you. I had to stay. I had to be here. You're alive. Oh my god, you're alive."

"Shh..." I say, keeping my voice calm as her voice grows louder between cries.

"I missed you so much. You have no idea how much it hurt me to see you like that. I tried so hard to be strong, but I couldn't be. You almost died."

"I know, baby. I know."

Something flashes in her eyes.

That's the first time I've ever called her that, and it feels so good.

Emiline lifts herself up and crawls into bed with me. One arm drapes over my chest, and her legs nestle beside mine, cautious of my cast. She carefully rests her head on my chest and just holds me.

She holds me like any minute she's about to lose me again.

After everything I've just been through.

After everything *she's* just been through.

There is no way in hell that she will ever lose me again.

I press my lips to the top of her head and she squeezes me a little harder, but weary of my fragile state.

"I love you, Emiline," I whisper into her hair.

She lifts her head, teary eyes looking up at me with shock.

"You love me?"

I nod, smiling down at her in my arms. "I know I walked out on you without saying it back, but I fucked up, Em." I swallow past the dryness in my throat, emotions taking over now. "I was on my way to you."

"You… what?"

"When the accident happened. I was on my way to the hospital to tell you all of this. I was in agony over the way I left your apartment that morning. It was eating me up inside and I needed to tell you how I felt."

Emiline cries again.

I don't give her a chance to feel guilty about it. My opposite hand reaches up to cup the side of her face while my thumb swipes away a tear that falls. "I don't think I could ever physically be without you in this lifetime or the next. I'm here and alive because of you. You never left my side. You gave me strength. I heard everything you said and fought like hell to get back to you."

Her head melts into my palm, and her eyes flutter closed.

"I was so damn scared," Emiline whispers.

"Look at me, baby." I urge her to keep eye contact with me. "I came back to you. I promise, I'm never, ever leaving you again. Do you hear me?"

She swallows, lifting herself on her elbow next to me.

"You came back to us."

I angle my head in confusion. "I came back to you and my best friends. Yes."

"No." She shakes her head, her hand coming to her stomach as I look down and see what she's doing. "You came back to us."

"I don't understand."

She pulls herself off me, and I immediately hate the loss of contact and feel an uneasy feeling in my gut. She looks ready to deliver the worst news of my life.

"After they brought you into the ER"—she winces, as if the memory hurts her to say out loud—"I had a panic attack after seeing you flatline."

My eyes fall closed as I release a sigh and think about how much I fucked up everything. How much it now hurts to know that I wasn't fucking there for her.

"I ended up passing out from it. When I woke up, the doctor told me they ran blood work."

I hate that I put her in this much pain, and the old me would've wanted to run so I could avoid ever putting her through that.

But I could never bring myself to be without her.

Falling in love with Emiline was the easiest thing I've ever done, and I never want to be without that feeling.

The corner of her lip turns up just slightly. "It turns out we've been having a little too much fun."

My eyebrows furrow as I continue to stare at her.

"We're having a baby, Logan."

Did she just say what I think she just said?

A baby?

We're having a baby?

I continue to stare at her in confusion. "A baby?"

"I was just as shocked as you are right now. I know we stopped using protection and I don't have all the answers as to how this happened. There was a day or two I missed a dose of my birth control, but I got right back on it," Emiline rambles. "I don't want you to feel like I trapped you. I've been terrified and anxious for you to wake up. I needed you awake and alive, but I knew that would come with having to tell you the news. I wasn't sure how you would react or if you would feel like I was trapping you. And I just..." She sighs, allowing herself to finally catch a breath.

I reach up and take her hand in mine.

"We're having a baby."

She nods.

I keep my eyes locked on hers as I slip my hand out of her hold, placing the palm of my hand over the lowest part of her stomach before my gaze lands on where my hand rests.

I say nothing because I don't even know what I should say.

The news ignites something inside of me I never knew I wanted... needed.

A life is growing inside the woman I love more than anything.

A life we created together.

A life that allows me to see the future so fucking clearly.

"All my life..." I start to say but choke on my words from the overwhelming emotion flowing through me. "I've never wanted this."

The disappointment on Emiline's face is evident, but I continue anyway.

"I never wanted to find someone to spend my life with. I never saw a future with a wife, kids, or *people* to come home to. My only focus has always been on my job. From being a little kid and following in my father's footsteps. But I see things a lot clearer now."

Her hand covers mine, still resting on her stomach, and she looks down.

"My dad was a good father. The best a kid could have ever asked for. He loved my mom and me with every fiber of his being. He showed up when it mattered most and never missed an opportunity to tell us he loved us."

She wipes a tear from her eyes.

I finally look up at her, tears blurring my vision.

"I love you, Emiline Ford. I never want to miss an opportunity to tell you that. You have been the greatest and most unexpected adventure of my life. No part of me feels like you trapped me. We did the dance, which led us here. Sometimes, the most epic love stories go a different route. It looks like ours is taking the road less traveled."

She laughs lightly. "You're okay with this?"

"I need three to five business days to process that I'm going to be a dad." I bark out a laugh myself. "But, yes. I want this. I didn't know I wanted this, but now that it's in front of me... I can't picture a life without it. Without you."

Her head falls back down on my chest. I allow myself this moment to close my eyes and soak this moment in.

A moment I never want to forget.

"You know, there was a time you asked me what I liked. You asked me if I have something I can't live without. You put me on the spot that day because it was a hard question to answer."

The lift her head to face mine, keeping it on my chest.

"The answer will always be you."

She smiles from ear to ear before pressing a kiss to my chest.

I may be stuck in a hospital bed for a bit longer.

But I'm holding my entire world in my arms.

With that thought, I smile.

Because what a perfect ending to our beginning.

EPILOGUE
Logan

Four months later

"CAN'T we just stay in bed all day?" I groan.

Emiline tosses me a shirt to wear for the night. "I wish, but nope. You know we've been planning this for a while now. It would be nice if the person we're throwing this dinner for showed up."

"Macey is cooking, right?"

"It's her restaurant, but no, she's not. She wanted to be there for this."

"It's not the same," I whine like a child.

Emiline leans over the side of the bed, gripping my chin in her hand. "You're so cute when you whine."

My hand reaches up to hold her by the waist, my thumb brushing her growing belly. I look down and back up at her; a smile stretches across my face. I lean in to give her a kiss. "Okay, Mama."

Her smile is soft against my lips.

I'll never get tired of calling her that.

Emiline hasn't left my side since the day I woke up in the hospital, and it was a long journey after that. I was there for another month before being transferred to a rehab facility for a few weeks to help me gain strength in my leg again.

I still struggle on some days, but I've made a lot of progress. I won't be running a marathon alongside Marc anytime soon, but by the time our little baby is here, I'll be able to keep up with him or her.

That's enough motivation to keep going.

Him or her.

I protested at our twenty-week anatomy scan over the fact that Emiline wanted the gender to be a surprise. As someone who has spent their life meticulously planning for his future, I needed to know so I could plan this.

Our baby needs the most perfect room.

Our baby needs clothes.

Our baby needs a name.

The unknowns have always scared me, but Emiline has been my rock every step of the way. While I knew she was strong before, there's something incredible about seeing the strength she holds growing a human inside her.

She's free, and it's clear who she is as a person today.

She doesn't hold secrets with her brothers or friends anymore.

The stress of school and exams doesn't linger in her head anymore.

Her last panic-inducing moment was the morning we told her brothers that she was pregnant. She didn't quite get to the point of having a full-blown panic attack, but I saw the way her breathing changed and watched as anxiety filled her features.

Trust me, I was nervous too.

But they all surprised us.

All three of them smiled from ear-to-ear and felt an overwhelming sense of joy for us. There wasn't an ounce of concern on their faces. It's like they knew Emiline changed me in all the right ways. They knew no matter what, I love her, and I wasn't planning on leaving her side anytime soon.

I finally concede to her demands and jump in the shower.

Tonight, the entire group is getting together to celebrate my completion of rehab and the start of a new life for myself.

Yup, you heard that right.

The start of a new life.

After waking up from my coma, I called the chief and told him I couldn't take the position. There was no way I could carry the workload of being chief while raising a child. I know my dad did it with ease, but I have a long way to go before I become even half the man he was. The thought of becoming a father is both terrifying and exhilarating. I'm not sure if I'm ready, but I'm determined to be the best dad I can be.

I let the water hit my back. Despite the emotional thoughts coursing through my head, I smile. Wide and with ease. Because even if I'm not following in my dad's exact footsteps… I believe he would be really fucking proud of the man I've become.

"Emiline," I shout. "Care to join—"

My words fall short when I hear her heaving in the toilet just outside of the shower.

"I'll pass," she chokes out over the toilet.

I wash the soap from my body and jump out of the shower as fast as possible, finding her sitting on the counter.

"Sorry. I would have joined you. But you know… morning sickness is actually now called all-day sickness. And it doesn't go away in the first trimester, it stays the. Entire. Time."

I take her face between my hands, staring at her, memorizing every minor feature, even if it is a mess from vomiting.

"I love you, babe. So much. It's not even funny."

"I love you too." Emiline smiles at me before pushing me away and jumping off the counter. "Now, get ready. We're going to be so late."

"You got it, boss."

———

I sit at Ollie's, one arm draped over the back of Emiline's chair, as I scan the table. An indescribable feeling washes over me, seeing everyone we love together to celebrate *me*.

Not too long ago, it was only me and the Ford brothers.

Late nights on the town.

Refusing to let ourselves get tied down by women.

Thomas sits at the head of the long table. Peyton sits on one side of him with her belly so round she can't fully sit in the seat. She's due any day now.

Thomas has always looked at her differently. From that first night he met her, everything changed in him, and I've loved watching him grow to be the man, dad, and husband he is today.

I continue around the table when I land on Marc staring at Avery like she hung the moon. At the same time, she goes on and on about closet organization tips. I'll never understand it, but watching how much she loves talking about it is funny.

Sitting next to her, engrossed in the conversation, is little Mackenzie. For a nine-year-old, she sure is fascinated with how Avery organizes her clothing by the sleeve length and color. At least, I think that's what she's saying.

I keep scanning the table when my eyes land on Macey and Oliver—my partner-in-crime, the man I thought would be single with me for the rest of our lives and sitting next to me in a retirement home. But Macey is the most unexpected thing to happen to him. I'll never forget when he brought her back to the city to live with him. What a turn of events that was.

Then I stare to my side and watch Emiline listening to Avery.

She's laughing and smiling from ear to ear.

After going through what I've experienced, I can never take that smile, or her, for granted.

Picking up the butter knife next to my plate, I clink it against my glass, drawing the attention of the table in my direction.

Emiline snaps her head toward me, not expecting this.

"I'd like to say a few things," I announce, rising from my chair. Out of the corner of my eye, I watch as Brooke, Silas, and the chief enter the room simultaneously, staying off to the side and giving me a silent nod to continue.

Great. Now I'm really going to get emotional.

"Thank you, everyone, for coming out tonight for this celebration Emiline has put together. The last few months have been some of the longest and most challenging I've ever faced. I wouldn't have made it through if it weren't for all of you in this room tonight."

I swallow past the emotions. It's too soon.

"As everyone in this room knows, I've worked my entire life to be the best I can be at my job. I've loved being a police officer."

Emiline gasps to the side of me, and I look at the chief. He smiles and gives me a silent nod to keep going.

"I've been given a second chance at life. I looked over all the reports of my accident, and I shouldn't be here tonight, standing in front of you and making this speech. But you can't get rid of me that easily." I chuckle.

The group laughs lightly, and I keep the grin on my face as I continue.

"That's why I've decided I'm going to officially retire as a police officer."

Thomas, Marc, and Emiline all stand up from their seats. They have shock written all over their faces and are unsure what to make of this.

"Are you sure?" Thomas asks first.

"But you've wanted this your entire life, Logan," Marc adds.

"Since when?" Emiline chimes in.

Avery tugs on Marc's arm. "Would you sit down and let him finish before rudely interrupting?"

"I've been thinking over this decision since the moment I opened my eyes in that hospital room. I was looking for you." I turn to face Emiline. "The first person I wanted to see was you. But instead, I came face to face with Thomas." I turn to look at him with a lopsided grin. "You told me something within that first half hour of being awake while waiting for her that stuck with me."

Thomas tilts his head to the side in confusion.

"You said, and I quote, 'If you ever hurt my sister, I'm going to murder you with my bare hands and make it look like an accident.'"

Thomas barks out a laugh, and everyone around us does the same.

"But then you also told me to take care of her, cherish her, and be there for her when she needs me. You asked me if I was serious about how I felt, and without hesitation, I said yes."

I turn to face Emiline again.

"I know this comes as a shock to you too. But after having that conversation with your brothers and thinking things through, I don't want to be the man who put work before you or our baby. I don't want to worry about not making it home to you two."

"So what will you do?" she asks.

I turn to Silas. "Silas and I have decided to open our own boxing gym. We're going to work with children and teenagers to teach them basic self-defense skills. It won't be as intense as adult classes, but we want to give the kids something to do and something to look forward to after school."

Emilie's eyes widen, and tears glisten in her eyes. Her features soften almost instantly as her palm delicately connects with my cheek. "You're the most amazing man I have ever met, Logan Bennett."

"I want to go!" Mackenzie shouts.

"Me too, Uncle Logie," James adds.

I laugh at them. "You two are welcome anytime, you know that."

Both cheer in unison as I scan the table again. It's taken me a lot to get to this point, to actually feel proud of myself, to feel like I'm doing something right in life.

I did it, Dad.

EXTENDED EPILOGUE
Emiline

February

"LOGAN! WAKE UP!" I shout through the dark room.

"What? Who? Where's the fire?" he says, sitting up straight in bed trying to open his eyes.

"My water broke!"

"How? You're scheduled for a c-section next week. Your water can't break when the baby is flipped upside down."

"Yes it can, Logan," I groan before pacing the side of the bed. "This can't be happening right now."

He rushes out of bed to my side, both hands gripping my shoulders. "We got this, baby. Let's get the bags and head to the hospital. They'll tell us the next steps."

I nod in response but still don't move.

I don't know how this works with a scheduled procedure.

I'm not ready to have a baby *today*.

What day is it anyway?

Logan moves effortlessly around the room, while I stay planted where he left me. Getting dressed and moving in and out of the room to grab the things we packed weeks ago.

I kept it light and only the essentials we needed.

Peyton having her baby a few months ago helped me to understand what I need to pack and don't need to pack. She assured me I didn't need three suitcases like people on the internet tell you that you need.

After what feels like forever, Logan comes back in the room with an outfit for me.

He knows me better than anyone does. Even without saying the words, he knows I'm currently in a state of shock that this is really happening. He removes my sleep shorts and tank top and slips on a pair of comfy sweats I had picked out for the day we planned to go in. Then he pulls a quarter zip sweater over my head.

I smile at him.

I can't help it because I'm so lucky he's even here for this.

I'll never take anything he does for granted because there was a time where I thought I would be delivering this baby on my own. Where I thought this baby would be without a dad.

"We got this, baby," he assures me. "I can't wait to meet this little boy or girl."

I wrap my arms around him, my round belly sitting right between us. "I still believe it's a boy."

"I say we get to the hospital and find out. What do you say?"

I lean in and press my lips to his.

Knowing out lives are about to change forever.

———

My nerves are through the roof as the bright white lights shine down on me.

My body is numb, and I'm hooked up to a ton of machines monitoring my heart rate and oxygen levels. A drape sits on my chest, obstructing the view of the surgeon and the rest of the operating room.

When we arrived, they confirmed that I didn't pee myself and my water did in fact break.

Since I wasn't having any real contractions and wasn't immediately about the have the baby butt first, they took their time. That alone eased my anxiety.

Having a baby via c-section was not in my plans for ever having a child. When I thought about this early on in my pregnancy, I couldn't wait for the moment I pushed the baby out and they placed him or her on my chest. When we learned that the baby was upside down and not planning to go anywhere, I felt a piece of that experience ripped from me.

But once I wrapped my head around it, I knew I would do whatever I needed to do to ensure the baby came out safely. Even if it was because I was cut open and baby had to come out through the sunroof.

I turn my head to my left on the table where I see Logan.

He's holding my hand and dressed in a blue bunny suit with a scrub cap covering his hair for the operating room.

He gives my hand a three pulse squeeze.

I got you.

And I know he does.

The surgeon goes through his pre-procedure checklist with all participants in the room. I hear the monitor pick up as my heart rate accelerates.

"I'm right here, Em. Baby will be here any minute."

I control my breathing because he's right.

I lose track of time and I hear a nurse call out 'baby' from somewhere in the room right before I hear the faint cries behind the drape blocking my view.

Tears erupt from my eyes.

I turn to look at Logan, squeezing his hand for dear life as he wipes away the tears from his.

"Dad, do you want to do the honors to tell us what your baby is?" the surgeon says behind the drape.

Logan stands from the chair next to me, not releasing his hand in mine before the doctor dips the drape down enough to hold the baby over it.

His other hand moves to cover his face before he looks down at me.

"It's a baby girl," Logan cries. He sits down again, bringing his face to mine and pressing kisses to my forehead before traveling to my lips. "You did it, baby. We have a little girl," he cries harder than I've ever seen.

I can't stop the waterworks coming from me.

I was so sure it was a boy this entire pregnancy, to the point I didn't even pick a baby girls name.

I turn to my right, and watch as they bring the baby to the warmer to do their assessment and clean her up.

Her.

I'll never get used to that now.

"Go," I tell Logan. "Go see her."

He gives me another kiss before walking over to stand with the nurses and neonatologist assessing her. Every few minutes he turns back to look at me, a grin spread across his face.

My face hurts from smiling as hard as I am watching him become completely obsessed with her in just a few minutes.

They wrap her up in a blanket and hand her to Logan.

My eyes go fuzzy from the tears and I think I just fell in love with him more than I did yesterday. I keep my eyes on him as he stares down at the tiny screaming human wrapped in a little pink blanket in his arms like she just became his entire world.

And I know she did.

He hesitantly walks over to me, sitting down careful like he's going to break her. But moves her face right next to mine.

"Hi, baby girl," I sob, staring at the most beautiful thing I've ever seen in my life. "I'm your mama. I love you so much."

She turns her head and the screams she was just letting out die down.

"I think she loves you too," Logan says.

I look up at him, with one arm nestled on her and my thumb stroking her head.

"She needs a name," I tell Logan.

"I had an idea," he says. I narrow my eyes in confusion but let him continue. "I was thinking Daisy."

"Yeah?"

"Daisy means new beginnings, among many other things depending on the color." He lets out a light laugh. "It symbolizes rebirth and a new day. Happiness and joy. Loyalty and the ability to keep secrets. They represent being sweet, humble and friendly."

"Daisy," I say, looking down at our daughter and processing everything he's saying. "Hi, Daisy. Welcome to the world."

"I love you so much, Emiline," Logan says.

I look up at him, knowing that no words I say can express how much I love him in this moment. "I love you too."

We both spend the next few minutes staring at her.

At our daughter.

No doubt thinking of everything we've been through that led to this moment.

Once we're out of the operating room and into recovery, I hold her tightly, unable to process anything happening around us.

She's beautiful.

She's perfect.

She's ours.

"Do you want me to text everyone and let them know?" Logan asks next to me.

That's when I realize everyone doesn't even know we're at the hospital. The sun is just peaking over the horizon now and they're all just likely waking up.

"No." I shake my head. "Let's stay in this bubble for just a little longer. Just the three of us."

"Are you sure?" he questions as his hand comes to stroke the top of her tiny head.

I nod. "Once everyone knows, our phones will be blowing up like crazy." I turn to look at him. "What's one more secret, right?" I joke.

Logan laughs, leaning forward to press a kiss to her head.

"She's going to be that last secret we keep though," he confirms.

"She is," I assure him.

Because just for a little longer, I want to take in this moment alone with my entire world both in my arms and sitting next to me.

Captain Crunch Chicken

How to make the chicken Logan loves to make for Emiline.

Prep time: 35 minutes
Cook time: 10 minutes
Total: 45 minutes
Servings: 12 chicken strips

Ingredients

2 lb boneless, skinless chicken breast
6 cups of captain crunch cereal
4 cups milk
6 eggs
3 cups vegetable oil
salt + pepper

Directions

1. Pour milk, 1 tsp of salt and 1 tsp of pepper into a large bowl
2. Add in chicken breasts and let sit for 15 minutes
3. While that's happening, pour cereal into a zip lock bag and ground it. I like to whack it with a spatula or use my hands to crush it through the bag
4. Crack the eggs in another large bowl and whisk together
5. Pour flour in a shallow bowl or place
6. Put crushed cereal in another shallow bowl
7. Take the chicken out of the milk one at a time.
    a. Mix chicken in the flour until well coats
    b. Then place the chicken in the egg wash and coat it well
    c. Then coat the chicken in the ground cereal mixture

In frying pan:
- heat the oil in a large skillet on the stove over medium heat. Be sure not to cook it at too high of a temperature because it will burn due to the sugar on the cereal.
- Cook for 4-5 minutes per side. Avoid tossing too much or it will get greasy

In air fryer:
- heat to 350 and bake for 20 minutes.

In oven:
- preheat the oven to 375 and place on a baking sheet. Cook for 30 minutes.

ACKNOWLEDGMENTS

Writing this acknowledgement feels different. It feels like I'm saying goodbye when I'm not. But then again, we're saying goodbye to the Firsts in the City universe, so in a way we kind of are.

I wanted to first thank Logan and Emiline. I know that feels weird to thank fictional characters. These two have been waiting since writing book one for their moment. They also were written through some of the most challenging times in my personal life. They took me the longest to write because of that and they showed patience through the process. While readers begged for these characters, they remained calm and hopeful that their story would measure up to what everyone expected. It took a few turns, but I couldn't be prouder to end the series with these two and this story.

Lauren Brooke – I'm not sure I could have wrote this book without you. Listening to me cry. Listening to me vent. Listening to me want to wipe the entire manuscript when it was halfway done and start over. You didn't let me of course, but you kept me focused and helped me in all aspects of life.

Mel – what is there to say that isn't already said through our daily phone calls? Nothing. Thank you for always being my rock and always picking up when I need to talk through something. One day you're going to get sick of me, and I'm thankful that day isn't coming any time soon.

Tabitha and Caroline – not only are you two and LB the best hype girls an author could as for, but you're always there to bounce ideas off of and encourage me to keep going. Tabitha finding pieces of the book to add the smallest something to that only enhances the scene, and Caroline for putting up with my overuse of commas and terrible grammar.

Amy – Oh my god… I could not have done this without you in the slightest bit. You came in during the final hours and offered some of the best suggestions to make this book what it is. It might have been tedious and felt impossible to make happen, but we did it. I hope you know that you're stuck with me from here on out.

My alpha readers (Kristen x2, Rachel, Jessy, and Shima) – I'm truly so lucky to have people like you in my life. This book was a disaster of epic proportions. I had zero timeline, zero organization and was a hot mess updating things left and right and you all went with the flow of my hot mess life. You have no idea what that means to me.

My beta readers (Jackie, Cait, Isabella, and Paula) – Thank you for reading early and being an extra set of eyes and doing it in the last minute for me. Your suggestions and love for this book only made me that much more excited to get this out in the world. I'm also really sorry for making you cry. Truly.

Salma – your tough love will always be my most favorite thing during this process. I doubt this book would be anywhere near as awesome as it is without your insight and eyes. Thank you will never be good enough.

Erin – my forever hype girl. I hope you never lose your sparkle and who you are as a person. Checking on me randomly and making sure I'm drinking my water and taking a breather here and there was everything. I love you my Philly girl.

Last but not least – Victoria Wilder and Ashley James – I hope you two realize the impact you've had on my life in just a short period of time. What started as just some accountability through writing sprints, has turned into a lifelong friendship. When I was at my lowest part of this writing process, you two came into my life and held me accountable. When I was stressed and anxious and didn't know what to do in the thick of edits, you both were there ensuring me that *'I've got* this.' Readers wouldn't be reading this book if it wasn't for you two because there is no way I could have finished this alone.

ABOUT THE AUTHOR

Jenn McMahon resides along the shore in New Jersey with her husband, Daniel, two children, Zachary and Owen, and two dogs, Cooper and Piper. She has spent the last couple of years engrossed in romance books, to now writing her own and sharing them with the world. When Jenn is not writing, she can be found reading, watching reruns of her favorite TV shows (Scandal, Grey's Anatomy and Friends – just to name a few), or petting her dog. She also loves taking trips to the beach with the kids, Atlantic City date nights with her husband, and thunderstorms.